The Cross and the Tomahawk Series

mark ammerman

RiverOak®

Good News in Fiction

COOK COMMUNICATIONS MINISTRIES
Colorado Springs, Colorado • Paris, Ontario
KINGSWAY COMMUNICATIONS LTD
Eastbourne, England

RiverOak® is an imprint of
Cook Communications Ministries, Colorado Springs, CO 80918
Cook Communications, Paris, Ontario
Kingsway Communications, Eastbourne, England

THE RAIN FROM GOD
© 2000, 2005 by Mark Ammerman

This story is a work of fiction. All characters and events are the product of the author's imagination. Any resemblance to any person, living or dead, is coincidental.

First Cook Printing, 2005
Printed in the United States of America
1 2 3 4 5 6 7 8 9 10 Printing/Year 08 07 06 05

Unless otherwise noted, Scripture quotations are the author's paraphrase of the King James Version of the Bible. Scripture references marked KJV are taken from the King James version of the Bible. Public Domain.

Library of Congress Cataloging-in-Publication Data

Ammerman, Mark, 1954-
   Rain from God : historical fiction / by Mark Ammerman.
      p. cm. -- (The cross and the tomahawk series ; bk. 2)
   ISBN 1-58919-048-3 (pbk.)
   1. New England--History--Colonial period, ca. 1600-1775--
Fiction. 2. Narraganset Indians--Fiction. I. Title.
   II. Series: Ammerman, Mark, 1954-   Cross and the tomahawk
bk. 2.
   PS3551.M56R34 2005
   813'.54--dc22
                                        2004026664

old:0-88965-134-5)
LOC Catalog Card Number: 97-70110

This book is dedicated,
with sincerity and great respect,
to the memory of

Brother Joe Hazard.
(September 9, 1901–March 15, 2000)

Oldest member of the Narragansett Indian tribe,
Joe believed in Jesus from his youth.
An elder of his people and an elder in the faith, Joe was an
artist, a farmer, a father, a miller, a road builder, a member of his
tribal council, and like his Savior, a worker in wood.

Look, all you his people,
to your father Joseph.
He is wise in all things eternal.
He is rich in all things true.
Look to him even after
his eyes have closed forever,
on this earth,
for his star shines brightly
in the darkness of our day.

Contents

Foreword

I am a Narragansett Indian who lives in a small town in a small corner of the smallest state in this great, big country. Not too long ago, into my little portion of the New England woods came a man filled with God's spirit, humble yet confident, apprehensive yet determined, moved by a willingness to serve the Creator. "A man sent from God," I thought as he introduced himself to me and shared his desire to write a book—a unique book—about the historical relationship between the Gospel and the New England Native American.

Mark Ammerman spent four days in my home, walked the woods with me, visited with other Indians on the reservation, read through a stack of books from my father's (the late Rev. Harold Mars) shelves, visited historic sites and various town libraries, compiled his notes, and then returned home to begin the book that you now hold in your hands.

The Rain From God captured my imagination and held my heart from beginning to end. In my lifetime of reading, only one other book besides the Bible (*The Hiding Place* by Corrie ten Boom) has kept me so glued to its pages.

The story of Katanaquat takes place over three hundred years ago, but its words ring true to my own life story in many ways.

When reading the beginning chapters of this book, I relived my childhood. Memories raced as I followed Katanaquat, Assoko, and Miantonomi in their romping, forest adventures. I remembered the exciting, youthful, and energetic days of hunting, exploring, and playing beneath the tall trees of the Charlestown woods; the friendships made and kept; the relatives who visited; the council meetings and powwows and Indian cultural events that made up our communal life.

I saw myself, like Katanaquat and his young friends, straining young muscles with those of my father as we rocked the Talking Rock together and made it "talk."

I heard the "talk of the gods" as my memory called forth the many wandering stories of old Bunk Stanton, a Narragansett man who lived with his two big dogs in a little cabin down in the woods on our reservation.

I heard my own "Song On The Wind" as I recalled the many Sundays at the Narragansett Indian Church where my father pastored. How we sang to God's glory in that little stone church in the woods! I can almost see those notes passing through the walls and blowing down across the reservation to be heard by other ears beneath the trees.

I felt the romantic heartbeat of Katanaquat and Silvermoon (whom the author graciously named after my daughter) as I remembered my own courtship with a very beautiful Indian maiden who lived on the edge of the reservation in a home without any modern conveniences. I saw myself carrying water to her house from the babbling brook where we often sat to talk. I married that maiden thirty-two years ago, and God has since blessed us with a son, three daughters, and a grandson.

The historical events that followed the childhood of Katanaquat were painful to review. Deception, division, hatred, abuse, violence, murder, war—the sin and the fruits of sin that are common unto man. Too many of these things I have also seen, and see still even among some who claim to live in the name of God.

But as the book came to a close, the joy of my salvation lightened my eyes anew. I rejoiced in the grace and Gospel of Jesus Christ as Katanaquat bowed at last to the mighty Creator whom he had long feared but had never seen or known.

The great message of this book is that one God is the Father of every nation, tribe, and tongue throughout the earth, and that he loved the world so much that he sent his only begotten Son to offer to us all—red and yellow, black and white—the hope of life eternal.

As I read *The Rain From God*, I sometimes found myself, like Katanaquat, puffed up with the pride of my heritage in the flesh. But then my heart recalled the words my father often spoke to me, "Roland, never forget that you're an Indian, but always remember that you're a Christian *first!*"

For there is no difference between the Jew and the Greek: for the same Lord over *all* is rich unto all that call upon him. For *whosoever* shall call upon the name of the Lord shall be saved (Rom. 10:12–13).

Neither pray I for these alone, but for them also which shall believe on me through their word, that they may be one, as thou, Father, are in me, and I in thee, that they also may be one in us, that the world may believe that thou hast sent me (John 17:20–21).

Rev. Roland C. Mars
Charlestown, Rhode Island
January 20, 1997

I'm Your Brother

A long-awaited rain fell steadily, heavily, loudly upon the shingled roof of the white-steepled clapboard church at the crossroads of a tiny village in the wooded, southeast corner of Connecticut.

It was September 17, 1995, "Native American Sunday," and the morning's guest speaker, the Reverend Roland Mars, stood smiling behind the raised wooden pulpit at the front of the sanctuary. But he didn't need a podium. At six feet five inches tall, the dark-skinned minister towered over the seated congregation like a full-grown oak over a stand of young white birch. His grin flashed like warm lightning in the sparsely decorated old church, and his deep, friendly voice added a low rumble of Indian-summer thunder to the droning patter of hard rain against the gray windows.

"I'm your brother!" he declared. And he meant it.

As I sat, rather self-consciously and alone, in a stiff-backed, noncushioned pew at the rear of the sanctuary, I reflected for a moment on the meaning of those words—to me, to Reverend Mars (with whom I had come to church that morning), and to our respective races.

Roland Mars is a Narragansett Indian. His early ancestors walked the vast wooded wilderness of Rhode Island, Connecticut, and Massachusetts long before my English Puritan forebears stepped from their salt-weary ships onto the rocky shores of New England. Amazingly, for nearly 350 years now, these two races have been able to say, in Christ, "I'm your brother!"

The story of the Gospel and the Native American—particularly of Protestant missions in the seventeenth century—is something like a secret still untold. It is part of a national history and heritage, shared by both red man and white, that is so rarely mentioned as to seem like a myth. Yet it is so fully documented (as you can see if you take even a shallow dip in the bibliographical pool at the back of this book) that it is a marvel we have been told so little about it in our schools or by our popular media.

The true stories of Pocahontas and John Rolfe, of Squanto and the Pilgrims, of Roger Williams and the Narragansett, of John Eliot and the Praying Indians of New England, of the Mayhews of Martha's Vineyard—and of many others—are as remarkable and full of heroic drama as any fiction ever written. It is apparent from the voluminous testimony of original historical sources that thousands of seventeenth-century Native Americans fully and truly embraced the Gospel of Jesus Christ, becoming Christians in the deepest sense of the word. That they were culturally influenced by the whites—both for good and for evil—is incidental to the reality of the spiritual and moral transformation that took place in the hearts of individuals who repented of their sin and trusted Christ.

But before the dawning of redemption was the long darkness of a people trapped in ancient paganism. The spiritual existence of the northeastern American Indian was a frightening one, filled with ancestral gods, benevolent giants, mysterious dwarfs, and the alarming daily presence of a vast pantheon of moody spirits.

Into this wild and savage world, this cosmos of cold superstition and hard existence, strode at last the white man with his gunpowder and his God of love and mercy.

To the Indian of the wooded northeast of America, the little Englishman—with his ships and his guns, his swords and his hoes, his pots and his pans, his books and his clothing—seemed at first a god himself.

To the English, the nearly-naked Native American—with his greased and painted visage, his crude weapons and bark-covered houses, his wild habits and meager existence in the midst of the shadowed forest—seemed, concerning his civilization at least, little removed from the beasts of the brutal wilderness.

But the most discerning among both red and white soon discovered a common heartbeat. Not surprisingly, they also found that blood ran red on both sides. Yet a remarkable reality exists in the shared historic record of these disparate cultures. A man of a third race, a despised and rejected Jewish prophet, laid his hand upon the hearts of both red man and white, bound them together by a spiritual covenant hitherto unknown in this New World, and turned them face-to-face in compassionate unity, so that the woods today still ring with those powerful and timeless words: "I'm your brother!"

Mark Ammerman
December 1995

For a further discussion of research and terminology, be sure to see the historical notes at the end of the book. You may find the glossary of terms and the bibliography, also at the end, helpful as well.

ACKNOWLEDGMENTS
Honor to Whom Honor Is Due

A book of this sort is far more than the overactive imagination and frantic research of one man. I have many folks—living and dead, friends and family, strangers and acquaintances—to thank.

First, I wish to acknowledge the great debt I owe to my father and mother, Clifford and Margaret Ammerman.

My father spent the days of my youth bent over a typewriter, standing in front of a teletype, overseeing the inking and the clinking and the clanking of an ancient letterpress as it spewed forth the latest edition of *The Wayne Independent*—my hometown newspaper and the "Nation's Largest Rural Tri-weekly." Dad was the editor—the boss—and he saw to it that my creative work (crudely scrawled cartoons that hometown folks seemed to like and still remember) was in print before I was even in high school. He continued in this way to encourage me in my art and my writing. Eventually, he even paid me. Thanks, Dad!

My mother spent the days of my youth bent over an ironing board, standing in front of a stove, planting pretty flowers, and overseeing the spiritual, moral, and grammatical education of three daughters and one son. Mom was a Presbyterian preacher's kid, a practically perfect mother, an English major, and a published poet. She made sure we learned how to pray, tie our shoes, mind our p's & q's, and write our *i*'s before our *e*'s (except after *c*'s). Mom is in heaven, where tongues of men and angels are mixed in perfect praise (and syntax) to the Author of salvation and all communication.

Second, I wish to thank my wife of twenty-six years, Terri Lynn Ammerman, for all her love and prayer and support through this wearying and wonderful "on-the-side" odyssey of writing a novel. Terri joyfully undertakes life with the commitment and creativity of a Proverbs 31 "squaw." Without her, I might not know the night from the day. Her husband and her children (Jandy, Kesha, Margaret, Bethany, Jonathan, Brooklyn, Micah, Danny, and Lemmy) rise up and call her blessed. For where would the blessings be without her?

Thanks, honey, for listening to all the words and helping to make them sound even better, for speaking balance into my life, and reminding me to go to bed.

Third, I wish to give thanks to a whole heap of folks:

David Fessenden, Dr. K. Neill Foster, Janet Hixon, and the gang at Christian Publications for their initial commitment to this project and their compassionate friendship. Jeff Dunn, Phyllis Williams, Diane Gardner, Michele Tennesen, and my new friends at RiverOak Publishing and Cook Communications for their passion for the republication of this book and its series.

Hope we can do this for a long time, guys.

Reverend Roland Mars and his wife, Starr, for opening up their hearts and home to me, for praying and encouraging me in my research and my work, and for letting me borrow Silvermoon's name for my book.

This book's for you, Rolly, and for all your people, red and yellow, black and white. Keep tellin' it like it is. I'm your brother!

The Board of the Narragansett Indian Church, for listening to my impromptu preaching, for giving me some insight into their rich heritage (both Indian and Christian), and for inadvertently fueling the fire of evangelism in my heart.

My prayer is that this book will turn your eyes anew upon the cross of the only begotten Son of the One Great God of all peoples and tribes. No white man's god here, just Christ for the nations!

William Scranton Simmons—anthropologist extraordinaire at Brown University, Providence—for all the hands-on and open-hearted research and writing he has done concerning the Indians of

New England (the Narragansett in particular), for his advice and bibliographic leads, and for his encouragement.

Without your books, Bill, I'd be stuck in the mud.

 Lancaster County Public Library, for wandering the electronic highways of interlibrary loan in search of obscure seventeenth-century books and pamphlets, for calling my home countless times when another ancient manuscript had arrived from some far-off depository, and for letting me renew their own books so many times that hardly any other library patron had a chance to read about New England history for a year!

Keep those shelves stacked, folks! And keep those computers hummin'. If not for your excellent service and assistance, I'd be up the muddy creek without a paddle.

 Steve Erk (and Carol Erk for giving Steve "leave"), for all the long walks and the listening ear, for the prayer and encouragement, and for that last-minute all-nighter before the manuscript was due.

Though your expertise with the English language is a delight to my ears, Steve, it was your willingness to make photocopies and punch holes in laser paper at 5 a.m. that got me through. Thanks! Let's not do it again.

 Dick Stipe and Liz Andes (my bosses at North Market Street Graphics, where I used to put in my weekly forty), for the privilege of the use of the equipment necessary to edit and print my home-grown manuscript.

 Marc Campbell for being the very first person to read what I wrote, and for liking it so much.

Hope your own dreams and imaginations end up on folks' bookshelves someday.

 Roger Williams for his great heart, for his much-writing, for his life-risking commitment to biblical truth as he saw it, for his love for the

Indians as sons and daughters of Noah, and for his being my great-great-great-great-great-great grandfather.

I look forward to meeting you, Grandpa, on that "larger, brighter day."

 John Eliot, Daniel Gookin, and the successive generations of the Mayhews of Martha's Vineyard for their uncompromising commitment to do good—temporally and eternally—to the Indians of New England.

Your lives and examples shine like lights in the darkness. Many whom you led into the narrow gate now stand with you in the wide gardens of the Courts of the King. Because of the foundations you laid, many more have passed through that gate behind you. May you have the great joy of seeing more follow still.

PART ONE:

The Children of Cautantowwit

"… they say of themselves, that they have sprung up and grown in that very place, like the very trees of the wilderness."

—Roger Williams

CHAPTER ONE

The Rain From God

My name is now Jacob. It means "one who replaces another by force."

It is a new name to me, for the name it has so lately replaced is the one I wore for season upon season until now when I am an old man with the sunset in my eyes.

My name is now Jacob, and I speak it to myself while by myself. When I arise. When I sit and look out of my window at the falling leaves. When I begin my prayers. And when I lay my head upon my bed to sleep, perhaps to wake beyond the river.

Soon, beyond the river.

I was Katanaquat, the Rain From God, but no rain at all, as I see it now. Just the promise of rain and the breaking of promises. A cold and bitter wind to both my friends and to my enemies.

I was Katanaquat, the strong one.

But the arms that stripped my name from me were stronger than my own.

Before the final blow, I wore my name like war paint, and I fought with all who dared to wrest it from me. Even did I hold at bay, for days and nights unnumbered, the one who now at last has laid me low.

He knew where I was weakest, for he followed me on every path I trod. And now he is the conqueror.

Strangely, sadly, had I known that my defeat would taste so much like victory, I do not think I would have fought so hard, so long, so foolishly.

But, no! This is the dead one speaking now. For how can a man know what might have been if one path had been chosen against another? And while he walks forward, how can a man truly know what lies in the thicket before him?

I lived my life a warrior. That is all I really know. Of my warfare I can tell you, for the warpath is a clear one through the forest of my memory. I walk it one more time with you before my knife grows dull and no tree can be marked to show the way.

My father was born two days south of the river Chipuxet in the village of the sachem Woipequand.

Mequaminea was his mother. Opponeechet, a sagamore and warrior of his people, was his father. They were Pequot, long-time enemies of the Narragansett.

As my father came forth from the womb of his mother, a strong wind lifted the door of the wigwam, scattering the coals of the fire, awakening flames that had been sleeping, bringing light and warmth into the room. And so the child was named Waupi, the Wind, because the wind had come to greet him at his birth.

When Waupi my father was a boy of eleven summers, strong and straight like the pine, he was able already to bend a bow with those who were many summers older. He had proven himself a hunter and had stood with his father and the other warriors when the village was threatened by the Narragansett during the Last Harvest. But no arrow flew, only the curse, the threat, and the angry taunt. The Narragansett returned to their country; the Pequot to their harvest.

Then it was the First Moon After The Last Harvest, the time of the Great Hunt Before Snow. Waupi wanted to go, but because many warriors were out on the hunt, he had to stay home with the women, the children, and the old men.

Opponeechet and forty Pequot hunters set out into the thick forest, eastward toward the land of the Niantic. For many risings and sleepings they hunted the woods, laying their traps and running the deer. Though they followed many herds, they killed but little and soon became discouraged. It seemed their arrows would not fly straight and that the beasts were fleeter of foot than was natural. The hunters began to believe the spirits were against them. They slept warily in the night.

Then Watoomish, an older man among them, dreamed a dream.

In his dream he saw the dreaded spirit Chepi leading the beasts of the forest eastward—always away from and always ahead of the hunters—until he brought them into a valley filled with the bones of dead beasts. There below the dark hills, the Pequot hunters were met by a huge powwow[1] with the legbone of a stag in each large hand. The powwow mocked them and pursued them from the valley. It was then that Watoomish awakened, sweating and trembling.

The dream upset the hunters much, and they counseled among themselves as to its meaning. Some were very frightened and wanted to return home. Others feared that if they went home their own powwow would chase them back into the woods with deer bones in his hands. Some felt they had angered the spirits and that the dream was telling them to fast and dance to appease Chepi and to win back the favor of the gods of the forest. Or perhaps they should carry the dream back to the tribe and ask their powwow to break the bad medicine that opposed them, for then they could start the hunt over with assured success.

But Opponeechet had an interpretation and a plan of his own, for he knew that it would be their shame to go back to the village empty-handed. He also knew that many of the men would not rejoin the hunt no matter how long the tribe danced, being content to fish the rivers and gather shellfish from the seashore. No! The Pequot needed the meat of a successful hunt, so Opponeechet had to put heart into his hunters.

He had strong medicine, everyone knew, for he had fought many battles and taken many scalps with never an injury to himself. An arrow once struck

---

[1] *Powwow* is a word which originated with the pre-European Indians of America's northeast—the Narragansett in particular—and has since spread in use across all of North America. Yet time and travels have nearly erased its first meaning. The current and most common use of the word denotes a large tribal or intertribal gathering. More colloquially, the word is used as slang for "gettin' together to talk things over." But in the historical context of *The Rain From God*, powwow means "medicine man" or "shaman." In short, the powwow was the tribal healer, prophet, magician, and priest of the New England Indian. Interestingly, among the Amish of Lancaster County, Pennsylvania, "powwowing" (also called "conjuring" or "charming") has sustained its original Indian "witch doctor" connotation. To the Amish, powwowing is folk-rooted faith healing, and some Amish condemn the practice.

him full in the chest, the force of it knocking him to the ground. But he was unharmed, for an amulet that he wore around his neck had taken the blow. That is why Opponeechet my grandfather was a sagamore, and why men were willing to follow him into the battle.

"Are we women that hide in our wigwams when we see the shadow of the enemy?" he challenged. "Do we run from the moose because he snorts at us in the night? Are our legs like those of children or our moccasins worn thin that we sit down after such a short walk? Watoomish has dreamed a dream, but why do we see in it only our defeat and not our victory? I say Watoomish woke too soon!"

He looked upon his hunters and spread out his arms as if to embrace the darkened woodland.

"We have crossed the Pocatuck," he said. "We are under the trees of the Niantic slaves of the Narragansett. This path walks in two days to the village of the brothers Mascus and Canonicus, chief sachems of the Narragansett. In that village dwells Askug the powwow!"

The hunters glanced uneasily about them as if each shadow beyond their fire hid an image of the hated Askug. Opponeechet scowled and continued his speech.

"The dog of a powwow sets his curse against us night and day! And so the spirits blow our arrows from their paths! But now Chepi is leading us to the wigwam of the medicine man!"

The hunters arose. "No! It must not be! We must go home at once!" they cried, grabbing at their weapons and pulling at their boots.

"We must not go home!" Opponeechet declared stubbornly, for there was hard purpose in his counsel and hot hatred in his heart against the sorcery of Askug. "We must not go home! We must go on! And I will go on, though none go with me. I will follow Chepi into his valley of bones."

The hunters shouted against this counsel, stamping their feet and waving their arms in the smoky air, as if to wake themselves from yet another dream of danger and defeat. Opponeechet spoke louder, above the fearful wailing.

"To the wigwam of the sorcerer I will walk. I will face him. I will lay his bones upon his own floor. I will bring his head home to Woipequand. I will have his medicine for myself. Then the Pequot will be forever free of his curses and his mockery!"

"I will not go!" was the united cry of the astonished hunters as they took up their weapons and gathered the meager spoils of their hunt. Without looking back they trod one behind the other through the bushes toward the Pocatuck, toward the country of the Pequot, toward the shoreline and the setting sun, toward home.

But Opponeechet was not wholly deserted, for two men stood with him beside the low fire—Nashemit his brother, and Wasqueek the One-eyed. Wasqueek had relatives among the Narragansett, and he knew well the way to the house of Askug.

Sometimes three are better than three hundred for a feat such as Opponeechet intended.

They threw more wood upon their fire, danced and chanted around the leaping, crackling flames and called upon the spirits to aid them in their mission. They put aside the heart of the hunter to take up the cry of the warrior, smeared their bodies with the blood of the black bear, donned the feathers of the owl, and boasted to fall upon their prey like the beasts of the night—of a sudden, in the silence, to devour.

Before the dawn had fully broken, Opponeechet and his warriors were upon the path that led to the chief city of the Narragansett. The sun climbed twice to the top of its mountain and came down twice on the other side. It was nearing its sleep after its second descent when the Pequot band found itself within sight of the campfires of Mascus and Canonicus.

The three warriors drank deeply from the waters of a nearby stream, settled themselves within the tangled shelter of the rhododendron, and slept the night in turns.

When the stars began to yawn, as the morning sky began to wake, Wasqueek led Opponeechet and Nashemit silently within the walls of the slumbering village.

No more than one hundred steps brought them before the door of the wigwam of Askug. As quiet as the opening of an eye, they raised their war clubs, set their hearts to the slaughter, and pushed aside the skins that hung at the door.

But the spirits were with the powwow.

Old Bones, the house dog of Askug, met the invaders at the door. They kicked their way past the barking guard and fell upon the startled, waking household.

Moatankunk the young son of Askug was killed immediately, his head crushed by the club of Wasqueek.

Satquag the nephew of Askug was slain in his bed, his scalp taken from him by the knife of Nashemit.

But the powwow rolled aside from the deathblow of Opponeechet, howling loudly to alarm the sleeping village, slashing at the leg of the sagamore with his knife, gashing him deeply below the left knee. Old Bones took the other leg in his sharp teeth.

Mishtaqua, the wife of Askug, rose to her feet shrieking. As Wasqueek swung toward her with his bloody club, she struck him with the leg bone of a stag. He went down for one brief moment, but that was all it took for him to know that it was time to flee. The sight of the bone in the hands of the squaw[2] was too much like the dream of Watoomish, too much like a nightmare come true. Nashemit saw it too.

"We must go!" shouted Nashemit as he brought his club down upon the head of Old Bones, freeing Opponeechet from the grip of the dog.

The men of the Pequot turned as one and fled the tent, running like the hare before the fox, as wakened warriors of the Narragansett tumbled toward the wigwam of the powwow.

"It is Wasqueek!" screamed Mishtaqua as the Pequot invaders mounted the wall that surrounded the town.

Then something happened to Wasqueek. Perhaps his one eye failed him and he did not see the logs that lay loose upon their sides just within the wall. Perhaps the spirit of Old Bones caught him by the leg. Perhaps his heart froze when Mishtaqua howled his name. No matter— he fell. And before he could rise again, the Narragansett had him in their grasp.

Mishtaqua held her dead son in her bloody arms, wailing the dirge of

---

[2] *Squaw*, a very popular Indian term in use across our nation, is in reality and origin a pre-seventeenth-century Narragansett word. First heard by the Europeans from the lips of the Indians of New England—and thus made part of the initial English-Indian vocabulary—*squaw* has worked its way west, all the way to Hollywood, through the centuries. Though some present-day Native Americans consider the word an offensive English invention, it is in fact an Indian term. In *The Rain From God, squaw* takes its place in a way that is linguistically, culturally, and historically accurate.

death, cursing the Pequot assassins, calling on her husband to avenge her. He must slay the killer of Moatankunk her son. He must capture a boy-child from the Pequot to replace her dear and dead beloved.

The village took up her dirge, blackening their bodies, pouring their tears upon the ashes of their mourning.

Then they took up her call for vengeance.

They tied Wasqueek to a pole within the center of the village, and Mishtaqua took the sight from his good eye with the sharp end of a burning brand. They broke all his bones, cut off his fingers one at a time, and burned his flesh slowly as he sang his own death song. Then they fed his charred meat to their dogs.

But before he died, he surrendered the names of Opponeechet and Nashemit.

In the Moon When The Leaves Have Fallen, Mascus led many warriors against the village of Woipequand.

In the fighting, Nashemit fell dead beneath the war club of Mascus, and Opponeechet my grandfather was slain by Askug of the Narragansett. I know this to be true, for my father told me so. He was there. He saw it with his own eyes. Askug told me so as well when I was young, and showed me once the dried scalp of the father of my father.

A young boy was captured and brought to Mishtaqua. It was Waupi, my father.

Mishtaqua bathed him in the cold waters of the Cawcawmsquick, clothed him in the skin of the beaver, adopted him into her family, and cherished him as though he were her own blood and of her own body.

He loved her in return, as an orphaned pup will love the she-wolf who takes it into her den and nurses it along with her own. He took upon himself the Narragansett name, the Narragansett pride, the Narragansett destiny.

To end the blood feud between the clans of Askug and Opponeechet, the Narragansett powwow paid one hundred arms of white wampum, with fifty arms of black wampum, to the wife and relatives of the slain Pequot sagamore. Thus he bought peace in the matter for a time, and secured the right to make Waupi his son.

But there was no love between my father and the powwow, for Askug would not have it. His hatred of the Pequot caused him to hold the heart of my father away from his own. Waupi was to him as the trophy of war, the living spoils of a conquest not yet complete, the smoldering brand from the fire of an enemy which must be extinguished before it can be carved as a weapon to be used against the foe.

Askug changed the name of my father to Nopatin, the East Wind, for the Narragansett wind had come from the east to fall upon the Pequot wind and had stolen it away.

From that day my father blew from the east, and he grew to be a brave and faithful warrior of the Narragansett.

In the seventeenth summer of his life, Nopatin—now a warrior who had spilled the blood of Wampanoag, Nipmuc, and even Pequot—married Taquattin. She became my mother during the Moon When The Snow Melts And The Rivers Run High. Yet in the year of my birth, the rivers ran low. For the snow of the winter had stayed frozen in the clouds, and no rain had fallen at all.

Mascus and Canonicus were worried that the soil would be dry and choked at the Moon Of The First Planting, and so Askug had prayed long for rain. Yet there was no rain.

A fast was called. A dance was held which lasted for many days. But still the clouds would not open.

It was almost the time for my mother to bring me forth when Askug had a dream.

He saw a squaw in childbirth—it was Taquattin. She brought forth a serpent and not a child. As the serpent came forth from my mother, the heavens clouded over and the rains fell.

The serpent is the sign of power with the gods. It is the sign of all powwows. And it is the name of this one powwow—for Askug means Snake. Askug declared the meaning of his dream to be thus: that my birth would be a sign from the spirits that they had heard our prayers, that rain would fall upon our fields as I was being born, and that I would be a powwow like himself, mighty in medicine and close with the spirits. My name, he said, would be Katanaquat, the Rain From God.

My father had much hope in this dream, for he had prayed for a son and he had prayed for the rain. But he was much troubled as well, because he feared the spirits would take me from him and give me to Askug as he himself had been taken from his own father many summers gone. He also half-suspected the dream to be a lie, concocted by Askug to place me under his power. He did not say so to Askug, but he argued long that it was not the right of the powwow to name the child.

Even today I do not doubt the power of the spirits, the supernatural nature of the dream of Askug, or the circumstances of my birth, but I know that powwows lie. Indeed, all men are liars.

My mother was captured by the vision, and "Katanaquat" was on her lips days before she began her labor to bring me to the light.

The night of my birth, thunder was heard across the waters of the Great Bay, and the salt sea and the dark sky were troubled together as a great wind pushed black clouds from the isle of Quinunicut to the land of the Narragansett.

Rain was truly falling as I came suddenly into the world, my mother shouting "Katanaquat!" and my father shaking his head in fearsome wonder. He took me gently in his arms and walked out into the storming night. He held me up to the weeping sky, his own tears mixing with the welcomed waters of the birthing clouds. And there he stood, while I bawled and squirmed in protest against the cold pelting of the eager spring rain.

At last, in sobered awe, he returned me to the breast of my mother and began to dance in gratitude and joy around the warm fire within the crowded wigwam. The village took up his song, rejoicing in the double blessing: warm rain for the thirsty earth and a boy-child for the Narragansett.

"A Narragansett!" they shouted.

"A Narragansett!" echoed Askug.

"A warrior is born!" they chanted.

"A warrior is born!" sang my father in return.

"Rain from God!" they thundered.

"Rain From God!" answered Askug.

"Katanaquat, my son!" declared my father. And he went out again into the blessed rain and bowed his proud head upon the puddled earth.

CHAPTER TWO

My Friends

The Fool was my friend. We were born one day apart. I was first and the Fool followed. But whereas I came forth with a dream and a destiny amid the lightning and the thunder and the freshly falling rain, Assoko arrived in the quiet grey shadow of the lingering storm, his feet first and his eyes crossed.

While I grew strong and fast within the wigwam of my father, Assoko crawled on all fours for so long that we thought he was part beast.

While I was learning to walk and run and think and talk like every other boy-child in the village, the Fool was still laughing and crying like a new papoose.

While I was dreaming of flying like Kaukant the crow, Assoko was pulling himself forward—slowly, so slowly—like the slug upon the rock in the dew of the evening.

But we lived our days together, the Fool and I, for his mother and mine were sisters. We breathed the air as brothers.

He first walked with his strong, clinging arms wrapped around my waist, stumbling at my side as I wandered over rock and root beside my father through the woods.

He first talked while lying at my feet, weeping as I scolded him for once again waking me by tumbling over my head in the early-morning dimness of the wigwam of my father. "Show me. Show me. Show me," he sobbed over and over as I tried to calm him, scolded him anew for his unmanly tears and shouted to my mother to come and hear the Fool speak. "I will show you," I sternly consoled him, though I did not know what my promise carried. All I knew was that I was the she-bear, Assoko was my cub, and life—for my poor Fool at least—was the hunter.

But the she-bear is not cruel to her young as the children of men are to one another, and I was often cruel to my Fool. He was in my power, and though I felt a strange and affectionate pride in every new step he took, I would often deride him for his failures. Then he would cry, and I would deride him for his tears. I had to make of him a man, you see, though we were only boys together beneath the green wood.

I kept my pledge. I showed him. I showed him everything my father showed me. I told him everything my father told me. I took him everywhere my father led me. And he followed until he was strong enough to walk, even to run, with the rest of us. With the best of us.

Still, he cried like a baby at each unfamiliar hill, each new task and trial. And always I would scold him for his tears, which only squeezed more rain from his sorrow-clouded eyes. At length he acquired a habit of his own design in which he would fight his tears to a standstill, pull the surrounding air into his chest in one long breath, and swallow his sorrow like one who swallows a handful of bitter water. Then he would stare, his dark green eyes to the sky, unmoving but for the nervous twitching of his short, round fingers. Not a breath—no, not a single breath—until his lungs were pleading to the spirits for relief. Then with a sharp cough and a loud caw, he would suck in the sky and begin to laugh.

Such laughter! It spilled out of him like waters from the broken dam of the beaver, carrying all before it. It bewitched me so that laughter was all I could answer to him. And then we laughed together, long, foolishly, and for no other reason than laughter itself.

Yet even his tears, at times, were so full of power that I could not bring myself to rebuke them. They welled up from a sorrow deeper than his own hurt, like the sea which holds within it something of the life of so many others. My own life—I now see—was alive within Assoko. Always his tears were clean, never bitter, washing him free of his chains each time they fell. They never muddied him. He was nothing like me.

I loved him—not for himself, I am ashamed to say—but for how he was the strong shield and the warm cloak of my soul.

When I was sad, he was sad with me. When I was happy, he was happy with me. When I was angry, he owned my cause as his own. When I was excited, he danced as though the springtime was alive within his breast. And when he danced, I felt the strength of life, the heartbeat of a river.

Yes, a river, clean and with nothing dead upon it or within it. A river without shores, flowing where it will, when it will, suddenly quenching the thirsty soil of some dry and dusty field. I was always thirsty, though I little knew it then. Assoko filled me up unselfishly and without complaint.

Others feared him. Some pitied him. Many believed he was possessed by spirits. Askug told me the Fool was part spirit, part beast and part man— that he would bring us favor with the gods, favor with the beasts of the earth and sea, and favor in war. I thought at times that Askug might be right, but I did not always believe the powwow, even then. Somehow I could always trust the Fool.

Assoko could think for himself. I knew he could, no matter what others said about him being a mere shell for the gods. Not quickly, not always correctly, but fully in the end. As the turtle walks, so does the Fool think— slowly, simply, carefully, purposefully. And, amazingly, always to the good of another, to the joy of another. This was so unlike the spirits that I was sure that Askug was wrong and that my Fool was a man indeed. Yet he was so unlike other men that I sometimes thought he must simply be a very different kind of god himself!

I have known other fools, but none like mine. Others are useless or stupid. Some are wicked and easily angered. But Assoko had a mind that bore good fruit in its own slow season and a heart that could break curses and join enemies in peace.

The boys mocked him, for we all mocked one another, and I would take his offense upon myself, fighting those who taunted him. The Fool joined me, and we would beat our foes together. None of us minded. This was our way, the way of the Narragansett. We were learning to be warriors. This was all we knew.

And I showed Assoko. We learned together.

For the Fool was my friend.

Miantonomi was my friend. Not like the Fool. Not like a brother. But like a father, though he was but a year my elder.

He was everything I wanted to be. A true Narragansett. Brave, strong, keen-eyed, self-controlled, and wise as a sachem, for his father was the grand sachem Mascus, brother of the great Canonicus. He knew who his enemies were, though they were few while we were young.

He liked me. Because I defended the Fool. Because I won my wrestling matches with the other boys. And because I laughed like the Fool. No one else dared laugh like the Fool.

I felt myself a warrior in the presence of Miantonomi, respected and somehow older than my days. I would follow him anywhere. Yet I wished it were he that followed me.

We learned to bend our bows together, Miantonomi and I, with the Fool. Miantonomi made his own bow from the strong branch of the hickory, while I could barely bend the one my father made of ash. The Fool broke his, and he cried.

Miantonomi sent his arrows straight into the dead birch that we used as our target. My arrows soon found his in the birch, and we knew that we would one day hunt together, fight together. The feathered shafts of the Fool stung his bow hand, sending the women ducking and scolding, and he cried.

But in time, Assoko too could pull the bow string to his ear, whittle his own arrows from the branches of the white oak, and send his shafts into the birch. Then he laughed, always laughed, until his laughter seemed to guide his missiles, and his aim at last surpassed our own. We were astounded. The Fool never missed. Laughing and leaping, running and dancing, he hit his mark. Many said that his arrows were alive, for how could a mere boy—and a fool at that!—shoot so well, so straight, so often? Miantonomi thought it was his spirits, but I felt that the Fool could shoot straight because he wanted to. More than anyone he wanted to. Because it gave him such joy. And so I thought that his heart would guide my arrows too, for we breathed the air as brothers.

I did not fear him. Why should I? He was my Fool. He was my friend.

But I feared Miantonomi. And as much as I loved him, I envied him.

His eyes were dark and deep, quiet and strong, keen and clear, but they hid a heaviness that could weigh another down with their stare.

His words flew swiftly on the moment, but straight as his arrows, true and to the mark. They were words you could hold in your hands, not like the fog that so many of us coughed up and blew at one another. They were words you wanted to remember. Words you wished had been your own. Words you were tempted to steal. But none dared steal the words of Miantonomi.

His anger was sharp and heavy like the tomahawk, but he held it tightly, used it wisely, loosed it only when justice could be served.

His arms were firm and long. His legs were supple and strong. At eleven summers he could pull up the three-summer oak by its roots. Like the ant which carries the beetle, he amazed me.

He was my idol. My prince. I was glad he was my friend.

In the summer when Miantonomi first uprooted the three-summer oak, we stalked off into the forest, three ready warriors of the mighty Narragansett, to test our courage and our strength against the foes of our imagination. And many they were.

The Pequot and the Wampanoag, like phantoms of all that grew beneath the shadowed forest ceiling, were behind every rock and tree. The Mohawk, like the howling storm, suddenly and mercilessly fell upon us from the north. The wildcat and the wolf, like the cruel lightning of summer, leapt down at us from the clouded heights of the cragged cliffsides.

And we took them all on!

We bent our green bows and shot our dull-headed arrows at the gathered hosts of our tribal enemies, shouting, howling, and threatening to hang their ugly heads in the branches of the hawthorn. We chased them through the underbrush and over the wooded hills, swinging the war clubs we had carefully chosen from among the fallen limbs along the path. We overtook them in their retreat, crushing their painted skulls as they ran. We caught their wounded in the rout, wrestled them to the ground, and exercised our wooden knives in the taking of their coveted scalps.

Then we turned to the forest beasts who were circling in around us. We grappled with the wildcat and kicked at the wolf until, shamelessly wounded and gloriously triumphant, we knelt in reverence as their lifeblood mingled with the rotted skeletons of the ancient fallen oaks.

All the while, Assoko laughed like the gamester who has just won the possessions of the powwow. Miantonomi played the serious warrior, as if he were already a sachem twice his age and the veteran of a hundred battles. And I found myself sometimes in our common world of war, sometimes in my private world of dreams, and sometimes—startlingly—at the double-edge of a fear that we might meet the enemy indeed or be lost in the woods and caught after dark by the skulking spirit Chepi.

We spent hours at our warfare, hunting the brush for our hidden foes—

and our misfired arrows. Only the Fool, even in the midst of his great, mad joy, hit his targets with consistency.

We chased the squirrel and the partridge. We sent fierce tribes of antlered deer bounding in graceful panic toward their homelands. And once, Assoko bounced a shaft off a startled porcupine, whose own arrows—if he could have loosed them—would have done far more damage than ours.

At the end of our chase we ate the conquered flesh of the blackberry and strengthened our hearts with the cold blood of the fresh spring that bubbled out of the ground at the foot of the Hill Of The Talking Rock.

"Tired! At last!" said Assoko, between giggles, gulps of water, and gasps for air.

"I took thirty scalps!" I boasted, holding up a thick handful of grass and sod that I had torn loose from the earth during the recent slaughter of our foes.

"You lost thirty arrows!" taunted Miantonomi playfully, splashing the cold water in my face. His challenge woke me from my fantasy and signaled the beginning of more serious games.

"You fling mud in my eyes, only to have your own blackened!" I replied, rising to my feet above the amused Miantonomi. The Fool was puzzled and waited to see what would come.

The arms of Miantonomi were instantly around my knees as we tumbled together into the thick weeds. "Wrestle!" shouted Assoko, and on my behalf he flung himself into the thrashing tangle of arms and legs.

"You are a weak woman!" I declared to Miantonomi as I pushed him back upon the rocky soil, pinning his shoulders to the earth. "Weak woman! Weak woman!" echoed Assoko as he lay sprawled upon the legs of our prince.

Our captive struggled for a moment and then relaxed. I knew well not to loosen my grip or shift my weight, but Assoko thought the game already won.

"Weak woman!" Assoko repeated. "Weak wo … Ow! Oh! What! Ha ha! Wup!" With a violent heave of his legs, Miantonomi had sent the Fool rolling into the blackberry thicket.

I braced myself, leaning fully upon the chest of my opponent. I dared not lose my advantage, or it was my turn to roll.

"Weak woman?" Miantonomi grinned, with such feigned malice that I nearly let go for fear. He lurched to the side, like an angry bear, in a powerful effort to throw me off. I held on, and we tumbled over. But only once. And then Miantonomi had the upper hand.

With one arm he pinned both of mine to the ground. With the other he pulled his wooden knife from beneath his belt. One more breath and he would take my scalp—for the twentieth time that summer. In all the years of our warring together, I had yet to take his even once! The repeat of my defeat was upon me. Though my lips were silent, my heart cried out in shameful anger and in futile and utter denial of the imminent conquest.

The Fool heard my heart cry. Did he not always? But what could he do?

"Ough!" groaned Miantonomi as a stream-soaked log connected with his temple, splintering into a dozen soggy pieces, and knocking him sideways into the gurgling spring.

"Weak woman!" shouted Assoko as he followed the dazed son of the sachem into the shallow waters. The two of them lay in the pebbled stream, limbs locked in a strained and determined contest of strength and endurance, and for a brief moment they did not appear to move. Then they came unwound in a wild whirl of arms and legs and water and sticks and stones. I imagined they were demons of the sudden storm, pulling down the woods around us, and I shrank back against the hillside in expectant fear.

They were on their feet now, thrashing to and fro like some multi-limbed beast that had arisen with the waters from beneath the dark earth.

But ho! I heard laughter.

My Fool, without a doubt!

They were on the ground again, grinding themselves into the black dust beside the muddied stream. Laughter again. A shout! And the Fool had his hand clapped upon the painted forehead of Miantonomi.

I laughed then too—a mad, pride-driven laugh of victory for my Fool. Were we not one? Was this not also my first scalping of the unconquerable Miantonomi? I got up and danced. I lay down again and laughed some more. Only the sobered eyes of the son of the sachem could bring my merriment to a halt.

"The spirits! They are strong in the Fool!" gasped Miantonomi as he rose from the streamside and threw himself in exhaustion upon the grass beside me. He was clearly shaken, but far from taken. He had not lost to a man, after all, but to the gods within a man. This was not an even warfare. This was not the struggle of warrior against warrior. This was a game of the gods. "Let them play it with someone else now," he said with resignation and the pained echo of injustice.

I did not argue with him, but I felt he had been rightly beaten. By my Fool. By me.

We lay upon our backs for a time, quietly, thoughtfully, on the hillside of the Talking Rock. It was Assoko who broke into our dreams.

"Does it really talk?" he asked.

"Oh, yes," I replied, "with many tongues."

The Fool was sitting up and gazing toward the top of the hill. The Talking Rock had caught his slow imagination, and it would not let him go. We waited for his next words. At length we forgot he had spoken.

I was dreaming of a dawn massacre against the Mohawk—in which I played the principal and princely part of war chief and sagamore—when Assoko spoke again.

"Will it talk to us?"

"We can ask it to," I suggested.

I was returning to the slaughter of the Mohawk, for I had not yet taken their sachem or given my victory speech, when Miantonomi arose and ascended the hill.

The Fool and I followed.

There at the top of the mound, in the midst of a grove of young oak and chestnut, beneath a towering, crooked, and crumbling old maple, sat a large egg-shaped rock upon an even larger table of flat stone. The ancient giant Weetucks had once used this stone table for his private meat, and the rounded rock had undoubtedly been the egg of some great bird from his own country. Now the egg was turned to stone—by time or sorcery, no one knew. It was one of several Talking rocks that were scattered throughout the countryside upon various hills and mountains of the varied tribes to our north, south, and west.

"Ask of it what you will, brave Katanaquat," said Miantonomi.

I walked to the rock and put my right hand upon its smooth surface. The eyes of Assoko were wide with expectation. Miantonomi smiled a knowing, curious smile.

"Oh, Great Rock With Tongues Of Many Tribes," I began, warming to the ruse, "we would hear from you this day. We have wandered far from home and fire and wish to send a message to our village. Can you speak for us from your table on the hill? Will you shout to the mountains and send your echo to the wigwams of our fathers?"

I stepped back and bowed upon the ground before the mute boulder. From the corner of my eye, I saw that Miantonomi was no longer next to the Fool. In fact, he was nowhere in sight. As I had expected.

Assoko, tensely standing at my back in tranced attention, stared at the stone as if he thought it might at any moment rise up and bellow. And it may as well have.

From behind the Talking Rock, the bushes began to swell and sway as a low, throaty moaning rose upon the hilltop. If Assoko had been a bird, he would have flown right then, but for lack of wings—or better instinct—he fell instead upon his face and began to wail. I thought that a good wail out of me would aid the cause, so I raised my voice with the Rock and with the Fool.

Gradually the moaning from the Rock died down and a rattling commenced—very much like the sound of dry sticks against stone— followed by a rain of acorns and chestnuts. By this time, Assoko was as a dead man, and even the pelting of the nuts from heaven could not move him.

Then the Rock began to speak.

Why should it cry to our fathers? it asked. *Who were we to call upon it for favors? Were we not mere children? Simply food for the giants who, like Weetucks, once feasted upon this mountain? Should it not lay us upon its table, crush us like dried corn, and leave us as meal for the birds?*

Why even speak to us at all? it continued. *We were less than children. We were old women. Our scalps were worth nothing for our cowardice. We would never be warriors, we who could so easily be lost so close to home.*

Our bows were like willow, it contended. *Our arrows like stubble. Our knives like wet clay. Our hearts like water. Our courage like the hare. Our strength like the chipmunk. Our dreams like those of dogs.*

And on and on.

As the insults continued, the Fool slowly lifted his head, a strange and righteous frown upon his dusty face. He stood to his feet and swept back his hair from his sweaty brow with his stubby fingers. His lip bent low. His hands fisted. He strode toward the Talking Rock.

As he passed me, he reached down and swatted me upon the shoulder, a signal for me to stand and follow. I did so.

When he reached the Rock, he stood defiantly before it, crossed his arms and said, "Weak woman!"

Had he guessed?

Miantonomi, believing himself at last discovered, stepped out from behind the talking stone, with a triumphant grin upon his broad face. But the smile froze as he beheld the Fool.

Assoko flung his challenge again at the Talking Rock, most surely at the Rock alone, as he had but a moment earlier.

"Weak woman!" he spat.

When the stone refused to answer, he placed both hands upon it and pushed his determined face against its sun-warmed surface. Speaking into the heart of the silent giant with a conviction that frightened me, he repeated his words: "Weak woman!"

"It fears you, Assoko," said Miantonomi. "Your spirits are stronger," he affirmed. He meant it.

Suddenly, strangely, I sank into a grey, misty world of my own. My Fool was not a house of spirits to be feared! Was he? *No, no, Miantonomi, no!* I shouted within myself. But I could not bring my tongue to say so.

Neither was this stone the voice of the gods! It could say nothing and fear nothing and was not to be feared or fought. It was a dead thing. A boulder on a hill. A great egg to be rolled this way and that upon its hard plate in order to raise a rumble that could be heard two hundred whoops away. It was a sender of signals. A way to talk to other men on other hills. A way to send a call for help, a call to war, a call to assemble in council, a call to the feasts and the games. That is all this rock was for and all that it could do. And it took men to make it speak! But something held these words within me.

My fears! They held me captive to the spirits. Our games had become the sport of the gods! The spirits intended to confuse us upon this hill, cause the sun to fall while we reeled in tired and foggy dreams, and then set upon us in the darkness of the night!

But why should the gods win? And why should I let them? I must not let them!

"We will make it talk to us!" I cried in a sudden effort to awaken us to a common moment of reality.

Both Assoko and Miantonomi turned to me in puzzled wonder.

"Not as the spirits talk! Not as you just pretended, Miantonomi!" I said.

"Assoko, did you not recognize the voice of our prince from behind the stone?" I chided.

"Miantonomi, my prince," I appealed, "we have made a fool of our Fool again, but he has risen to defend his honor—our honor—nonetheless. Is he not the brave warrior? Have we not taught him as much?"

I continued in earnest, "Will not the dog bark when he hears the sudden noise outside the wigwam, even though it be the footsteps of his master? Will he not receive the reward of his vigilance, though he howl at friend instead of foe? Hooray for the howls of the Fool!

"Come, Miantonomi. Come, Assoko, let us make this stone talk as our fathers make it talk, not as our imaginations make it talk."

Miantonomi shook himself for a moment and pulled back his shoulders. As our fathers make it talk! Now that was a challenge worthy of the son of the sachem! But it took several grown men to move the Talking Rock. He was about to say so, but my words were not done.

"Are we not able? Cannot our arms together make it speak? Is our strength truly that of the chipmunk and no more?"

"We shall make it talk!" declared Miantonomi, and I knew I had won half my battle. "Let us make this stone grumble, Assoko!" Miantonomi said, as he laid his thick hand upon the shoulder of the Fool.

Assoko relaxed and stood back to look upon the rock anew. Long he stood, finally closing his eyes as if asleep, waiting for the dawn to open them to familiar shapes and forms and colors. "You were the rock, Meentomi!" he said at last, and he sat down to cry.

"Stop that weeping!" I insisted, for I felt pulled by his heart again, away from the sun, the trees, the Rock, and the coolness of the wind against my face.

"Weak woman," sobbed the Fool, and I knew at once that I had robbed him of the victory against the foe. We could have subdued that stone together, he and I. For my honor alone, no doubt, and nothing more. Now the Rock had beaten him—beaten us—and I had no means of vengeance. But still we might have victory.

"Up, up!" I shouted, tugging at his arm, slapping his chest. And so he rose, took a deep breath, set his lips tightly—and waited. Waited for the anxious wind within him to cry out for release. I held my breath with his. It was my habit now as well.

With the tears still damp upon his face, the laughter started burning in his eyes. Soon he was down in the dust, twisted and doubled and laughing like the fool he was, pulling at the legs of Miantonomi as if to say, *Come into my joy. It is yours, if you'll have it!* This was no spirit! This was my shield against the spirits! This was my Fool. And as I joined him in his laughter— our laughter—I was free again.

We leaned against the Rock, the three of us, straining to melt our hearts and muscles and wills into one. We growled like the bear together. We howled like our fathers together. We pounded ourselves against the hard stone together. We chanted and sang and pushed together. And as our breathing grew heavier, as our sweat and our blood began to stain the grey skin of the Talking Rock, it began ever so faintly to click and whisper, tap and titter.

We moved when it moved—or it moved when we moved—forward a little, backward a little, the wakening rhythm of its heavy heart communicating strength to our own.

"Talk, Rock, talk!" commanded Miantonomi, as we gasped and pounded, grunted and shoved, fell back and pushed forward, finally following the slowly growing momentum of the great swaying stone.

Cracking and groaning, in time with our chanting, the Rock began to tell us its story. The Fool was laughing now, his roaring—like a war cry—sending blood to our heads, strength to our arms, medicine to our souls. We leapt upon the Rock as it leaned away from us, jumped back when it turned to strike at us, pursued it again as it fell away, gave way to it as it rose once more, pummeled it again in its retreat until it was reeling like a dazed and wounded bear. Falling on its hard knees as it rolled forward, banging its bare buttocks as it staggered backward, it set the earth to shaking with its mad rhythm.

"Talk, Rock, talk!" we shouted, triumphantly riding the reeling giant as it thundered its pained message across the valleys and the hills. We made it talk! As our fathers make it talk! We made it shout! Made it cry out to the very heavens! We were mighty! We were men!

"Aaaaaaieee!" shrieked Assoko, in a flash of terror.

"Waughoh!" cried Miantonomi, as the world turned upside-down.

"Father!" fired my tongue, just once, a weak and distant plea in the midst of a sudden, dull, and heavy pain. Then darkness.

CHAPTER THREE

My Foes

The bees were humming in my head, but I could not see them. My mother was there, a comforting, invisible presence, singing quietly. Her song was like medicine, stronger than the buzzing of the bees. Sweeter than the honey.

My father was there, formless but strong, lifting me from the hard earth, holding me to the heavens, laying me down again upon the cool grass. Lifting me up. Laying me down. Lifting me up. Laying me down.

No! Not upon the stones! Please, not the stones! They tear my flesh. They bruise my bones. They whisper frightening things to my soul. They rise up and shout at me with strange rumbles and clatters. They fall upon me. They break themselves into pieces, grow legs like the beetle, crawl upon my face, and crumble to dust in my open mouth.

I cough. I choke. The air is full of poison! I cannot breathe. I gasp. I plead. I stumble and fall in a dark, dusty fog. Where am I?

I see nothing. Only red. Then black. Then red.

The bees are back! They sting me with fire. They suck the water from my bones. I thirst. I thirst. I thirst.

A maiden is singing. She moistens my lips with water. Her music is like the soft breeze of autumn in the reeds beside the bay. Why can I not wake to see her face?

Snow. Naked I lie in the snow! Cold. So horribly cold. Where is my clothing? Where is my home?

Oh, Father! It is so good to see you. Hold me. Warm me. Rock me in your arms.

* * *

A rattle. A moan. A shriek. A clamor of spirits. Dark shapes dancing, clawing at my soul. And the bees have returned. Hornets and wasps! Knives and tomahawks! They puncture my skin. They carve my flesh. They chip my bones.

I run. Somehow I run. I leap and fly like the hawk, drifting above the earth. Above the hills. Above the sea. But the bees follow. They swarm all around. They drive me to the ground. Upon the rocks. My bones are broken.

There are snakes in the rocks!

Askug! Askug! Send them away. Chase them away. Use your medicine. Use your magic. I hear you singing. I hear you howling. I hear snakes hissing! Are they your snakes? Why are they biting me? Call them away! Call them away!

How can I be so helpless? So weak? Where is my bow? Have I no medicine of my own?

Miantonomi, my prince! Are you there?

Assoko, my Fool, my friend! Cry with me! Pray for me! Mourn for me!

Mother! Father! It is so hot! Keesuckquand the sun god comes down from the sky to assail me! My eyes are on fire! My skin is aflame! I drift upon the boiling sea in a lone canoe. The merciless sun beats me into unconsciousness.

Night comes at last with the sound of the surf. With the silver moon. With the fall of a soft, warm rain.

I am wet with the sweat of my body.

Like dew upon the morning grass, it is cool. It is fresh. It is sweet.

I can breathe. I can see.

Am I home?

"Mother?" I said, and I didn't know my voice. It was like one who spoke from beneath the earth.

My mother turned at the sound. Her hands went to her mouth and she knelt at once beside my bed. With hope and fear in her eyes, she dried my wet brow with my blanket, but it was soon wet again with her tears.

I tried to smile, but I felt as if my face would crack. I tried to sit up, but my arms were useless and a searing pain in my left side pulled me down upon the bed. The knives of the hornets.

"Katanaquat, my wounded little warrior!" cried my mother. "Do not try to rise."

"What ... what happened to me?" I croaked. "How long ...?" And I began to cough, which set my side afire with pain. But I did not moan. I did not cry out. I lay very still.

"Do not try to speak," said Mother. But I had to know.

"What happened?" I asked again at last, with the voice of the drowning dog.

And then my father entered the wigwam. Beholding me, the fire of strong joy flashed in his eyes, but he did not speak of it. He knelt beside my mother and placed his hand upon my head.

"The fever is gone," said Father, his face next to mine. "Chepi has taken his curse away!"

His hair fell upon my neck as he spoke quietly in my ear. "I was outside and I heard you, my son. Your words are awake!"

I remembered.

The Talking Rock.

"The Fool?" I asked. And I was quiet for a moment, catching my breath. Biting my lip. Swallowing my pain.

"Miantonomi?" I asked. And I looked anxiously into the eyes of my father.

"The Fool is well," replied Father. "Miantonomi too is well. But you, my son, have been hanging between two worlds!"

His hands hovered over my pained abdomen. "When the Talking Rock fell, you fell beneath it. It tore your flesh. It broke your bones. It dashed your head upon the stone table. It stole your waking. But before it fell on you, it called us to you! We came and I carried you home. But the wound in your side became poisoned. You would not wake. For three suns and three moons, you have been far from us in your dreams. We did not know if you would open your eyes in this world again."

Mother held a cup of water to my parched lips and I drank a swallow. It went down like broken shards of bone. Tears came to my eyes but I could not move my arms to wipe them. I was ashamed.

"Your ribs are broken," Father continued. "Your left arm is broken. You must not move for many days. Askug has been with you often. He set the bones in your arm. He looked to your wound. He has called upon the spirits daily. We owe him much." And then Father glanced toward the door cautiously. "Indeed we owe him too much!" he said, and I understood. The powwow charged heavily for his services, even to those who were of his own household.

"But your mother has been with you every hour. And the daughter of Potachiq, young Silvermoon, has cared for you much," Father said. "To them, as much as to Askug and the spirits, we owe your life!"

He then took Mother in his arms, and together they wept. I sighed deeply, staring up through the smokehole at the moonlit clouds in the midnight sky above us. In spite of my pain, I smiled.

"Silvermoon," I whispered to myself and closed my eyes.

When next I awoke, I became more fully aware of my condition. My hair had been shorn so that the wound on my head could be tended. My left arm was splinted and tightly wrapped from my elbow to my wrist so that the broken bone might heal. On my left side was a bandage of pelt soaked in a potion of herbs, held tightly by strips of animal skin which encircled my waist. Hidden within me, beneath the bandage, were several broken ribs. I felt their confusion as they cried out for reunion with their brothers. My side throbbed with a painful life of its own. The muscles of my arms and legs were weak and tight and sore. My stomach was captive to a gnawing hunger, but I was unable to free it because I could eat nothing but the thinnest broth, and only a little at a time. My throat felt as if there were a fish stuck in it. And my head ached incessantly.

In a looking glass, a remarkable invention of strange gods which my father had won at gambling, I saw a frightful ghost: a pale, swollen, black-eyed face beneath a hairless, gashed, and purple scalp.

When I first go to war, I said to myself, *I will paint myself thus, for surely no enemy can stand before such a sight!*

And so I lay in my painful imaginings, grateful to be alive but wishing with all my heart that I could fall asleep and wake again whole.

On this fourth morning after the Talking Rock fell, Askug came to see me.

"You are with us at last!" he said, taking my hand in his. I felt the warmth of his pleasure.

Though not by blood, the powwow was my grandfather. He looked after my needs like a father, for which my own father was sometimes grateful, sometimes jealously annoyed.

"Does the boy need two fathers?" Nopatin my father once challenged Askug.

"Does the boy need two hands, two arms, two eyes, two ears, and two legs?" Askug replied.

"Yet only one hand bends the bow," returned my father. "You may sharpen the arrow, Askug, but I will bend the bow!"

I was the son of my father—the only son of my father and the only child. He would have me in his hands as long as wisdom and the gods allowed. Then he would loose me to the world.

But this day the powwow held me in his hands. Or so he wished.

"Your dreams, Katanaquat," he said, looking deep into my eyes.

I did not like his gaze, for it often was not his alone. There were others within the cavern of his soul. I saw them sometimes, and they chilled me to the bone, but I had learned not to blink or turn away. No one stared me down. Neither man nor spirit. I was neither dog nor wolf. I was Narragansett.

"Your dreams," he repeated. "Were they visions from the spirits? Did the gods come to meet you in your sleep?"

Askug longed for the day of my vision. Without a vision, I could not be a powwow. Without a visitation, I could not walk in his moccasins. This meant more to him than I knew, but I was fully aware that it was at the heart of our relationship. As my father taught me to walk like the hunter and the warrior, Askug taught me to think like the medicine man. As my father taught me to sharpen stone to tip my arrows, Askug taught me to sharpen the flint of my soul.

The spirits. They were everywhere. This I knew better than most. I could see, I could hear, I could sense what others could not. This is not the great advantage that some may think, but none may choose the eyes with which they are born. The choice is whether to close them or leave them opened. When I was young, I was very frightened by the spirits. And indeed they can surprise me still. But as I grew, I decided I would not be bullied. I had both a body and a spirit, so why let a ghost have the best of me! No matter how powerful were the gods, I was a man! A Narragansett! I would have my life in my own hands and live it in victory.

Askug had powerful medicine, and I wanted that of course. But Askug had to shame himself—or so it seemed to me—in order to win his power. And even then he did not win it! He had to ask it of the spirits.

They came to him and gave him what he asked, but they stole from him as well. The strength of his body sometimes failed him completely, especially after healings. Then he would collapse in a heap like the dead man. Sometimes he babbled for hours like the sick old woman. Sometimes he thrashed about the ground like the wounded snake. And none of this of his own will. Yet he accepted these indignities as though they were the scalps of an enemy. And so we accepted them too. For this was the way and the calling of the powwow. This was the tradition of the Narragansett.

Other times, Askug had the strength of ten men! I have seen him throw off many strong warriors in battle. I have seen him shatter stone upon his forehead. And once, when I was a boy of five summers, he became so angry with my father—over what, I still do not know—that he uprooted the wigwam of Nopatin in the dead of winter, as the child flips the turtle on its back, sending my mother and me screaming out into the drifted snow. But these were not the work of the man—this was the spirits. And as much as Askug had them, they had him. No one could tell what he would be like from one moon to the next, not even Mishtaqua, his squaw, who remembered a day long past when Askug was the gentle man, the caring man. Now he was driven by an evil passion for power and authority.

I was heir to that passion.

But I did not want the spirits. Not on their terms. I would be my own man. This I decided when I was young. But I did not say so to Askug. I feared him too much to cross him in that way.

A vision? I did not want a vision.

A dream? I had dreams in plenty, but none that called me to medicine and sorcery.

Nightmares? I knew their cold grasp. Some were of my own mind. Some were of the spirits, taking advantage as I slept. Perhaps they knew I resisted them. I resisted even in my dreams.

But the Talking Rock dreams, the fever dreams of the past three days and nights, had nothing in them to hold me. Except, perhaps, the sweet singing of the gentle maiden. But that had been no dream.

"The gods did not come," I whispered hoarsely to the anxious pow-wow at my bedside. And if they had I would not have told him.

"No beast spoke to you? No bird or serpent?" Askug asked.

I closed my eyes that I might better speak my own mind.

"The only creatures I saw," I rasped, "were torturers and tormentors. My pain and my sickness wore wings, bore fangs. I had nightmares. Nothing more. And they are now gone."

I opened my eyes again to look at my grandfather. His eyes spoke plainly of the disappointment in his heart. Perhaps I should have felt his sorrow. Instead I felt my anger. Who was this man to wish me bound by serpents? And yet I understood. Should I not be grateful for his medicine toward me while I dreamed of death?

"Thank you," I said, "for chasing the evil ones from me."

He smiled sadly. "I could not let them steal The Rain From God," he said. "Your life will be long, young Katanaquat. Your medicine will come with time. Rest now, for you have been in the hot and tiresome battle."

He rose to leave, and as he lifted the door, his shadow fell across my face. He turned back toward me for a moment to bless me. But his words were lost to me. I heard only the hissing of the snake.

My next visitors were those whom I longed for most. And one more.

Miantonomi and my Fool came warily, curiously, amazedly to my sickbed. They had seen me in my tossings. They had stood in fear for me as I writhed in my fantasies. They had joined the chant of Askug in the frantic fervor of his medicine over me. They had sat quietly as my mother sang, as Silvermoon changed my bandages. But that had all seemed to them a dream. Now I was returned from the shadows. Now I was something to gawk at. Gawking with them was Uncas, Pequot cousin of Miantonomi.

"Kat?" said Assoko, not quite sure that I was me.

"It is Kat," I said hoarsely, "though it looks like the scalped bear beneath the deadfall."

The Fool crossed his legs and sat down smiling. He began a slow back-and-forth rocking with his upper body.

"Weak Woman was the deadfall!" he said.

"He calls the Talking Rock 'Weak Woman' now," explained Miantonomi, sitting down beside the Fool.

"If it is a weak woman," I replied faintly, "then I am an infant daughter of the Niantic."

Uncas stood over me, grimly staring.

"You look awful," he commented with a candor not born of empathy.

The great grandfather of Uncas—Weesoum—had been Chief Sachem of the Narragansett. Both Miantonomi and Uncas were of his line: Miantonomi through the sons and grandsons of Weesoum, and Uncas through the daughters and granddaughters. But Uncas was born west of the Pocatuck. His Narrangansett grandmother had married a Pequot.

"We made her talk!" said Assoko proudly, still speaking of the Rock.

"We made her angry!" added Miantonomi.

"You roused the woods for miles," commented Uncas, sitting down at last, "and nearly caused a war between the Nipmuc and the Pequot! They say the Rock shouted insults back and forth between the hills of their villages, taunting them with remembrances of past injustices and blood feuds. They painted themselves for combat because of the slander of your rock. When they found out it was all your doing, both tribes declared war upon the Narragansett!"

"Your own tongue is better suited for such work, Uncas son of Meekunump!" fired the voice of a woman from behind the curtained door. My mother entered our lodge with a scowl and an armful of firewood. "Such splintered tales are no good greeting for a boy in need of comfort!" she said with a critical eye upon Uncas. "Either speak like the friend or be silent at the bedside of the wounded!"

Uncas set his mouth straight like the arrow. "I meant no ill, good Taquattin. I have come to wish Katanaquat well."

She was not convinced. Nor was I. Though I had not the hatred for all Pequots as Askug had, I knew Uncas to be far less than an honor to his people.

I did not like him. Though he was my age, I could not be his friend. For he would have no friends, only slaves! He imagined himself a sachem to his peers, a tyrant in the kingdom of our childhood. He was a bully with brains who had a ready excuse for every injustice he inflicted on those weaker than he. He was a liar and a thief, though he denied it with brightly painted words. When he came to our village to visit, I hid my best arrows.

At first, for the sake of Miantonomi, for my father, and for the Pequot blood that flowed in my own veins, I tried to respect Uncas. But that was impossible! He held his head high by standing on the heads of others. His taunts were never in jest. He cheated at snowsnake and other games. He chanted loudest at the feasts. He had an answer for every question, even those not put to him. But he could be as silent as the stone when it served his purpose. For he knew that even the fool, when he is silent, is considered wise.

And in our games together, he played Miantonomi against me.

But Uncas was a thin curtain to the son of Mascus. My prince was seldom fooled by his scheming cousin. Yet Miantonomi treated Uncas with a grace that amazed me. I could hardly bear the presence of the liar!

The worst of it was the way he treated Assoko. He knew that we loved him and so looked for ways to embarrass him. He used this abuse as a stone in our moccasins to make us stumble. It was a torture to me. Many times his cruel words nearly brought us to blows, which is what he really wanted!

I wondered why his heart was so hard against all men. My own heart became harder the longer I hated him.

"Weak Woman," said Assoko, still thinking of our Rock.

"How did you really tip it?" asked Uncas.

"Weak Woman," echoed Assoko.

"With these strong arms!" I answered firmly, raising my bruised limbs in painful and ironic display.

"Weetucks did not help you?" asked Uncas, repeating the rumor that had spread throughout the country.

"Perhaps he did," replied Miantonomi, simply.

"But we did not see him," I added.

Assoko rocked quietly, smiling.

"Some say you placed the branch of an oak beneath the Rock," continued Uncas, pushing a small stick into the rug upon the floor, "and rolled it from its table thus," he said, flicking a piece of shell from the rug to my bed.

"These were our branches," I said, lifting my legs in determined demonstration.

"The son of the sachem has much medicine, I know," said Uncas, looking to Miantonomi, "but this Rock is too large for one young heir of the king!"

"I was not alone," said Miantonomi calmly.

"But your only help was this murmuring Fool and this infant daughter of the Niantic," argued the Pequot, shaking the backs of his hands at Assoko and me, a thin smile upon his face.

I squirmed on my bed, lost for a reply worthy of the insult.

Assoko rocked silently, lost upon the hill of the Weak Woman.

Miantonomi grinned. He had an answer after all!

"We are Narragansett, my foolish cousin!" he replied finally, slapping Uncas upon the back. Then he arose. With a gentle touch upon the shoulder of Assoko, he signaled their departure. Uncas rose last.

"You will soon be well enough to chase the rabbit again," said Uncas, looking at me with empty eyes.

"Or roll hills into the sea!" said Miantonomi, putting strength into my heart.

"Kat?" said the Fool.

"Assoko?" I replied.

"We made her talk!" said the Fool.

And they left me for a time.

I slept—a restless sleep, but without dreams. When my eyes opened again, the moon hung high in the heavens. I could see it through a small opening in the door of the wigwam. A warm fire was burning not far from my feet. It sang its song pleasantly, pushing twisted vines of dark smoke upward through the hole in the roof.

Mother was asleep, but Askug and my father were conversing on the other side of the blaze. At first I could hear only the growling of their voices, but at length their words grew louder. I strained my ears to hear above the crackling of the flames.

"The Pequot have always been women!" railed the powwow.

"Am I a woman?" asked Nopatin my father.

"You are a Narragansett," replied Askug.

"Am I a woman or a warrior?" asked Nopatin.

"You are a warrior," said Askug. "And a Narragansett," he repeated.

"If I were a Pequot, would I be a woman or a warrior?" challenged Nopatin my father.

"You are not a Pequot!"

"I was born a Pequot!"

"You are not a Pequot!"

"I was born a Pequot!" repeated Nopatin, standing to his feet. "My father was born a Pequot!" he continued, swinging his arms wildly through the swirling, rising smoke. "Opponeechet was a warrior, not a woman! To his dying day! As you well know!"

"Do not speak that name in this house!" shouted Askug, staring madly at Nopatin. I thought that those eyes alone would silence my father. But nothing could still him at that moment.

"It is the name of my father," said Nopatin. "And you drive me to speak it, though I would keep it in silent honor!" His own eyes followed the smoke to the ceiling. "And this is my house!" he added.

"Your father is dead!" replied Askug. "I am your father now! And you are a Narragansett!"

"Of course I am a Narragansett! I would be nothing else!" pleaded Nopatin, leaning toward the face of the powwow. "But you hate the Pequot so much that you never cease reminding me of who I was! And you want me to hate them as you do! I cannot. I will not. How can I hate what I loved? How can I hate those who loved me?

"But I am no longer a Pequot. I do not so much as wish to be a Pequot. I am a Narragansett! You yourself taught me all that it is to be a Narragansett. You tell me constantly that I am a Narragansett." Nopatin knelt before the powwow, his hands clenched in angry frustration. "But you will not let me be a Narragansett! You make me into two people and let me be none!"

Askug sat unblinking, more like a chiseled stone than a man. The flickering flames sent eerie shadows sliding across his face. He was silent.

"You took my father from me. You took me from my people," accused Nopatin. "You made me your son—and I would be your son gladly! But you have never been a father to me. Never held me in your arms. Never given me one small bit of your heart or soul. Yet you ask of me what none should ask of any man."

Askug did not look upon my father. His eyes were cold like ice, though the fire burned warm.

Nopatin my father stood tall, looking down upon the silent powwow. "Since Katanaquat my son was within the womb of his mother, you have wanted him as your own!" he spat bitterly. "And you would dream a dream to take him—if you could!"

A wind came down the smoke hole, chasing the smoke back into the room. For a moment, all was amber and grey, and I heard my mother coughing. In the haze, I saw that Askug had risen. The two men stood face to face in the choking shadows. I closed my eyes for a moment because of the clouds.

"This is my house," I heard my father say. The wind shifted, or perhaps it was the door being opened, but when I opened my eyes, the smoke had cleared and Askug had gone.

CHAPTER FOUR

The Blood of My Brothers

My wounds healed. My hair grew long enough to fall across the scar upon my head. My ribs no longer cried to me. My arm could be trusted.

I carried much wood for my mother. I pushed much snow from our door. I made myself a new bow. I sharpened many arrowheads. I carved tiny faces in the war club of my father. I played snowsnake and the moccasin game. I listened to many stories around the fires of many wigwams. I ran in three marathons through the thick forest—one in the deep snow before the Melting and two within the Moon Of The New Green.

I laughed with Assoko. I arm-wrestled with Miantonomi. I chanted with Askug. I smiled at Silvermoon. I cried with my mother. I followed my father into the lair of the sleeping black bear. And I longed for the full warmth of spring.

Just after the Melting, the village moved from the Valley of Winter to the Planting Acres by the shoreline.

The cornfields were prepared for seed, and the Fool and I helped my father and some of the men in the repairing of the scare towers. Many would take watch in these towers from the time of the planting until the Moon Of The First Harvest in order to scare the birds from the seeds and the beasts from the corn. Only Kaukant the crow was given freedom of the fields, for Kaukant had brought our first corn from the garden of the great god Cautantowwit. Sometimes, when I took my turn at the scare tower, I dreamed I was a big black bird in flight, fanning and drifting upon the southwest wind, heading to Sowanniu, to the courts of Cautantowwit. It was always summer there.

But my dreams of summer were often interrupted by the irreverent Kaukant and his lesser brothers.

I liked the watch, for it gave me time to plan contests and conquests, time to imagine myself as the warrior that I knew I soon would be. Not soon enough for me!

This season, while upon the watch, I carved my first war club.

While I sat in the tower one misty morning, my father came to me.

"Katanaquat, I want you with me on the hunt today. I have brought your new bow and your straightest arrows." He set them at my feet.

"May I bring my war club? It is almost finished!" I cried excitedly, holding it up for him to see. Carved from a piece of soft maple, it was decorated with moons and suns and the faces of ugly creatures and wild animals. At the top I had bound a large stone with a strip of raw deerhide.

"A fine weapon!" said my father admiringly. He ran his long fingers across the carved handle. "You have the gift of your mother for images."

"And your gift for war, Father!"

"I have danced for the hunt, Katanaquat, not the war," said my father with an understanding smile, "but you may bring your club."

I was glad, and I was proud. I pushed the club under my belt, gathered my bow and arrows, and leapt down from the platform. A younger child who had come to the fields with my father climbed up into the tower and took my place at the watch.

Father and I headed north into the woods along the Pochassett, where soon we met a small band of hunters from the village. Several of them had sons with them, friends of my own age, and I knew at once that this was a special rite of our coming manhood. The unexpected privilege of this hunting expedition warmed my heart and filled me with joy. As we filed quietly through the newly greening woodland, I felt at peace with the spirits, at peace with the land, and at peace with my destiny. I quickly fell into a daydream in which my father and I were co-captains of a raiding party, heading deep into the dangerous country of the man-eating Mohawk. If only Miantonomi had been with us!

"He is with Mascus and another group of men, heading west," my father told me.

At a certain crossing of a swift, cold stream, we halted for a rest. The men took out their tobacco, and the woods soon filled with the sacred smoke of many pipes. Father gave me his pipe, and I smoked a little, but my mind was on the Mohawk.

My father showed off my war club to the members of our party, and there were many grunts of affirmation.

"Where did you find the stone?" asked Apponeaque, the son of Chipetauck, as he examined my workmanship.

"It is just a piece of a Weak Woman," I replied.

"What do you mean by that?" asked a curious hunter.

"It is a piece of the Talking Rock which broke off when the Rock fell on me," I said. "Assoko has named the Rock 'Weak Woman,' because we made it talk."

"Aha! Your head was hard enough to break a finger off the Weak Woman, was it?" laughed the hunter. "Perhaps that finger will fall upon the head of an enemy someday."

"I know that it will!" I declared, dancing menacingly, club in hand.

"With you in our band," said an old brave who was drinking at the stream, "we shall have no need of our bows. You can chase the beasts down yourself and strike them to the ground with the finger of the Weak Woman!"

All laughed warmly, for it was not an insulting jest. It was meant to put strength in my heart. And so it did. As we continued on our way, I ran even more assuredly along the warpath that would lead to the destruction of the Mohawk.

Just as I was creeping in my imagination upon the enemy village at the break of dawn, our band came to a fork in the path. Several of the older hunters talked quietly while the rest of us settled for a moment upon the moss-covered rocks beneath the trees. The mid-afternoon sun, a warm and reassuring presence, filtered through the thick evergreens and the freshly budded branches of an ancient stand of oak.

My father roused me from my fantasy, pointing through the forest to a faint outcropping of rock that was nearly two shouts from our present position.

"When the sun has fallen below that hill," he said, "many deer will come down the right-hand path to drink from the quiet waters of

Ashanduck Pond. If the deer sense our presence, they will retreat to the left-hand path and head eastward over a bend in the Pochassett. The band will split now into two groups in order to surround and intercept the deer in a small glade not far from Ashanduck.

"You must know where we are going," Father said, "but you must not think about the deer. They might hear you thinking and turn back on the path."

"I will not think about them, Father," I promised, "for I am on the warpath in my mind!"

"Very good, Katanaquat," Father replied. "You will be ready when we come upon our quarry!"

Father and I went with eight others along the left-hand path and shortly halted to take up silent vigil downwind from Ashanduck in the rocks and bushes at the appointed bend of the Pochassett. There the men took nokehick from their backbaskets and belt pouches, and we each mixed a handful of the parched cornmeal with a handful of the waters of the river. In quiet, hopeful anxiety for the coming kill, we had our simple supper.

The longer we sat, the harder it was not to think about Noonatch the deer. I tried to think of Miantonomi, but I then imagined him downing a great buck. I dreamed of home, but the vision that emerged was of my triumphant return from the hunt. And the more I tried to conjure up my massacre of the Mohawk, the more I longed for the sight of the antlered herd. As I struggled vainly to direct the arrows of my imagination away from Noonatch, my father suddenly stood up straight.

They are coming! I said within myself, and a joyous anticipation sent a shudder through my body. Then I heard the whooping. But hunters do not whoop, I knew, for then the prey will flee!

Father swiftly knelt beside me, pulled an arrow from his quiver and set it to his bow. With one quick jerk of his head, he signaled me to get behind him. I saw other men reach for their bows, as boys took cover behind rocks and trees. Like Pussough the wildcat before it leaps upon the fawn, the hunters were poised, tensed, bows readied. Hands moved automatically to belts and backbaskets, affirming the ready presence of war clubs and knives. Heads turned toward the approaching sound of shouting voices and running feet. Eyes scanned the thick forest before us, glancing quickly at the shallow waters behind us. The air was full of whispering spirits, and small, frightened animals came bounding toward us through the brambles and the brush. The hunters around me were transformed into warriors in a moment. A sudden chill ran up my back, across my shoulders, and into my head. Could the Mohawk be coming?

Shaking, I shafted my bow and felt for my club.

The shouting was no longer confused noise. It was words we all could hear. Our names were being called. There were cries for help. We heard sharp words of woe and disaster. And in a breath, about three bow shots away, the forest came suddenly alive with a wall of men running. It was the other half of our hunting party—some of them. Two things I saw clearly: blood and fear.

With a shout of our own, we rose from our cover to meet them. They fell into our arms, and for one heavy moment there was only the sound of gasping and groaning. Then, as one, we lifted our voices in a raw cry of anger, pain, and sorrow.

One of the wounded, a warrior named Pequawus the Grey Fox, held a bloodied arrow in his hand. He had pulled it from his own chest, and he flung it at the feet of my father.

"Wampanoag!" was all he said.

"How many?" fired Father.

"Fifteen! Twenty! They fell on us as we sat in wait for the deer!" said Pequawus.

"Ahyaiiee!" we cried. And then the forest echoed with our words.

"Where are Waucho and his son?"

"Neemaut, my brother!"

"You are wounded! Are you killed?"

"Who escaped?"

"God is against us!"

"Curse the Wampanoag!"

"Are any of the enemy killed?"

"Do they follow? Are there more?"

"Must we run?"

"Can we overtake them?"

Within my mind, I wanted to fly like the partridge out of the woods and down the river toward home. But within my heart, I had been captured by the blood of my brothers. I no longer heard the words that blew around me. I no longer saw the fear upon the faces of the boys. Instead I heard the voice of my Fool shouting, "Weak Woman!" I saw Miantonomi standing tall upon the table of the Talking Rock, saying, "Come, let us make this stone talk!" I saw the Talking Rock topple. Then I knew, without knowing, what I had to do.

"Follow me!" I cried as I swung my war club above my head, pushing my way past wailing warriors and bewildered boys.

"Katanaquat!" shouted Father as I ran toward the trees from which the fleeing party had just come. I did not stop. And then Nopatin my father raised the war whoop which became the cry of the entire party, and I found myself overtaken by the swift-running warriors of the avenging Narragansett. Single file, we moved determinedly toward the thicket of the battle. Though I had long dreamed of war, and though my dreams had seemed so real to me, this was no shadow, no vision now. My heart pounded like the surf upon the shore, pushing me forward like the waves of the sea. The setting sun flooded the forest with a golden light. The tall trees were silhouetted sharply against the red and yellow sky. The line of grim warriors moved like the black snake over the rocks and through the ferns. I felt wonderfully awake.

When we came upon the scene of the ambush, we could go no further, for the scalped bodies of three of our dead brothers called us to the earth beside them and held us there in tears. The Wampanoag were gone. We did not pursue them.

Mascus, and Canonicus his brother, called for war against the Wampanoag. Though the Wampanoag, under their chief sachem Massasoit, had trespassed on our lands before, as we had on theirs, lately they had become much bolder. They stole from our traps. They dug up our corn caches. They came in large numbers and disturbed the hunt. Sometimes there was fighting. But not until now had they taken scalps in ambush. It was time to return their blood upon them. Time to bend them low like the birch beneath the snow.

Many sachems from scattered villages of the Narragansett took up the call. Much warpaint was mixed. Many arrows were fashioned. Forts were built around our principal towns. War parties danced and took to the trail every new moon for the next four moons. Sometimes our warriors crossed eastward over the waters of the Great Bay and moved north through the lands of the enemy. Sometimes we entered the Wampanoag country across the Pawtucket and the Sneechteconet. But always we hunted, raided, and fought when the advantage was ours. Once a band of Narragansett and Nipmuc fired arrows even into the city of Massasoit.

But the Wampanoag did not hide in their wigwams. They did not bow the knee. Instead, they increased their raids into our country. There were battles, and warriors of both tribes died. None called for the truce. No wampum was offered for the peace.

Another summer came, and the fighting continued like rain which sometimes falls and sometimes passes over. My father led several raiding parties, and I wanted desperately to go with him. But I was not allowed. Not yet. Even Miantonomi, though a young man of thirteen summers, could not go, and this made him sullen. He was not interested in play. He sat at home sharpening his arrows, greasing his bow, chanting his war chant, smoking the tobacco of Mascus his father, and bringing the vision of war always before the troubled eyes of his mother. She could only wish him younger. Or older. Anything but an almost-warrior who would not bring in wood for the fire!

Assoko asked daily if he might go to war. And daily he was told that he could not. Daily he cried about it. Daily he laughed about it. Daily he sharpened his arrows, greased his bow, and sang of battle.

I sat with him one morning, and we sang together. We sang of the ancient battle between the great, good spirit Cautantowwit and the evil spirit Chepi, a song that was carved in our memories, for we had heard it since we lay at the breasts of our mothers. When our chant ended, Assoko wept.

"Why now do you cry?" I asked him. "Is it because our song is done?"

He wagged his head, no.

"Is it because Chepi tread upon the young corn in the garden of Cautantowwit?"

He wagged his head, no, and wiped the tears from his face with his long black hair.

"Is it because you cannot go to war?"

"Kat cannot go," sobbed the Fool.

It was me for whom he wept! But I did not want his tears. I was angry with him for reminding me that I was not yet a warrior. I was angry with Miantonomi for sitting alone in the smoke of his wigwam. I was angry with my father for not taking me on the warpath. I was angry with Askug because it was easy to be angry with Askug. I wanted the fight. With any-one!

"Even if I could go, I would not take you with me," I said sharply, intending to turn his tears sour. "You are just our Fool and not a warrior. You cannot think fast enough to war against the Wampanoag."

Assoko rocked quietly, sadly, breathing my words.

"Your spirits would confuse us in battle," I continued. "We would shoot at each other instead of the enemy. We would all start laughing and crying and rolling on the ground, and soon our scalps would be hanging in the lodges of the women of Massasoit!"

Assoko looked at me, the pain of his heart within his eyes. My shafts had hit their mark. But victory tasted like ashes, and I was more angry than before.

"Oh, Fool!" I shouted, rising from the ground beside him. "You are not to blame if we are not yet men!" I kicked the dirt floor with my heel.

He hung his head, saying nothing. Then he rolled onto his knees, lay face down in the dust, and did not move.

"Get up!" I chided, slapping his legs. "You are not the dead man! You are Narragansett, and you will go to war as surely as I will!" But he would not stir.

I knelt beside him, stung in my conscience. "I spoke like Uncas! I am the skunk! I am sorry!" But he would not be roused.

I lay down in the dirt with him, penitent, angry only with myself. "I am the sick old woman!" I declared. "And Assoko is the mighty conqueror!" But he would not so much as turn his face toward mine.

A thunderous clap! And both of us were on our feet in an instant.

The sky was as blue as the breast of Peshauquaog the bluebird. No clouds could be seen above the tall fir trees. No wind blew to bring the summer storm. But it had thundered! Very loudly. Very near us.

Women and children came out of their homes. Dogs barked. Shouts could be heard from across Red Creek. A war party returning? In a breath, the Fool and I were racing to the tent of Miantonomi. But he was not there. He was over the creek with his father, Mascus, said his mother. They were meeting with Dutch traders. "Had we not heard the Dutch thunder?" she asked.

Dutch thunder! The Dutch gods! Here!

A curious crowd cautiously forded the shallow waters of Red Creek to join our sachem. To gaze upon the white spirits. To seek their favor. To touch their thunder sticks. To barter for their magical inventions.

I only wanted to see them with my eyes. That would be enough, I thought. To see with my own eyes what others feared and marveled at. Then I would know better how to be the man. Better how to be the warrior. Better how to hold my own against these new gods—if it came to that. Had Askug seen them yet? I wondered.

As we came upon the clearing in which the council of trade was being held, we huddled in the shadows of the surrounding trees. Within the Council Rocks, I saw my prince Miantonomi, standing tall beside Mascus and Canonicus. And then I spied the gods!

They had to be gods, I thought, for never had I seen men like this! Their legs and arms were fully clothed with smooth skins of bright colors. Their chests and backs were protected by a large shell like the sea turtle, which glistened like calm waters in the sun. Their eyes were like the sun-splashed bay, deep blue and green within their wide faces. Each head of hair upon the gods was of a different hue—some yellow like the spring flowers around the wigwam, some brown like the chestnut. Some curled like the vine around the dead oak; some fell straight like my own. Many of the spirits had much hair upon their faces. It spread out upon the upper lip and wrapped itself from ear to ear upon the cheeks and below the chin. Upon their heads were round, glistening bowls, like the shell of the sea urchin. Upon the bowls, from front to back, rose a single thin blade.

They had weapons. Broad knives as long as their arms, silver like the icicles of winter, were tied to wide skins that were wrapped around their waists. And thundersticks! The long, straight, dark clubs must be their thundersticks. With those clubs they could call down the storm, I was told. They had only to aim them as we point the arm, and lightning leapt forth to strike down their foes. With just one of those thundersticks, I could chase a whole band of Wampanoag! Perhaps even a band of the Dutch gods themselves.

They laid some of their goods upon a scarlet skin which they spread upon the ground. There were tomahawks and hoes made of a marvelous stone called iron. Small knives, like our own but sharper, made of a stone called steel. Small boxes made of wood and filled with beads, like our wampum, but rounder and more colorful. Bags filled with white sand called sugar, pleasant to the taste like the boiled sap of the maple and able to make bitter foods sweet. Looking glasses, like the one my father had, of several sizes and shapes. And strong water in bottles made of glass. The glass, we were told, was made from the sand of the sea!

I understood nothing that they said, but men were there of the Montauk of the Long Island, and they could speak to the Dutch and for them. We traded many furs for their inventions, and we gave them much corn.

When they had gone, Mascus called a feast to thank the spirits for this visitation. There was much dancing and much giving away of personal goods. My father danced the longest and gave away even the looking glass he had won at gambling. But much was given back to him as other men danced. Among his new possessions was a knife of the Dutch gods. I wished it were mine.

Late that night, as men still danced, Assoko and I sat with Miantonomi at the edge of the dance circle, drinking the songs and speeches of our elders. A warrior danced wildly around the fire, chanting as he moved. His song was of the Dutch:

> *Across the great salt sea they float*
> *Upon the great white bird.*
> *The thunder and the lightning come*
> *To do their bidding at their word.*
> *They come to bring us wampum,*
> *And they come to bring us sugar.*
> *They come to bring us medicine,*
> *They come to bring us favor.*
> *They come to bring us iron,*
> *And they come to bring us steel. ...*

I leaned toward Miantonomi, who was gazing intently into the fire. "Father won a steel knife in the dance," I said.

"My father wanted one of the long knives," he replied. "But the gods would not part with any."

"I want a thunderclub," I whispered, loudly enough for only Miantonomi and my Fool to hear. "To fight the Wampanoag."

My prince looked upon me gravely. "Without the medicine to call down the lightning, it would do you no good," he said.

"I would have the medicine if I had the thunderclub," I insisted.

Assoko rocked silently between us, waving his arms gently like the wings of a gull.

"Do you think they really fly upon a great bird?" I asked.

A boy named Wunnauquit, sitting to our left, heard my question. "Moosoog, one of the men of the Montauk, says no," he answered. "He says that they ride in great canoes made of wood, large enough to carry half a village. The canoes have trees growing upon them, with great skins upon their branches. The wind blows upon these skins and pushes the canoes across the waters."

"They control the winds as well as the thunder and the lightning!" said Miantonomi. "And they have come here among us!"

"But we can see them and touch them," I reminded him. "Unlike Chepi, who hides in dreams and visions!"

"Will their favor always be toward us?" my prince wondered aloud.

"Perhaps not," replied Wunnauquit. "For the Montauk told us that white gods landed on the isle of Capawack and took by force a man named Epinew of the village of Chappiquidick."

"Took him where?" I asked, with a sudden chilled shudder in spite of the torrid blaze that rose before us.

"Back to their home in the clouds. Or across the sea. Or wherever they dwell," continued our informant.

"To make him a prince among their people?" asked Miantonomi.

"Perhaps to eat him!" I answered. "The gods do eat men, you know!" I stared at the madly dancing flames. I could almost see the spirits whirling around the circle of the dance, blowing hot air in our faces, touching us with their invisible tongues. Fire was a god, as we all knew. And we had seen it eat men. We had offered it several Wampanoag of late.

Wunnauquit continued. "Moosoog also tells of several Patuxet who went aboard the great canoe of the gods. They too were taken. There was fighting. Thunder and lightning fell from the great canoe upon the Patuxet who were within their boats upon the water. Then the great canoe sailed away."

"The white gods will not take a Narragansett," stated Miantonomi confidently. "For we have Askug, and he will not let them take us."

I was not so sure. Askug had not ever called forth lightning from a stick!

Miantonomi continued. "And we will make friends of the white gods, for we can speak to them face-to-face, and they to us."

"But we do not understand them," I argued. "Can the raccoon speak to the wildcat?"

"The raccoon and the wildcat are both beasts," he replied. "The Narragansett are men. The gods understand men. And have these gods not made themselves understood to the men of the Long Island?" At this he stood up tall to finish his speech. "And we are warriors like the Dutch gods. We make weapons. Weapons for war. But we can also make peace. We can make friends. We will be friends with the white gods." He spoke like the son of the sachem. Strong words. Good words. "Their friendship will give us strength!" he said. Then he sat back down.

"Strength to fight the Wampanoag?" I asked.

"To fight the Wampanoag," he answered.

It was a private council of war. Just the four of us—Miantonomi, the Fool, myself ... and Uncas. He was visiting again with his mother and his sisters, quite often since the war with the Wampanoag. When in the village he always came looking for Miantonomi. Thus we found ourselves together at our private council rock, an outcrop of stone beneath Old Willow by the side of Red Creek.

Upon the rock, with heavy rounded stones that we fished from the stream, we crushed small slabs of red shale into fine powder. We mixed this powder with water and streaked our faces and bodies with the dull red mud. Our war paint.

Upon the rock, with the paint we had mixed, I drew an image of flames. With a black stone, I scribbled the smoke that arose from the imaginary blaze. Our war fire.

Then upon the rock, we sat to hold council.

After many heartbeats with no words spoken, Uncas rose. He should have given place to Miantonomi, for the son of the sachem should have the first speech. My own mouth was shut against this ignoble act only because it was not my place to defend the honor of my prince unless he could not do so himself. I saw fire in the eyes of Miantonomi, but the flame was not a dark one. The Fool sat smiling.

"The Dutch gods have gone away!" said Uncas. "And though we have not learned their tongue, our fathers have embraced their shoulders. Though we have none of their thundersticks, we have their steel knives." At this, he pulled a shining blade from beneath his girdle.

"How did you get that?" I asked enviously.

"A Dutch god gave it to me," he said. And though I expected the lie from Uncas, I found that I believed him. "I gave him the stone knife which I chiseled myself, and he traded me this," he said, lifting it up and turning it from side to side for all to see. It was a thumb longer than the knife of my father.

"May I hold it?" I asked.

"No," he replied, "for I need all its medicine. You have Askug."

"I only want to hold it!" I argued with unhidden irritation.

"Put it away, Uncas," said Miantonomi, "and continue your speech."

"But," I countered, "I only want to look at it!"

Miantonomi flashed an understanding glance at me. His eyes spoke to my heart. I would be silent. I would wait my turn at the speech.

Uncas tucked the knife back in his belt and continued.

"Together we have much medicine! Miantonomi and I are of the line of great sachems. Katanaquat is under the shield of the powwow. Your Fool, your elders say, is full of his own spirits. And," Uncas then drew the blade again, "with this, and others like it, we can fall upon the Wampanoag with victory assured. Our eyes will be like the eyes of the eagle, our feet will fly like the wings of the eagle, and the knives of the Dutch gods will be like the talons of the eagle in the bodies of our prey! We need not the protection of our elders nor the strength of their arms. We have enough of our own!"

His words put strength in us, and we grunted our assent. With a proud gleam in his eye, he sat down.

Miantonomi rose. "Though I do not fear the enemy, I will not go out against him without the consent of my father, Mascus. He has forbidden the warpath to me. Though all the medicine of the powwow were within me, and though I were armed with every weapon of the white gods, I would not defy my father."

My heart weakened. I had hoped for a rallying plea for the battle. Did not Miantonomi spend his days and nights dreaming of the warpath? Surely Mascus would not deny us the blood of our enemies forever. Would he have us play these childish games around chalked fires until all the warriors of the Wampanoag were old men and their daughters all taken as squaws for the Narragansett? Then I saw the lips of my prince bend slowly like the bow. A smile. A plan.

"But," said Miantonomi, "my father has not forbidden the hunt!"

"Yes!" I said, forgetting tradition and leaping to my feet. "We will arm for the hunt, fully and in case of any enemy surprise, and we will go into the woods only a few hours behind a Narragansett raiding party! What could be safer, if our fathers and mothers should ask? We will be like the river that runs between two strong mountains: the village behind us and our warriors ahead. No enemy could come upon us! How can anyone object?"

"Exactly, quick Katanaquat," said my prince, laying his hand upon my shoulder as we stood face to face. "And if our warriors come upon the Wampanoag, we will soon be there to help them! Who will object to the aid of four young hunters with ready bows?"

"Let us fight!" I shouted to the waving willow and the passing wind.

"Fight!" echoed Assoko, and he jumped up and began an awkward shuffle around the weeping willow.

Miantonomi and I followed him in the dance, but Uncas sat watching, a strange smile upon his face. Suddenly he scrambled up to the top of the council rock and announced loudly, "One thing more!"

Reaching into his back bag, he pulled out a small glass bottle filled with a pale liquid.

"Strong water of the white gods!" he proclaimed. "I will take this with us on the warpath. When we are in need of its strength, I will share it with you. Together we will drink the death of our enemies!"

Putting the bottle back in his bag, Uncas slid down from the rock and joined us in the dance.

CHAPTER FIVE

The Song On The Wind

T oo many moons we wait!" I complained to Crooked Tail the pup dog as he rested in the shade beneath the hollowed trunk. Absently, impatiently, I chiseled at the blackened stomach of the charred oak that would one day be my own canoe.

"Wait for what, my son?" said Nopatin my father. I started with surprise, for I thought I was alone. Except for Crooked Tail. Except for the spirits.

"For the Harvest!" I blurted, pulling the lie from the air.

"Ah!" replied Father. "It will come! And with it the games." He knelt beside me to inspect my work. Smiling in approval, he continued his thoughts. "This year you may run with me in the foot ball races upon the shore," he said. "Yes, too many moons we wait. But it will come."

As I grumbled in my anxiousness to follow the war party into the woods, much work went on in the village. The Moon Of The First Harvest had nearly arrived, and the women were busy making bark bags and willow baskets in which to gather and store the crops. They would then dig large pits to hold a portion of the harvest through the winter. But the store seldom lasted through the season of the snow, for the men would come back from the long hunt, dig up the corn and feast until it was gone. We would all eat well for a few days, and then the women would send the men back into the trees, hoping the spirits would quickly lead the beasts of the wood within sight of the bow of the hunter.

Mother was always prepared for the snow. She made our moccasins and our snowshoes. She gathered wood for the fire. She made sure we had rabbitskin blankets and robes, perhaps even a pair of moosehide boots. And she prayed to the spirits that her hidden corn cache would remain hidden! Sometimes I followed her to see where she buried it. Once I told my father. He laughed loudly, whispered the secret to my mother, and she scolded me terribly. But food was for eating, not hiding, I argued! And did men shiver for the winter while the leaf was yet green? Was this not the job of the woman? Was this not the way of the Narragansett?

At last the First Harvest arrived, and with it came plans of a raid against the Wampanoag. I had early news of it, for my father was to lead the party. I told Miantonomi, and he sent word to Uncas, who pestered his mother for leave to come to our village for a short stay. When he arrived he found us in the midst of our people, at the edge of the dance circle in the center of the village. We were gathered to chant and to sing for the success of the raiders. My father led in the dance, and a growing band of warriors followed. But my eyes were upon Askug.

Within the circle, near a whining, popping blaze of pine, the powwow was lost in a dance of his own. Like the nervous deer he pranced, his arms chasing one another around his head in a blur of sweaty flesh, his hands tightly gripping his bone-handled rattles. For a time, he leapt up and down—like the dog trying to grab the piece of meat that the hunter has hung from the branch of the tree—barking loudly each time his feet left the earth. Then, like the rattlesnake an instant before it strikes, he pulled himself down in a hunched position, still as stone but for the rattles in his hands which shook themselves furiously as though alive. "He is a snake!" I said aloud. Then he whirled around in a dizzying spin, his hair and his robes flying from him like the fallen leaves of autumn when the wind suddenly tears them from beneath the trees and scatters them abroad. For a moment I imagined his hair leaving his head altogether. But then he froze in place again, howling like the hungry wolf. Uncas stared at him as though he were a spirit clothed in flesh. The powwow, my grandfather. The spirits were with him. This we knew. And thus they were with the Narragansett.

Long into the night men danced. The fire burned.

When the moon at last retired to its wigwam and the sun began to wake upon its bed, tired men, women, and children lined the wood's edge and chanted quietly. They watched the single line of warriors walk behind my father as they disappeared into the great, deep green. While the men continued singing and the women wearily set about the work of day, four young hunters slipped away to the wigwam of Nopatin to make ready for the hunt.

"I have been sharpening my arrows for so long," said Uncas, "that I wore ten arrowheads down to nothing! Now they are invisible, and the enemy will not see them coming!"

Miantonomi smiled while I searched my mind for a clever reply. I found none, though I had sharpened my arrows for just as long.

"Fight!" said Assoko, his face a curious contradiction of scowling eyes and grinning teeth. "Fight the Wampanoag!"

"Not so loud, Fool!" I chided. "Taquattin my mother is outside beaming a hide. She may hear you! She believes we are preparing to hunt the rabbit."

"The rabbit may wear war paint," said Uncas quietly behind his hand. "How shall we paint ourselves?" he asked.

"We have berries in our bags," answered Miantonomi. "We will squeeze them for paint if it is our fortune to fight. If not, we will eat them!"

Uncas pulled his steel knife from his belt. "Do we have any more of these?" he asked. Miantonomi had one which his uncle Canonicus had given him, and he took it out to show us. The Fool had none.

"What about Katanaquat?" said Uncas. "Did Nopatin already lose his blade in the games?"

The knife of Nopatin. Had he taken it with him? I took his knife basket from the wall where it hung. It was filled with many stone blades— some old and chipped, some new and sharp, some raw and waiting to be shaped by the hands of my father. At the bottom of the basket, my fingers closed upon a leather sheath. Within it I could feel the cold, hard steel of the Dutch gods. Hurriedly and without display, I removed the knife from the sheath, wrapped it in a small piece of deer hide and put it into my back bag. I would return it as soon as our "hunt" was done. If it happened to be stained with the blood of the Wampanoag—as I hoped—my Father would surely not be angry with me for taking it.

"The Fool has his spirits," said Uncas.

"Yes," said Miantonomi.

"And you have the strong water," I said to our Pequot companion.

"Yes," he replied.

Armed well for both the chase of the hare and the possibility of conflict with the Wampanoag, we ducked warily out of the wigwam.

Twenty strides from our tent, Mother was beaming the skin of the buck upon the stretching frame. Her strong arms forced the beaming club from one side of the hide to the other, stretching it, softening it. Soon it would be ready for smoking. Then it could be made into new leggings for my father. Or a blanket for our bed. Or a door. Or many moccasins. Perhaps it would be traded for tools or corn. Or for the inventions of the Dutch gods.

The long, black hair of Taquattin my mother was unbraided, and it clung to her bare back with the sweat of her labor. She was not so pretty as she had once been in the days when Nopatin my father first took her as his bride. The life of the squaw is a hard one, and she wears out much sooner than her man. Mother was now stooped from the weight of each long day. Her arms were thick, but her hands were calloused, thin, and bony. Her teeth had begun to loosen from the chewing of the hide to make the leather. And though it was the summer of her life, the autumn could be seen within her eyes. Yet she always carried springtime in her heart, and soft songs fell from her lips like the quiet waterfall in the midst of the forest of pine. She was a good woman. A good mother. But she had borne my father only one child, and lately he spoke of taking a second wife. Yet Taquattin my mother would always be his love.

"You will not go more than ten whoops from the village, Katanaquat," she cautioned, as our small party approached her.

"The hound must follow the hare, Mother," I grinned, looking into her dark eyes. I hoped she thought me joking.

"You will not be very long, Katanaquat?" she said.

"As long as it takes to catch the rabbit by the ears," offered Uncas, yawning nervously at the morning sun.

Mother glanced at the golden ball hanging in the blue sea of the sky. "When Keesuckquand has begun to climb down from his mountain, you will turn homeward," she suggested.

"We will!" I assured her. "Yes, we will!" echoed the rest of the young hunters, with little intention to either keep our word or heed hers. Mother kissed my forehead and blessed me for the hunt.

As we wound through the village toward the northern woodlands, a young maiden came out of her wigwam to meet us.

"Your mother told me you are hunting today, Katanaquat," Silvermoon said to me, smiling. "Last night I sang for the victory of your father, and I have just finished singing for you!"

I wanted to thank her, but as I looked into her deep eyes, I could think of no words. My heart was making too much noise, and it confused my tongue. Uncas had no such problem.

"Your songs can surely calm the spirits, fair Silvermoon! Your presence puts strength into my heart," he said, looking upon her fully. I felt my face getting warm, and I found my tongue.

"We must go, my brothers," I said suddenly, "for the hare will not sit in the open field and wait for us."

"I believe it might," said Uncas, all the time gazing upon Silvermoon, "if the maiden would sing for us once more." Silvermoon hung her head slightly, her dark hair falling over her eyes. Her smile fell as well.

"She sings beautifully," I said, half to myself. Her smile returned, but not her gaze. And in that moment I wished I were yet bedridden, lying quietly in the wigwam of my father with my mother stirring soup over the fire while Silvermoon wrapped my side in clean bandages, humming.

"I will sing again for you, Katanaquat," she said quietly, and she backed slowly into her wigwam.

I had to pull Uncas away as we turned to leave the village.

"She is a woman!" he said as we entered the green shadows of the tall wood.

"She is my friend," I said. "And I do not think you should stare at her as you did!"

"Your friend!" said Uncas. "Though I have seen her often with your mother, you have never spoken of her as your friend, Katanaquat. Is she promised to you?"

"No! She is just …" I hesitated. "She is just a maiden!" I said. "And I do not think you should stare at her as you did!"

I did not wish to talk about her. Not with Uncas. But I was angry with him over her, and I wanted him to know it. Yet where did this anger come from? Many young braves of the tribe thought Silvermoon beautiful. That had never bothered me. But Uncas! The Pequot was a thief! His eyes, like his hands, would take what was not his. Silvermoon was ours! Not his! I wanted to strike him.

My heart beat heavily, and my breath came noisily as we strode through the ferns and pushed through the bushes on our way to the glade beside the Great Swamp. The warpath of my father would begin there, but I could not think of that battle now.

Uncas and I walked in the lead, side by side, Miantonomi but a stride behind us. The Fool was ten strides further to the rear, humming to himself, swinging a big stick through the branches and the ferns. My prince was silent. He knew these moments belonged to the Pequot and me.

"Has anyone taken her into the woods?" Uncas asked.

"She is a maiden! She is a Narragansett!" I said, clambering over the rotted skeleton of an ancient oak.

"Have you never taken a maiden—a Narragansett maiden—into the woods?" Uncas asked with a haughty cough of disbelief.

"I …" What could I say? We laughed and plotted and boasted about such things among ourselves. The young women belonged to us all until they married or were with child. Any maid who wanted any brave, any brave who wanted any maid—it was just a matter of consent. Miantonomi had his maidens. Others boys did too.

"Of course I have!" I lied. "But Silvermoon is …"

Why was she different? Why did I feel differently about her?

"Silvermoon is a woman!" asserted Uncas. "And I shall take her myself—if she will have me—when we return!"

My right hand swung out from my side and slammed Uncas square in the chest. We both stopped in our tracks. I could hear Miantonomi breathing behind us. The swishing and the swatting of the club of Assoko suddenly ceased.

"Silvermoon is mine!" I heard myself say, and I knew for the first time that it was so. I faced Uncas now, and his eyes settled coldly upon mine. His face was relaxed, but his legs and arms were tensed. For many heartbeats no one spoke. Then Uncas broke the silence.

"Why did you not say so from the start?" he asked. Still he did not move.

"Kat?" I heard the Fool say, but I kept my gaze upon the eyes of the Pequot. I did not speak. My heart was hot.

Assoko leaned toward us with a puzzled expression, gazing at the unmoving statues of his friends. He touched my arm. He touched Uncas. He pinched my arm. He pinched Uncas. He stood for a moment as still as the Pequot and I. "They breathe," he said at last to Miantonomi. "But they are like stone!" What magic had thus frozen us?

With a look of disgust, Uncas turned his head toward Assoko. "You are a fool!" he barked. The eyes of the Fool grew wide, and he stumbled back a step. Then he broke into laughter.

"I am the Fool!" he said between his merry chuckles. And Miantonomi started laughing too. Uncas shook his head in disbelief. A sharp sigh escaped my lips.

"You should have said so from the start," Uncas repeated to the trees and the stones. He glanced at me once, snorted through his nostrils and started off ahead of us through the brambles and the brush. We spoke no more of Silvermoon.

As we continued our movement toward the Great Swamp, we came forth at length from the wooded shadows into the brightness of a sprawling, grassy glade. Beyond the glade rose the majestic heads of the tall cedars of the dark swamp, their roots anchored deep in the thick, black mud beneath the still, green waters that lay at their feet. We did not wish to enter their domain. Even the grown man, with the memory as sharp as the quill of the porcupine, could be lost in there for hours. Days. Or always.

Somewhere at the edge of that swamp, winding through the green glade, was the path that we were seeking, the path that led to the land of the Wampanoag. As we moved down a long slope into the heart of the meadow, the tall grasses snaked in the wind like the waves of the salt sea. From a line of low blackberry bushes that stood like a wall before the Great Swamp, a squealing cloud of passenger pigeons rose suddenly, darkening the sky as they passed over us in search of a meal apart from the presence of man. Nearing a line of low blackberry bushes, we found our path. Upon it were the faint prints of the moccasins of the Narragansett raiders. They had taken the path farther to the south and had passed this way not long before. Heartened by the familiar tracks, we stopped briefly to fill our mouths several times with the bittersweet fruit of the thorned thicket.

Before long, the meadow ended once more at the door of the deep wood, and the path wandered beneath the trees with the Great Swamp to our right and the waters of the Shickasheen upon our left. Under the roof of the great green forest, we soon came upon a group of moss-covered rocks that rose like a pile of giant grey clamshells from a cluster of trampled ferns beside the stream. There were signs that the raiders had stopped here to rest, to drink from the Shickasheen and to smoke. We decided to do the same.

We all had pipes and a good supply of the tobacco we had helped our fathers grow. But none of us carried any fire.

"I meant to bring a fire pot," I said. "I thought we had remembered everything!"

"We have not the time to start a blaze now," said Miantonomi. "We shall have to wait until our night fire to drink our smoke."

"I have something to drink that is better than tobacco!" said Uncas loudly. And he lifted the bottle of strong water from his backbasket.

"Before we continue the hunt of the long-eared Wampanoag, we shall sip the medicine of the white gods!" he said, holding the flask up for all to see. My hand moved toward the bottle, but Uncas held it back. "The prince must have the first taste," he said. "And then I will drink. Then the Fool. And then you, Katanaquat."

"I only wanted to touch it," I murmured.

Uncas handed the strong water to the son of the sachem. Miantonomi took the bottle and ran his fingers across the smooth glass. He held it up to the sunlight, gazing through it. He pressed it gently against his cheek, his lips, the palm of his hand. He shook it so that the liquid frothed within. Then he grasped the wooden stop at the top of the bottle and pulled it out. Pop! He smelled the opening with a curious frown and ran his tongue across it.

"It is very strong!" he said, looking long at each of us.

"Drink!" said Uncas. "It is not poison! I saw my uncle drinking it last night and he was not dead this morning!"

Miantonomi hesitated, like one who tests the cold waters of a deep pool with his toes and is then not so eager for the bath. He took a mouthful, held it for a moment, then swallowed. His eyes widened, he coughed slightly and his face became flushed. He sucked in a deep breath and blew it out his cheeks. He handed the water to Uncas.

Uncas took a deep draught and immediately bent over like one who has been kicked in the stomach. Rolling his eyes, he sat back up. He wiped his mouth. Breathing through his teeth, he passed the bottle to Assoko.

The Fool looked at me with a grin, stood up, spilled the liquid into his mouth and swallowed it. "Ha!" he said. "Ho!" he said. "Oh!" he said. Water came to his eyes. He blinked, and the tears rolled down his nose. "Strong water!" he gasped and took a second drink.

"My turn!" I protested, taking the bottle from his hand. He sat down and began to rock.

I lifted the vial to my lips. The strong water tasted like the skunk stinks! It was sharp and heavy, and it wrapped itself around my tongue. It was like hot fire and smooth honey going down, painful and pleasing all at once. I could not stop myself from crying out. "Phaw!" The blaze faded to an inner warmth. This water truly held within it the power of the spirits! I returned the bottle to Uncas.

We passed it three times, and each time I felt myself growing bolder, stronger, taller, like the giant. Like Weetucks. Like the mountains from which he came. I began to dance, giggling like the young maiden, stumbling over the pebbled earth beneath the mound of stones. How could I act so foolishly, reeling about with no more control of my limbs than a toddling child, and yet feel my heart so full of strange strength? But why should I reason? Why should I worry? Let my legs dance as they will! Let my head dream in the daylight! This is really quite a pleasant dream! A new sort of daydream. And it is all so very funny, though not so very clever. What will happen next? And does it matter?

I saw Assoko doubled up on the ground in a joyous lump, rolling on his back at the feet of Uncas. I saw Uncas sitting with his head in his hands, rocking like the Fool. I saw Miantonomi standing unsteadily, swaying slowly like the birch in the wind. He looked upon the rest of us with a strained bewilderment that pulled coarse laughter from my chest. I stumbled toward him as he leaned toward me, lost my footing, and we fell heavily each into the arms of the other with a laughter that surprised me with its force and with its freedom. We danced. We fell. We got up to examine our wounds, and danced again. The Fool rolled in the dirt. Uncas sang himself a song of war, rocking with his head between his legs. And I, my

senses marvelously confused, imagined the world to be something altogether different than it was.

The low-hanging branches of a creek willow, swaying in the breeze,
appeared to be a vast, silent fall of green water. The form of the Fool,
writhing upon the ground, became at once a tumbling stone, then a great
red snake, then a growling, rolling bear cub. Miantonomi was a spirit, dark
one moment, full of light the next, twirling in the air behind the waterfall.
The sons of Keesuckquand passed through the green waters and became
dancing shadows that swam about our heads.

Uncas stood. As I came toward him, jerking and chanting, I saw him
loom before me, a dark brown blur against the afternoon sun. His face was
one massive grin. But the grin had eyes, and they held strange fire. The eyes
of the mad dog hold the same fire, and it smiles before it bites.

He struck me full in the face with the back of his hand, and it felled
me like the war club. For a heartbeat I thought I was fallen beneath the
Talking Rock, but then the world returned to me. And as I touched my
thumb to my pained nose, I saw my own blood. Then I saw nothing but
the mad eyes of Uncas.

"Son of a stinking rat!" I cried and threw myself at his legs. But I tackled only tree roots. The swinging foot of Uncas found my ribs.

"Oogh!" I coughed. My ribs shouted at me angrily. *Would you break us
again?* they cried. *Get up! Get up!*

I took hold of the thick bark of the willow and pulled myself up, turn-
ing at the same time to face my foe. He was still grinning. Was he mad?
Did he think this a joke? Or was I mad? Why could I not think straight?
Why could I not stand straight?

The strong water! It was full of the spirits! And I had poured them
down my throat!

Uncas had something in his hand. The bottle? No.

He swung the sharp steel at my head. My hand caught his wrist and we
fell against the willow, our faces a foot apart, the blade of the gods quiver-
ing a thumb from my scalp. Behind the shining silver, I saw the grin, the
mad eyes. I would shut them forever if I could! The knife hovered. Our
muscles strained. A blurred motion. A sickening thump. The mad eyes
widened, the grin fell, and Uncas tumbled sideways onto the stones.

"Weak woman!" shouted my wonderful Fool, waving the stub of a thick branch he had just broken against the side of the head of Uncas. He would have brought it down again upon the dazed Pequot if Miantonomi had not stepped in front of him.

"Out of my way, Meentomi!" shouted Assoko, but our prince did not move. He put his hand upon the shoulder of the Fool.

"Assoko has won," he said. "Kat is not harmed. Uncas is defeated."

The Fool looked at me. He looked at Uncas. He looked at Miantonomi. He looked at me. He looked at Uncas. He put down his club.

Uncas sat up, his head in one hand and his knife in the other. He was shaking as he put the blade away. The madness was gone from his eyes. But not from mine.

"He tried to kill me!" I cried, and I moved to pick up the club of the Fool.

"Stop!" said Miantonomi, his foot upon the branch. He turned to Uncas. He pulled him roughly to his feet and put him up against the tree. "What crazy game do you play, Uncas, with your water and your steel?"

Miantonomi spat upon the willow near the face of Uncas, and then forced the nose of his cousin to within a hair of the spittle. "That is how close you have come to dying this day!" said my prince. "For I would have killed you myself if the steel had touched Katanaquat!" These were hotter words than he had ever spoken to Uncas. They flared up from his heart by themselves. Miantonomi would not have spoken them otherwise.

Uncas straightened himself against the willow, his own heart bringing fire to his eyes. But he did not speak.

Miantonomi loosed his grip and stepped back. The anger drained from his face and he sighed. "The hot water of the gods is within me," he said. "I am not myself." With a look of frustration, he sat down upon the rock pile, but he did not take his eyes from Uncas. The shaking Pequot slumped wearily against the trunk of the willow, sliding slowly to his knees. Assoko stood beside me, murmuring something which I could not understand.

Uncas looked to me, a sad and pained expression upon his face. What was this look? From where did it come? Did he want my pardon? He would not have it! How I hated him! His hand moved toward his belt.

"You dare not touch that knife!" I said.

"I ... I want to give it to you," he said.

"You have tried that once already!" I said. "With the sharp end at my face! I do not wish to see it—or you—ever so close again!"

"Katanaquat, my brother ..." he began.

"You are not my brother!" I fired.

"The strong water," he said, "it took control of me! It made me crazy. It made me want to kill you. I am sorry. I am very sorry." And he took the knife out and laid it at my feet.

I wanted to kick it into the creek. I wanted to kick Uncas into the creek. But he appeared truly humbled. Like the foe defeated in battle, he lay before me in hope of mercy. Could his heart be true in the matter? No! His heart was a rotted gourd. He feared me, that was all. Well, let him fear me! That is what I wished for all along. The dog!

My head swam. The cursed water! Did it move Uncas against me after all? *It surely may have,* I thought. The spirits were tricky. Would they not throw the Pequot against me if they could? Uncas was a bad dog, a stray who wandered in from moon to moon to eat my food and keep me from my sleep. But the spirits were my enemies night and day! I picked up the knife.

"I will not have a bad heart against you," I heard myself say. I did not believe my words. Nor did Uncas. But I would put this moment behind us. I pushed the knife up to its hilt in the soft soil beneath the willow. "As the earth hides the sharpness of the blade, so I will bury these memories." I helped Uncas up and looked him in the eyes. I saw no fire, for it was hidden by the black smoke of his soul. I pulled the blade from the ground and wiped it clean upon my loin cloth. "As this blade is clean again, so may our friendship be from this day."

Uncas apologized to Assoko. The poor Fool was very confused, but Uncas finally convinced him. Then Assoko gathered the pieces of his broken branch, laid them at the feet of Uncas and kicked the dirt upon them until they were covered.

The Pequot apologized last to Miantonomi, asking forgiveness in very humble terms. My prince listened, and then offered him his hand.

"You are my cousin," said the son of the sachem. "You are my brother. Your blood is my blood. Our knives must never taste the blood of our brothers. Though you made me very angry, the strong water made the anger boil hotter still. I take my anger back. I forgive you."

As I looked upon the waters of the Shickasheen, they began to turn like the whirling of the sea when it pulls its tides away from the rocks beside the shore. I closed my eyes, but the spinning did not stop. A nauseating fire rose from my stomach to my head, and my senses reeled as I fell to my knees beside the stream.

"I'm going to be sick," I muttered.

When my stomach had emptied itself four times, I crawled to a dry, mossy table of rock and lay there, face down, my chest heaving as if I had run a marathon. Exhausted I was, but my head was clear, the spirits were gone. I had spat them all up, and good riddance! They could keep their strong water. It was not meant for the Narragansett. Not for me, at least! I would not be captured in that way again.

Though we still walked under the weight of the strong water, we took up the trail again, moving faster now as the sun began to roll down the far side of its mountain. I heard the words of my mother but they were only empty echoes in the far-off hills. The wigwams of Mascus and Canonicus were behind us. The warpath was beneath our feet. The long afternoon was before us. We must race great Keesuckquand to the edge of night. And before the moon ruled we must know for sure where my father and his warriors had camped.

A small fire warmed us beside the gurgling waters of the Tuscataucket. Upon it we cooked the flesh of the red hare. We had hunted rabbit after all. The smoke of our fire fled to the south, as did the smoke of the fire of Nopatin one hundred whoops northward among the scattered rocks of Elk Point where the waters of the Weweonke meet the Tuscataucket. We kept our fire in a low pit, in the midst of a palisade of thick rhododendron. We kept our conversation low as well. Our elders to the north did not suspect our presence, and we did not want them to.

When our meal ended, we sat long without words, staring into the dancing flames. My thoughts were many and troubled.

The haunting eyes of Silvermoon. The ache of longing. The crooked heart of Uncas. The smoke of jealousy. The honey and the sting of the strong water. The snare of the spirits. The mad eyes of Uncas. The fire of

anger. The fear of my father discovering us here. The fear of the night. The
fear of the gods. The fear of madness. The fear of death.

"Why do the spirits try to kill men?" were the words which awoke me
from the wandering of my soul. I heard the words first in my heart, then
they fell from parted lips—my own. I saw the faces of my friends, the face
of Uncas, the amber-tipped leaves of our viny fortress, the blue and yellow
flames and curling grey smoke of our sputtering fire.

"Do not talk of such things!" said Uncas, shifting his body closer to
the fire. "Even your powwow would not talk of such things in the dark of
the night in the midst of the woods!"

"I did not mean to speak aloud," I said, feeling a sudden chill. But I
sensed now that to back away from my question would be to run from the
gods. I would not run. And if speaking of the spirits could make Uncas
squirm, I would talk all night! "But why do you fear?" I asked him.

"I do not fear!" he insisted. "I am not so afraid of the spirits as the
Narragansett are. The Pequot know how to live with them. We honor
them. We respect them. We seek to please them and to win their favor. But
we do not look for them behind every wigwam as your people do!" He
glanced nervously over his shoulder as he spoke.

The Fool was rocking close to the fire, humming. He shook his head
gently from side to side as he rocked. By this I knew that he was listening
to our words.

Miantonomi sat thoughtfully, holding a green stick to the flames, feed-
ing it little by little to the fire. "Only the fool walks with his eyes closed,"
he said, tapping his thin brand against a stone. Tiny sparks leapt in all
directions, then died.

"Eyes open!" declared Assoko, wide-eyed, with a frown.

"The gods are many," said Uncas, "and we cannot know them all. Why
trouble ourselves about them, especially tonight? And who has seen them
but the powwows?"

"I have seen them," I said. And all heads turned at once to look upon
me. *Mad fool!* I said to myself. *Your mouth is too quick to spill the secrets of
your soul this night! Does the strong water still boil within you?*

My heart was bloated with the subject. I wanted to boast of the shadows I so often sensed and saw. But I must not! I would not! The war with
the gods was mine alone. I would fight it alone. Win it alone.

A thought flew to me. "Have we not all seen them?" I asked. "Have we not all seen the Dutch gods?"

"Dutch gods!" said Assoko, his mouth opened like the drooping smile of the panting dog.

"Oh!" said Miantonomi. And I hoped my ruse had won.

"We have all seen them," I affirmed.

"They are not really gods!" declared Uncas suddenly.

"What do you say?" inquired Miantonomi.

"It is what the Montauk say," continued Uncas.

"They must be gods!" countered Miantonomi. "Or how else could they call forth thunder and lightning? How else could they cross the great waters upon great canoes? Make glass from sand? What man has ever done these things?"

Uncas was unmoved. "Perhaps they are the children of greater gods than our own. As Cautantowwit carved our first father and mother from the great oak within the center of his garden, could not another god greater than Cautantowwit make men and women across the sea?"

"We have seen no women among the Dutch gods," reasoned Miantonomi.

"They have women. Across the sea," Uncas insisted.

"Did the Montauk say it was so?" asked Miantonomi sincerely.

"They said it was so," said Uncas.

We sat for many moments as the fire burned low. New gods. New men. New women. Strong water. What a very strange day!

"And who is this greater god?" asked my prince. His heart was clean in the matter. He wished to know because knowing was good, not because he wanted more arrows in his quiver than his brother or his foe. Miantonomi wished to know so that he could lead others into knowing—as the hawk leads its young to the edge of the nest so that they may finally fly—not as I wished to know, so that I could arm myself better for the warpath and the war. So that I could win.

"The greater gods are three," said Uncas, holding his head high with the import of his news. "One is a father whom none can see. One is his son, who appears as a man. And one is a spirit."

"One appears as a man?" said Miantonomi. "As a Dutch god?"

"I have not heard," said Uncas. "But I do not believe it anyway."

"If the Dutch gods have said as much to the Montauk, then it must be true," said my prince. "And why would you not believe it?"

"Because the Dutch gods are not gods!" said Uncas. "And so they may be liars. The Montauk say they are liars."

"Men do not lie about the gods!" said Miantonomi. "For then the gods would be against them. The gods would slay them!"

And why do the gods try to slay men? came my question back to me. Is it because the spirits are evil? Are they jealous? Do they fear us? But Cautantowwit is not evil. He made us. He gave us all that we needed to live. Yet we speak so little of him. And we do not fear him as we fear the shadows of the night. As we fear Chepi. As we fear the manitoo within the beasts, the trees, the winds, the waters! And now there are three more, greater than our own gods, who make Dutch men and give them clothes and steel and boats with wings! What will Askug say? What will he do? Is his medicine strong enough to face new gods? We are Narragansett. We face east! If new gods come from the east, we will face them too.

Suddenly, the cool of the night was pushed from us by a strong, warm, southerly wind. Had our fire awakened? No. It was nearly gone. But the shifting wind pulled new fire from the logs, and in its light I saw our faces. Amazement was etched upon us all. And fear. Was this wind an ill omen? But it came from the south! Was it from the fields of Cautantowwit? Then it would be a good omen.

I stood up. I do not know why, but I stood up. Miantonomi and the Fool were on their feet too. But Uncas cowered near the fire pit, trembling as though the wind blew cold and bitter on him alone. *Stand up! There is nothing to fear!* I thought. But I did not say so. Words would have been wrong just then. They might have shattered the magic.

The strong, warm breeze was comforting and welcomed, like the voice of my father calling me to his side. What spirit was this? What presence was this? Was this a vision? But we all felt it! And Uncas! What was wrong with him? Why did he not stand to share in the sweetness, the lightness … the incredible sound?

The sound of the wind. It shifted ever so slightly from the familiar whistling and rustling of the air among the trees. It began to hum. To sing. To sing without words! A song in the air! A song on the wind! A song from the gods! A melody that rose and fell with a mysterious beauty and rhythm.

The forest was full of it. You could hear it over the hills and in the valleys, I was certain. Surely my father could hear it! This was not a song within our minds. It was right here, right now, in the air, all around us!

Assoko fell to his face on the ground, arms outstretched. Miantonomi knelt silently beside him. I stood, amazed and entranced, my eyes searching the treetops, staring into the deep darkness. I wanted to rise up and ride upon the wind, upon the song itself. I felt it enter my heart, and I did not fight it. I took its melody upon my lips. I sang. We sang. All but Uncas. He moaned. He cried. Was he dying? Were we all dying? Would this song take us to Sowanniu? To the beautiful courts of Cautantowwit? I did not want to die! But the song would not cease.

And then it did. Yet a silent echo kept it ringing in my heart.

We did not sleep at all that night. Our hearts were full of fear and wonder. The wonder was an aching thing which troubled our souls with a strange longing. There was nothing to which it compared. The fear was a clean fear, without terror, so unlike the fear of the spirits which drove us daily to avoid the shadows and cleave to the sunlit paths. But for Uncas, the fear was like that which we lived with always, a weight and a burden, a dread and a foe. Could he have heard another song entirely? But no. As we hummed the tune together, he knew it well. The same song! Yet he closed his eyes and held his ears. He would not bear it. The song had been to his soul as the howling of the hungry wolf pack. The darkness of the stormy sea. An evil omen. So very strange that he could be laid so low by that which gave wings to the hearts of the rest of us!

In the first light of the new day, we left our camp to pursue Nopatin my father. I had to tell him what we had heard. I had to ask him if he had heard it too. Within a short space, we met the party returning noisily in our direction. They were all talking at once, and when they saw us they threw their arms in the air and ran to meet us. They had heard it too. Many were affected as Miantonomi, Assoko, and I had been. Some were downcast and sullen, like Uncas.

We returned to the village together and found that all those who had been abroad in the forest had been touched by the wind, filled with the song, moved by the melody. Those for whom it was an ecstasy were carried with a joy like at the time of the harvest. It is a sign of great favor, they said. Those for whom it was a curse were frozen with a deep foreboding. We must humble ourselves before the spirits or some terrible disaster will surely come upon us, they said. We were a people divided. Was this a trick of the gods?

Askug had not heard one note. He had slept soundly within his own tent the night before, and the winds which had visited the village had been cool and full of the threat of rain. The powwow had little to say as the tales were being told, but talked with my father in our wigwam late into the night. He would pass no judgment upon the mysterious song, he said, for none could tell him what it really was. There were no words. The spirits had not spoken. There was only music upon the wind which delighted some and brought great fear upon others. What could be made of that? He would let each man do with it as they saw fit before the gods. He asked my father to repeat his experience several times. He asked for the melody. I fell asleep to the song of two men humming.

CHAPTER SIX

The Dying

The corn and the beans of the harvest did not last long beyond the Longest Day. The snows were many and heavy and the winds were hard and cold. The streams were frozen like rock and too thick to break through for fishing. Even the Great Bay of the Narrangansett was covered with ice and layered with many white blankets. Though the village had moved to the shelter of the Valley of Cedar, the snow moved with us.

The beasts wandered north and west, away from the sea, away from the Narragansett. The hunters came home too often, too soon, with too little. Those tribes which were our tributaries—the Coweset and Shawomet to the north, the Niantic to the west, and the island tribes to the east—were no better off, and were unable in their want to even pay small tribute to Mascus and Canonicus. Our forays into the lands of the Mohegan and the Wampanoag produced little spoil.

"I can no longer sing the Song On The Wind," Miantonomi told me, as we huddled near the fire of his father on a bitter morning in the Moon Of The Deep Snow. "Though I long to hear it as we first heard it, it brings me warmth no more," he sadly said. "For how can I sing the song of summer when summer may never come again!" His head and his heart were bowed low, not for the weight of the snow upon the wigwams, nor for the hunger that gnawed, but for Mascus his father. The great sachem lay upon his sickbed, weak and full of fever.

"The summer will come, my prince," I said quietly.

In the cold days that followed, in spite of the medicine of our powwow, in spite of the songs of our people to the gods, in spite of the constant care of many squaws, the great sachem wandered further into the valley of the shadow of death. For two risings of the sun he did not open his eyes, but on the third he sat up suddenly and called for his sons and his daughters.

"We are here," said my prince. They had not left the bedside through four days and four nights.

"My children," said Mascus with the voice of the distant wind, "I am going away."

"Where are you going, my father?" asked Miantonomi, brushing tears from his eyes.

"I do not know," he replied.

Fires snapped and hummed within the long wigwam of the grand sachem. Men chanted quietly. Women sobbed. Dogs barked somewhere in the village. We waited for our chief to speak again, but he did not. At length his eyes rolled upward, a deep sigh blew forth from his lips, and the soul of great Mascus of the Narragansett crossed the Last River to bow before the gates of the Gardens of Cautantowwit. The gods had taken him. We could do nothing but mourn.

One clouded morning in the Moon Of The First Planting, I came to the grave as I had each day for many moons. The weathered mat upon which the sachem had died lay across the resting place. Upon the mat, his face blackened with the soot of the last fire of the great sachem, sat Miantonomi. His hair was matted with wet ashes. His dark cheeks were striped by the trails of his tears. His arms hung at his side, and his shoulders stooped, as he sang a low song of lamentation. I sat down before him.

"My father is forever gone," he chanted.

"I grieve for you and with you, my prince," I replied.

"I shall see him no more," he continued.

"I grieve for you and with you, my prince," I repeated.

"His name is buried beneath this earth."

"I grieve for you and with you, my prince."

"None shall speak it evermore."

"Yet it lives in our hearts, and we shall not forget it."

I rose from the ground and stood by the side of my prince. *"Kutchimmoke, Kutchimmoke. Be of good cheer,"* I said, stroking his head and his cheek. He put his arm around my legs and pressed his face against them. His grip was weak. His face was wet with his crying.

"It is time to rise from the mourning," I said, "and live again."

Miantonomi looked up at me with weary, reddened eyes. After a long moment, he offered me his hand. I helped him to stand, and we walked from the grave without looking back.

It was a double feast and a grand ceremony. Canonicus, who had ruled with his younger brother for thirty summers, was hailed as the new chief sachem. And Miantonomi—my brave friend, my only hero, my idol and my wise prince—inherited the calling of his father and was exalted to the rank of under-sachem to great Canonicus. At fifteen summers, never having killed a man or been to war, my prince became the second-in-command of the great nation of the mighty Narragansett.

Ambassadors from all our subject tribes, as well as men from the Pennacook, the Massachusetts, the Mohegan, the Pequot and the Pocomtuc, came to honor the new sachems and to join in the reveling. Uncas was there, but he did not speak with us. Assoko and I danced with the braves until we could no longer stand. There were many grand speeches, much gambling, much giving of gifts, much blessing and much feasting—for each tribe had sent what meat it could spare for the royal occasion.

There was much drinking of strong water, and this was not good. It brought evil spirits into our midst. Drunken men fought one another, women and children hid, and two wigwams were set afire before Canonicus and a band of warriors wrestled the wild men to the ground and bound them. They remained tied to the trees until the strong water grew weaker within them. For three days we feasted. On the night of the third day, with torches and song, we followed Canonicus and Miantonomi into the forest to the Circle of the Council Rocks. There we threw our torches upon a great pile of wood in the center of the circle. The fire spirits united in a roaring, towering blaze that stretched toward the sky like the bloody arm of a great giant, its fingers twitching violently, clawing at the stars. The night faded from the clearing as the fire rose higher. The stars fled. Only the moon could be faintly seen above the shadowed tops of the shimmering pine. We sang. We chanted. We danced.

When at last the fire had fallen to its knees among the ashes, the people began drifting toward their wigwams and their beds. It was then, in the darkness of the midnight hour, that we saw there were two moons in the sky! One was Nanepaushat, the familiar god who had watched men through each night since time untold. But the other! It was the size of the full moon, but not as bright. And it moved faster than our moon. You could not see it crawl, but if you watched it long enough you could tell that it had wandered further on its path. It had a tail! Like the whale that swims in the deep waters of the salt sea, its tail flowed out behind it as it swam slowly across the dark waters of the heavens.

Many ran to hide within their wigwams. Others sat or laid down upon the grass within the clearing of our village to gaze upon the heavenly twins. Canonicus called on Askug to stand with him and watch. Miantonomi stood by them, and I stayed at his side. The Fool hunched next to us, glaring at the sky. Every few moments, he glanced at me and quietly muttered, "Kat sees it!" My mother stood apart from us by ten paces, and I saw that Silvermoon was with her.

Three moons! I thought. *And the one upon the ground shines brightest in my eyes.* She saw me looking upon her, and she shyly hung her head and smiled.

Askug grunted, his gaze tied to the heavens.

"Good sign!" he declared at last. "Two moons. Two sachems. Nanepaushat walks the heavens as he always has, and Canonicus continues to rule over the Narragansett. But a new moon appears beside Nanepaushat, just as young Miantonomi has risen in the sky of our people. Together, Canonicus and Miantonomi will light up the night and make it as the day. This sign in the heavens is a good sign! The Narragansett shall prosper!"

When the Great Dying began, Canonicus called for a fast. Though the plague had not yet come to our doors, we begged the gods to stand as a wall around our people. Askug danced like the wild wind when it turns in circles upon the salt sea. He cut himself with stones, shrieked like a wigwam full of scared papooses, and sang every song he knew until he fell from exhaustion and had to be taken to his bed. There he lay unmoving for two risings and two settings of the sun. The elders danced in his place and chanted until their voices were like the hoarse barking of the dying dog. The men tossed their tobacco upon the flames of their fires, offering the sacred smoke to the spirits. And everyone prayed.

Across the Great Bay, the Wampanoag wailed. All along the eastern seashore, northward the length of many days walking, people lay dying on their beds, yellow and covered with sores. No matter how warm the fires within the tents, they shivered like hunters lost in the snowstorm. Sneezing and gasping, turning in feverish anguish upon their mats, their skin peeled off them like rotted bark from the dead birch. For many, many moons the Dying raged. Men and women, young and old, sagamore and fool—all fell before the invisible foe. People fled their villages. Tribes left their lands. Thousands of the dead lay unburied in wigwams, on the rocky shores of the salt sea, beside the marshes and beneath the trees of the great forest. Whole nations perished.

But the Dying came not to the Narragansett. The double moon. It had been a good sign indeed! The stricken nations sent ambassadors to the Long House of Canonicus and Miantonomi. Sachems of the Nipmuc came from both sides of the Blackstone and as far north as Mount Wachuset. Our great leaders promised corn, beans, squash and the protection of our warriors to all who bowed the knee to Canonicus of the Narragansett. At last, Massasoit himself crossed into our country with ten of his chief counselors and humbled himself before us in the Court of Canonicus. It was not war that reduced him thus, but the Dying. He had too few warriors left to stand against his foes.

CHAPTER SEVEN

Squanto

Tisquantum of the Patuxet was back. He was one who was taken by the white gods several summers before the Dying. But now that he was home from over the great salt sea, none of his people were anymore upon the earth. The Dying had struck the Patuxet at the roots, and they had fallen like the swamp cedar in the storm, never to rise again.

Like the man who has been scalped and yet lives, Tisquantum was a man without a soul. His country was filled with the sun-bleached bones of his people, and he was forced to find sad haven among his neighbors, the Wampanoag.

It was during my seventeenth summer, in the town of Sowams, the chief city of Massasoit, that we first met the last man of the Patuxet. Canonicus and Miantonomi, with myself and a band of warriors in attendance, came to Sowams to collect our tribute and to see this Patuxet ghost who could speak with the tongue of the gods from over the sea. He had not been with the Dutch but with a tribe called English. He had lived as a servant in their great stone houses, had dressed in their marvelous clothes, and had been treated lovingly. He had sailed with them upon the endless salt waters and had come home again to our shores only to be taken anew by a wicked boat prince and sold as a slave to a tribe of black-robed powwows in a land called Spain. He escaped and found his way back to the land of the English. Then he sailed to a vast, cold island to our own north, beyond the lands of the Pennacook and the Abnaki, where he fished night and day for cod. And now, having been returned once more to our shores by an English boat prince named Dermer, he was among his own again. Or as nearly so as the gods had allowed.

His stories were fantastic beyond dreaming, and so I did not know if I believed them. In some ways he reminded me of Uncas, though he did not seem a bad man. Or a madman. His tales were not heavy like lies. Certainly the spirits were with him, and his medicine was strong to have brought him safely home after so many adventures among the children of the gods.

But the English were not gods, he said, nor were the Dutch. Neither were the priests of Spain. Nor the priests of the land called France—many of whom had come already among the Algonquian and the Abnaki. They were men like us, said Tisquantum, for they came forth from the womb of woman. They first were children and then men. They married and had children of their own. They planted the earth and hunted the forest and the field. They sailed the rivers and the seas, fought and bled and died like we do. But their gods had given them many things that we had never seen or dreamed of.

The English lived in vast cities of wood and stone and clay and glass. Their weapons were more and larger and stronger than we had seen among the Dutch. They had long thundersticks, short thundersticks that could be held in one hand, and even great thunderlogs that spat fire and stone and could knock down many men at once.

Their clothes were of several kinds and colors, and they wore them upon their bodies fully, even upon their heads. They had beads and jewelry like ours, but of metal and of many strange and wonderful stones. Their homes were filled with marvelous inventions. They had curious bundles of magic skins called books, in which much knowledge was contained. The books could talk to those who knew how to listen. They traveled on wide paths of dirt and stone in great rolling baskets pulled by animals called donkeys. They rode on the backs of swift, tamed beasts called horses. The horses were like elk or moose, but stronger and without horns. They didn't eat them.

Their lodges were like several of our longhouses piled upon one another, which had steps within that you walked upon to go from one floor to the next. Their forts had towers that rose like cedars into the sky. Their great rivers were spanned by long, wide bridges made of stone. Even upon these bridges were their houses built! There were thousands and thousands of English living within the cities and without. And one great sachem, called a king, ruled over all the cities and all the houses and all the English. How I longed to be like that king!

But they did not have great trees like ours or many deep forests near the cities, for they had cut much of the wood down long ago.

We marveled at these tales!

* * *

When it came time for us to return to our country, Canonicus asked Tisquantum to come and live among us. But he did not wish to part with the Wampanoag or the boat prince Dermer who was upon the sea nearby. Nor did he wish to leave again the shores of the great salt waters that had been his home in a past and happier season. Yet he would walk for a time in our company, he said, to tell us further of his life among the English.

"Speak to us of their women," said Miantonomi as our path led us westward from Sowams toward the neck of the Great Bay of the Narragansett. We crowded together as we walked that we might hear him, and this slowed our going. The path was narrow, and the brambles were thick at its side, not having been burned away for many summers because of the Dying.

"You have been talking much of women lately, my prince," I said. "Is it time the Narragansett had a princess?"

"An English princess!" he laughed. And we laughed with him.

"The young English women are pleasant to look upon," said Tisquantum, "and they make good wives. But they do not work like your squaws. You could not treat them so much as slaves. And you would have to hoe your own gardens!"

"Lazy women!" I said. "Do they think they are men?"

"They are not lazy," countered the Patuxet. "And they do not think they are men. And they do not get ugly so fast as your women do." Several braves grunted in protest. But we knew it was so. Our women faded quickly, like the dandelion that blooms bright as the yellow sun one day and is white and withered and scattered on the wind the next. Was not this the way of all women? Of all life?

Surely the English women are not as pleasant to look upon as Silvermoon, I thought. *Surely she will never be ugly. Not to my eyes!*

"Nor do they lie with men as our maidens do," Tisquantum continued.

"How can there be children?" asked Miantonomi.

"I do not mean that they never do," said Tisquantum. "But most of them marry first."

Uncas would not like the English! I thought.

"And the men take only one wife."

"Only one wife?" echoed many voices.

"Only one at a time," said Tisquantum. "If one leaves or if she is put away and so is no longer a wife, then they may take another. It is their way."

"It is very strange and very hard," said Canonicus, who had been listening in silence as we walked. "For how then can a man become great? How can he stay warm at night? How can he have many children? And who will do his work for him as he sits with the elders or goes on the hunt or to war?" Canonicus had four wives.

"The work gets done," said Tisquantum. "Men till their own fields and sometimes hire other men to work for them. And men work together to build their houses and to make their goods. But they do not hunt as much as our tribes do or take their houses down to move them with the seasons. They do not need to. Much food and clothing come from many nations and tribes, from across many waters to the English. They always have all that they need."

"Then why do they come here?" asked Miantonomi.

"They want more," said Tisquantum.

The sun had climbed near its summit when we reached a small village of the Wampanoag where the Wanamoiset empties into the bay. The cool forest opened onto a wide plain of thick stumps and waist-high corn. The smell of salt was in the air, and sea birds circled the fields as we followed our path through the corn to a cluster of wigwams that sat along the shore. The barking of dogs and the shouting of young children greeted us first. Then several warriors came forth and led us to the house of their sachem. He had us in and was very happy to know that the famed Tisquantum was among us. Food and tobacco were brought to us, and many more tales were begged of the lauded Patuxet.

"Of their gods," said the sachem, our host, "I would hear." And I saw that Miantonomi stopped his eating for a moment and set his meat aside. He stood.

"Miantonomi of the Narragansett," said our host, with a slight bow of his head, "you wish to speak?"

"Only to ask our host to beg Tisquantum to tell us first of the English god who appears as a man," said my prince, and then he sat down.

"Tell us of this god first," commanded our host to the Patuxet.

Tisquantum rolled his head back and stared at the hazy ceiling of the large wigwam. The smoke from his pipe drifted upward and joined the twisting billows that climbed from the small fire in our midst. A warm summer wind, rolling off the bay, pulled the grey clouds out of the hole in the roof and flung them eastward.

"They call him Jesus Christ," said Tisquantum at last. "And all who seek to appease him are known as Christians."

"Are they powwows?" someone asked.

"Not those who are English," said Tisquantum. "There are Christian powwows among the Spanish and among the French but not among the English." He looked thoughtfully around the room. It was filled with many warriors. Many women. Many children. There were many more standing in the door and surrounding the wigwam. Everyone wanted to hear the stories of Tisquantum.

"The Spanish powwows—the priests—do not dance and wail like the powwows of our tribes," the crosser-of-the-waters continued. "They dress in long black robes. They burn sweet-smelling clays and long, white sticks to their gods. They ring bells and chant. They pray many somber prayers. And they turn strong water into blood and drink it, bread into flesh and eat it."

"Water into blood! Bread into flesh!" exclaimed the warriors who were packed into the wigwam. "Have you seen them do this?"

"I have watched them work this magic in the houses of their gods. Many times. But never did I see the strong water become blood or the bread become flesh."

"Then their medicine is weak!" I said.

"Or their god is weak!" another added. And I was glad the words were spoken, for they put strength in my heart against this new god.

Tisquantum looked upon us with a pained fire in his eyes. His lips turned down and moved without words. Then he spoke again.

"Their medicine is not weak," he said. "Nor is their god. It was my eyes which were weak, for I had not the Spirit."

So they had to be taken by the spirits in order to see! And then they could drink their blood and eat their flesh! Always the spirits must have their way, even with men from over the sea.

"But who is this Jesus Christ?" asked Miantonomi, leaning forward in the circle that surrounded Tisquantum.

"He is the only Son of the English God," said Tisquantum with a strange tremor in his voice. "He is not like our gods," he said hesitantly. "He is not like our gods," he said again.

"What does he do?" asked the sachem our host.

"He tells the English how to live," said Tisquantum, "that their souls might not suffer after death but go instead to be with his Father."

"He tells the English how to live!" scoffed a warrior of the Wampanoag. "I could tell the English how to live!" There was a low rumble of rude laughter within the wigwam. "But what does this god do to show his power?" the warrior challenged our teacher the Patuxet.

"He dies and rises from the dead," said Tisquantum quietly.

"The gods cannot die!" we shouted.

"He dies because he is a man," said Tisquantum.

"And men do not rise from the dead!" we shouted.

Even the Fool would not dream such foolishness, I thought. *Can the English truly have such a god? Would the Dutch have such a god? He is not like a god at all! A god who dies! Who would fear such a spirit? Let this god come here as a man! I would face him!*

The floor then was taken by an elder who began to speak of the gods of the Wampanoag, the gods of the Narragansett, the gods of the Massachusetts and ...

"We have not heard all there is to hear of this Jesus Christ," Miantonomi whispered in my ear, "but I am sure we will hear no more today!" He was disappointed and so was I. But when I looked into his eyes, I was surprised to see that the disappointment ran so deep. I was wading for sunfish and was glad to throw them back. Miantonomi was spearing for whale.

We stayed the night with the Wampanoag of the Wanamoiset and awakened the next day with the light of the dawn. Our Patuxet friend bid us farewell before the sun had climbed above the wood, and walked off alone toward Sowams. The Wanamoiset sachem lent us two canoes to cross over the Great Bay to our country. Four of his warriors rowed with us to bring the boats back. The crossing was a silent one, the sleepy waves of the Great Bay rolling gently beneath us, the unbelievable tales of Tisquantum singing strangely in our heads.

In the moons that shortly followed, we met Tisquantum again while traveling among our tributaries. It was in the village of Nummastaquit of the Massachusetts. The Patuxet was there as guide and tongue for the English boat prince Dermer, who had walked the woods with his men to trade English inventions for the skins of Nóosup the beaver.

Dermer was a pleasant brave, tall and strong, with much goodness in his heart and much medicine from his gods. His tongue could speak as our own, but only with the words that a small child speaks. Yet it put strength into our hearts to hear our own words fall from the mouth of an English. His men were like the Dutch gods. I could see no difference.

But the medicine of Dermer failed him at last on the isle of Capawack. Tisquantum was not with him. There, Dermer and his men were attacked by a band of warriors led by Epinew, who was once captured by the English himself and who bore them only malice for his treatment in their lands. All the men of Dermer were killed but one, and the boat prince was badly wounded at the hand of Epinew. He escaped in an English flat canoe, fled to his ship, and sailed south to a land called Virginia where the Powhatan dwell. If he were a god, though his wounds were sore and many, he surely would not die, I said. But there he died.

After this, Tisquantum went to live quietly among the Wampanoag.

More English ships came to the eastern shores of the great salt sea. More Dutch boats crossed from the Long Island to the lands of the Pequot, the Niantic and the Narragansett. Many skins were traded for many knives, many hoes, many tomahawks, and axes. Much wampum was exchanged.

I now had an English blade a hand longer than the Dutch blade of my father. My mother had an iron hoe which turned the soil faster than ten hoes made of shell. The new axes were a wonder! More fields could be cleared for our corn, more white pine felled for our canoes than ever before. My father bought my mother a black metal comb with which to straighten her hair. She sang as she pulled it through the long locks that fell to her hips, before gathering them to her back or braiding them.

My favorite English invention was the tomahawk—the cutter—for it warmed in my hand like a weapon from the gods! Let others dig out their canoes with it—I would fit it for the field of battle. It was a club whose bite was worse than that of any beast, a sharp hammer whose blow was deadlier than the talons of the wildcat. The Fool and I practiced long in the use of the tomahawk. At last we could swing it so that it sliced the trunk of the six-summer birch at one blow. We could throw it so that it buried its narrow face in the hard oak. We kept it so sharp that none dared run a thumb across its nose. We were certain it could swiftly take the head of the man from his shoulders—if only given the chance!

But we were not at war, for the Dying had reduced our enemies and thus we were made victors by the gods. Even those tribes that had not fallen to the plague were now at peace with us, for our numbers were increased by all our tributaries. Yet I longed for the warpath and the war. My heart ached for the glory of the triumph. Even for the pain of wounds or loss, for then would come revenge and war renewed. Anything would be better than this long wandering from town to town, listening to grand speeches of the greatness of our ancestors and the glory of our sachems, only to gather wampum into baskets and wander home again. Could not women do as much? This was not the manhood I had dreamed of. If I were in the moccasins of Miantonomi, I would look for new warpaths to run. My prince did not agree.

"Why does your heart cry for blood when no blood has been drawn from you?" he asked one day in the Moon Of The Falling Leaves, as we sat together upon the rock beneath Old Willow. The thin, yellow leaves of Old Willow still held tightly to her boughs, though the ground at her feet was alive with the warm, shifting colors and the strengthening odor of the loosed coverings of the maple, the oak, the chestnut, and the elm.

"Why does not the heart of my prince leap at the thought of battle as it did when we danced around this rock as children?" I countered.

"We are no longer children, Katanaquat," he said. "And we are now lords of the wood! It is our place, my place especially, to keep peace. Not to break it."

"I want someone to hate!" I heard myself say. "Not for the sake of hate," I quickly added, "but to be the man!" And I looked to my prince, for I needed to see his words as well as hear them.

"You speak like Uncas," he warned, and he looked away from me.

"Do not insult me, my prince!" I said. "I do not breathe as the Pequot! I only want to fight."

"And to win," said Miantonomi.

"To win," I said. "Of course."

"But you have never lost," he said, looking upon me again. "You have never fled an insult. You have never begged off from the fight. You have never run from my side. You have walked with me into many dangers. You have been the man. Though our knives have not been wet with the blood of our foes, still we have subdued them. We have won."

"Why does it not seem so?" I asked. "Not like the Fool and you in the stream beneath the Hill of the Talking Rock. Not like the Weak Woman herself! Not like Uncas and the Strong Water. Not like my dreams."

Miantonomi sat without speaking.

"I would that the Pequot would break the peace!" I said at last.

Miantonomi stood without speaking.

"Sometimes I dream of meeting Uncas in the battle," I continued. "You and me and the Fool together."

My prince looked at me without speaking.

"I have often killed him in my dreams," I admitted. "But then I must dream him back to life so that I may kill him when next I dream."

Miantonomi laughed, but not to scorn me. It was laughter born of love and of many summers together fighting phantoms in the forest. He knew my heart. His heart beat as mine. But his soul was cleaner. Where was the rain from god to wash mine as clean?

But why trouble my spirit with such things? I was The Rain From God! I needed no other waters.

"Katanaquat, my brave," said my prince, "you take more delight in the anguish and the terror of the falling of the tall tree than in its stately beauty and its strength while it stands! This is where our river divides." And he kicked several stones into Red Creek before speaking again. "If the tree must fall, it must fall, and glory to him who fells it. But if it stands on its own lands, blessing those who dwell beneath it, woe to him who fells it in the night!"

"So then I dream him back to life that I may have him to kill again when next I dream," I said stubbornly.

"Will his brothers revenge him who is felled unjustly?"

"The brothers of Uncas?" I asked with a start. "Unjustly?" I added. "I marvel that the gods have not slain him!"

"Not the brothers of Uncas," said my prince, "but the brothers of the tall tree of which I speak."

"The tree!" I said. "Its brothers can only wave their arms in sorrow." I pulled at a near-hanging branch of Old Willow, shaking loose a brief shower of wispy dry yellow. "Like this old giant, they can only weep."

"No, Katanaquat, though it takes many generations, they will have justice."

I looked at him in wonder.

"They can send their seed far away upon the wind, so that when they themselves die, there will be no offspring to give shelter to the sons and daughters of the murderer."

"They can do that?" I asked, for I had never thought it so.

"And they can drop their seed upon the grave of the killer, sending new roots down to where he sleeps, slowly crushing his bones beneath the earth."

"Would this cause his spirit pain?" I asked. I wondered also if the spirits of the trees were planted in the garden of Cautantowwit. Surely they must be, for that is where they came from.

"What do I know of such things?" said Miantonomi suddenly. "I only hope we never face Uncas in war. And I would not be so quick to splinter the bark of the tree that shades your wigwam!"

"The Pequot does not shade my wigwam!" I returned.

"But the peace does!" said my prince.

A marvelous thing occurred. In the midst of the Moons Of The Snow, a ship, filled with one hundred English, men, women, and children, came to the haunted shores of the Patuxet. Unafraid, they built their wigwams and their houses upon the cursed earth. Their medicine was strong, but not so strong as ours had been in the Dying, for half of their tribe perished before the Melting. Yet they stayed. Their axes felled the trees with which they raised their homes. Their thundersticks echoed in the forest as they hunted for their meat.

Though the path was less than half the morning from the English, the Wampanoag did not go among them, for they feared the evil spirits who had slain the Patuxet. Then Askug received news of a recent great gathering of Wampanoag powwows, summoned by Massasoit and held for three sunrisings and three sunsettings in a deep swamp south of Sowams. The magicians called upon the spirits to either destroy the English as they had the Patuxet or to leave the land clean for the coming and going of the Wampanoag. When the English did not die, Massasoit went to them with a grand train of his warriors. Without consulting Canonicus, he took himself out of the hand of the Narragansett and placed himself into the hand of the English! We did not know this until all had been accomplished in a council between Massasoit and the sachem of the English—whom they call a governor. His name was Carver, which means "to cut," and it was thus that Massasoit was cut from us and bound by treaty of friendship to the English. But this was the doing of Tisquantum, now called Squanto, who became the tongue of each for the other, so that their hands were clasped as one man and our lordship spurned.

"Squanto must be stilled, for his tongue turns the nations against us!" Askug cried, as we sat at council in the house of Canonicus. The council fire rose hot and high as our hearts burned and our voices were lifted against the rebellion of Massasoit and the meddling of the Patuxet. There were many old hunters and young warriors seated in the council. I was there with my father, Assoko at my side.

"But I fear to call the spirits against him," our powwow continued, "for he has crossed the Salt Sea, survived the Great Dying, and has the medicine of the English within him. If all the magic of the Wampanoag did not bring the English down—not one of them—we must take other means to silence Squanto. Then the English will know that the Narragansett are men, and not women like the Wampanoag. Then they will treat for peace with us and give Massasoit back into our hands, who is our rightful vassal."

Askug turned his head violently from side to side, looking to the eyes of all men present, snorting through his nostrils like the maddened moose. "Who among the sachems of the Wampanoag bears no love for Massasoit?" he asked. "Who can we call upon to help us take Squanto in a snare?"

Tantumquag, a warrior whose mother was born among the Pocasset, arose. Askug sat down, folding his legs about him like the cat upon the rock.

"Corbitant, sachem of the Pocasset, is subject to Massasoit," said Tantumquag. "But he grumbles under the mantle and would not pay tribute if the choice were his. He boasts of a day when his people are many again, but he might like something else to boast of sooner!" Tantumquag sat down and Askug rose again.

"Let us offer Corbitant much wampum to take and cut out the tongue of Tisquantum the Patuxet. Then Massasoit will have to speak for himself to the English, and can we not do the same and with sweeter words?" There were many grunts of assent, and many heads wagged in approval.

Miantonomi rose.

"My sachem!" said the powwow, who had not finished speaking, but who seated himself again in deference to our prince. This time the medicine man appeared rather like the snake that is coiled and ready to leap. *Will he one night go to bed a man and wake the next morn a serpent?* I wondered.

My prince looked respectfully upon Askug, then upon Canonicus our chief, and then carefully upon us all.

"The tongue of Squanto," he began, "as a pleasant trophy for the necklace of the powwow would not serve us as well as the tongue of Squanto speaking for the Narragansett." He looked again upon Askug, addressing him personally. "Your words are strong, brave Askug, but I propose that Corbitant be hired to bring the Patuxet to us, that we might win him to our side. If we take his tongue by force we win his enmity, and thus the same of the English. Would not his mouth serve us better if it were eating from our hand rather than seeking to bite it in revenge?"

My prince was wiser than my grandfather! Though I would have enjoyed the sight of the severed tongue of the last of the Patuxet, I would rather see it stolen from Massasoit to serve my prince. I spoke my assent aloud, as did many around the council fire. Askug nodded his approval, but his coils did not relax. Canonicus stood as Miantonomi retired to the shadows at his feet.

"The son of my brother speaks with words that are older than he is. I would make his words mine," said the grand sachem warmly. "Why stick our hand into the tree for the honey when we can send the bee into the tree for us?" He turned to Tantumquag. "Your mother will visit her relatives in Pocasset. She will bear our message to Corbitant, with a small gift in token of fifty arms of wampum. If he wishes to play our game he will bring us the honey."

The mother of Tantumquag made the trip, and Corbitant accepted the gift. Encouraged by the boldness of our plot, the Pocasett sachem soon confronted Squanto in a wigwam in the town of Nemasket. But instead of entreating him to meet with us, he threatened to stab the companion of the Patuxet, a Wampanoag named Hobomock. Hobomock broke free of Corbitant and fled to the English governor.

"Corbitant kills Squanto!" cried the Wampanoag. "Quick! Save him!"

Standish, the war captain of the English, a very small brave with hair like fire and a very big heart for battle, took fourteen men upon the warpath to

Nemasket. They surrounded the house in which Corbitant had captured Squanto, but the Pocasset sachem had fled. Squanto was found to be well, though Corbitant had promised to stab him also. Three men of Nemasket were sore wounded when they broke out of the house to escape the English guard, but the English took them home and dressed and cured their wounds. So our agent failed us, and worse. For fear of the English, he too made peace with them, as did as many other sachems—even those of the islands about Capawack.

Another ship came into the harbor of the English, into the waters of Plymouth—for so their village was named—with many more men from over the sea. The more were the English, the bolder would Massasoit become against us. We must speak to the English ourselves!

"I would go to them," said Miantonomi at a small council in the house of Canonicus, "for they have a new governor named Winthrop, and he may not love the Wampanoag as Carver did. I would tell them we are the Narragansett. I would tell them we would be the friends of the English. I would tell them we are mighty and many and that our medicine is strong. I would tell them that our gods and their gods could be friends. That our tribes could rule the country together. That we could share in the bounty of the land and in the tribute of the smaller tribes. I would ask for an English maiden. We would give them one of ours. We would marry our tribes in peace. We would win back the spoils that are ours, the sagamores who have left us, the lands that have escaped us."

"And if they say no?" asked Canonicus our chief.

"I would say the same things again. I would boast of our ancestors. I would bring the English to our city. I would walk them through our lands. I would show them what the strength of our arms has won us. I would offer them much wampum, many skins," said Miantonomi. "How could they refuse?"

"They have already been poisoned against us. By Massasoit. By Squanto. And now by Corbitant," replied Canonicus. "And even if they take our hand in friendship, why do they need our arms to hold the land? They have their own, and those of the men of Massasoit. They have their thundersticks. Their medicine. And they may be gods themselves, no matter what some say!"

Askug stood. But Miantonomi would not sit down. He did not want to give the floor to another. He wished to speak and be heard. He wished to carve out a peace with the English with his own hands and hold it. He wished to win back the lands and the peoples that were ours. He wished to stand and keep standing. For his people. For the Narragansett. This had always been in him, this call to be our father. *Raise the war cry, my prince! I shouted within myself. That will bring your people to your side!*

For an awkward moment both men stood, and the dark eyes of Askug flared with an anger that rose from the pride of his days, the honor of his station, and the violation of tradition. Then he turned stiffly to sit down, but our prince would not let him. "Speak, powwow! It is your right. I am like the tree which will not bend with the wind. But I must bend. I am not a god. I am just a sachem. Speak!" And our prince sat down instead.

"Would you go, my sachem, to the English, after so soon attempting to steal their tongue?" said Askug. "And would not Massasoit suspect our purposes? Would he not try to stop you? Let us first send a message, not by the hands of a Pocasset sagamore or a Narragansett sachem, but by a faithful warrior of your choosing. One from among us who will pick two or three more. Together they will speak to the governor and treat of peace. They will go before you, as the summer wind goes before the rains that bring life to the land."

The smoke of many pipes hung like low clouds in the wigwam of Canonicus. The words of Askug were like clouds within my heart. Why should we crawl like shamed children into the presence of the English? Why should we slide like shadows through the lands of our tributaries? Why should we fear sachems or governors when our cause is just?

I stood. And the smoke was so thick in my standing, I could barely see the feet of my father. Or the face of Askug, though I saw him sit down.

I took a deep breath, which clawed at my nostrils but cleared my head.

"I will go," I heard my mouth say, which was not at all why my heart had moved me to my feet. *Let us follow our sachem in force—a royal train like that of Massasoit when first he entered Plymouth!* was what I wished to say. But my tongue had overruled my heart. And all I could do was sit down again, an indistinct fear stirring sickness in my stomach.

"I would send none other," said Miantonomi. "And the choice of companions is yours."

CHAPTER EIGHT

Plymouth

The deep snows of winter lay like a heavy blanket of white fur upon the forest floor, covering every rock and bush, every path and thicket. Our first night was passed beneath a cold outcrop of rock, our skins wrapped tightly about us as we lay together beside a small fire. A freezing rain fell at midnight, but the sky cleared by dawn. As the sun climbed its hillside in the heavens, it flung its bright arrows into the silver woods. They bounced from every ice-encrusted branch of every tree, colliding with each other, confounding the eyes of all who forced their way through this slippery, strange, and shining world.

Assoko broke through the crusted ice into the softer snow beneath, stumbled forward and sank to his knees. Smoking and smiling we waited—my father and I—for the Fool to overcome the foe. Thrusting his red, raw hands to the leafy floor below the cold carpet, laughing loudly the while, he freed himself—and a thrice-loosened snowshoe—from the snare of the storm.

"Falling!" gasped Assoko, out of breath from his wrestling. "Always falling!" he grinned.

We were many whoops from Plymouth, and the day was cold in spite of the bright sun. But Noonatch the deer had broken the trail for the three of us, and Nopatin my father knew the way.

In my backbasket I carried a gift for the governor of the English. It was a bundle of finely painted arrows, straight and sharp, wrapped in the skin of the blacksnake. It would tell the English that the Narragansett are a strong people, fit for war and the hunt, full of the medicine of the gods, worthy and willing to strike the hand of friendship with the men of Plymouth.

In my heart was the message that Canonicus bade me speak in the ear of the governor. It was a tale of our honor and our lordship over the tribes of the bays and the shores. A call to smoke the pipe together as warriors who are brothers. An invitation to come to Narragansett to feast with our sachems and to treat of peace and friendship.

My fear of the mission had flown, for my father was with me. And my Fool. Together we would stand in the courts of the English and declare the purposes of the Narragansett. But now I was very tired, and this caused me more to dream as we plodded through the white and wintered forest.

Yet I did not dream—this time—my dreams of war, but of peace. Of days of sunshine and quiet drifting in a lone canoe upon still waters. Of wading and digging for oysters among the salty grasses off the bay shore. Of sitting in the watchtower while Kaukant cries to his brothers above the tall trees. Of roasting popcorn beneath the white, shining face of Nanepaushat. Of laughing with Miantonomi and Assoko. Of my mother singing. Of Silvermoon.

I heard the gulls at last.

"We must lay our weapons here," my father said, and I smelled the salt winds of the Great Salt Sea.

We placed our weapons into the hollow of a large old elm. Only our knives were yet upon us. For the English asked this of all who would come among them. We covered the hollow with the branches of the soft pine and covered the pine with snow. No one would know that the proud work of the hands of the warrior lay hidden within the heart of the elm. No one could take the tooth of Weak Woman—which I had long-since grafted to a larger, stronger war club—from the closed mouth of the old tree. But I felt weak and naked as we walked from the spot, the shoes of the Fool in my tracks, the shoes of my father in the tracks of the Fool, dragging a pine branch to cover our trail.

Within a few whoops we came out of the woods upon a stump-covered hillside. My heart rose to my mouth as our feet brought us closer to the low squared fences, the flat wooded walls, and the smoking stone chimneys of the English. We saw no one. I feared an ambush, and my fingers were wrapped tightly around the handle of the cold English steel at my belt. Suddenly the sun was darkened, and a shadow moved across the flat, white field before us. Were the English gods coming down from the heavens upon us? No. It was only clouds of winter from off the sea.

"Ho!" came the shout. And we saw an English approaching.

"Ho!" answered my father, and we raised our empty palms to show we walked in peace.

The English was clothed with skins of brown and green from his neck to his toes. His shirt came to his waist, and was held to him by a thick brown belt. His leggings were in pairs—one from his waist to his knees, the other from his knees to his feet. At his wrists and below his chin were wide skins of white. A long pelt covered his shoulders and hung behind, like the black wings of Kaukant. His head was covered by a tall, black trunk with a circle of dark skin, like a mushroom upside-down, which kept the sun from his eyes. His feet were clothed like the hoof of the moose with a shoe that was thick and strong and shiny. I would have traded my bow for those shoes! His hands were not clothed, and his face was unpainted though covered with hair below the nose like the Dutch gods. His belt held an English long knife. He carried a thunderstick. When at last we stood face to face, I saw that his eyes were clean. This put me at ease, though I did not know what lay behind the eyes of an English.

To our surprise, he spoke words that our ears could understand. Though they were few, though they were words we spoke mostly among the Wampanoag, and though they broke strangely in the air, it was delightful to hear them. Assoko laughed until the English himself was laughing. And thus the gods were with us.

He called himself Winslow, and he led us to a roofed shelter beside one of their homes where a low blaze burned within a ring of stone. There he gave us water and beer, and there we warmed our hands and feet. We made him to understand that we had come from Canonicus of the Narragansett. That we had come in peace and friendship. That we wished to speak to the governor Winthrop, and that we bore a gift for the same.

He said we must wait a bit by the fire, for it was the Sabbath, a special day upon which the English worship their gods. Shortly they would break from their prayers to take meat. Then we might speak with the governor or with one who would take our message to him. We had a word of peace for Squanto as well, if he could be found, though our hearts still strained against him. Would the Patuxet hear us after the threatenings of Corbitant? We believed so, for we came not as the deceitful hireling, but as those who had breathed the smoke of the council fire of Canonicus.

Winslow left us and ascended the hill to a longhouse where many tracks led through the snow. We wished to see where he had gone and so we followed. It was our way. All who come to the Narragansett may wander where they will and may stand at any door. If they are welcomed, they may enter and share in whatever bounty the house may hold. Would the English ways be otherwise? Could we imagine them so?

As we neared the longhouse we heard voices raised in song. What strange notes and sounds they were—but filled with a beauty and a power that I longed to share. Like Squanto, perhaps I would one day learn the tongue of the English—if only to sing! I would sing to Silvermoon. Songs of love. Songs of bravery and battle. Songs of the Narragansett, but in the strong tongue of the English.

And then we heard it. But could it be?

Yet it must be, for there was none other like it ever! The Song On The Wind! They were singing the Song On The Wind! The melody was unmistakable. It gently rose and fell and rose again, calling to us as it had that magic night so many moons ago. Yet with words we heard it now! Strange words that surely held something glorious and grand! Was it a message from the gods? Which gods?

Of course! It was the English gods who sent the song upon the wind! Yet they knew we could not understand the words and so they whispered but the melody. That haunting melody! It played in the heart and set the man seeking the singer, like the meat that roasts upon the open fire calls to the hungry hunter. But now the meal is cooked, and we are called to the bowls!

We must enter the longhouse! We must see the English singing. We must know the meaning of the words.

Almost unconsciously I rushed against the strong, oaken door. It did not open. It did not move. It could not be lifted, pushed aside or parted. It had an edge and my fingers found it, but I pulled at it in vain. My father pounded on the wood, and Assoko fumbled with the strange metal pieces that were hung upon it. Suddenly it swung inward. Winslow had worked its magic from within, and there he stood. But his face was darkened, and at his back were several men who had not the look of friendship.

"The Song On The Wind!" I shouted.

"Sing it for us," pleaded my father.

The Fool was laughing and leaping and swatting at the air. *Dance!* his eyes cried.

They did not understand our words—or they did not like them—for the singing was stilled and the room was filled instead with the gasps of women, the startled sounds of the English tongue, and the frightened cries of children.

"No!" I shouted, as strong arms pinned me to the wall, "Sing! The Song On The Wind!" It hardly mattered that I was wrestling with the English. I wanted only to hear those notes. Those words. Once more. Once more.

Assoko swung his arms wildly, holding several men at bay, while the eyes of my father ran through the room in search of ...

"Squanto!" he cried. But I did not see the Patuxet, for my eyes were upon Assoko as he fell to the floor beneath a tangled heap of brown clothing, shiny shoes, and hairy, shouting faces.

Squanto sat with us in the lodge of Winslow, as Standish and two English warriors stood over us with thundersticks crossed upon their breasts. I was much frightened, but I buried it within my heart and caused my eyes to look upon the English with strength. Assoko was silent and still, like the stones beneath the snow, but his nostrils flared like the moose before the charge. He was reaching for me in his heart. He watched my eyes. He listened to me breathe.

Nopatin my father was angry, and his fire was smoking. We had been wrestled to the floor of the longhouse and our knives had been taken. Only upon the words of Squanto had we been released. Under guard of many English braves we were led to this room and made to sit.

But warm meat was laid before us, and we ate. Water in abundance was poured, and we drank. Our hearts began to beat without fear.

"Why did you break in upon the Sabbath gathering?" asked Winslow through the tongue of Squanto.

"We heard the Song of the Gods!" my father answered. And Squanto fed these words to Winslow in the tongue of the English.

"But why did you cry out so and leap about?" asked Winslow.

"Because the Song stirred up our hearts and we could bear our silence no more!" said Nopatin my father.

The English braves looked very puzzled, and Standish shook his head as though he thought us mad. I wanted to stand and face him. To pour my feelings into his soul. To make him understand. For what was so strange about our passion? Did they not feel the same about the Song?

"Tell Winslow about the wind!" I said to Squanto. "Tell him what the Narragansett heard in the night. And the Wampanoag. And the Massachusetts. What you yourself would have heard if you had been among us in the wood."

The Patuxet told Winslow the incredible tale which, since his return to these shores, he had heard many times within the wigwams of the Wampanoag. The English listened with widened eyes and raised brows, and the face of Winslow glowed with the tiny spark of understanding.

"Please sing it for us again!" I begged, leaning toward our host. And Squanto passed my plea along. The English braves laughed and counseled for a moment with each another.

"We will sing it," said Winslow. And as he rose to his feet, I rose also to mine. But Assoko sank to his knees. And Nopatin sat erect in his chair, his eyes upon the English like the man who watches the thundercloud to see if lightning will leap forth upon the earth.

They jostled one another and laughed nervously like young maidens in the presence of young warriors from another tribe. But then Standish raised his voice, and the singing began. I was in a dream. Surely I was in a dream. For strange gods filled the room, and my breathing came with difficulty. Light broke into my heart like the midday sun through the clouds of the summer storm. This was the Wind Song. And the English knew its words!

"What do you sing? What does it mean?" I shouted above the chant.

And the singing ceased.

"It is a song to their gods," said Squanto.

"Where does it come from?" I asked, and I noticed that Assoko was still upon his knees, his face to the wooded floor. My father sat with wonder in his eyes.

"It comes from England," said Winslow through the tongue of the Patuxet. "We sing it there in our worship in the lodges of our gods and in our homes. Now we sing it here. But is this truly the song you heard upon the wind? For how could it come to your ears without the English to sing it?"

"The gods of the English flew here ahead of you!" I declared, speaking like the grandson of the powwow. "They brought us the Song so that it would play in our hearts. And now they have brought you here so that we may know its meaning and sing it too!"

Winslow looked upon his fellows with amazement and ran his white fingers through his brown beard. He shook his head as though my words had chased his thoughts away, and then at length he spoke.

"This is too wonderful," he said, and he sat down.

"The words," I heard my father say. "What are the words?"

"They are words of praise and gratitude to God the Father, to God the Son, and to the Holy Ghost," Winslow explained. "It is a song of thanksgiving for the great goodness of our great God, for we love him because he first loved us."

And I wondered at this, for the Narragansett did not sing such songs to Cautantowwit, though his goodness was known to us through the things he had given us. He was a distant god. A dim tribal memory. The untouchable shadow of a long-forgotten dream, rather than the hard, dark presence which surrounded us daily, laughing through the walls of our wigwams as we spilled hot soup upon our laps or cut our fingers on the flint while chipping our arrows. Thanks to the gods? Only when they had mercy upon us in the midst of plague, aided us in the hunt or in war, cut down our enemies, or kept their curses from our doors. But never from a heart in love! For did the gods love men? How could any man think so?

And who was this god which had a son? A son who walked as a man and died as a man? *He is not like our gods,* echoed the words of Squanto in my heart. How very true! But how then could he be a god at all? And what was the holy ghost? My questions were many, and I wished at once that Miantonomi were there. But as it had been in the wigwam of the sachem of the Wanamoiset, the answers would not come this day, for Squanto spoke suddenly and led us down another path.

"Do you not come to speak for Canonicus, your sachem?" he asked, and I remembered the message. The gift. "Winslow told me you have words for Winthrop," said the Patuxet with the winter in his eyes.

Assoko still had his face to the floor, and some of the English were trying to rouse him. My father spoke to him gently, and he staggered to his feet before sitting once again upon his stool, a full and foolish smile upon his painted face. "He is a fool," explained my father, but the English did not understand.

"Canonicus has brought violence upon me," said Squanto quietly, facing us squarely, his visage grim and his eyes cold.

"No, my friend," spoke my father to the Patuxet, "This is not so. It was Corbitant who twisted the purpose of Canonicus. It was the Pocasset sagamore who bore you ill. Our sachem and our people only wished to counsel with you, to speak of matters of honor and justice."

"Why does Canonicus send a crooked-hearted Pocasset to call me to his fire by a knife to my throat?" challenged Squanto. "Why does he not send one of his own, bearing gifts and sweet words?"

The question struck the heart, for here we were!

"We feared to come among the English," said my father, "for they had smoked the pipe with Massasoit. And we thought Corbitant to be a man who could easily bring our sweet words to you. But he betrayed us. And now we come with our own lives at your mercy."

"He swore to kill me," said Squanto, "but he fled when he knew that the English would revenge me."

"We will punish the sagamore if it wins your heart to us," said my father. "He has dishonored us as well as you."

Squanto stepped back, and his eyes warmed briefly. "We will not treat of this any more today," he said. "And upon the words you have spoken, I will hold Canonicus guiltless."

How strong was the tongue of this lone Patuxet! How right was Askug in fearing it! But was the strength his own, or did he stand behind the rock of the English and the Wampanoag?

He spoke to Winthrop, and our host bade us sit with him again. Our knives were returned. Standish spoke to us briefly in his own tongue, bowed slightly, and left. His two warriors moved themselves to a corner and talked quietly over a bottle of strong water. Could they drink it and not be taken by the gods?

"Speak to me as your sachem has bid you," said Winslow through Squanto, "and I will take his words to Winthrop myself." For we were not sachems to speak to a sachem. It was right and just for our words to reach his ears by another.

"We have come with a gift, and our heart is in it," I said as I removed the snakeskin from my backbasket. I held it out to Winslow, who took it from me gently. "It speaks of our strength and the strength of our gods. Of our heart for peace with the English. Of our love for the prosperity of Plymouth. Of our desire to walk as brothers and lords in the lands and forests of our fathers and our grandfathers, and among the tribes of our rightful tributaries. Our great sachems, Canonicus and Miantonomi, beg you to come and see us, to eat our meat and smoke our tobacco, to embrace the shoulders in unity for all the days of our breathing upon the earth."

Squanto then spoke for us, and Winslow quietly considered his words.

His eyes remained clear, but they grew cool, and his brow turned upon itself. His lips drew themselves together, and his fingers slowly plowed the curled hair upon his chin. He spoke with the Patuxet and the Patuxet with him. My eyes looked to my father. His eyes cautioned me to hold my tongue.

At last Winslow rose and held out his hand. I felt a strength in his grasp that was clean, but his calm stare caused me to shut my soul. Had I offended him? Had my words failed to pass the good heart of Canonicus into his hands?

He spoke, and the Patuxet changed the strange sounds into those we understood. "Go to your great king the sachem and tell him the English will think deeply upon all that he has said to us. Within four days we will send a messenger to bring our answer." With that he showed us to his door. We would have begged more meat for our journey or a bed for the night, but Squanto called us out into the setting sunlight.

"I will come to you myself with the words of the governor," he said, "and you may feast me at your fires."

"Did he not like our gift?" I asked with trouble in my heart.

"He likes it well," assured the Patuxet. "But the English do not rejoice so quickly at such things. They eat their meat slowly and so enjoy it longer and more fully. You will hear their pleasure if you are patient."

"Night is coming, and we hoped to lodge here until the dawn," said Nopatin my father.

"Cold!" coughed Assoko, rolling his eyes. He puckered his lips and blew his breath like smoke into the air.

"You must go now," said Squanto, "for the time is not yet for you to lodge among the English."

Was this the English way? Or were they poisoned against us as Canonicus had said? We started off into the icy woods. But our journey home was not a harsh one, for our eyes had been filled with hope and wonder. We had carried the heart of Canonicus to the table of the English, and we had eaten well at that table. We had come away with our scalps and our tongues. We had found our weapons in the old elm where we had left them. And we had heard again the Song On The Wind from the lips of the English themselves! With words. Words of thanksgiving to the strange gods from over the sea. Askug must give us such songs for Cautantowwit. Then perhaps the winds would carry our songs to the courts of Sowanniu, to the ears of Cautantowwit himself. Would he not be pleased? Would he not bless us?

* * *

Squanto came to us as he had promised upon the fourth rising of the sun. We feasted him and smoked long together as we listened to more tales of his life beyond our shores. At last we called upon him to give us the words of the governor of the English of Plymouth.

"He is displeased with the Narragansett," began the Patuxet, and loud cries of anger and confusion arose within the longhouse of Canonicus. But none stood to challenge the words. We would hear them all first.

Squanto walked a slow, full circle around the crackling fire, looking upon each brave assembled in the smoky chamber. Lifting his head as if to peer above ours, his eyes fell downward upon the Narragansett. *Look!* I said within my heart. *It is the spirit of Uncas!* The spirit of contempt and high conceit! Was this the Pequot in another form? No. For Uncas was among us even then, seated with his uncle among the warriors. From that moment, I did not trust the Patuxet.

"The governor Winthrop does not fear the Narragansett," continued Squanto. "Neither your muscle nor your medicine. The English have done you no wrong, and they do not intend any as long as you bow to them in peace. But if you would rather have war than peace, then you may begin when you will."

There were many sad moans and angry murmurings among us, but we waited on Squanto for the whole of it.

"You will not find them weak or sleeping," said Squanto, "nor do their gods sleep." At this he stood before Canonicus and held out the snakeskin which we had delivered to Plymouth. The arrows were now gone, but the skin was bulging as though filled with sand and pebbles.

Canonicus recoiled with cold terror in his eyes, causing a gasp to escape the lips of many. "What is in it?" demanded our sachem.

"Thunder powder and the stones thrown by the thundersticks of the men of Plymouth," Squanto replied.

"Take it away!" shouted Canonicus with an angry wave of his large hand. "I will not touch it. Send it to the sagamores and sachems of our tribes. Let them look upon the answer of the English. But let it not rest in the lands of the Narragansett. Send it at last to Plymouth unopened. We do not wish war with the English!" His eyes were filled with anguish and confusion. "Why do they step on our heart in this way? Why do they twist our arm when we reach it to them in peace?" The grumble was echoed like low thunder throughout the longhouse.

Suddenly Squanto lowered his head and looked upon us as a man does his brother. His eyes grew warmer, and I wondered at the change. "I can help you," he said. "For I have much medicine with the English."

I saw his game. I stood.

"The Rain from God," said the Patuxet in veiled mockery of my name. With a grim smile he sat down.

"The Patuxet gambles with our lives!" I accused, and the eyes of Squanto flashed like the thundersticks of the English. Could those eyes kill? My own were a shield! I looked upon him until he turned his gaze away. "It is this 'tongue of the English' which has twisted our words, not the governor of the English who has twisted our arm!" I declared. I did not know this for a surety, but the sentiment was welcomed by many in the house.

Squanto began to rise, but Miantonomi stood first. He held his hand up, and all became quiet but for the sharp spitting of the hot flames and the low whispers of the watchers standing packed outside the door. I sat down, my eyes upon the Patuxet, my ears upon my prince.

"Tisquantum has come to us alone, with no arms but those that any warrior would carry to the wigwam of a friend," said my prince. And many heads were nodded in assent. "This we can all see," he declared.

"But Katanaquat has seen something else, a sharp knife hidden in the heart of the Patuxet," our prince continued. "And we must know if this knife simply guards the life of the messenger or if it is borne to do us harm." He turned to face Squanto. "Do you twist the words of the English against us?"

"No," replied the Patuxet, and I felt his denial carried truth. But not without the shadow of a lie.

"Do you twist our own words when you speak them to the English?"

"No," answered the Patuxet, but my ears did not receive it. I stood again, for my complaint was not complete.

"Why did the eyes of Winslow darken when we offered our hand in love and peace?" I fired. "Was it because our heart was hidden in the hands of Squanto? Was it because our words died in the ears of Squanto? Was it because Squanto invented his own tale for his own gain? That he might play the one against the other and win favor with both? That he might make promises to the English in return for strong water? That he might make promises to the

Wampanoag in return for wives? That he might make promises to the Narragansett in return for meat and tobacco, wampum and ..." I could speak no more, for my blood had risen to my face, and I feared my hands would take the Patuxet by the throat. Many voices were now raised in appeal against him. Had he not carried the Wampanoag from us?

Squanto stood. And many others.

"I am my own man!" said the Patuxet. "The last of my people." And he looked around him as the fox looks upon the circling wolves with a clean fear but a sharp eye and no dismay. "I have taken no wives! But many are the gods who stand with me, for they know I stand alone among men. Lay not your hands upon me for the words I have brought you. Or the gods will strike you down!"

"You speak as a fool!" shouted Askug, who came forth from the mass of anxious men to stand beside Miantonomi near the fire. "Do the gods strike down whole nations?"

"They did so in the Dying," replied the Patuxet. "And this I know better than any man here." Troubled grunting filled the air. Many sat down, pulling their arms and legs around them in protection against the spirits. "And they can do so again if they are called upon," said Squanto.

"But who can summon this of them?" challenged our powwow. "For not even all the medicine of the Wampanoag could bring down one head of the English. Though I have killed men by the spirits, never have I caused whole peoples to fall."

Squanto drew himself tall. He wore the coat of the English always, which now he pulled apart at the breast, exposing his heart to us all. "Here dwells the greatest god of the English!" he declared. We shrank from him in caution and in fear. "Because he dwells here, I may call the plague upon any whom I will."

"You cannot!" spat Askug hotly, stepping toward the Patuxet with a madness in his eyes. He shook his black rattle in the stormy face of Squanto.

"The English have the plague buried beneath the floor of their storehouse!" shouted Squanto. "They will loose it upon the Narragansett if any harm befalls me!"

"Is it true?" we cried with one voice, and we pulled at our hair in terror of the thought.

"It is not!" declared Askug.

"We cannot know," said my prince.

"Send the Patuxet away!" cried the people, and as one we fell back from the door, opening a pathway from the fire of our sachem to the wet, cold snows outside. "Leave us!" we begged the Patuxet. "We will not touch you." Some held forth gifts to buy their safety, but Askug forbade it.

Squanto took the snakeskin filled with shot and powder, bowed his head to our prince and our king, lifted his face to look down upon our powwow, curled his dark lip at me, walked slowly into the frosted air, strode proudly through the city of Canonicus and—with a loud and lingering chant upon his tongue—disappeared into the wide, white woods to the east.

It came to us later, by many messengers, that Squanto was playing the same game among the Wampanoag and the tribes of the eastern islands. Massasoit sent his own knife to Winthrop, demanding the hands and head of the Patuxet for stirring up rebellion. The governor begged for the life of Squanto, for otherwise the English would lose their tongue. But he agreed at last to forfeit the Patuxet, for this was just and according to the treaty between Massasoit and Winthrop. Squanto was saved from death only by the arrival in Plymouth Bay of another great ship from over the sea—and this on the very day his head would have bloodied the earth! The ambassadors of Massasoit went home in great anger, but the sachem of the Wampanoag finally let the matter rest.

After that, the Patuxet no longer went among the tribes to win his own way. And if the gods of the English truly lived within his breast, they grew weary of him but two summers later, for a fever came upon him, his blood left him through the nose, and he died. With the last beatings of his heart—we were told—he begged Bradford to plead for him that he might go to the heaven of the English man. Surely his soul feared the spirits of our own shores, having forsaken them. Upon his deathbed, he gave many of his possessions to many of his English friends as remembrances of his love. They felt his death a great loss, for though he had caused them much trouble with their neighbors, he had also done them much good, teaching them how to fish the rivers and plant and eat of the good of the land, for they knew not how to live outside their great cities of wood and stone.

But I could not mourn his passing. He had been to me a thorn of trouble and a strange weight. He had taken the sweetness from my memory of the Wind Song. He had pulled my teeth out when I laughed at the table of

Winslow. And my heart was harder within me for knowing him. But he armed me much against the spirits, for I saw better now how they could use a man and then cast him away.

Before the death of the Patuxet, Miantonomi took his first princess—Wawaloam of the Niantic—more closely weaving our destiny with that of our tributaries to the south.

"Do your dreams not fly to a woman, also?" asked Nopatin my father as I ate with him one evening in the Moon Before The First Harvest. Moapitug, the second wife of Nopatin, sat beyond the fire, nursing her papoose—my brother and the son of my father.

"They do," I admitted, stirring the hot broth that Taquattin my mother laid before us.

"And does she shine like the silver moon in your heart?" asked my mother as she watched the pot upon the blaze.

"She does," I said with an embarrassed smile, glancing at my father anxiously, hoping he might rescue me from this slippery bank upon which he had set me. But his grin betrayed his treachery. "The soup is delicious, Mother," I said, in a vain attempt to climb the bank myself and keep my feet dry.

"There is one whose soup is as good as mine," she said, "for I taught her how to make it!"

"I have tasted that soup," I said, remembering the days when I lay upon my bed after the fall of the Talking Rock.

"You have only smelled it!" my mother declared. "It is time for you to make new bowls and new spoons. It is time for you to take those bowls and lay them at the feet of this woman of your dreams. She will fill your bowls for you. She longs to do so."

The baby cried, and I looked at him through the rising flames. His mother was good to look upon, fresh and full of the life of the squaw when she is young. Moapitug was not much older than Silvermoon.

"And she will fill your quiver with arrows," said Taquattin my mother. "It is time to wake from dreaming!"

CHAPTER NINE

Silvermoon

Silvermoon. Light from the heavens to brighten and soften the blackest night.

Silvermoon. The strong medicine of Nanepaushat, wrapped in the dark skin of the maiden.

What secret chant did the girl sing that gave her the strength to capture the heart of the strong young hunter? What charms lay within the woman that enabled her to bleed all the cares from the soul of the man? How could the smile, the touch, the words of this creature so sap every cold, hardened impulse from the proud veins of the warrior?

I made my bowls and laid them at her feet.

My twentieth summer stands tall in my memory with a life of its own. I can see it. I can smell it. I can hear it. And if I close my eyes and turn them inward upon the paths now grown over with the grass of many generations, I can feel it.

We were wedded in the Moon Of Midsummer, and many gifts were given to us, some of which I gave away again in the marriage dance. But the greatest gift, and one I would not dare to part with, was the wigwam that my father built for us with the help of many friends. This was a great surprise, for I expected only a bed and some baskets within the wigwam of Nopatin. Askug blessed the house with much loud chanting and prayed for the fruitfulness of the womb of Silvermoon my wife. He prayed also for the dream of the powwow to come upon me and upon my children and the children of my children.

But my only dream was Silvermoon. I cared nothing for the hunt, for it only took me from her. I thought little of the battle, for what is a handful of bloody hair when a woman sings upon your bed? The warpath was for children, not men, a creek too shallow to swim in. But a woman! A wife! She is life and the mother of life, a wide river and a deep sea. And when a man loves a woman, his life means more to him than ever it has. Why should he bare his painted breast before the foe if it means he may never lay it again upon the soft breast of his beloved? I did not long for my friends, for what were they but dull-headed arrows? Place them in a basket where I can find them if I need them. Sharpen them another day. But not today! Today is Silvermoon.

This is the blessed foolishness of the young man with his woman. This is the dream that will one day wake and wonder at itself. This is the spell that causes the scalp-laden warrior to wander in the garden with his wife, whistling like the bluebird and hoeing the beans. This is the magic that keeps the tired brave up at night, walking barefoot with his love in the dew beneath the stars. This is what makes the bedridden old hunter chuckle and shake his addled head, the toothless squaw wring her wrinkled hands and weep for her youth. This is the song of spring when the bud clings to the branch with full promise of the green of summer. This is the soft rain upon the new corn. This is the pounding heartbeat of every young brave, the bone in the throat of every proud warrior who watches the sun go down upon his life. And for some men, even after waking from the dream, this is the sap that binds the bark and keeps the canoe from sinking to the bottom of the sea.

In the first year of our love a son was born. His name was Kattenanit, the Night Wind, for he was born in the night while the cool winds of the Great Bay pushed dark, grey clouds across the face of the silver moon.

"I am a man!" I cried as I stood alone upon the shore of the dark, rolling bay. "My son lives, and I am a man!"

The great clouds floated high above my head like greyed gulls flying one behind the other on an unseen pathway in the heavens. The white light of the full moon fell upon the giant gulls and threw long, dark shadows over the glistening billows of the deep, dancing waters. The night winds stroked my face, ran their fingers through my hair, and tied my locks in damp tangles about my neck.

"I am a man!" I shouted to the crashing waves and the silent moon. "My son lives, and I am a man!"

Silver-tipped fish bounded like deer upon the shadowed waters but a bow shot away, leaping and lunging until they were out of sight. I laughed, for the sight reminded me of the Fool dancing for battle. And I suddenly awoke.

The wind now carried the whisper of the spirits, and my skin became sensitive to the chill of the night. A son is born. A Narragansett. A boy-child who will grow to be a man. A hunter. A warrior. A boon to his tribe. A terror to his enemies. A man!

And a man is more than the husband of a woman. More than a brave with a squaw. He is lord. Lord of the land. Lord of his lessers. Lord of his heart. Lord of his soul.

I was the Rain From God, but I must not sprinkle the gardens of women! I must fall upon the beasts of the wood. The heads of my enemies. The skulking spirits. The shadows of my fears.

I must fall where I would, when I would. This my son must see, for this my son must do. All my sons, for surely this was only the first bubbling of the fresh spring from out of the fertile earth.

Silvermoon, my beautiful light, my faithful friend, the mother of my son, the medicine of my days and nights. You are my squaw. I am your brave. I must not hoe beans! I am awake now.

PART TWO:

Dog Eat Dog

"A ... storm of war blows ... until the Lord Jesus chide the winds, and rebuke the seas."

—Roger Williams

CHAPTER TEN

The Warpath

Assoko!" I cried. "Do not dance so close to the quills of the porcupine!" Running and leaping within twenty paces of the logs of Sowams, he was as dark and as big a target as any bowman could wish for. Yet no arrow touched him, nor any other missile from the enemy. In fact, where he ran, painted heads disappeared behind the cover of the high wall. The Wampanoag thought him a witch. Or a demon in flesh! He shouted and laughed in his mad joy, turning hand over head in front of the frightened foe, like a gleeful child in the games at harvest. But his flint was feared more than his medicine, for he fired his arrows so straight and so true that he already had killed two warriors and wounded three. Few of the rest of us hit any, for we shot our missiles in a high arc, waiting to see where they landed before shooting again. This was our way. We could little afford to lose our arrows. Nor did we wish for too high a count of vengeance against us. But the Fool! He leapt and laughed and fired his swift shafts like the hungry hunter chasing down his supper. *If I could forget myself,* I argued, *I would do the same.* But now the battle seemed a useless thing, for though we had the trees, the foe held the town.

We had crossed the Great Bay in silence, many canoes filled with many warriors. In the early dawning of the cold green morning, we fell with great cries upon the city of Massasoit. His warriors came out to meet us upon the wooded shoreline and arrows flew. But little blood was shed. The Fool advanced ahead of us, like the dark cloud before the storm, and his bold taunts and wild shouts chased the foe back to the door of the city. There they raised a bloodcry of their own and ran toward us as one, loosing a rain of sharp flint upon us. But the Fool—like the spear that is thrust into the water to take the porpoise—pushed into their midst with his war club whirling. A warrior fell beneath his fury, and the rest turned to flee into their city. In an instant, Assoko cut the scalp from the head and flung it over the wall, laughing. We rushed to his side, loosing our missiles at the defenders who faced us from behind their walls.

"Weak women!" shouted the Fool, whose hands had already armed his bow with sharp death. His first shaft crossed the wall and buried itself deep in the chest of a young brave of the Wampanoag.

Then thunder started barking as small clouds of smoke arose from behind the logs, and a man fell at my side. My heart cried aloud, but my lips were still as I knelt to touch the deep wound. The blood was warm like the soup of Silvermoon. A warrior of the Narragansett was dead.

"Guns!" cried the voice of Miantonomi from the far side of the field. "Thundersticks!" And our warriors fell back to the cover of the trees. From there, we kept up a slow and futile barrage of the palisade of Sowams. Only Assoko braved the field. Even the stones of the thundersticks could not fell him. At length, fewer arrows flew in our direction and the thunder ceased.

Miantonomi made his way through the trees to my side.

"Massasoit flees," he said as I called to the Fool to come to us. "Yotaash my brother and a few of his warriors have been on the other side of the city, and they have seen the grand sachem and many of his warriors leave the walls and head east toward Plymouth. There are three English yet within Sowams. It is they who hold the thundersticks."

I called to the Fool again. He started at last to stumble in our direction, and a sudden shower of arrows pursued him like angry bees out of the troubled hive. But they did not sting him, for they fell around him harmlessly.

"Let us send for Canonicus," I said to my prince. "With more warriors, we can surround the city and win it by numbers, if not by arrows. It will surely surrender when the Narragansett make it an island and threaten to cover it like the cold sea."

"Perhaps," he replied. "But I do not wish to fight the English."

Assoko, like the squaw picking flowers, squatted in the low grass collecting the arrows that had followed him toward the woods. A few more fell around him as he went slowly about his work. He swung his arms at the whispering shafts as if they were mosquitos singing in his ears.

"We will tell the English to leave," I said, "for why should they send death against us or invite it upon themselves? It is Massasoit we want."

"And it is Massasoit who is gone!" said my prince. "Gone to sit at the door of his masters the English, to wag his tail and beg for a sharp bone to strike the Narragansett. Standish will come with many English warriors, and we will have to run home without scalps or captives or spoil!"

Men of the Wampanoag began to congregate at the wall of Sowams, shaking their fists at us, cursing and tossing the waste of dogs over the logs in our direction. "They have defied us for so many seasons!" said Miantonomi to the spirits and the winds. "I do not know what to do."

We set a small guard along the edge of the woods and on all sides of the city, and turned for a time from the taunting to gather by our boats upon the shore. There we lit our fires and took our meat. Ninety warriors of the Narragansett were set against Massasoit that day, but whether or not we stayed was in the hands of Miantonomi our sachem.

"If it were not for the English, we could bind our vassal to us again," I complained as we sat beside our blaze. Assoko rocked slowly at my side, numbering his Wampanoag arrows aloud. Missing count often, he started each time anew with a short grunt and a long laugh.

"The English love Massasoit," said my prince, "and we dare not draw them into this. Yet so many sachems follow him in his rebellion! And now that more English have come to the shores north of Plymouth, even the Massachusetts are striking hands with the white man." Miantonomi rose to pace around the fire, kicking the salted sand with the heels of his moccasins. His heart was heavy. His hands did not rise to declare the glory of the Narragansett. Nor did they swing in defiance of the Wampanoag. They were held to his side by the cords of his love for his warriors and his people.

"Must we go to the English governors to beg what is ours?" I asked in disgust, recalling the day so many winters ago when Squanto had disgraced us before Winslow.

"No," said my prince, looking out over the Great Bay. "We must show them our strong arm."

"We will fight them!" I cried, leaping to my feet. For though I feared them, I wished with all my heart to bury that fear in their blood.

"I will not fight them," said my prince darkly, turning to face me. "Their gods are too strong, and they have done us no wrong beyond spreading their strong wings in friendship over the tribes that surround them."

"Tribes that once lay beneath the wings of the Narragansett!" I added bitterly.

"But I will not tremble before them," continued my prince, "or run from this battle with the Wampanoag." He turned again toward the salt bay. "Yet there are too few of us!"

"Canonicus! And Nopatin my father and his men!" I said.

"We will send for them," said Miantonomi softly, and he called for a messenger to cross the waters to the city of Canonicus while the day still held light.

We sat again while the fire burned low and the sun walked down its mountain toward its wigwam and its bed.

"The Narragansett are ugly women and old dogs!" shouted a warrior of the Wampanoag from his cover behind the logs of Sowams. "Their teeth are rotted and their breath stinks! They chase their tails and bark at shadows!" None could see the lips that hurled the insult, for a heavy dawn fog wandered like smoke along the shore and among the trees, blurring our sight of the city and our foes. But the waking sun smote the mist until it fled, revealing at last the long shadows and glistening green of the early spring morn. It was then that we saw, upon the sparkling waters of the bay, the canoes of Canonicus coming to our aid. A great shout of greeting arose upon the shore, but this did not still the taunts from within the city. The Fool and I joined our guard at the treeline.

"Miantonomi of the Narragansett is a broken bow!" continued the chief taunter. I could see him now, a tall brave with his face painted red and black, his wide mouth opened like the hungry young bird, coughing his insults into the wind. His head wagged like the tail of the dog above the sharpened logs of the palisade. "The men of Canonicus paint themselves with moose dung!" he continued. "Their arrows are winged with the tail of the moth! They fight with spoons and bowls!"

My heart burned against this ugly face at the wall as it continued to sing our shame.

"Their courage is like the fleeing fawn! They soil their clothes as they run! Their bows are made of birch! Their aim is like the blind old hunter!"

The eyes of Assoko flashed. He armed his bow.

"Hit him," I said through my teeth, and I saw the Fool draw his string to his cheek. The shaft hissed like the snake as it leapt from the bow. In a heartbeat it crossed the field. I saw the foul mouth bellowing curses, the blurred form of the speeding shaft. I heard the sharp collision of flint and wood, the astonished gasp of the mocking warrior. I saw white eyes widen for an instant, then disappear beneath the shielding wall. The Fool had missed by a thumb, but his arrow was firmly impaled at the top of the palisade. It shivered for a moment, chattered like the woodpecker, and then was still. Still, too, was the tongue of the taunter!

By now the canoes of Canonicus had been emptied upon the sands of Sowams, and the woods surrounding the city filled with two hundred screaming warriors of the Narragansett.

Canonicus came to me.

"Nopatin your father will come behind me over the waters with fifty men," he said, peering from the fresh cover of the new green toward the walls and the wigwams of Sowams. "But many of our warriors have come to watch before they fight," he continued, "for they have heard that there are English in the city."

"Only three," I said with disdain in my voice for warriors who would not war.

"Three English with thundersticks could mean many dead Narragansett," said my sachem, sad rebuke within his eyes. "Whom would you send first against their lightning?"

His heart for his men was as the heart of the father for his children. My heart did not beat as his, though my son was the apple of my eye. Kattenanit had now lived ten summers, was strong and full of medicine, and could well bend the small bow I had made for him. If my heart were law, the boy would have been with me even then. But this was not our way. And Kattenanit did not lust for the fight as I did when I was young. This I could not understand.

"We will not have to bare our breasts for the shot," I replied with resignation, "for even watching eyes, if they be many, may convince the Wampanoag to bend the knee."

"That is my hope," said the great sachem, and his gaze searched the trees for his nephew, my prince. "Miantonomi?" he asked.

"He is with Yotaash his brother in the woods beyond those wigwams that stand highest within the walls." I pointed eastward into the spring green. The sun had risen above the treetops. The warmth of the day was a comfort and a strength. The blossoming bushes filled the air with the strong smell of the perfume of the earth. And the winds came off the bay with a gentle force that seemed to urge us out of the wood and into the field against the foe. Yet who but the Fool would dare the ready missiles of the Wampanoag and the swift lightning of the English? None, even though the spirits crowd us from behind! Our own blood was not the sight we danced for.

Then came Yotaash, bounding like Noonatch beneath the low boughs. "Canonicus my king!" he cried. "Standish comes!"

We circled Sowams to the east—Canonicus, Miantonomi, Yotaash, a small royal guard and myself. Out of all shot of the city, upon a hill that leaned into the tall cedars at its feet, we stood across the path that walked from Plymouth. We laid our weapons upon the grass and sent a messenger of peace down the hill ahead of us to meet the English captain as he came. Would the English have an ear for us? Would they leave us in peace to fight our own war? Would they honor our complaint against the Wampanoag? Would they admit us justice in our cause? They must!

Many seasons, many feuds, many scalps, and many breakings of ties and trust had set the Narragansett and the Wampanoag against each other. Nothing but arms could decide our destinies. Nothing but blood could seal our fates. Nothing but the subjection of Massasoit could wash the warpaint from our flesh. Surely the English would understand. Their hearts would tell them that our cause was just. They would go home.

Soon our man returned with a warrior of the Massachusetts. He was the ear and the tongue of Standish. They would not go home, he said, but were coming on with arms. They would not turn their backs upon their neighbors and friends the Wampanoag. Neither our claim of lordship over Massasoit nor our bloodfeuds with him were reason to break the peace, he said. For peace was their heart, and they would not sit still while any made war with their neighbors. But if blood must decide the peace, then we would see blood, he said.

Canonicus was shaken. Standish might come forth from the cedar at any moment. And could his purpose be changed? I was for running, for nothing could be gained in falling to the powder and the stones of the English. But the matter was decided as a messenger came flying from our men upon the shore.

"Canonicus my sachem," gasped the breathless brave, grasping the firm shoulders of our king. "Nopatin has not come, for he stands at home alone against the Pequot. He begs that you return at once!"

The Pequot! Sassacus their sachem had been lurking at our western door for many seasons, harrying our hunters, bullying the Niantic our allies and tributaries. With our forces weakened by our sally against the Wampanoag, the Pequot chief had entered our lands with a large body of warriors. Only my father and his men stood between him and the towns of the Narragansett.

"We row immediately," said Canonicus.

When Standish emerged from the trees to climb the hill toward Sowams, the forest around the city of Massasoit was empty of the Narragansett, as were the fields and the rocky shoreline. Except for warm ashes upon the sands and the broken shafts of the two tribes scattered upon the land, none would know that the battle had been forced the day before. The lone shaft of the Fool, fixed high upon the palisade, pointed its feathered fingers westward across the Great Bay.

Small brown flies swarmed around the bodies of the dead and wounded as women wailed, men wept, and children wandered curiously among their mourning elders.

Nopatin my father paced the village of the Chicamug Niantic, encouraging the warriors, comforting the grieving, chanting curses against the enemy, reciting the names of the Pequot warriors whom he knew to have been among the marauders. His keen eyes swept the surrounding forest for anything foreign. His right arm was bandaged with a wet, crimson strip torn from his own loin cloth.

"I wish I had been here, Father," I said. Bloodying my fingers with his bandage, I unwound it gently.

"You were right to be where you were," he said. "I would have been there too had not the mother-in-law of Miantonomi come to beg help against the Pequot. Two battles did I fight before arriving here." He grimaced as I touched the flesh near his wound, an ugly, deep gash from the bone of a war club.

"The tooth of a 'weak woman,'" he grunted with a grim smile. "But I took the head!" And he pointed to the spoil lying at the foot of an old maple. Its bloodied mouth was a silent cave, its black eyes empty windows. "Tackamissic," he said of the head. "My cousin on the side of Mequaminea my mother. I did not like his harsh greeting, and so I bid him farewell!" The soul of the Pequot would now wander a prisoner in the heart of Nopatin, and thus it would not haunt our wigwams or trouble our dreams. Nor would it ever fly to Sowanniu, for surely Cautantowwit would not let it in his gates. None of our enemies would find rest in the courts of the great god of the Southwest. But then they said the same of us.

"Was Uncas among them?" I asked.

"He was not," replied my father.

"The spirits are like wasps beneath our blankets!" I said. "And our enemies surround us like the trees about our villages!"

Nopatin turned his gaze into the forest again, setting his teeth firmly as I wrapped a fresh skin around the wound. "Your mother will see to my scratch when I get home," he said.

"And Askug will flap his arms like the hummingbird against the Pequot!" I added.

"I would flap with him if I could!" he said, shrugging his pained limb. "But tell me of the Wampanoag. Did they weep like women when they saw the strength of the Narragansett?"

"No," I replied, looking about me at the weeping warriors of the Niantic. "But they ducked their heads whenever Assoko bent his bow!"

"Aha! Then they are not fools," he chuckled. "But what do I hear of Standish and his warriors?"

"They came to stand with Massasoit," I said, "and we would have faced them had we not heard your call." I lied, for this was what my pride declared to me. "If our people had long knives and thundersticks, we could hold every mountain and tree to our lordship."

"But not the hearts of men," said Nopatin my father, and he rolled the head of Tackamissic his cousin into a basket and lifted it with his good arm. We joined Canonicus and Miantonomi and, together with a large body of weary warriors, we walked silently home through the sweet-smelling forest, serenaded all the way by bands of singing birds which flitted about the boughs of the newly budded trees.

"Roger Williams of the English was among us in your absence," said Askug to Miantonomi as we sat at soup within the wigwam of the powwow. "But I would not treat with him."

"I like the man," said my prince to the powwow. "And he has won the love of Canonicus. He learns our tongue that he might do us good and not evil. And he comes among us with a clean heart and no fear. He warms my heart to the English and would warm their heart toward us!"

"I do not trust him," said the powwow my grandfather, "for he goes also among the Wampanoag. And he asks about the Pequot!"

"Do not many of us go among the Wampanoag and ask about the Pequot?" said Miantonomi. "Do not many of us have relatives among our enemies? Relatives whom we visit in times of war as well as in times of peace?"

I thought of Tackamissic. I did not know what to think of Roger Williams. For the man was a mystery. An English, but not one! A hunter. A trader. A brave. A lone walker of the many paths of the great forest. A man with many tongues that spoke from one heart—a clean heart, said my prince.

"And he speaks of the gods of the English!" spat Askug. "My heart grows dark when I hear of them. My soul is troubled like boiling waters."

"Do you fear the gods of the English?" I asked, as I looked upon the boiling waters of the soup of the aged Mishtaqua. She stirred the brew slowly over the hot fire, adding powdered herbs and crushed beans. She listened to our words in silence.

"I do," admitted Askug, "for I know them not. They do not come to me in the night. They do not whisper in my dreams. Nor have I seen them in my visions." He frowned deeply and his lips rolled one upon the other. "And so I fear them."

"But why fear Williams for his eagerness to speak of his gods?" asked my prince. "If we listen, we may learn and no longer fear!"

"I am warned against these gods by my own spirits," mumbled Askug, and I saw within his eyes the black flame of something dark and cold. I did not want that kind of warning. I would trust my own eyes. My own ears. My heart. My mind. And I wished to learn, as Miantonomi said, that I might no longer fear. For the fear never ceased. It rose within me at any given hour and had to be beaten down by my will, subjected by my soul, threatened by my own hard dreams of mastery and manhood. New gods were not welcomed news to me! They were snares hidden along my path, foes to be avoided as I walked each day beneath the heat of Keesuckquand and lay each night beneath the cold light of Nanepaushat. Even Silvermoon could no longer sing my soul to sleep, for I knew now that I must keep it ever waking, ever watching, ever strong. The powwow had surrendered and become a slave. I would be no slave.

"Father?" said Kattenanit my son, as we lay upon our bed together in the cool of the night. "Do the gods love men?"

Silvermoon turned toward him to answer, but I laid my palm upon her lips. Cold Tongue our pup dog lay by the warm ashes of the fire, whining in his dreams.

"No," I said. "But your father and your mother love you. And it is time you slept." Silvermoon took my hand to her breast and smiled. The boy rolled over and entered his dreams.

War with the Pequot was hot like the summer. That long, bloody summer. That thirtieth summer of my long, bloody life. Canonicus summoned all his vassals to our aid, even Chickataubut and John Sagamore from the Massachusetts near the English town of Boston. The tomahawk of the Narragansett must fall, said our grand sachem, upon the heads of all foes and rebels, that we may live again in peace and safety upon the lands of our fathers.

The Pequot were aliens and cruel invaders. They had come down among us from the Mohican and the Mohawk, many fathers ago, absorbing some small tribes and pushing many more to the west and to the south. The Narragansett held their ground, like the mountain that will not move though the wild storm tears all the trees from her by the roots. But the Pequot were ever pushing their lines. Now they wanted the lands between the waters of the Weekapaug and the Pocatuck. The lands of our Niantic neighbors and allies. We said no. Though our blood stain the harvest and our skulls lie in the streams, no! Nopatin my father led many warriors into the embattled territory, wrestled in deadly combat with men who were once his companions in the Pequot village of his youth, and championed our name against Sassacus the son of Woipequand. Would not Askug take my father to his heart at last? Call him a true son of the Narragansett? A true son of his own? But the powwow was beyond such sentiment. His eyes were dark continually. No candle of love or loyalty could lighten them.

To our north, the Nipmuc revolted from our rule, thinking to slip from our hold while blood ran in the Pocatuck. But we had two hands. With one we fought the Pequot. With the other we struck at the Nipmuc. Again our subjects among the Massachusetts strengthened our arms.

To our east, across the Great Bay, Massasoit kept watch from his wigwam, paying us small tribute while clinging to the cloak of the English at Plymouth.

In the Moon Of The First Harvest, Miantonomi and his squaw, with twelve warriors—the Fool and I among them—walked the long path to the Massachusetts. We went among our subjects, giving them gifts and strengthening their hearts against our foes. Many English were living in the country with their pigs and their cattle, their fences and their houses. Others were abroad in the woods, hunting. We greeted one another in peace when our paths crossed, but I always looked behind me as we passed.

"I would go among them," said Miantonomi while we sat in the house of John Sagamore. "But I need one to be my tongue to them. Not a Pequot or a Wampanoag …"

"Or a Patuxet," I interrupted with a slight bow.

"… but one of our own," my prince concluded. "And I have not heard of any Patuxet rising from the dead," he said to me with a gentle jab of his elbow.

Nor of any god dying, I said within myself.

John Sagamore, so named and known by the English, told us of one of his braves who went to Boston often to trade. His name was Ouxamit. He understood the English well and was able to speak some in their tongue. He would be glad to bring us to the house of the governor Winthrop.

"It is good!" said Miantonomi. "It is time for the sachem of Boston and the sachem of the Narragansett to smoke and treat of peace and friendship."

The town of the English at Boston on the Bay of the Massachusetts was much like Plymouth when first I had seen it. There were rows of English homes and longhouses of one and two stories, built of flat wooded planks and roofed over with bundled hay and straw or with squares of wood and bark. There were fences around each house, and between the rows of houses was a wide path upon which the English walked and moved their goods and their beasts. Wigwams were planted here and there at the edge of the town. Upon the shore and in the waters near the shore were boats and canoes of many shapes and sizes.

We were welcomed by the governor Winthrop and feasted greatly at his home for two settings of the sun. Many things amazed me, but none so much as the tenderness I saw between this Winthrop and his wife. I felt a darkness wrap itself around my heart when I beheld their love, for this was not my way with Silvermoon. Not since our first summer. Nor was this the way of the Narragansett. Yet our squaws knew that the English wives were better loved, and they complained about it long and often. And so we had to learn a new way to be men. In this the English caused much trouble in our homes, for who knows how many arrows went unsharpened while the mighty warrior kneaded his heart anew toward his squaw! And how low could a man stoop for his woman and still be a man? But I did not stoop. I simply smiled more and growled less. For a while.

Yet Winthrop was a man, and a strong one.

After two days was the Sabbath, and Miantonomi and his squaw desired to go with the governor to see how it was that they worshiped their gods. I begged the privilege also and was allowed to go, for I longed to hear the Song On The Wind once more. Miantonomi and I had spoken of it as we walked the path to Boston but did not tell this to Winthrop. Ouxamit would go to the worship with us while the rest of the Narragansett were given food and drink and the freedom to walk about the town and eat upon the shoreline where the boats were tied. But they must not make any great noise nor smoke their pipes near the longhouse of the gods.

To the loud heartbeat of the drum, the people of Boston were called to gather at the longhouse of their gods. The whole city came. I had never seen so many English.

Outside the longhouse, upon its grey-wooded walls, hung the heads of many wolves, killed by the hunters of the English. The wolf was hated, for he slaughtered the English beasts. Those who killed the wolf and hung him upon the longhouse were given English wampum. Upon the doors were skins with many strange symbols. These were the skins that spoke to those who knew how to listen. They told the English about goods that were for trade, said Ouxamit, about marriages that were planned, and about councils that were to be held. What incredible magic! Skins that talked! Surely the gods of the English were mighty!

Within, no skin hung. No wolf head. There were none of the bright colors and the dark smells of the houses of the powwows. None of the bones and rattles, feathers and herbs, snakesticks and shells. For as Squanto had told us, they had no powwow. There was no fire, and no man danced. There were no rugs upon the walls to tell the stories of the gods, no pipes, and no tobacco with which to please the spirits. How did they call upon their gods?

The room was large and cool but light, for Keesuckquand could enter through the many windows. Each window was covered with a thin skin that had been oiled to let in the sun while keeping out the winds. The English were seated upon long wooden planks. The men sat on one side of the house while boys sat together behind them. The women sat on the other side with the young girls at their feet. Along the wall of the men was a wooded floor about the height of the beds of the Narragansett. Upon it stood a robed man who began to call upon the gods. Yet he did not speak in the way of Askug, for the powwow had to scratch when the gods itched. Dance when the shadows tickled his feet. Moan when the fangs of the spirits struck his soul. Shriek when his heart grew hot with the brands of the gods. But the god-sachem of the English—whom they called the preacher—spoke to his gods as the warrior speaks to the captain of war. As the child speaks to the father. As the brave speaks to the great elder. As the man speaks to the man. What kind of god could be summoned thus? Was the preacher speaking to the god who walked as a man? Yet if this god walked as a man and could be talked to as a man, where was the god?

We stood. Another man led in song, as our powwows do, singing words to the people which the people sing back to him. But there was no fear in the faces of the English. No pain. No anguish. No twisting of the heart to wring forth waters with which to cool the unquenchable thirst of the spirits. There were tears in the eyes of many women, yet behind those eyes was strange joy and a mysterious awe. Though my ears did not hear the Wind Song, my heart heard its echo from the lips of the English. The melodies, though not the same, rose and fell with the same deep calling to my soul. I wondered if their gods would come.

And what if they came to me? Their tongue was not my own. Their shadows were strange. Their hearts were not known to me.

What are you doing here? they would say, and I would not know how to answer them.

Why do you come here? they would ask, and I would have no tongue to speak to them.

We will slay you! they would declare, and I would not even know that my blood was in their eyes.

How could I fight? I had no weapons. Where would I run? I looked to the door, and it was closed. Men stood by it with poles. English surrounded me, front, back, and sides.

But my prince was near. At my left hand. Untroubled. Unafraid.

I must not fear! Yet I felt myself in the unseen grip of a great snare as though the hand of Weetucks—made invisible by the gods—was enclosed about my body. As though I were under the waters of the great sea, held down by a great stone tied about my legs. I must loose myself! I must rise! I must breathe the breath of life before my lungs force open my mouth and I swallow the sea!

Why did I fear? Why did my soul cry out so desperately for the wooded path and the open skies?

Was it Chepi who breathed his dark threats in the ears of my soul? Was he angry that I stood in the house of strange gods? Was he jealous? Can the gods be jealous?

The gods can be whatever they wish to be!

And so can I.

Thus I wish to close my ears to the plaguing spirits!

I slapped my chest to clear my soul. I ran my hand through the hair upon my forehead to clear my eyes. My hand was shaking. My forehead was damp with sweat. And I noticed then that the singing had ceased and that the English were seating themselves again. I reclined upon the groaning wood, a thin sigh escaping through my clenched teeth. *I will not fear*, I said to myself. *My prince is with me. And I am The Rain From God.*

The preacher began to tell of the gods. Or so I believe. What he said, I do not know. All I know is that the room was warming, the flies were buzzing, my stomach was growling, my legs were twitching, my bottom was tiring, and my eyes were begging me to close them. But we must not sleep in the house of the gods, Winthrop said.

So I slapped my chest again to wake myself, and many frowning eyes beheld me.

"Perhaps we also must not slap our chests in the house of the gods," I whispered aloud to Miantonomi, and the English boys giggled to hear me speak.

More eyes looked upon me, and heads wagged against me.

Perhaps I must be as the still hunter who sits and waits for Noonatch, I thought, and so I stopped my tongue and watched the preacher.

His mouth opened and closed with the strange noises of the English tongue. His hands turned the magic skins of a large English book. He pointed his finger at the ceiling, at the people, at the book. His arms moved all about as he spoke, and I thought he must be conjuring the spirits to either come or go. His eyes flashed with the passion of his speech. He might have been speaking of great wars and of ancient medicine and of caverns filled with demons and dwarfs. Of the land beyond the seas with its houses on bridges, its forests without trees, and its great king in his great stone fort. Of the great English gods which made the great English lands and the great English people. But I did not know if he spoke of any of these things, for his words were to me as the chattering of the chipmunk. When he was finished—and the sun had climbed much since he began!—we stood again to sing.

Then at last the doors were opened, and the golden eyes of Keesuckquand peered curiously in upon us. Quietly we walked out into the autumn afternoon.

"Did you see the gods?" I asked my prince. "Did you hear their voices or know their presence?"

He stopped for a moment and turned back to look upon the long-house. The heads of the wolves stared back at us with dark, empty eyes. Their mouths hung open in silent laughter, though I heard no jest.

"I did not see the gods, nor did I hear them," he replied, "but I felt the same longing as on the Night Of The Wind Song. That longing which …" He tossed his hands into the air in an effort to shake words from the heavens, as a child would shake the brittle, golden leaves from the trees of autumn. "That longing which has no name," he said at last. "No face. No object I have ever seen. No place that I have ever been. No pleasure I have ever known." And he looked into my eyes to see if my heart was as his. "Do you know that longing, Katanaquat?" he asked.

"I have known it, but I do not understand it," I said.

More feasting. More drinking. More smoke and talk of trade. And the governor was glad that we should live in peace with him. But he desired also that we walk as brothers with the Pequot and the Wampanoag, a thing hard to hear because of the blood which yet lay unavenged upon our lands. But we would take the words of Winthrop with us, said my prince. We would carry these things in our hearts. We would counsel with our elders. And we would come again one day to feast and smoke and speak of peace.

CHAPTER ELEVEN

Uncas

Uncas came among us in the summer that followed from the land of Mohegan on the Connecticut. Yet not of his own will did he come, but he fled the heavy threatenings of Sassacus his sachem, for the cunning cousin of Miantonomi was caught stirring up rebellion against the grand sachem of the Pequot. When his plotting was discovered, Sassacus warned him that his head would be taken some dark night if he did not behave. So Uncas ran to the Narragansett to recline in our wigwams while the anger of Sassacus cooled.

Uncas was now a sagamore at Mohegan, with many seasons behind him since he had taken a daughter of Sassacus as his bride. But such was the crooked heart of our old companion that not even marriage could bind him to any man in loyalty. He desired more of Sassacus than his daughter. He wanted his wigwam. His seat. His power. His people. For Uncas could live without love—even without air, I declared—but not without power.

I was not happy to see him.

"Are you not a sachem yet, Katanaquat?" said the Pequot, scratching the skin of my pride with the bloodied edge of his sharp tongue. We sat with crossed legs before the fire of Miantonomi, four grown warriors of the eastern woods—Assoko, my prince, myself, and Uncas. The lips of the Pequot were frozen in a smile that held no joy, nor offered any. His eyes were as clouded waters, within which I imagined the dim, moving shadows of some strange monsters of the deep. The blaze that rose between us cast a crimson glow upon that dark sea, and the monsters fled, leaving only waters filled with blood. My own hot blood was rising to my head, and I wondered for a moment what kind of lively entertainment might be had in kicking the burning logs into the lap of the Pequot refugee.

"Meentomi is our sachem!" declared the Fool with a grin. For he loved our prince and thought it a grand thing to follow him.

"And are you not a sachem yet, my Fool?" Uncas said, tearing the taunt from my taut hands and throwing it to Assoko. The Fool sat rocking. His face mirrored that of Uncas, with the same dead smile and the same red, clouded eyes. It appeared as mockery, but it was not, for the Fool played the looking glass unconsciously. I saw myself often in his visage, and it much surprised me, though it was an outward image only. For I did not think myself so dark and dirty. Within, the Fool was clean, and even now his black smile hid bright fire and deep strength. He was thinking. We would wait.

"Meentomi is our sachem!" he said again at last. "Cancus is our sachem!" he added. "Two moons. Bright nights."

"Two moons," said Uncas, "are one moon too many! Nanepaushat needs much room to roam." And he pushed a small slug into the fire with his toes.

"The sky is big enough for two moons," I said, as I watched the sad slug shrivel and shrink within the flames.

"The old moon is tired of shining, I hear," said the Pequot, speaking of Canonicus, who had lately cast the mantle of leadership more heavily upon Miantonomi. "Does the new moon find pride in the view from on high?"

"The new moon does not fly like Nanepaushat," said my prince calmly, holding his cousin in a strong gaze, "but walks the woods with his brothers. When he looks down from any hill, he sees the same trees as his brothers." Miantonomi pulled his moccasins from his feet and tossed them to Uncas. "If you wish to see what we see, then put these on!" he said.

"I'll wear them one day," said the Pequot to the dancing flames. And then he turned his eyes on me. I stared into the swamp of his soul. There were no spirits in the crimson mist. Only bloody waters. Beneath the waters lay the sucking red sands, pulling me slowly down. I could not fight them. I had to turn away.

My grandfather and I pushed our way carefully through the blackberry brambles beside the Crying Swamp. The thorns of the boughs tugged at our leggings as the branches attempted to enclose us in their bristled arms. Angry spiders shook their webs at us in defiance. Frightened rabbits fled the cover of their prickled wigwams. Wary serpents slid beneath rocks and took up watch against our heels and toes.

Beyond the thorny wall lay a soft, wet carpet of short grasses, tall ferns, bright flowers, and scattered herbs. A swarm of hungry mosquitos met us there, falling upon us like the spears and arrows of the Mohawk. We paid them little heed, and they found little to their liking upon our thickly greased skin. The fat of the bear with which we had painted ourselves confounded their purposes. And so we went quickly to our work.

We were after the herbs, for Askug needed a fresh supply for the ills of our people. Here were the cures for many rashes and fevers, the banes of many sad shadows and angry spirits. Here too was the path that led deep into the Crying Swamp, to the dark wigwam of the black demon Chepi. Few ever wandered beyond this green, shadowed doorway into his domain. It was bad enough when the black spirit wandered out! Better to face ten warriors of the Mohawk in the bright light of day than be caught by Chepi under the half moon. But I did not fear him in that moment, for I had walked the green gauntlet around his swamp many times since my boyhood. First with Askug, then alone. And thus one tall terror was conquered by a thin brown path worn by the Snake Of The Narragansett and the Rain From God. Still, I always heard the crying. But that is a tale for another time.

"The English will no longer beg us to keep peace with Sassacus!" announced Askug as we knelt in the wet ferns, our fingers deftly pulling at the roots of the feverleaf. I stopped my labors and looked into his face. His wrinkled eyes shone with a dark joy. His mouth was set in as firm and as true a smile as the old man then knew. I seldom saw the pleasure of Askug in those days, for the joy of the powwow had narrowed sharply to the pain and destruction of the people of the Pequot. I waited for him to say more.

"A band of Pequot has murdered an English boat captain named Stone. And seven of his men as well. On the Connecticut," Askug exulted. "Will the English hold back our hand against Sassacus now? Will they not rejoice instead when we dance for war against the Pequot dogs?" The powwow turned back to the earth, pushing his long fingers into the soil like many small hoes in the hands of many squaws. "Soon, very soon, we will pluck

the cursed nation of the Pequot out of the ground by the roots!" he proph-
esied. With a quick jerk, he held a large feverleaf to my face, its dangling
roots covered with the black mud of the doorway of Chepi. Mosquitos
danced in the air.

"Will the English not avenge the death of Stone themselves?" I asked
as we crawled among the cool ferns. "And would it not be better to let them
do so? Why should the Narragansett die and mourn when the English can
reduce the Pequot with no danger to our people?" My words filled my heart
like the words of Miantonomi, but I was not counseling peace. I was playing the part of my prince to the powwow. For Askug needed none to take
his side. He was a gaggle of gods and a tribe unto himself.

"Let them avenge Stone!" said the powwow, scattering the hovering
insects with his wildly swinging arms. "And when the fog of the thundersticks blows away upon the wind and the Pequot limps home with its tail
between its legs, the arrows of the Narragansett will fall like sleet upon the
whimpering dog!"

"Nopatin my father will soon push the Pequot back over the waters of
the Pocatuck," I said.

"Nopatin your father …" and the powwow hesitated, but I knew his
thought.

Nopatin your father is a Pequot, were the words of his heart. For the
powwow did not want victory against the Pequot to come at the hands of
a Pequot, even though that Pequot be the adopted son of the Narragansett
powwow!

"Nopatin will triumph!" I declared. For my father was a Narragansett.
A man. I would see him in no other way.

"But," reasoned Askug, with the cunning of the serpent, crawling from
under his rock in a new direction, "his heart calls for you to stand with
him. For he must not stand alone against the foe." Askug wished the triumph to be mine, for only then could the powwow claim the triumph and
the vengeance for himself. Nopatin was just the war club of the
Narragansett. I was the Rain From God. And Askug danced for rain.

The powwow set his plants aside and rubbed his muddied hands upon
his loincloth. "You are the strength of the right arm of your father," said the
powwow to my heart. "The knife of his will. The son of his youth. The medicine of his Narragansett father. The vengeance of his Narragansett mother."

I saw myself at the side of my father, painted for battle, armed for blood. My tongue could taste the cool waters of war.

Askug stood, and a cloud of winged bloodsuckers rose with him. "You are The Rain From God, my son, and though your father stands as a strong wall against the Pequot, you must cross that wall to fall upon the foe so that his foot slips upon the wet ground. So that his eyes cannot see the sun. So that his nose cannot smell the fires of the Narragansett or his ears hear our feet in the forest. You must fall on him, Katanaquat! And the spirits will fall upon him with you. Your rain will so blur the senses of the Pequot that he will shoot his arrows into his brothers!"

The vision rose larger within me. The vision of my own right arm held high, the deadly tooth of the Weak Woman biting deeply into the flesh of the foe. The vision was like strong water, melting the fear and firing the heart.

Askug was stomping among the ferns, his feet sinking into the soft soil, turning the green carpet brown in his dance. "Katanaquat! Katanaquat! Katanaquat!" he chanted. "Fall upon the Pequot! Fall hard upon the Pequot! Fall upon the Pequot!"

My blood rose hot and my heart beat hard as he whirled upon the doorstep of Chepi. How could this stiff, old man become so quickly like the wolf pup, chasing his tail and leaping high for bloody morsels from the hand of his master? But vengeance is a hard master who demands all from his slaves. He calls even the dying to dance to his tune, so that they have not even a breath to look to their own souls before they fly! Still, he is a master willing to fill the heart full! As the bitterness of Askug against the Pequot clouded the air like the mist and the mosquitos, the face of Uncas rose before my eyes. My own deep hatred leapt from my heart to strike hands with that of my grandfather. I joined in the chanting, and our loud shouts shook the vines and rattled the hollow dead cedars that stood like sentinels at the door of the dark swamp. My feet followed the feet of Askug, and the mud of our stomping splattered our leggings like the blood of our enemies.

I danced again. This time around the war pole within the city of Canonicus. Many followed me in the fire-lit circle, pledging by their song and their dance to follow me further in the battle. My Fool was among them.

Uncas had returned to the Mohegan, upon the vain promise to sweeten his tongue with the sap of the maple and busy his hands with the carving of canoes. I wondered how long it would be before the chief sachem of the Pequot spit the Mohegan poison out of his mouth completely. Or was Uncas merely a clever spy for Sassacus, gathering news for his father-in-law while eating our soup and chewing the meat of our hunt? No matter. Whether in league with Sassacus or not, he was the fool of none but himself. He did nothing if it did not please his own foul heart. I did not know if it were safer having him within our walls or without.

Miantonomi gave me blessing as I stood with thirty warriors at the side of Red Creek. Canonicus promised wampum for a victory. Askug promised chants and dances while we were gone. And Silvermoon promised songs for my safety. *I no longer need her songs,* I thought, *for they are simply the wind-blown whispers of a woman.* But they were ready melodies within my heart when I wished to dream of home. Kattenanit my son, my only son—for Silvermoon was as my mother Taquattin and had borne me only this one child in fifteen summers of our marriage—was now a strong young brave of fourteen years. He gave me two arrows of his own making—fine, straight shafts with yellow feathers and tapered flint.

"Shoot as the Fool shoots," he counseled quietly with a warm smile. And it was good counsel, given with love, more like the words of his mother than the heart of his father. But Assoko heard it and thought it a jest, and laughed so long and so loud that my pride was wounded. I stepped on his foot to still him, but it did not stop his laughter. Instead he chuckled while hopping on one leg, which caused others to ask of his behavior. Thus the counsel of Kattenanit became public, and I was shamed before my brothers. But this did not cause any to leave me, for none could shoot as the Fool shoots! So at last I laughed too as we walked the warpath toward the Niantic to join Nopatin my father in the battle against the Pequot.

Nopatin my father with his warriors, and I with mine, had followed the waking sun to the edge of a large camp of the enemy. The Pequot party, under the sagamore Mattacoomuck, slept in the stolen wigwams of the conquered Niantic of Tishcatuck. Some would wake that day but for a moment, never to sleep again beneath the oak and the sycamore.

With the loud war cry of our people, the Narragansett fell upon the tents of the foe. Some of us opened their doors to strike them upon their beds. Others stood in the shelter of the trees, bows bent, waiting for the scalpers to fall back into the woods with the Pequot in pursuit. I, with half my men, entered the village first, for my heart was hot for the bloody flesh of the Pequot. I entered the first wigwam I came to.

"I will kill you!" I shouted, as the tooth of Weak Woman bit into the head of a dazed and dreaming warrior. With the swift and practiced hand of the squaw who cuts the meat of Noonatch for her family, I slid my knife above the ears, across the brow and over the head of the dying man. With a sudden jerk, his hairy scalp came loose in my hands. With a shriek of triumph, I forced my knife into his heart and released his life blood upon the floor of the wigwam. His companions shrank in waking terror at the sight of their dead brother and the sound of my loud cries.

"Katanaquat!" I shouted, shaking the severed scalp before their wide eyes, washing us all in the sticky shower of red rain. Raising my bloody weapons above my head, I threw one last cry in their faces before rushing from the tent toward the cover of the trees.

The Pequot rose as one to follow us, but our arrows drove them back to their tents and the protection of a small grove of water willow. For a time, we exchanged shrieks and shafts, but none was killed on either side. Then I heard the laughter of my Fool and the loud voice of Nopatin. To my right, rushing from the cover of the oaks, was Assoko of the Narragansett. Behind him, to my great surprise, was my father. All eyes were upon them.

When the Fool fought with you in the battle, it was hard to fix upon the foe. For the Fool commanded the attention of all, especially those who lay within sight of his bow! Those who fought against him must either fly like the fox before the wolf, cry upon the spirits for a great shield, or leap into the deep hole like the groundhog.

Those who fought at his side could forget the war and enter the dream of every warrior for his own pride and valor. Who could but wish to throw off fear as the Fool did? Chase the foe like Keesuckquand chasing shadows?

Dive into the thick of the enemy like one playing foot ball on the shores of the Great Salt Sea?

Yet none but the Fool had the protective eye of the spirits and the strong wall of his own mad ignorance!

My father! Was he now a fool himself?

Assoko ran toward the Pequot like the starving dog bounding upon the pack of young rabbits. But he was not armed! My father ran behind him, his bow pulled to his chin, the Fool playing the shield in a wild display of flying limbs and loud laughter. Several Pequot warriors fled the cover of the wig-wams to join their brothers in the willows. One of them fell with the shaft of Nopatin through his thigh. Pequot arrows began to fly toward the Fool and my father. To my amazement, Assoko caught one in mid-air and flung it back toward the willows. The bow of Nopatin was armed again, and his shaft soon followed the shaft of the Fool, but with greater effect. A warrior of the Pequot fell to the ground with Narragansett feathers decorating his painted chest. Nopatin was shooting as the Fool shoots!

"Shoot as the Fool shoots!" I cried, and I loosed an arrow of Kattenanit upon the thicket of the Pequot. It flew swift and straight, sticking fast in the hard willow, spitting a spray of shattered bark into the faces of the star-tled foe.

"Shoot as the Fool shoots!" echoed the Narragansett. Nopatin tackled the laughing Fool, and the two of them tumbled behind the shelter of a large stone. The Pequot saw them fall and came forth as one body to fall upon them. The arrows of the Narragansett flew at the Pequot like the owl when it takes the bird in flight. The enemy tumbled like the cornstalk before the sword of the English. Never had I seen such a sight!

In a breath, with our knives and tomahawks in our hands, we ran from the oaks, a pack of howling wolves racing toward the wounded deer. There was no tomorrow for any of us. Only the shrill wail of battle and the deadly crush of stone and steel and flesh and bone.

Many Pequot reeled toward the Pocatuck, seeking to cross its waters to their own country on the other side. Some waded into its deeps to swim for their lives. Some slipped and scrambled over the wet rocks and fallen trees that formed a bridge between the lands of the Niantic and the lands of the Pequot. Some pulled wounded brothers through the red-stained waters. Others ran along the shoreline through the woods, looking for the shallows and a way to cross swiftly on foot. We did not follow them, for we were busy with their fellows at the foot of the weeping willows.

Eighteen heads of the mighty Pequot swallowed flies upon the palisade of Canonicus. My tomahawk had taken two. Three of the Pequot wounded, including Mattacoomuck their sachem, perished bravely beneath the slow tortures of our children and our squaws. I will not tell you how Mattacoomuck died, for I no longer take delight in some things that once fed my soul. Yet never did I see a man endure so much and still sing! So great was our admiration and amazement that at last we made a stew of him to share his strength with all.

Nopatin my father was honored for this great victory. The Niantic begged him to come and live among them. So Miantonomi and Canonicus bestowed upon him lands and a sachemdom along the Pocatuck.

The Fool was offered a wife by the Niantic. He took her to himself and loved her.

My father asked me to come with him and set up my wigwam by his, but I told him privately that I longed for lands and a sachemdom of my own. I did not say so to any other, but my prince knew my heart.

"I need you here for now, my Rain From God," he said to me. "But much wampum will be yours and many skins to trade with the English. Take also another bride to give you more children. And I myself will help you build a larger wigwam."

We built my wigwam. I traded my skins. I put my wampum in many baskets. I displayed my scalps upon a high pole. I wore a new shirt that I bought from the English. I hung a steel knife about my neck. I took a new bride. And then another.

I sharpened many arrows. I told many tales of battle and blood. I took Kattenanit often into the woods to put strength into this heart against the spirits, to be the man, to hunt, to shoot, to swing the tomahawk, to stalk the shadows of Pussough the wildcat, to tread the path outside the swamp of Chepi, and to walk tall among our vassals and among the English and their gods.

A daughter was born, and then a second son. Was I not like a child of Weetucks? Was I not a giant among our people? Had I not come forth from the womb with great prophecies upon me? Had I not, even as a child, toppled great stones and risen up against the enemies of the Narragansett? Had I not, as a man, led many warriors into battle, taken many scalps, even the heads of my enemies? Did I not have many wives? Did not children now begin to flow from my loins like the river from the wellspring in the hills? Was not my father now a great hero and a sachem? My grandfather a feared powwow? Had I not shot my bow like the Fool? And was I not his closest friend? Did I not sit in the inner council of our people with my prince Miantonomi and our great sachem Canonicus? Had I not risen above the poison of Squanto to walk among the English and the Dutch, and to know their favor and their friendship? And did I not have much medicine—my own strong medicine—against the power of the gods?

Uncas returned to us, with eleven warriors of the Mohegan. He was no longer welcomed by Sassacus. For he had risen once more against him, even to the dawn of battle. But no battle was fought, for Uncas, outnumbered by the Pequot of many villages, fell back to the Mohegan. Sassacus came to him there with a train of many warriors. "You will leave this land," the great sachem told him, "or we will do to you as Canonicus did to Mattacoomuck. But your flesh will feed the buzzards, instead," he threatened. "Now go, and do not come among us anymore!"

Thus Uncas was no longer a Pequot, and no longer allowed at the Mohegan. So he made himself sachem of the few who would follow him. With their wives and children, fifteen men of the Mohegan moved with Uncas further north along the Connecticut, out of the lands of the Pequot. There they made their home and their tribe. And they called themselves Mohegan, for that was their name when they had been Pequot.

Now that he was among us again, his proud and crooked heart could be seen by all. With his men around him, his boasting was no longer in jest, his threatenings no longer veiled in riddles. He started much trouble with men of the Narragansett, trouble that nearly came to blows. But he thought himself our ally, for now his heart was as fully against Sassacus as was ours. But none among us wished to share his heart in even this. Only Askug could rejoice that Uncas now hated the Pequot.

Yet Askug hated Uncas. In this, at least, my heart beat with the powwow.

One day, as I walked the forest with Kattenanit, I heard the noise of men laughing. We stood still to listen to the sounds upon the wind. Voices came to us from the east, beyond a low hill covered with pine and carpeted with the soft needles of many seasons. A small stream flowed beneath the pine, and we could hear its gentle music. Words did not come to us fully, though we heard eight tongues.

"Do you know them?" I whispered to Kattenanit.

"They are not of our village," he quietly replied. "But I think I hear the voice of the Mohegan who sticks closest to Uncas. The one named Wequash. Listen, for he is loudest of them all."

We were silent again. And, yes, it was Wequash. For his tongue was strong and strange, with a piece of the song of the English upon it. Wequash walked often to Boston, I knew, and went once with Miantonomi to Salem, where Roger Williams had his house. My prince liked Wequash, though the Mohegan was like the hand upon the arm of Uncas.

I motioned for my son to follow, and we moved swiftly up the hill. The men were not moving, we knew, for their voices were neither closer nor further than when first we heard them. I thought they were seated, smoking and talking, upon the flat rocks that lay scattered beside the stream. The smell of tobacco met us as we crested the hill, downwind from the chattering band. Here the pines began, and though the brush was sparse beneath them, the boughs were low. Many large rocks pushed their faces above the earth, chest high to the grown man in some places, higher than his head in others, obscuring our view of the warriors along the stream. We kept the path, for we would not show fear. I felt it my place to discover their purpose, to see that the black hand of Uncas not muddy any waters of the Narragansett!

As we rounded a slight bend, between two needle-covered mounds of stone, we met the braves.

"Greetings, friends," I said, even before they were fully in our sight. "We are Katanaquat and Kattenanit his son. What good can we do you?"

The warriors started suddenly to their feet, and by their faces I feared mischief. Yet I walked to within ten paces of them, no weapon in my hands. My son stood behind me in the path. "Greetings, friends," he repeated, and we held out our palms in peace.

"Greetings, friends," repeated a few of the Mohegan, and now we saw them to be the men of Uncas indeed. Eight of them, as we had guessed. Palms were extended by most, but some moved toward their weapons.

"Do you need your clubs when two braves of the Narragansett come to smoke with you by the laughing waters?" I asked, looking at the men who had moved to arm themselves.

Wequash motioned them to stand away from their weapons. And so they did—nervously, I noticed, and with strange embarrassment.

"Katanaquat," said Wequash rather loudly, reaching his arm toward mine. "Come and sit with us." Though I suspected the motive of his hospitality, I saw no violence in his eyes.

Wequash and I clasped arms, and I sat at once upon the rock against which the many war clubs rested. I picked one up. As its master started toward me, I held it up to him and said, admiringly, "Well-carved! Is it the work of your hands?"

At this he stopped, and his body relaxed. With a sudden smile, he said, "Yes! My grandfather made many clubs for the Pequot and the Niantic, and he taught me how to do the same."

Kattenanit seated himself beside me and asked to see the club. I handed it to him, and he spoke many good words about it. In this way, we fell to showing off our weapons, and the tension faded into good will and much laughter. But for all the proud chatter of warrior with warrior, I saw that Wequash was yet on his guard. His eyes, though they moved casually upon us all, fled often—in a wink—beyond the thick brush just over the stream.

I rose to demonstrate the use of my club in hitting pinecones in the fashion of a game. This was met with much delight, and soon we all were knocking cones into the woods. When at last all cones were gone which had been near at hand, I suggested crossing the stream for a fresh supply. A clamor of dismay arose from the men of Uncas, and I looked upon them with surprise.

"Do you not wish to play any longer?" I asked. "Or do you not wish me to cross these waters?" With a quick leap, I was on the other side of the stream. Kattenanit followed like my shadow, pulling several war clubs into the stream behind him. Just as swiftly, he armed his bow.

"There is danger beyond the bushes!" shouted Wequash loudly enough to chase away all danger within one thousand paces.

"I would see this danger myself," I said, and I started through the brush toward the quiet pines beyond. "Kattenanit will guard the creek for you," I shouted back at the men of the Mohegan, "so that you have no need to fear!"

My son stood as an armed sentinel between my bare back and the men of Uncas. They made no move for their weapons, but they made enough noise to cause the rocks to roll!

Within three paces beyond the thick brush, I found my danger. And it was danger indeed!

Uncas crouched upon the fallen needles, black fire in his eyes, a sharp knife held to the throat of a terrified young maiden of the Narragansett.

"Supauchem!" I whispered gently to the girl, for I knew her well, the oldest daughter of one of my chief warriors.

Her clothing had been torn from her, her flesh was dirtied with the sticky needles of the pine, and her face was smeared with the dust of the earth and the trails of her tears. When she heard her name, she burst forth weeping, like the sudden letting of the waters of the summer storm. Her tongue stuttered, her breath came in gasps, and she could spit out nothing but the sounds of her great anguish.

"You are a dead man!" I spoke quietly to Uncas. And then there was no sound but the sobbing of Supauchem. Even the men of Uncas had ceased in their shouting, for they knew their sachem was discovered.

"If you turn one toe in my direction," said Uncas through his teeth, "this child will be the first to die. After that, Katanaquat will be the dead man—not Uncas."

Then my shadow stood at my side, his bow leveled at Uncas.

"She will die," said Uncas, coolly to my son, "though your shaft splits my head!"

"If you are a man," I said to the Mohegan, "you will let her go and face me only."

"You would fight without your Fool?" he taunted. And he pushed the girl from him and sprang to his feet. I saw then Wequash and the rest of the Mohegan standing in the wood with their arms, but they were not poised for battle. They had crossed the stream to watch the contest. As any man would. Perhaps they even whispered to the spirits for the triumph of the Rain From God. For who could love Uncas?

On this side of the creek, the pines rose like giants above the earth, their distant heads topped with the only green that saw the sky. Below the dark ceiling, dead branches hung like skeletons above our heads. Below the bony boughs lay the dried cones and curled needles of uncounted seasons. The sun touched the thick carpet rarely, in small, scattered patches of muted white light. All else lay in a shadowed blend of faded yellows and twilight browns.

Uncas moved slowly into the darkness of the shade of a massive pine, rolling his steel in his right hand, flexing the fingers of his left hand. I could hear him speaking lowly, but his words did not reach me clearly. *Like his heart,* I thought, *like the shadows of this ancient wood, his words hide themselves from true light.* Had they ever been clean?

"What of your own heart?" I heard the Mohegan say, and I wondered if he heard my thoughts! "Does it not fear death?"

"I fear death, as any man," I replied, moving closer to the dark form of the tensed Mohegan. "But I know that it will come, and I am ready to meet it."

Did I believe that? Or did I simply hold up the hard bark of the warrior, the shield of pride, and foolishness which shouted to the soul, *Though death meets all men, surely I will never die!* Not today, at least. Never today.

"Here I am," said Death through the tongue of the Mohegan, and it leapt upon me.

My arm pushed the bladed hand of Uncas from my chest, and my hand found the wrist. Thus I held the weapon from me as I sought to shake it loose. But the free hand of Uncas took my hair in its grip, and with a violent wrench it pulled my head to one side. My own free hand held my own long steel, and I swung it now toward the arching torso of my foe. But though I trusted it to strike home, it passed through the air to claw the needled carpet on the forest floor instead. Uncas had thrown me.

I rolled wildly away from the leaping Mohegan and vaulted to my feet at the base of one of the pine giants. High above us strong winds rattled the rafters of our wigwam. Suddenly a window flew open in the green ceiling, and Keesuckquand let loose his bowstrings. White arrows shot through the hole into the room in which we fought, and then the window closed again. My eyes were assailed by the battering, bright beams. For a heartbeat, I stood in dazed display against the dark tower of pine at my back. Death took the moment and flew at me from the blackness. But my foot came up like the sprung snare, catching Death in its swift flight, sending it tumbling into the twisted branches of a fallen pine. The shadows blinked, and I ran from the spot to take my stand in the open ground.

So I am outnumbered! I said within myself. *Death is upon me. Keesuckquand is his ally. And Uncas is Uncas. Be the man, Katanaquat. But don't be the fool.*

"Kattenanit!" I shouted, and I heard the sharp buzz of the arrow as it slides from the bow. I heard the hard rap of flint against wood and the embittered cry of the angry Mohegan. My blindness left me and I saw the form of Uncas, reeling in a half circle in front of the tree where Keesuckquand had struck me. His loincloth was pinned to the pine by an arrow beneath his groin and between his legs. It had missed his person but had made him its prisoner. He tried to tear himself from the trunk, but the shaft held fast, and the cloth would not let him go. The force of his leap threw him face-first to the ground, violently plowing the soil with his chin.

Before he could raise himself, I was at him. I fell with my knee upon his right wrist, grasping the arm and pulling it behind his back with all my force. With a raw cry of pain he released the knife, and it rattled into the dead branches from which he had climbed some moments before. I saw that he was still fastened to the tree by the loincloth and the arrow, and so I stood back from him to recover my wind. Kattenanit was at my side, his bow rearmed. The men of Uncas were like the still stumps beneath the tall pine.

"Loose me and I will finish this game!" growled Uncas as the blood of his nose trickled over his curled lip into his mouth.

"Loose yourself," I said quietly, for somehow the lust of death had drained from me, "and crawl back to the Connecticut. We have fought over Narragansett women too often, my Pequot. My Mohegan. The cousin of my sachem. My enemy and the darkness of my heart!" I spat upon the ground near his head. "Crawl back to your own women and your own wigwams and be glad that the shaft did not end forever your dreams of sons and daughters! I will kill you on another day when we can stand in the light and see each other face to face!"

I walked from the pines into the gaze of the sun upon the murmuring stream, splashed my face with the waking waters, ascended the hill from which we had come, and passed through the oak and the maple toward my wives and my children and my wampum and my prince. By my side was the first son of my first love, having proved himself the man. By his side and covered with his cloak was the shamed and weeping daughter of a doubtless worried warrior of the Narragansett.

Chapter Twelve

Pequot Deadfall

*E*ven among the pines and under the tallest trees, the snow lay heavy. Rivers were hardened paths of ice and crusted snow. The wind blew strong and without mercy through the leafless forest. Cold were the days and frigid were the nights. We slept with our dogs in our beds.

In this moon of much hard winter came Roger Williams to the country of the Narragansett. He came not to visit but to stay.

"Will you not miss your people? Will you not miss your gods?" asked Canonicus to the English god-preacher.

"My God is with me even here," replied Williams. "There is no place that a man can go that God is not already there."

I did not wish to believe this. Was the English god standing among us in the house of Canonicus? I could not see his shadow. Nor did I see any spirit behind the eyes of Williams. But the English gods were not as our gods, Squanto had said. Perhaps they had no shadows.

I sat with crossed legs beside my prince. The north winds fought hard to climb into the tent of Canonicus. But they were frightened by the many blazes of the many fires of the grand sachem, so that they ran instead in circles on the ceiling, chasing the smoke like the dog chases the cat.

"And my people …" Williams hesitated. He needed time to find the words of our tongue. He spoke them well, better than any English I had ever known, but slowly like the turtle walks. "In time I will send for my wife and my children," he said. "And we will make our home in peace by the rivers of the Narragansett."

Beside Williams sat a young man called Angell, the same age as Kattenanit, a hardy boy of fourteen summers, who had walked with Williams through the wild white woods from Salem to the warm wigwams of Sowams. From there, the two of them broke the icy trail to the city of Canonicus and

Miantonomi. They had no goods to trade and no weapons but one English musket, one tomahawk, and the knives of their belts. Why had they tempted the spirits by this mad journey? Williams did not say. But he would not go back, he said, for his god had placed us in his heart, and then had torn him from his people that he might then give his heart to us. He would live by us as a brother and a neighbor, learn of our ways, show us the ways of the English, and do us good with all that came into his hand.

What a strange and wonderful man he was! But I feared him, for I saw no fear in him.

Canonicus was delighted, for he loved this Roger Williams much. He gave him land beyond the Seekonk near the little mouth of the Great Bay. There Williams built his house. He called his lands Providence, for this meant that his god had surprised him with good. Some other English came to join him, to build their houses and to plant their corn. And they walked the woods with us in peace.

Silvermoon combed her long black hair, humming the combing song she had learned long ago from Taquattin my mother. Her locks, thinly streaked now with the color of her name, fell below her knees like a glistening wall of dark, waving water. If I closed my eyes I could see her as I saw her on the first night of our marriage, strong and beautiful, clean and shining like the full moon. But I did not close my eyes, for I did not wish to dream of things that once were.

The moment was ours alone, for the rest of my squaws and my children were out in the fields under the spring sun. I pulled a flea from my leg and cracked it with my teeth.

"Your light has faded in my eyes," I said to the memory of my first love, but the words were spoken aloud. Silvermoon turned to me slowly with a still sadness upon her painted face.

"Your light is as strong in mine as ever it was, my warrior," she declared quietly. "But it hides within your heart behind many clouds."

"My heart is not clouded!" I said. "It is clean and strong." I spat the flea into the fire.

"It does not love as it once did," said Silvermoon, standing before me with her strong eyes upon mine.

"It cannot love as it once did," I returned. "For the heart of the great warrior is not as the heart of the child. It carries mountains in its back bag instead of seashells and turtles. It walks over great rivers and sits in the council houses of great sachems. It does not lie beside quiet waters with its young bride. It cannot look back and live again the summers of another day."

I rose to pace about the low blaze. Why did squaws always talk of love? Why could they not just be squaws and be quiet? We gave them all that was ours to give!

"The wife of Roger Williams is a squaw of my own years," said Silvermoon. And I knew I must hear again about the wives of the English. "Yet she is the only love of Roger Williams, the only wife ..."

"You are not the only wife of Katanaquat!" I said, impatiently. "And I am not an English! I am Narragansett! I am a great warrior! Great warriors take many wives! This is right and it is good! This is our way!"

Silvermoon hung her head, and her hair fell over her eyes as the hair of the young maiden when she looks shyly upon the young brave whom she loves. My heart was stricken with an ache and an anger. But my pride would not bow to the ache. It rose to embrace the anger.

"I did not promise to love you only or to love you best!" I shouted, waving my arms in the air like the powwow in his dance. "Nor did I promise to carve you new spoons each summer! It is enough that I bring you meat from the forest, fish from the waters. It is enough that I sharpen my arrows to chase the foe from the lands of the Narragansett. It is enough that I teach our son to do the same. You are fed. You are warm. You are safe." I took her hair in my hands and wrapped it tightly around her bosom and her back. "You are my squaw, and I do not beat you. Why do you ask for more?"

She swallowed heavily, and her eyes were like clouds full of rain. But she did not weep. She looked at me once more, unwound her hair from her dark flesh, turned to the wall and resumed her combing. Her humming entered my heart like a dirge, and I left the tent with shadows in my eyes.

The summer of my thirty-fourth year was the pathway to the deadfall for the Pequot. They could not know it, nor could any of us. For what man, while he walks within the flowered green of summer, can dream of winter and the end of the world?

"I will punish them," said my prince as we sat at the table of Roger Williams in his house at Providence. "I will take many warriors and punish them. Though they are sagamores of the Narragansett, they act as rebels in this matter and not as subjects to Canonicus and myself!"

"I believe you must do as you now say," replied the preacher. "Otherwise the governors of the English will hold you as guilty as the murderers themselves."

"Askug says that it is the work of the Pequot," I offered. "Though the clubs were swung by our own braves, the powwow believes the deed was paid for by Sassacus."

"I cannot think so," said my prince, "for the murdered was a friend of the Pequot sachem and had opened trade with him. Why would Sassacus want him dead?"

"Because his blood, shed by the hands of the Narragansett, would cry for vengeance," I said. "And thus lightning would fall upon the city of Canonicus from the thunderclouds of the English."

"This is why I must punish the rebels!" said Miantonomi. "But I hold not the Pequot at fault."

"I think as your prince does, Katanaquat, and not as your powwow," said Williams. "Sassacus begged long for this trade with the English. John Oldham was a respected Englishman and a fair trader. You know this to be true. For he shared meat often with Canonicus and Miantonomi, did he not? His murderers were probably angry that he now traded also with the Pequot. Were you not angry yourself?"

I was, for I did not want the Pequot to prosper. But I would not split the skulls of the English for selling glass bottles and wooden chests! This I declared as we sat in the kitchen of the preacher of Providence.

"I know you would not," said Williams, "but others would. And they have."

"I will punish them," said Miantonomi.

The slayers of Oldham dwelt on Manisses, called Block Island by the English. Their deed was done upon the ship of Oldham as it took its rest off the Manisses shore, having been recently upon the Connecticut among the Pequot. Nearly twenty warriors came aboard pretending friendship. When they saw their chance, they buried a hatchet in the head of Oldham and attempted to cut his limbs from his body. But they were discovered in their work by another boat of the English. In a short battle, some of the murderers were slain. The rest fled.

Though the peoples of Block Island were Narragansett, they were ruled by sachems who pulled hard against the long leash of Canonicus. Jealous against us for our friendship with Oldham and wishing to test the strength of the leash, they killed the trader. Also they wished for English guns and powder, glass bottles, and wooden chests. And a taste of English blood. Would it not bring them much medicine? Perhaps. But with a heavy dose of woe!

Miantonomi set out at the head of seventeen canoes with two hundred men to punish the under-sachems. But they had fled—to the Pequot! Miantonomi would not seek them there, and the English would not find them there.

The English of Boston were alarmed, for it seemed to them that a league of sorts was struck between the men of Block Island and the men of the Pequot. This fear was like dry leaves upon the hot coals of the English pride.

Two sons of Oldham had been captured alive by the Manisses Narragansett, and they were held upon the island still. Once more we crossed the waters, this time with the men of Wepitamock the sachem of our Niantic tributaries. We brought back the boys without battle, and Canonicus sent the sad and fatherless young braves safely home to Boston.

But the English of Massachusetts were not satisfied. They would have justice against the warriors of Block Island and against the Pequot who harbored them. And there was yet the undone matter of the slaying of Captain Stone, whose murderers also slept in peace within the tents of Sassacus. There must be blood for blood—this we understood. Yet the English feared that we would stand in their way, for the rumor falsely flew that Canonicus and Miantonomi also plotted for the death of Oldham.

In the heat of the Moon Before The Harvest, the English came to us to hear the truth and to treat of peace. Among their chief men were a war captain named Gibbons and a god-preacher called Higginson. With them too was Cutshamakin, a sachem of the Massachusetts. We laid before them the roasted flesh of the deer, the bear, and many kinds of fish, and also the best of our chestnut breads, corn puddings, and soups. We gave them pipes and tobacco and blankets of fine design. We walked to our longhouse with

Canonicus our great sachem and Miantonomi our prince. We sat with our elders and our kings in solemn council and listened to the speech of the English. The meaning of their words was given to us by the tongue of Cutshamakin. It was the pledge of our friendship that they wanted. And a free hand to strike the Pequot if Sassacus did not give up the slayers of Oldham and Stone.

It was the will of Canonicus that Miantonomi receive the message and give the answer. Thus when the English had spoken, my prince rose. For many heartbeats he stood in silence, his clean eyes walking through the longhouse. They found each face of each dark warrior and searched each heart. They declared his covenant with us all, his call to stand first and always for the good of his people. His gaze fell at last upon the ambassadors from Boston who sat sweating upon thick skins in the center of the hot room.

"I do willingly embrace peace with the English," Miantonomi declared to each listening ear. To the spirits of the fire and the smoke. To the memory of his father and the father of his father. To the winds that would carry his words to every tribe and tongue beneath the tall trees that walk forever from the sea. "For though the English are but a few grains of sand upon the shores of our great lands, and though they are strangers to these woods, these swamps, these rivers, and these hills, yet they are a great people in the eyes of their gods, and their weapons of war are a great terror to all peoples around them."

A grunt of assent was passed from warrior to warrior within the house. Our prince continued. "We have heard and we do believe that the English have come to us from a great land where there are more men than there are trees. If they wished, they could come upon us from over the salt sea like the ants that swarm from the anthill." His eyes flashed with a puzzled darkness, for he spoke of things that were hard to conceive. Yet he spoke from a heart convinced.

"We know too," he said, "that the Pequot, whether at war or at peace, are a cruel and restless people. If Sassacus should fall upon us with all his might, though his men are fewer than ours, our nation would sink like the rock in the waters of the swamp." At this the warriors of the Narragansett growled like the angry dog which protects the door of his master. But Miantonomi spoke above the growling, and the dog fell silent once more. "You know this to be true, my brothers! For many of you tell me that you tire of war. Our sagamores hunger for the hunt and the harvest and the games. And our tributaries wish to lay down the bow at the feet of the English governors. Peace is like strong water to the Narragansett. It is like the dream of summer. And who among us, weary from the long winter of war, wishes to rise from his bed in the midst of such a dream?"

There was no answer from the sleeping dog.

"I would have peace with both the Pequot and the English, if peace will be had," cried our prince. He threw his right arm across his breast and then held it out to the center of the longhouse, opening his palm toward the English braves from Boston. "As for the punishment of the Pequot by the English, this is their matter. We shall stand aside from it. We have our own grievances with Sassacus, and time will tell the end of those. But for now, and for as long as the sun rises in the east, let us strike hands with the English in peace."

Sassacus was greatly dismayed when he heard of our council with the English, and so he hurried his own ambassadors to the wigwam of Canonicus. The Pequot sachem begged us to join him in league against the English. If the Pequot were subdued, he said, then the English governors would come against the Narragansett with their guns and their long knives. He warned that Cutshamakin and his Massachusetts, with Massasoit and his Wampanoag, would fight against us for the English. Thus they would have our lands for themselves. The English were liars, he declared, and their gods were thieves. We were much troubled by these words, and knew not what to believe.

Then Roger Williams came among us, alone and full of strong purpose. He rowed his canoe over dark and stormy waters to our shores. In the midst of our council with the Pequot, he entered our longhouse with courage and a clean heart. For three risings and three settings of the sun, he argued for the English and against the Pequot. Though he heard daily the threatenings of the ambassadors of Sassacus to put their knives to his throat, he did not flee. I marveled at the man, for he came to us with empty palms. And he was but one man among so many who might do him ill if so they chose. But the Narragansett loved him, for his heart was toward us in all things.

His words won us fully, and we crossed our arms against an alliance with Sassacus. Canonicus called the Pequot ambassadors to council one last time. He laid his heart before them.

"I have lived long," said the great king of the Narragansett, "and I know well the hard rain and the sad song of war. Sometimes even the victor walks for seasons in mourning. But always the vanquished must lie in the ashes and weep." None could deny this, though my own heart wished it were not so. The warrior must harden his heart to the cries of loss that shade each season of his life. Yet even the hardest heart can break, and then the sorrow spills like waters from the cracked jar.

"The English are strong and very wise," said Canonicus to the men of Sassacus. "Their armor is like the shell of the turtle against the tooth of the grass snake! You would do well to avoid all war with them. If you are wise you will give them the murderers of Stone and Oldham. Then the knife will be buried in the sand, and there will be no war."

The Pequot went home in anger. And Sassacus wrapped his coat around the slayers of the English.

Sassacus renewed his thrust across the Pocatuck, and Nopatin my father begged more men to pitch their wigwams beside his.

"We will fight sooner than later," said my prince, "for the Pequot cross our rivers and take the hunt from our snares. They curse us from behind their trees and throw stones across our rivers. They call us women and promise to lift our skirts."

"Should we put our braves in danger for the barking of a Pequot dog?" asked Canonicus, who favored the peace that his nephew had so recently declared.

"The dog bites as well as barks!" said Askug, "Unless we take its teeth, it will have us for supper."

"The mad dog heeds no master," I added. "And so it must be slain. If we join with the English against the Pequot, both the biting and the barking will cease at last."

"Sassacus is not a man. He is a manitoo," declared Canonicus, looking grimly upon the small band of council members who sat with him around the evening fire. "Though men fall at his left hand and his right, still he will stand. And then his children will rise up and strike us in the night."

"They slither now into our beds like the poison snake!" said Askug angrily, "Shall we fear their sachem for his medicine? I do not fear his medicine!"

"Though he be a god," I argued, "yet the gods can be beaten." This I believed. This I would declare. For otherwise the fear would take me and the spirits would toss me about like the ball in the games at harvest. I would rather be a dead man! My heart must be a rock. It would not be moved.

"The English gods and the god of Roger Williams will fight with us," said my prince. "Are these gods not stronger than the sachem of the Pequot?" Perhaps they were. And better to have them on our side than plotting our demise!

Canonicus our king laid his head to his knees, a strong sigh falling from his parted lips. His eyes were closed, and he appeared as one who sleeps. But then he lifted his face to look upon us all.

"Miantonomi," he said. "You are the oldest son of my brother. His heart beats on in you. If that heart cries for war against the Pequot, then my heart will beat the drums of war with yours. Though my old legs would throw me in the bushes if I asked them to run the warpath with you, still I may dance for the victory."

The English of Massachussetts, with Cutshamakin, sailed to Block Island. A battle was fought, a Pequot warrior killed. Cutshamakin flayed the skin from the head of the Pequot and sent it as a gift to Canonicus. Our king returned thanks to the Massachussetts sachem along with four fathoms of wampum. The war had begun.

Along the Connecticut, Pequot hornets swarmed from the hive of Sassacus. Many of the English felt the deadly sting of the arrow and the tomahawk. Men fell while cutting hay in their fields. Women fell while carrying water from the rivers. Children fell while standing before the doors of their houses. Some did not fall but were slain in their beds.

In the midst of their mourning, the English raised up many warriors from their towns along the Connecticut and along the Bay of the Massachussetts. Uncas, in full and final rebellion against Sassacus his father-in-law, joined himself and his men to the English.

* * *

On a cool and windy morning in the Moon Of The New Green, before the summer of my thirty-fifth year, Captain Mason, Captain Underhill, and the warriors of the English, with Uncas and his braves, landed upon the shores of the Great Bay and marched from their ships to the house of Canonicus. We did not know they were coming, and so with guarded hearts we met them upon the soil of our city. It was hot smoke in my eyes to see the hated Uncas standing haughtily at the door of my king, painted and armed for war, his feet planted on ground from which I had forbade him. But I could do nothing.

Captain Mason spoke to our king. "We have come to you with much love between us to ask that we might walk through your lands to the country of your enemy the Pequot. You know that this enemy is also ours, having lately done us many intolerable wrongs and injuries. We are now come, with God assisting, to avenge ourselves upon them."

Canonicus accepted their coming and agreed fully with their purpose, but he doubted their strength to stand against Sassacus.

"Your numbers are too weak to deal with the enemy," said Canonicus our king, for the English were only ninety men. Uncas had his Mohegans—and some men of the Connecticut tribes who held no love for the Pequot—numbering sixty in all.

"Sassacus is a great captain among many great captains, and his men are very skillful in war," Canonicus warned Mason. "Yet if you go forth against him, you will see this for yourself!"

The English were not afraid, they said, for their god would be with them. As they headed west into the woods, we did not follow them, for it seemed to us a mad thing to leap into the fire. No man throws himself upon the towering blaze to quench it! He lets it burn down a little. Then he casts water and dirt upon it from many sides. Then he beats it with wet, heavy blankets. At last he spits and urinates upon the hot ashes. And thus it is reduced little by little until it is no more. Yet how was it that Uncas did not fear the fire? Had he seen Chepi in a vision of victory? Or was it true that the Narragansett were women?

Miantonomi was at sea when Mason came to us. Our prince had rowed with many of our men and Wequash the Mohegan to Block Island to fall upon some Pequot who had gone there to gather food and to find haven for their women and children among the rebels of Manisses. There our prince was joined by forty English under Captain Patrick. Together they surprised and defeated the foe. Our warriors came home with fine wounds and great tales of the slaughter. Then Patrick sailed to Providence. And our prince came home too late to treat with Mason.

"We must follow this Mason," said Miantonomi, the fire of the Block Island victory burning in his eyes, "for I have seen the English fight. They are stronger than their numbers tell, and we do well to fight by their side. Yet I would walk the path with Patrick, and he has gone ashore at Providence."

"I will run ahead of you to Mason," said Wequash the Mohegan. "For I know the paths of the Pequot, and I can lead many warriors through the forest to their doors." Though the Mohegan had once walked long with Uncas, their paths were now parted, for their hearts were not brothers. Wequash was brave and strong, a sagamore and a man with a straight tongue. Lately he had come to live among us. Roger Williams trusted him. Miantonomi too.

"Go then," said our prince. "Take as many as will follow you. I will wait for Patrick."

But we would not go without the release of our powwow. For who could know the end of the path but Askug and his spirits?

Askug sought the knowledge of the gods and was soon convinced that we should go. Further encouraged by the hearts of Wequash and Miantonomi, and curious to see the warring of the English, the Fool and I, with nearly two hundred fighting men, ran the long warpath in the dusty tracks of Mason and Uncas.

We found them encamped about the fort of Wepitamock of the Niantic. The sachem had shut his gates upon them, for he feared the English. And though they wished only to pass through his lands to the country of the Pequot, they now suspected some treachery from his hands. Since the sachem would not let them in, they surrounded his town and would not let him out. They did not want him falling upon their backs as they marched toward the Pocatuck! But when we arrived, the Niantic were encouraged, and they opened their doors. Nearly one hundred and fifty men of Wepitamock volunteered to join us against the Pequot. Before we moved on, the sachem summoned them to kneel before him. He spoke strength to their hearts, reminded them to be men, and blessed them as the father does his children.

As we neared the Pocatuck, Nopatin my father met us with many of his warriors, and our numbers grew to five hundred strong. We gathered in a great circle, and many warriors—one by one—declared their valor and boasted of the number of Pequot they would kill. Then we moved on.

The day was very hot, and some of the English fainted from the march, by which we thought them weak like children and mocked them in our hearts and with our tongues. We told them that they dared not even look upon a Pequot, but that we would strike the enemy with daring and much death. We would show the English how warriors fight! But when we reached the river and the spirits of the roaring waters cried against us, many of the Narragansett would not cross. For we remembered the wounds of wars past and the tales of terror and torture. And if Sassacus was god indeed, then who besides the Fool could stand against him? And even the Fool was just a man graced by the spirits. What could he actually do against a grand sachem, a great warrior, and a god? What did it matter that he could shoot straight if his shafts turned to straw as they flew? What protection was his laughter and his dancing against the dark frown and the sharp teeth of the mighty Sassacus?

But if Uncas crossed, I would cross. This I declared to all.

The Mohegan sachem clung to the English captain as the itching vine encircles the oak. None else could reach the ear of Mason. "The Narragansett will all leave you," Uncas told him. "But as for me, I will never leave you." And many of the Narragansett left, while Uncas stayed, and thus we were darkened in the eyes of the English. I waded the Pocatuck with Wequash, Nopatin, the Fool, and but seventy of our warriors.

Wequash took the lead as our guide and as our eyes upon the leafy paths of the enemy. Roger Williams recommended him to Mason for this very task, and the English captain found none better suited from among the warriors of the woods.

We marched on in silence, the English at the fore. When we had walked the ground beneath our own trees, the Narragansett had boasted at the head of a vast, painted party. Now we trod fearfully behind the men of Mason, our eyes searching the forest for the dreaded demon dwarfs of the Pequot. And for the Pequot themselves.

A short time into the night, we came to a little swamp between two hills, and there we made our camp. We were much silent, for we believed ourselves quite near to the strong fort of the enemy. The night was clear, and the gaze of Nanepaushat strong. Guards were set about us, and sentinels were sent some distance from us. There, as they sat in the shadows of the Pequot pine, they could hear the enemy singing within their fort until midnight. Afterward we learned that the Pequot had seen English ships sail by them some days before. And because the ships did not land upon their shore, the Pequot thought the English dared not come near them. So they sang in their fort with much rejoicing, casting great insults against the English and their gods.

Early in the waking of the new day, the English gathered to quietly call upon their god. Then we moved as one body in a silent march toward the fort of the foe. The forest was cool with the dew of the dawn, and dark beneath the many boughs of the last green before the colors of the fall. All about us on the forest floor, beasts both great and small moved from our path to a curious distance, watching with wary eyes as we walked to our war.

What will happen when we come to the hill of the Pequot? I wondered. *Will Sassacus himself meet us? Ambassadors of peace? A giant powwow with stag bones in each hand? Has the enemy been warned by dreams in the night? Do they see us even now?*

Will the English run when fired upon? Will they knock us down in their flight? Should we run first?

Is Cautantowwit pleased with us? Have we begged him long enough for victory? Will Chepi strike at the foe for us? Or will the spirits rise up against us and cause us to entangle our feet in the roots of the wood of the Pequot? Will our own medicine be strong enough to make us stand and not run? Fall like the Rain From God? Hard like the Rain From God!

And what of the god of the English? Is he like a flea, as Wequash thinks him to be, a mosquito that draws only enough blood from a man to keep itself alive?

I did not know. And I did not want any longer to swat at the flies of my fears. Yet they kept buzzing about my head, and I could not ignore them.

We came to a great field full of the second planting of the corn at the foot of a large wooded hill. Wequash and Uncas were called to the front.

"Where is the fort?" asked Mason.

"At the top of that hill," said Wequash. Uncas confirmed it.

"Where are the rest of your men?" asked Mason.

"Behind you," answered Uncas, "very much afraid."

"Tell them not to flee no matter what!" said Mason, though he little knew that none could force anything upon us beyond what our hearts declared. "And tell them to stand, at whatever distance they please, to see now whether English men will fight or not!" We did not much mind the mockery, for we thought it mad to walk first into the snare. But we also did not wish to miss the game entirely, and so we cautiously followed the English as they left the path and started up the hill.

Mason ascended from the direction we had come, while Underhill took some men around to the other side of the rise to climb toward the wooded palisade of the sleeping Pequot. They had much courage. They trusted in their god, in their strong weapons, in the justice of their vengeance. Would these things give them strength when the arrows of the Pequot fell like acorns from the oak tree in the storm?

A dog barked, and we heard a Pequot shouting, "English men! English men!" Soon would the acorns fall!

I heard chuckling at my side, and I turned to see the Fool. Rocking on his squatted legs, he grinned his strong grin while the English flew to the fortress wall like woodchucks running for their holes. They stuck their muskets through the cracks between the upright logs and fired. We held our ears against the loud thunder.

"They fight like the Fool!" declared Assoko as the guns of the English echoed in the hills behind us.

"There is only one Fool," I said to the wind, "and less than ninety English. But there may be a thousand Pequot within that fort!"

Though I am no stranger to the blood of men, and though my own weapons have torn the life from the flesh of more than many, I still stand in awe of that morning on the hill. For though the odds were ever against the English, the battle fell to them in a way that I have never seen again—but once—in all the long, dark seasons of my life.

The doors of the fort were covered over with brush which was quickly pulled away by the men of Mason. Cries arose from the Pequot, as cries will always arise within the town of the sudden-besieged. Shouts could be heard among the English. And then, to my amazement, they pushed their way in, Mason at their head, with only their longknives in their hands.

And so the fight began upon the streets and in the wigwams. I heard the shrieks of many warriors, the commands of the captains of the English, the clash of steel and stone and wood. My blood rose for the battle, and I climbed the hill in haste. Assoko ran with me.

At the top we stopped at the backs of the armed English who stood outside the palisade. Beyond them, through the gate of the fort, in the midst of running men and screaming women, I saw Mason step out of a wigwam with fire in his hand. He put it to the mats that covered the house, and the flames began to nibble at the door. Soon the fire had eaten the wigwam whole. But its hunger was no less, and it leapt from the first house to another. The southwest wind, blown no doubt from the lips of the great god Cautantowwit, carried the cruel flames from one house to the next until the hot tongues were licking the very sand of the streets.

The Pequot raced about like crazed and frightened squirrels, some climbing to the top of the palisade, some running into the fire itself and falling beneath the hot, deadly blows of its wildly waving arms. The English came forth from the burning fort, having only a few wounded, and surrounded it with their readied weapons. As the Pequot shot their arrows into the midst of the English, Mason and Underhill repaid them with shot from their small guns. Some of the stoutest of the warriors of Sassacus came forth in a force of forty men, and though they fought with great cries and much strength, they all fell dead before the longknives of the English. Within the fort, the fire rose supreme.

For an eternal moment, the world was one roaring storm of blinding flame, blistering heat, black smoke, blurred violence, and blunt and bloody terror. I could do nothing but stand amazed. The Fool was upon his knees at my feet, a deep moan rising from his heart to his lips. Tears rolled down his cheeks like the waters of the bubbling spring. The paint of his face dripped from his chin like blood. Behind us, the warriors of the Narragansett had decided it was a fine time to head for home. Only Wequash and Assoko and I, with Uncas and a few of his men, stood with the English when the storm was finally over. Two of the English were dead, with twenty wounded. But seven hundred of the proud and mighty Pequot—warriors and women, old men and children—lay slain upon the smoldering mountain of their strength. A handful were taken alive. A handful more escaped.

Sassacus was not there that day. No one had to face the Pequot sachem and his medicine. Had he been there, would things have been different? I did not think so. For now a new and terrible god of war was among us. And who could stand against the great god of the English!

The war did not last long after this. Though the Pequot struck back, they were defeated on all sides. Another fort was taken, but with less violence.

Bands of Pequot were set upon in their villages and upon their paths by Narragansett and Mohegan alike. Many Pequot warriors and squaws gave themselves and their children up as slaves to the Narragansett, the Wampanoag, and the Massachusetts for shelter and for safety. Many more were captured by the English and kept as slaves and servants. Some of these were given to the Narragansett and a few to the Massachusetts. From time to time, Miantonomi sent the spoils of some fresh battle—Pequot squaws and the hands of Pequot warriors—to the governor at Boston.

Meanwhile, the crooked tongue of Uncas was busy against us, whispering to the English that Canonicus harbored Pequot captives and murderers. In reality, it was the mad dog Mohegan who was swiftly and secretly enlarging his own tribe with the armed refugees of Sassacus.

Sassacus himself, the gods having left him, his people threatening to kill him for their great defeat, walked northward toward the land of the Mohawk, with twenty of his bravest warriors. He carried with him five hundred pounds of wampum. But Askug sent a message to the Mohawk, offering one thousand pounds of wampum and the favor of the English for the head of the Pequot sachem.

We heard nothing for many moons. But one day a small band of Mohawk descended the Connecticut with a gift for the governor at the English town of Hartford. They brought him the scalps of Sassacus, of one of the brothers of Sassacus, and of five of his slain Pequot warriors.

The proud Pequot. Once he stood tall like the dark spruce of Chipachuac. Now he lay beneath the dim shadow of the sand willow. Once he was the strong terror of all who lived within reach of his tomahawk. Now he chopped wood for the squaws of the Narragansett. Once he was master of the lands from the bay that sees the Long Island to the borders of the lands of the Nipmuc and from the Pocatuck of the Narragansett to the eastern shore of the Connecticut. Now he carried water from the Eel River to the kitchens of the English.

I saw it happen. With my own eyes I saw it happen. But I did not understand. For how, in the short life of the butterfly, could the tall and mighty mountain be reduced to a back bag of pebbles that is scattered and lost forever beneath the fragile ferns of the great, dark forest?

CHAPTER THIRTEEN

Wequash

He is a most dreadful god!" groaned Wequash. "And I thought him an insect and the god of weak and silly men!" The Mohegan paced my wigwam like a wolf in a cage. "I ate at the table of Roger Williams and listened to the tales of his god. But when I closed his door behind me, I vomited the good meat to clean out the bad, for I thought that the god of Williams was foolishness and poison to my soul. But the tales were true! This god of the English is the One Great God. He is a most dreadful god!"

Silvermoon offered more soup, but I waved it away. My youngest son, Winaponk, a child of one summer, crawled toward the fire and was pulled back by Ohowauke his mother. Young Quanatik, my daughter by Ohowauke, helped Silvermoon pick up the bowls near our feet. She set them by the door, and Cold Tongue our dog licked them clean. My third wife Teeshkatan, nursing our newborn girl-child upon the bed, hummed a low song to the hungry papoose. At my side was Kattenanit.

"I am a dead man walking," moaned the Mohegan. "I do not know how to appease this terrible, terrible god!" He sat and rocked like the Fool, sighing like the wind when it walks through the woods in the Moon Of The Fallen Leaf.

My heart too was heavy, for I had no defense against this English spirit. My soul was a straight, sharp wall against the entrance of our own gods. But if I were to bow to the English god, I knew my wall would break as I bent. And a city without walls is soon taken by the foe! Where could I run? Where could I hide from the god who is every place a man can go? I must stand strong. I knew no other way.

"Come with me, Katanaquat," pleaded Wequash. "Come with me to the trading house of Smith at Cocumscussuc."

"Roger Williams comes there, does he not?" I asked, my eyes upon the crawling Winaponk. The restless little fellow was determined to take fire in his hands. His mother was determined that he not.

"Yes," said Wequash, "and I wish to hear his tales!"

We walked the woods to Cocumscussuc, Wequash, Miantonomi, Assoko, Kattenanit, and I. There, in the heart of the lands of the Narragansett, stood the house of Richard Smith, a straight-tongued English trader and a friend of Roger Williams. Miantonomi gave Smith land to build upon. Williams came often to the house of Smith to resupply his store of goods and to preach to the Narragansett about the English god. He was there when we arrived, and it was good to see his good heart within his good, strong eyes.

"Why do the English call us Indians and savages?" a young warrior asked the preacher as we stood in the longroom of the trading house.

Williams brushed his brown hair from his face and smiled. It was not the smile of one who fools you with crooked words or mocks you in his heart. It was the smile of one who is glad to have you at his table that he might put before you warm meat and cold water.

"We call you Indians because we once thought this land was called India," he said. "And we call you savages because you live more like the beasts of the wood than the English are used to living," he continued, "and because you do not know the One Great God."

"We have one great god," said another, "He is Cautantowwit and he is the maker of all things!" Many grunts of assent echoed from the bare walls of the long room.

"How many other gods are there?" Williams asked.

"Many! Great many!" said a roomful of voices, my own in chorus with the rest.

"Friends," said the preacher, "it is not so. There is only one God."

"You are mistaken!" shouted Watumps, a powwow from the tribe of one of our under-sachems. "You are out of the path! I know that there are many gods, for I have seen them! And five dwell within me!"

"Devils!" said Williams. "Evil spirits! But not gods. There is only one God!"

At this there was a great noise of troubled murmuring among us, for we had not heard these things before. Then Wequash stepped to the front of the room.

"Were you there?" he asked the men. "Were you there on the hill of the burning fort? Did you see? Did you hear? Do you not fear?" He looked upon us all, a pressing weight upon his soul. It was hard to face his pleading eyes. "I cannot sleep at night!" he cried. "Let Williams speak!"

We would let Williams speak. Let Wequash be still! Did he think we were children?

"I will tell you news," said the preacher. "One God only made the heavens and the earth. Five thousand years ago and upward, he alone made all things."

This was not hard to believe, for we knew that the god of Sowanniu had made the lands of the Narragansett. Whether he made the moon and the stars we did not know, but surely he could have. Perhaps he made the many gods as well.

"In six days he made all things," said Williams. "The first day he made the light. The second day he made the sky above us. The third day he made the earth and sea. The fourth day he made the two great lights, the sun and the moon and also the stars. The fifth day he made all the fowl of the air and the fish of the sea. The sixth day he made all the beasts of the field." The preacher stopped to see if we were with him. He spoke these things in our tongue or we would not have heard him. We were with him, though we knew not where he took us.

"Last of all, on the sixth day," said the preacher, "God made one man of red earth ..."

I heard within me the echo of a memory, and I saw myself sitting upon the lap of my father beside Red Creek, beneath Old Willow on the fishing stone. With one hand the fingers of Nopatin traced the deep wrinkles of the face of Old Willow, with the other he stroked my hair. "Cautantowwit made the first man and woman, long ago, in the land of Sowanniu," said my father. "He made them of a stone, like the one we sit upon. But the breath of life was trapped within their hard hearts and so they could not live. So he broke them in pieces, and the breath came forth to blow upon the branches of the oak tree. Then Cautantowwit took the oak and carved from it another man and woman. They lived. They became the father and mother of all peoples of the earth."

"... and on the seventh day he rested. And therefore Englishmen work six days, and on the seventh day they praise God."

So that was the reason for the Sabbath of the English and the Dutch! It was a good word, we agreed. Perhaps we would follow it. For resting one day out of seven was a grand idea! And the English god would be pleased, would he not?

"No," said Williams, "He would not. For he wants men to love him and fear him. Resting one day out of seven will not cause you to love him and fear him."

"Why would he not be pleased if we honored him in this way?" we wondered aloud.

"God is a Father," said the preacher. And this was hard to hear. For what god could be a father? The gods were ghosts and shadows. Dark mysteries and strange dreams. Fire and light. Wind and rain. Some wandering souls may have once been fathers, but never the gods!

"He is a Father who desires the hearts of the children to beat as his," said Williams. This was a desire I well knew, for I longed that Kattenanit love the warpath as I did, that he build his wall against the gods and be the man. But if this great god was a father, then a door must be broken in the wall, a door to let a father in. For how else could two hearts beat as one? But no! A door is a dangerous thing in a world filled with foes!

"And what father among you is pleased with the son who cares not for your heart, your counsel, or your company, but who thinks he honors you by lying down upon your bed once a week to sleep?"

A god who is a father. What a foolish dream! This must be another invention of the English! And not a very good one. How could this father be the same god who crushed seven hundred Pequot in the cool of the morning upon the tall hill beyond the Pocatuck? The English must have more than one god after all.

And what of the god who walks as a man? This Jesus whom Squanto spoke of? Was Williams trying to make fools of us? Did his gods use him to confuse us?

* * *

"Souls do not go up to heaven or down to hell, as this Williams declares," cried Askug within the wigwam of Miantonomi. "For as our fathers have told us, our souls fly to the Southwest, to Sowanniu!"

"You do not need to preach to me, good powwow," said my prince with a wave of his hand. "I know well what our fathers say. But do you know for yourself that our souls go to the Southwest?"

The powwow gasped in amazement. Could the sachem of our people even pose such a question in earnest?

"Did you ever see a soul go there?" asked Miantonomi with no malice and without a breath of a challenge. He simply wished to know.

"When did Williams ever see a soul go to heaven or hell?" fired the powwow, his face drawn tight and his dark eyes wide.

"He has books and writings, and one which God himself made, concerning the souls of men," the sachem replied, his own eyes as still as the deep waters of Watchaug pond on the day when the winds sleep, "and therefore he may well know more about these things than we that have no book from God. For we must take all upon trust from our fathers and the fathers of our fathers."

"And should we doubt them who have held these things in their hearts from the beginning?" cried Askug. "You would bring the frown of Cautantowwit upon us with your words, my sachem!"

The powwow whirled around in a circle, his arms outstretched, his thick, dark hair waving like the wings of the bat. I glanced at the shadows to see if he scattered them, but only his own were flying.

"The whole world will soon burn," cried Wequash in distress. "And then where shall we be? And what will become of the courts of Cautantowwit?" His questions were troubling, and I wondered at them. But I could not understand the depths of his woe. And I would not wash my face in the waters of his fears! It was enough to keep my head above my own.

"The whole world will burn?" exclaimed the angry powwow. "Perhaps the world of Williams will burn first!" And he leapt into the air beside the flames, pulling them toward him with his gestures. They came to him, dancing about his face, and I marveled at their obedience. Was he calling down fire upon the house of Williams? Did he dare? But then the blaze fell back to the wood again, and I thought I saw within its shifting colors the smoking wigwams of the conquered Pequot.

The whole world will burn! I thought. *Could this English god make such things happen? Could he?*

"I am sinking," said Wequash as I walked with him beside Red Creek. "For I know not God. Nor do I love him."

"Neither do I," I said to Wequash and the laughing waters.

"But I have been a thief and a liar and a murderer!" cried the Mohegan. "And so I will go to hell when I die. To the deep darkness where I shall always lament!" And he wept as we walked.

Was this man like my Fool that he wept like the child? But I could not stop the weeping. The sighing. The dread. His sorrow could not be undone. It had begun to weigh me down.

"I am sinking too," I said, "but not beneath the stones of my dark deeds! The wringing of your sad soul drags me to the bottom of your black deep while yet we both live!"

Wequash halted. He pressed his sad lips tightly together in an effort to pull himself up for a brief moment. His red eyes cleared as he looked into my own. "Surely God will see my sorrow," he said quietly. "What other hope have I?"

We moved on, crossing Red Creek on an old fallen pine, and soon found ourselves in the clearing of the Council Rocks.

"Why do you not light a fire here?" I suggested, desperately searching for a way to pull the man out of the bog. "And invite the village to a dance. Throw your goods into the blaze, with all your sorrow and your sighing. Give them up to this god. Declare yourself his man. Give yourself a new name. Call him to come to you. Will he not see? Will he not hear?" The thought of this ritual repulsed me, for it was the kind of surrender that I counseled myself against forever. But it seemed to fit the heart of the Mohegan. "Does not the powwow do the same? And do the spirits not come?" I reasoned.

"Do they not come?" echoed Wequash to the shadows and the tall pines.

"They come!" I declared.

Wequash stood upon the Council Rocks, staring at the bare, black earth within the fire circle.

"Though it seems the right path," he said at last, "I do not know if it is how God wants it."

"Who can know what the gods want?" I said. "Who can ever know?"

Miantonomi loved Roger Williams. And the preacher loved my prince. As often as it fit the calling of a sachem, Miantonomi traveled with his warriors to the house of the good man of Providence.

Williams entertained us well, though his house was not the great and decorated wigwam of the grand sachem. Some of us sat at his table while some of us reclined beneath the trees within his fences. Some of us slept upon his floors while some of us dreamed beneath the stars. His wife and his children did not fear us but spoke with us, laughed with us, and did our hearts good.

And always he had news. News of the English upon our shores and of the English over the sea. News of weather and war, of sachems and sagamores, of goods to be traded and goods to be had.

Always he turned our hearts toward our neighbors. He heard our sorrows with the English and wrote them to the governors. He brought their grievances to us and showed us ways to make things right. Ways that seemed good to our souls. Ways that made us want to walk in peace.

He was like the powwow, but without the shadows, knowing things that it seemed none else could know. He gave advice that it seemed none else could find, put strength into our hearts that seemed to stay there, and gave us shields against the woes of life, the wiles of the gods. He said that his god could protect us against all other gods, for the others were not gods.

He was like the father who explains the world to the son. Who unties the vines that entangle the soul. Who reads the rings on the fallen tree and knows then the years that it reached for the sun. Who knows even the reasons that it reached for the sun.

And his god! This god who was three gods yet one. This father. This son. This holy spirit. He was in earnest that this god was one and not three. And he almost made me see. Or almost made me want to see. I wanted to believe him, not for the sake of his god—for what was one more spirit among so many, true gods or no?—but because I wanted to trust the heart of the man. For if the heart of one man could be trusted, then perhaps there was hope for my own. The Fool had a heart I could trust, but the Fool had a heart like none other ever, and so it was not the heart of a man. It was something different, something beyond a man. Miantonomi had a heart I could trust, if I would. But I would not. For to trust his heart fully would mean that my own heart would be open to his eyes. Then he would see all the dark and envious secrets I had hidden from him all the seasons of our days together.

He would see the wall. And he would not understand. And he would wish it were torn down, for how could a man stand against the gods? And what if the gods should come in force to beat upon the wall themselves? Take it down, Katanaquat! Strengthen your arm instead. Be the man as your father is the man. As your prince is the man. Does the Fool fear the gods? Ha! So take it down!

But I did not think much on such things. Rather the thoughts leapt at me suddenly in my times at Providence, catching me unawares, sending me down strange paths in my soul. *There is another life somewhere!* these paths called. One which I glimpsed only briefly and imperfectly, like the deer who bolts across the open meadow when your back is turned. You hear the swishing of the grasses, and you turn to see the white tail disappear within the thick woods. It was there! And you could have had it! But now it is lost.

This other life, this shadow of the running deer, called to me at times like the Song had called upon the wind. But the shadow was not real. For dreams do not call you to wake. They beg you to sleep. And I would not sleep.

"His god has come to fight with our gods!" said Askug darkly as he wiped his wet forehead with the blanket of his bed. "Whenever Williams is among us, I can see no spirits! They hide from me! And when he is gone home, they come out of the shadows and fly at me in my dreams. They accuse me! 'You let him walk freely among the people!' they say! 'You let him call us false gods and no gods and demons and evil spirits and ...'" The old pow-wow buried his sharp chin in his bony hands. "... and I wake with the headache, the fever, and the sweat! How can I dance to cure the sick when

I stumble around in the fever and the sweat?" he mumbled through his brown, crooked fingers. "Ohhh! I need a powwow to cure the powwow!"

I laughed. Not because the old man had the headache and the sweat, but because the fever removed his fangs and stilled his rattle. It made him more the man and less the wolf, more the child and less the powwow. *Even his wife, though he beg for soup upon his bed all day, could stand him like this!* I thought. But it would not last. He would soon be up again, skillfully cursing the Pequot and the Wampanoag, the English, and the English god, sharply slapping the young boys of the village upon their heads in blessing, strengthening the hearts of the warriors of the Narragansett.

In the meantime, I would enjoy the game.

"Let the gods fight!" I said. "And let the best god win!"

"Words of war are easily spoken by one who is not on the grounds of battle!" Askug moaned with a crooked frown, dragging his fingers through his damp, matted hair. He knew not that my heart was daily besieged, that I knew the war well, and that he himself was more the stranger to this battle. He had surrendered long ago. It was not war that now rattled his soul, but the feuding of too many gods under one roof!

"He treats me well," the powwow said of Williams. "And I hate when he does so! It is like hot coals upon my head." His eyes flashed dimly. "My poor, aching head!" he added.

"His heart is clean," I said.

"His god is our enemy!" spat Askug, but the moment of venom made him cough for many moments more. "Cold drink, woman!" he barked hoarsely. And Mishtaqua my grandmother handed him a pewter cup filled with cool water.

"This is the cup that Williams gave me!" gasped the powwow. "Do you mock me, squaw?"

But she had left the wigwam.

Wequash was gone from us for four risings and four settings of the sun. He went to the house of Roger Williams. He sighed and he moaned and he poured his bitter waters into the heart of the good preacher. Let the preacher drink them if he would! Perhaps his heart could sweeten them. All the better for Wequash. All the better for me.

The Mohegan asked many questions. Williams gave him many answers. They ate and drank. They slept and rose. And Wequash came home to us with a new fire in his eyes. Though he still cried out against his own heart, he called on God daily. He prayed, not as the Narragansett pray, but as the English pray, to the One Great God. It was very strange!

"He does not only pray," accused our powwow, "but he preaches like Williams! And the spirits cry evermore against him in my dreams! They bid me to kill him, and that I would do! For I will have no peace otherwise, nor will our people know the favor of the gods! But what do my sachems counsel? What does The Rain From God think?"

Miantonomi and I, with Canonicus our king, listened to the bitter contentions of the medicine man. His words made our hearts heavy, for we loved the Mohegan who had come to dwell among us. He had shown himself a brother to the Narragansett and a strong arm to strengthen our hearts. And, but for his late moanings, a wise tongue to lighten our eyes.

"Are we to call him our foe who has been our friend?" asked Canonicus, leaning into the small circle of our council.

"His god is our foe!" said Askug, tossing his head from side to side, as if to dislodge the water of the bath from his ears. "As long as he walks with this god he calls father, he is no longer our friend. Did we trust him when he walked with Uncas? No! So let him forsake his god as he forsook the rebel Pequot, and then I will bury the hatchet!"

"Why do you say that his god is our foe?" asked Miantonomi.

"Because the spirits have said so!" declared the powwow. "And do you not believe them, my sachem? Do you think they would lie who have so often done us good?"

Of course they would lie! my heart cried. What fool could trust them? They made their own rules. They played their own game. Our thanks for their good to us today was no insurance against their dark arrows tomorrow. Hope and fear. Sacrifice and powwows. A careful eye and a hundred thousand guesses. But not trust! I knew well why I had built my wall.

"Since the English have come among us," said Miantonomi, "their god has brought us much favor. And more good than the spirits."

"You are mad, Miantonomi!" shouted the powwow, spit flying from his dark lips. My prince held up his palm.

"I do not speak against the spirits," he said with a clean heart, "nor against our great god Cautantowwit. But the god of the Southwest dwells far from his people, and it is often long before our cries reach his ears."

The powwow glared in silence as my prince continued.

"The god of the English is near them, and he smiles upon them often. Does he not smile upon us, too? Does not the ground yield its corn in greater measure than it did for our fathers? Are not the storms of the heavens much less in all seasons? Have not our enemies the Pequot fallen at last like the dry corn beneath the hail? And do we not now know the favor of many good and wise men, like Roger Williams?"

"I love Williams as a son!" declared Canonicus with a finality that nearly shut the mouth of the powwow. Nearly.

"But Wequash," argued Askug, "is not an English! And he is not a Mohegan. He is a Pequot still, like his bloody Pequot brother Uncas, no matter what he calls himself! If I paint myself blue tomorrow, instead of black, I am still Askug!"

"And Askug hates all Pequot," I said, with the heart of Nopatin my father. I thought it was him speaking. I almost turned to look behind me.

The powwow my grandfather arched back and bent himself toward me like the wolf who would leap upon the hare. Was this his true heart toward my father? Toward me? But my prince played the shield with the words of his mouth.

"Wequash lodges in my wigwam. He plays with my children. He eats from my bowls. He picks fleas from my dogs," said Miantonomi. "The stripes of war are upon his chest from wounds he invited on behalf of our people. You are right, bitter powwow, when you say he is no Mohegan. He is a Narragansett!"

Askug lowered his head against us and shook it slowly back and forth. Only his eyes wandered upward, and they stared upon us through his thin, dark brows.

"Wequash may preach his god among us," said Miantonomi.

"Just as Roger Williams may preach his god among us," added Canonicus. "Has our English brother ever begged us to still our tongues when we speak of the spirits? No, he asks us of them freely, and tells us freely what his own heart does declare. This has always been our way. It must be our way still."

* * *

We walked the path from Providence, Kattenanit my son and I, stopping only to eat the ripe berries that called sweetly to us from their laden branches. The sky threatened rain, and the air was cool with the coming storm. The trees bent to the west, as the birds stumbled through the sky in the face of the strong breath of Paponetin, the west wind. We did not speak, for the words of Williams held us in counsel within our own souls.

Jesus. The son who walked as a man. Kattenanit my son had an ear for this god. Wequash spoke often of him now, for Miantonomi liked most to hear of him. And truly, though I told no one—and though I swore never to strike hands with any god—this one called to my heart with a voice that was clean.

But how could this be? He was the weakest of all gods! A weak woman and a flea, as Wequash had once said! For what strong warrior ever gave himself up to the enemy without a battle, without a taunt, to be bound and tortured and killed? What mighty brave ever called upon his brothers to lay down their knives when the enemy was upon them in force? And what kind of fool would let the foe kiss him! Should Uncas come near me with his lips, I would tear them from his face!

"Father?" said Kattenanit my son. "Would you give yourself up to the fire of the foe to save my life?"

"I would," I said without hesitation. For the days of my son were the joy of all seasons. What would life be without him?

"Would you give yourself up to the fire of the foe to save the life of Askug?" he asked.

"I would not," I said. The days of the powwow were many and dark and nearly done. Another would take his place, and few would mourn his passing.

Our thoughts were our own again as we tread the darkening forest floor and crossed the blackening waters toward the wigwams and the fires of Canonicus. *The spirits must wonder,* I thought, *at the words they cannot hear within our hearts. For they cannot cross the wall.*

Let them puzzle. Let them guess. The winds would blow us home.

Wequash died in his house along the Connecticut.

He had been gone from us for many moons to the lands of his birth and the river of his childhood. There he raised his wigwam beside deep waters where the fish swam in large bands. He grew his corn, his beans, his squash, and his tobacco in a small field on the other side of the river. He called his wife to him from the village of the Mohegan, and she came with her children and the children of her children.

Then came Uncas also, claiming the land as his own. But Wequash withstood him, for the ground had once been the sachemdom of the great grandfather of Wequash. An old sagamore among the river tribes remembered this was so, and many stood with Wequash against the Mohegan. Uncas went home with empty hands and a vengeful heart.

The powwows of the western Niantic and the Mohegan then rose against the praying Indian, claiming that Chepi had appeared to them in the form of a moose, warning them to chase this man from the western shores of the Connecticut. Again he withstood them, saying that he feared not their gods and that he would stay, for this land was his own by right and tradition. They tried to slay him by magic, but one of them died instead. And so they left him alone.

But Askug the snake hated Wequash. He went to him alone and in secret to do him ill. When the startled Wequash found the weary powwow at his door, he bid him welcome and gave him meat and drink. Yet he wondered why the man had come.

"I was visiting Nopatin my son," said Askug in deceit, "and I followed the path from there to here. Though I have not called you friend, and I love not your god, yet I came at the bidding of our prince, Miantonomi. He would know how things go with you and your squaw, for he thinks of you often."

Wequash believed him, and they spoke together of the harvest and of the weather, of fish and of game, of wives and of children. The squaw of Wequash brought them strong water and tobacco, and they sat by the fire to share it. Askug spoke of wars past and of the tales that were still told of the strong arm of Wequash. The powwow remembered an old war club that Wequash had carved long ago. "I used to admire it," said Askug, "and I would like to look upon it again before I go." While Wequash was gone to find the old weapon, the snake spit his poison into the cup of the praying Indian.

I had seen the powwow make this poison only days before. A finely ground powder of roots and herbs, the mixture melts in strong water until it cannot be seen. It was the slow death of our good friend. For after the powwow was long upon the path to home, Wequash began to vomit. For seven days he lay in his house in pain. Though he ate, his stomach would not keep it. A strong, weakening fever held him to his bed. He knew that Askug had done this, but he did not curse him.

We knew nothing of his dying until it was too late.

"You were with him?" I asked Roger Williams as we stood outside the trading house of Smith at Cocumscussuc.

"Yes," replied the preacher. "Two days before he died."

"And did he still hold to his god though the spirit of death was upon him?" I questioned.

Williams put down the bundle of skins which he held in his arms. His eyes wandered upward for a moment to the treetops and the blue sky. His dirty hands pushed his brown locks backward from his face. Then he looked straight upon me and gave me his answer.

"He told me he was dying," said Williams, "and that he was much afraid."

"Then his god did not strengthen his heart!" I said.

"I do not know," replied Williams, and I heard much sorrow in the words of the English man. Had the god who was a father turned away from the dying son?

"Wequash spoke much of God while we were together," said the preacher at last. "He told me that his heart was full of the words of God that I had often spoken to him. He told me he knew that God was the Maker of all things, the Maker of all men, and that man has stumbled and fallen, because of the weight of his sins, from the mountain of God. He told me he knew that man is now the enemy of God and that each man, until he repents and believes in the One Great God, lies beneath the skies of God's anger. He told me all these things, Katanaquat."

And your heart should tell you these things, too, Katanaquat! spoke the eyes of Roger Williams with silent strength. I dropped my gaze to the ground.

"Wequash said that he prayed much to Jesus Christ," said Williams.

"Then why was his heart afraid?" I challenged. "For you have told us that death is not the enemy of the one who trusts this Jesus Christ!"

"Many people pray to Jesus Christ who have never turned to God nor loved him," said Williams.

"And Wequash?" I asked. And I found I did not really want an answer. But Williams did not really have an answer.

"I do not know," he said, his eyes filled with grey clouds of doubt. "For he said that his heart was very bad. That it was all one stone."

"And thus he spoke always since the fire upon the hill of the Pequot!" I said. And I pushed the toe of my moccasin into the dirt at my feet. "But did your god come to him ever or not?" I asked.

"I believe he did. But I am not a powwow," said Williams, "that I can see the gods."

And my heart cried loud to me, *Look! His god has given him up as he gave up Squanto. And he has died alone, a stranger and an enemy to his people, with only his squaw and her children at his side.* I said so to Kattenanit my son. But he grieved much and walked the woods with Miantonomi to lay a stone upon the grave and to weep. Then my prince brought the wife of Wequash, with all her children, into our city, and they lived among us as our own.

We hated Askug for the foul deed. Though the squaw of Wequash laid the blame at the door of the powwow, he kicked it from him. "I did not kill him!" he declared, but his lies were like smoke from the fire that cannot be hid, and none could breathe free in his presence.

CHAPTER FOURTEEN

Bitter Water

I will kill him," said Miantonomi. "It was murder. No wampum can buy the deed free."

"The powwow has brought us strong medicine for moons beyond counting," said Canonicus firmly.

"But he is gone bad!" cried the younger sachem. "Like the dog that is rabid! His hatred of the Pequot has driven him out of our hearts! Who will he poison next? The squaw of the dead Mohegan? Nopatin his own son? Katanaquat his grandson? Me? You?"

Canonicus frowned deeply and waved his large arms in the air above his head. "You speak from your own hatred, son of my brother!" he declared. "And so your waters are not clean! The powwow will not turn against his own!" The old sachem planted his elbows upon his knees and leaned his head in his hands. "He will not turn against his own," he said to the fire and the dancing shadows.

"You speak true. He will not turn against his own. I will kill him," said Miantonomi again. "It was murder. And there is no justice but for the blood of the powwow."

Canonicus looked upon my prince with dark sorrow. His lips were set hard like stone. His nose flared wide like that of the horse of the English. The burning green pine sang a high mournful song as it slowly bled within the melting flames. "It is your right," said our king, in dark harmony with the dying log. "It is your duty," he said at last.

When Askug next went to the forest for roots, Miantonomi followed. Only our prince came home.

None cried against it. It was blood for guilty blood. And by the hand of the sachem. This was our way.

* * *

Teeshkatan my third squaw sat in labor. It was hard. Harder than any which our people had seen for many seasons. She wailed in pain, and the child strained much to come forth. But it would not be born. For two days Teeshkatan sat with tears and much blood. I could do nothing. Nothing but walk alone beside Red Creek and chant. The powwow my grandfather lay beneath the gate of the swamp of Chepi. He could not chant with me. From other towns more powwows came, but their medicine did no good. Silvermoon sent them away. The prayers of Wequash, which had raised my son Winaponk from the fever and the cough, were gone from my memory. I could not repeat them. I called for Williams. But when he came, he found me with my face upon the ashes of my mourning.

The boy-child died in birth and took his mother with him.

The brightest day was as the darkest night. The sweetest water was as the bitter puckerberry. The sorrowed, gentle faces of those who would comfort me were as the dry and empty skulls of the dead. My heart was swallowed by a cold, black grief, and my eyes refused to open to the morning.

The gods! They could not breach my wall. And so they came through the door of my wigwam and slew my wife and child. Was their lust satisfied? Or did they want more?

"I must give them all that a man can give," I said to Silvermoon, "before they take all that a man can never recover."

I set the torch to my house and burned all that lay within it—the work of my hands, the work of the hands of my squaws and my children, the English and the Dutch. I sacrificed all the summers of my life, the winters of my days. I gave the gods the new green bow I bent for Winaponk, the bowls I had carved for Silvermoon, the pipes I had smoked with the Fool, the scalps I had taken in battle, the bed upon which my children were conceived, the wooden chest from Williams, my club with the tooth of Weak Woman.

Cautantowwit! my heart cried. *Great god above all gods! Look upon me from your far-off mountain! See the smoke of my sacrifice! Command the spirits in my favor! Call the wolf from my door! For I have ignited a great fire, a mighty blaze, and it burns away the darkness in my soul.*

Look upon me, oh great god of the Southwest. And call me Nétop! Call me Friend! I am the Rain From God! Give me strength to fall again upon the enemies of the Narragansett. Restore to me the joy of my pride. The pride of my life. The light of my eyes.

Or I am turned to sleet. To hail. To stone.

Nopatin my father had become a great sachem, and many of the tribes along the Connecticut looked to him for protection against the growing strength and wandering violence of Uncas. As warriors and sagamores came to Nopatin to pledge themselves to his leadership, the jealousy of the Mohegan burned hot against the Narragansett.

"Nopatin builds an army for his prince!" said the braves of Uncas.

"Miantonomi desires to be sachem over every Indian!" declared the men of the Mohegan.

"Miantonomi is trying to unite every tribe against the English!" whispered the scattered people of the Pequot.

And thus the twisted words of the heart of Uncas were repeated in the ears of red man and white man alike until at last the English at Boston were so filled with suspicion that they summoned my prince to come speak for himself. He hurried to Boston to give them his heart.

"I declared my love for the English once, and my feet have not moved," Miantonomi told the governor and his sagamores. "It is the lying tongue of Uncas that you hear in these tales! Bring the Mohegan sachem here before you and let him accuse me to my face. If he cannot prove his charges, then he should be put to death. For he stirs up brother against brother. This is a black deed, and it shows you his heart!"

The men of Boston believed my prince, and we went home in peace.

Miantonomi sold much land, for the English desired it of him and paid him well. There was plenty of soil for all men, said our prince.

But his words fell short of truth, for our lands began to shrink. Two of our subject tribes among the Massachusetts, led by Pomham and Soconoco, gave up their countries to the English of the Massachusetts, throwing off our cloak for the shield of the white man. Block Island and the people of Manisses, no longer ours since the war with the Pequot, were under the lordship of the English. The lands of Roger Williams, though we were welcomed in them, were striped with fences and fields, and the beasts were not as plentiful beneath the tall boughs. Most of the islands of the

Great Bay were sold as well, and only the Cowesets and the eastern Niantics still paid us tribute. Our paths were fewer through the trees, our journeys short upon the waters.

"I see at last," said Miantonomi to the men of the Montauk upon the Long Island, "that the forest grows only to the shores of the sea. Where the saltwaters lie, no tall tree takes root. The English came to us from over the sea with much salt in their pockets. Wherever they walk, the salt falls to the earth and the forest flees."

Our prince stood in the open circle within the village of the Montauk. The winds of the bay rushed past him, pulling at his long black hair as they flew.

"I see too that we are all Indian, we who were here before the Dutch and the English. And as the English are one people and call one another 'brother,' so we must be. Otherwise, like the snow that melts before the sun, we shall soon all be gone," said the sachem of the Narragansett to the people of the Montauk. They listened, for they knew how quickly the tree falls to the iron axe.

"You know our fathers had plenty of deer and skins. Our plains and our woods were full of turkey and fowl, our coves full of fish," my prince continued. "But these English now hold our lands. They fell the trees with axes. Their hogs spoil our clam banks. If we do not shake the salt from our blankets, no shade will be left above our heads. And we shall all starve!"

We had crossed the waters to the Long Island to speak of trade and friendship, of alliance and unity. We did not wish the English harm, for they meant us no harm. But we must now be wiser than the foolish children we had shown ourselves to be. For though the brave would give up his best bow in the dance, he had found that the English did not give it back. Their way was not our way. Especially with the land. We must plant our feet more deeply in the soil. We must hold what is ours against the rising tide.

Uncas renewed his whispers of a Narragansett plot against the English, and Miantonomi was called again to Boston. He asked if Roger Williams could come with him, but the magistrates refused. Our prince went without him and found the chosen ear of the English to be a Pequot.

How could we trust our words to a Pequot? he said. But the English would not move.

Hearts were cool among us, and though we promised our faithfulness, the hands of the English remained in their pockets. No meat was laid before us, no drink poured in our cup. Was this the way to treat a king? Was this the love of the English? Or was this the poison of Uncas?

"The Narragansett will all leave you," Uncas told Mason at the dawn of the death of the Pequot nation. Perhaps the English believed him still.

"But as for me, I will never leave you," said the Mohegan. And it was a rare truth from his tongue. Though it was all for himself, he was like the shadow of the English till the day he died.

Nopatin my father then began to play his part against the tribe of the Mohegan and their sachem. Some of his warriors killed a Mohegan sagamore. Others laid in wait for Uncas himself, shooting arrows at him as he sailed in a canoe down the Connecticut. Uncas growled about these things to the magistrates at Hartford. And so the governor of the English at Connecticut, wishing to bring peace, called Nopatin and Uncas together. But there could be no peace, for Uncas demanded six braves of Nopatin to be put to death for the one slain Mohegan. Nopatin would give up none, not even the one whose hands were guilty of the blood.

"I will stand with my brother against the Mohegan," said Nopatin my father, "with sharpened arrows, if I must. For my man has brought down one Mohegan, but Uncas would lay his axe to the roots of the whole people of the Narragansett!"

And so my father went back to the Pocatuck, and Uncas planned his own revenge.

"I have failed my people," said Nopatin my father. "I gave them my pledge to be strong, to protect them from the enemy. I would set myself and my warriors as a wall about our women, our children, and our old men. Now the wall has fallen. Cautantowwit is angry with me. I have failed my people."

The smoke of the village of Nopatin could be seen beyond many hills. The stench of the charred and broken wigwams filled the forest. The wailing of the mourners could be heard for a hundred whoops up and down the Pocatuck. Eight warriors lay curled in their graves beneath the new-turned soil, facing east. Thirteen braves were wounded. The harvest and the hunt were plundered.

"Uncas may eat his stolen meat, but he will choke upon the bones!" Miantonomi cried.

We came forth from the woods, six hundred warriors of the Narragansett, and forded the Shetucket about four bow shots north of its meeting with the Quinnibaug. Mohegan watchers were upon the hills, and we saw them run.

Let them run! Let them shout the alarm! Let the villages of Uncas flee before the fire!

Better yet, let them come to meet us in the battle! We were more and we were mighty! Let them meet us in their strength and in their numbers! We had come to fight.

We crossed the Yantic and came out of the trees at the hilltop that looked down upon the grey-green level of the Great Plain. There, on the other side of the great table of low grasses and flat rock, stood the waiting warriors of the Mohegan with their sachem our foe. They were many, but we were twice more.

A messenger came to speak to my prince, and Miantonomi walked with him into the valley between the two armies. Uncas came forth to meet him there. This was our way, for our kings must speak their hearts before the arrow flies.

"This is the foolishness of children," spoke Uncas to my prince, "that we come against each other with our quivers overflowing. Many squaws will weep tonight, and many young boys will hunt with their fathers no more!"

"Shall I go home and wait for the Mohegan to fall on me in my sleep?" countered Miantonomi. "Or shall I be the man and stand with my eyes opened to my foe? Either way, the squaws will weep."

"Then stand," said Uncas, "but face me alone. If you kill me, my men shall be yours. If I kill you, your men shall be mine."

My prince was tall and strong, like the oak. Uncas was big and mighty, like the bear. Does the oak fear the bear? Does the bear fear the oak?

"My men came to fight," said our sachem, "and they shall fight."

Suddenly Uncas threw himself upon the ground. Just as suddenly, the warriors of the Mohegan pulled their readied bows, and the air was filled with the whine of the swift, sharp swarm of painted shafts. Upon our hill the deadly rain fell, and we stumbled in astonishment toward the trees. Uncas rose with the bellow of battle upon his twisted lips, and the men of the Mohegan, their tomahawks raised high, rushed toward us like the great wave of the sea that runs before the hurricane. We fled. And so would any man. For death raced toward us over the Great Plain.

Behind us they came with a fury that was fed by our fear. The spirits wailed. Miantonomi fled with us. The Fool and I kept him in our eyes. We saw little else.

Two Mohegan captains, men with legs that run like the elk, were the only foe within our sight behind us. But they came swiftly on, like the eagle that falls at last from the sky upon the mouse in the field. They caught up to our prince first. But they did not pull him down. They sprang against him as he ran, so that he reeled into the brush and stumbled over the trail. I turned to help him, and the Fool with me, but our hearts could not save him. For Uncas arrived within the moment, with many of his warriors, and we were altogether caught within the snare.

Uncas seized Miantonomi by the shoulder. And my prince, when he knew it was the hard hand of his cousin upon him, stopped his flight and sat upon the ground. I heard his heart cry with grief and shame, yet his lips were closed and his eyes would not speak of his misery.

Many warriors of the Mohegan surrounded us. I saw too that others of our people were captives of the men of Uncas. With great insults we were herded before our silent sachem.

"I see The Rain From God has fallen at last," Uncas said to me with a dark and cruel smile. "And the Fool is not laughing! Is something not right with him?"

But Assoko did not hear him, for his eyes were on his prince. His heart was reaching for his chief, to drink his sorrow and to be his shield. Suddenly he broke free of his captors and staggered forward to fall upon his buttocks beside Miantonomi. There he sat rocking, a strange and sad reflection of our conquered sachem. Uncas sneered. But his men laughed gaily at the sight.

"Now!" said Uncas to my prince. "Now you do not have to lie in fear upon your bed, wondering when the war club of the Mohegan will fall. It has fallen. Yet not fully." He spoke low words to a few of his warriors, and four of the Narragansett were led before Miantonomi. As we watched, the tomahawk fell upon their heads, and their bloodied bodies tumbled into the tall grass beside our sachem and the Fool. Still my prince was silent.

"Why do you not speak?" asked Uncas in amazement. "Why do you not beg for your life, for the life of your braves?" he asked in angry disappointment. "Why do you not put your face to the ground and confess that you are weak? That you are a flea!"

The Mohegan sachem looked upon his own men, upon the captive Narragansett, and last of all upon me. "Would you not beg if it were you, Katanaquat?" he asked. But I did not speak a word. "I would!" he declared of himself. And he kicked the earth in frustration and contempt.

We were taken in triumph to the Mohegan fortress. And my prince, though hated by many, was hailed by all as a brave and mighty warrior. He was ushered to a large wigwam and given drink. A guard was set about the house, and within.

But the rest of the Narragansett captives, nine of us, were led to an open field outside the village, and there we faced the sharp teeth of the sour and maddened people of the Mohegan. Uncas put me last in the line of the gauntlet, with Assoko one in front of me.

How could this be? That we stood one behind the other as men walking to the summer games, but that the game was such as meant our life or death?

How could this be? That we walked not in victory and joy and freedom toward the city of Canonicus, our belts laden with the scalps, the wampum and the women of our foes, but that we stared down the long, doubled lines of cruel and howling young men, squealing children, and mocking squaws of the Mohegan?

How could this be? That the sun had risen upon six hundred proud warriors of the Narragansett, but that it would go down upon the blood of our shame?

Oh, where was the strong bow of Kattenanit my son? Where was the medicine of Askug my grandfather? Where was the strength of Katanaquat? Where was the god of Wequash the preacher? Where was my wall against the spirits? Where was the door that opened from this nightmare into the smoky dawn of my own warm wigwam?

How could this be?

Three of our men had run the bloody trail, thorny boughs falling like whips across their backs, knotted sticks falling like war clubs on their heads, wails and curses raining upon their souls. They ran it all the way, to lie at last upon the grass, gasping and heaving, while young squaws tipped water to their lips and set damp skins upon their wounds.

The fourth fell midway and was dragged from the shrieking fray to await the slow death of torture.

The fifth and the sixth each stayed upon their feet beneath the flogging.

The seventh broke out of the way by his own violence. Several warriors pursued him to the woods-edge and struck him from behind. He died quickly beneath their swift blows.

It was the turn of the Fool, and I feared for him. More than I feared for myself. My legs, when my turn came, would carry me down the long lane. But to stand and watch, tied like the dog to my own limbs! I would rather go down beneath the knives of ten deaf, toothless squaws!

They cut his bonds, and he turned to look upon me. His eyes were full of wonder, almost wild anticipation. I marveled at the heart of the Fool! Like the anxious arrow that rests upon the full-drawn string, Assoko waited only for the loosing. And I must do the loosing.

"Run, my Fool!" I shouted to his heart and to the gods who watched. To the walls of wicked women with their cruel staffs and their sharp clubs. To the chuckling, crooked Uncas. To the braves of the Mohegan. To my prince within the wigwam. To the stinking winds of death that blew their hot breath in our faces. "Run!"

He threw back his head and laughed like the jester. A laugh that was thunder. A laugh that was music and magic and murder. And he ran. Like the Fool he ran! Not as the arrow flies to the heart of the beast of the hunt, but as the frenzied powwow in his dance. As the rolling wolf cub with his brothers. As the merry gamester on the seashore. Leaping and reeling. Dancing and whirling. Laughing and shouting. Drooling and howling.

Arms swinging wildly. Hands fisted tightly. He ran. And the lines drew back in fear.

Young children dropped their sticks and began to cry. Young men stood still with wide eyes. Women crossed their clubs over their breasts. And the warriors beyond the gauntlet cried aloud, "The spirits are loose in the form of the Fool! Who can stand against him?"

But this was my Fool! He could be none else. I should have known. Like the wind, who could hold him? His laughter struck me like the sharp spear. It pulled the breath from my lips. It opened my heart. And my joy poured out like blood. I could not stand. I sank to my knees in my laughing, and bowed my head to the dust.

Does the morning sun rise out of the dark swamp? Only in the soul of the Fool.

Uncas stood at the end of the long, scattered line, his mouth opened like the starving wolf, his clenched hands white upon his war club. "Assoko!" he cried. "I wait for you!" But I saw that his hands were shaking.

"Weak woman!" wailed the Fool, and he charged toward Uncas like the angry moose running down the dog. The two men met in a collision of flesh and bone, and fell like the bear beneath the rocks of the deadfall.

Upon the pebbled soil the strange bear rolled, a hairy, howling beast with two heads and too many limbs. The beast bit itself, kicked itself, struck itself, and threw its useless war club into the brush. One head laughed. One shrieked. One cursed. One laughed the more.

At last a head arose and tore two arms and legs from off its body, rolled away a smaller beast and sprang up as a man. It was Uncas. His club leapt from the earth to his hand, swung itself around once and fell with great force upon the wildly kicking half-beast at his feet. It was caught in the grip of the half-beast, torn from the hands of the man like the spoon from the hands of the child, and swung once more in a hot circle. It smashed into the legs of the man and knocked him to his side upon the rolling stones. Then the half-beast rose to fall upon the man, and the many-limbed bear was whole once more.

"Weak woman!" cried one head with the voice of the Fool. And the bear began to bleed.

"Weak woman!" cried one head with the voice of the sachem. And the bear unwound its arms and legs. It rolled apart, and then became two bloodied, still, and gasping warriors.

Assoko lay upon his back in the settling dust, a circle of blood turning the soil red about his head. His eyes were open. His mouth moved without words. His hands raised and lowered the war club of the Mohegan. His forehead was raw. His wide, astonished eyes were small black islands in a sea of rising red. He sat up. His eyes found me.

"Kat?" he said.

Uncas rose from the stony ground, a horrid grin of triumph on his face. In one hand he held his bloody knife. In the other was the scalp of Assoko my Fool, my friend, my shield, the light of my heart, the strength of my childhood, the mate of my soul.

I did not run the gauntlet. For Uncas knew I was already fallen. With one scalp he had taken two. The Fool and I yet lived, but we were dead men both. Assoko had no soul, for it had slipped from him on the straight edge of English steel at the crooked hand of the Mohegan. And now my Fool was a shell for the gods, indeed! The hot winds howled in my head.

And my own soul. Surely it flew from me in that moment, that dirtied, bloody moment. It flew to the treetops like the frightened pigeon, sobbed in the boughs of the weeping willow, buried its sorrowed head beneath its sad wings, and slept through the long, dark night.

In the morning it woke as the buzzard and returned to me to gnaw upon the dead flesh of my hardened heart.

Uncas sent us into the woods together, two corpses walking the shadowed path toward home. Why did he not kill us? To return us to our people in this way was worse than the stake and the fire.

My prince was kept a prisoner within the strong fortress of the triumphant Mohegan.

"Not a dead man," said the form of Assoko as we wandered eastward beneath the tall green. "I breathe. I walk. I see."

I could not speak. For I knew not who walked beside me in the shell of the Fool.

"Kat?" said the man-thing, and I wanted to look upon him with the eyes of yesterday. But I was afraid. And I wondered if I would ever wake.

"Could not the English god give a man a new soul?" asked Kattenanit my son.

"No god can give a man a new soul," I mumbled in my darkness.

"Roger Williams says it is so," spoke my son. And Kattenanit wished it to be so. Otherwise the Fool was lost to us in that world beyond the reach of our hands. That world which the powwow sees only in his visions. Which the old man sees only in his dreams. Which the Rain From God sees often in the shadows, in the eyes of other men, in the flames of the fire, in the moving and mysterious waters of the Great Bay.

Roger Williams was gone. On great white sails across the great salt sea he went, to England, the land of his birth.

He would be back, he said. But now he was gone. Thus were his eyes and his ears and his heart and his tongue gone also.

Oh! That he had been here!

The eyes of the preacher were as the eyes of Wompissacuk the eagle, to see all that wanders the marsh and the field. His ears were as the ears of Noonatch the deer, to hear the twig break beneath the heel of the hunter. His heart was as the shield, raised between the wildcat and its prey. His tongue was like much wampum, pleading for the lifeblood of the beloved, playing its strong magic on the ears and the hearts of the hearer.

But he was gone. And thus the moons of the captivity of our prince were neither in his eyes or in his ears. Nor could his heart know that the hunter was hungry still.

"*Kitonckquêi! Kitonckquêi!* He is dead! He is dead!" they cried. And I came forth from my darkness to hear the dark news.

"*Kitonckquêi! Kitonckquêi! He is dead! He is dead!*" they cried. And I asked in my darkness just who now had fallen. A great one, I thought, for the village was weeping and wailing as one.

The answer, like cold wind, passed through me and shook me. But still I was sleeping, for surely the words were the words of a nightmare.

My hands found the arms of the brave closest by me. I seized him and held him and turned him to face me. "Speak straight to me, brother," I said. "For my heart will not joy in the jest!"

He looked upon me with great grief, and I knew that no jest was alive upon his tongue. So I asked, "Who is dead, my brother, that the Narragansett mourn like the wolf pack in its howling?"

"Our prince," he said with the voice of the vanquished, and he fell on his face at my feet.

Still I did not believe it.

It was our way to declare, in deceit, the death of our great ones, the falling of our friends, only to have them come home from the forest alive and full of strength! For when we mourned for that which was not, how much more did we rejoice for that which was? Great was our suffering beneath the weight of the night of deceit, but greater was our joy at the rising of the sun of the truth.

It was dark, and my prince! Did he live? Did he die?

I went to Canonicus, and the sachem called me in. His eyes were full of the lean moons of winter. His fire was low in the depths of his heart.

It was dark, and my prince! Did he live? Did he die?

I went to Silvermoon, and she would not look upon me. Her tears fell like sleet in the moons of much snow. Her light was gone.

It was dark, and my prince! Did he live? Did he die?

I went to the Fool, and he cried like the Fool. But he was not the Fool. And I could not believe him.

It was dark, and my prince! Did he live? Did he die?

I went to my son, to Kattenanit my son. And he knew of my darkness. He knew of my doubt. He knew of my fears and my wall and my shame. He knew of my sorrow which none could break into, and the hard-trodden soil of my heart, bare and rocky. He knew the fever of vengeance that burned in my eyes. He knew of these things, and he sat down beside me. My firstborn. The child of my first love. My son.

It was dark.

I laid one stone upon the many stones that rose upon his grave. The tall trees that had witnessed the capture of our prince stared down upon the mound of his burial. Their leaves fell like great brown tears. My tears could fall no more, for my heart was dry.

"He sat here in his defeat, and the Fool sat at his side," I whispered to the falling leaves and the frantic breeze that fled before the coming storm. "That Uncas would bring him back here to spill his blood is …" I leaned against the rocks, my face pressed hard against their cracked and chiseled stares, my arms outstretched in one great, cold embrace.

"Kitonckquêi!" I howled. *"He is dead!"*

"Michemeshâwi!" wailed my son beside me. *"He is gone forever!"*

The faces of the mute, impassioned stones absorbed my cries as Kattenanit knelt weeping in the yellowed grass. The skies wept too, like the spirits of the dying as the forest loosed its covering in the cool rain of the autumn. Low thunder rolled in the distance. I could howl no more.

My tired soul was emptied. My numbed limbs would not lift me. I almost fell to sleeping there upon the rain-washed tomb.

But the clouds then parted, and for a brief moment the sun of the evening awakened the gold and glistening colors of the wet and wearied forest. My heart awoke too in that single heartbeat, and it nearly cried aloud to rise above the clouds and stand again within the warm rays of the light of day.

My prince bid me stand. Or so it did seem to the ears of my soul. He bid me to stand like the man. To open my eyes. To walk straight. To sharpen my arrows against the foe. To do justice to the spilt blood of the son of the brother of Canonicus our king. To bend the bow to that end. To lead the Narragansett on that path.

Chepassôtam. It means "the dead sachem." Chepassôtam. For we could no longer speak his name. Not for many, many moons. To do so would be a shame and a dishonor. Wars were fought for the taunts of a foe who dared to name the name of the dead.

Chepassôtam. I knew his voice even now.

I would fight for Chepassôtam.

Though the whispers of vengeance woke me each new day, and my eyes now saw the sun, my darkness did not leave me.

"It is still a man, somehow," I said within myself, as I sat with the form of the Fool. "Though the soul is gone, it is still a man!"

"I will go," said the one who had been Assoko, the one who might be Assoko still. For I saw no shadows in his heart. And love had bid me look at last into his eyes. There were no spirits there.

"Where will you go?" I asked.

"To Sowwaniu," said the Assoko-man. "To find my soul."

This was my Fool, or I was a fool!

"You cannot!" I said to it. To him. To the hope in my heart. To the man without a soul. "For none can walk that path while he lives!"

"But I am dead," he said, and my fears returned. I looked away. But why did I fear? Was not this the voice of Assoko? Was not this the heart of Assoko? I could not—I must not—look away. And if this Assoko-man was just a ghost, could not my wall stand against it even so? I must trust in the strength of my own heart. I had nothing else.

"I am dead," he repeated. "For they say so, all of them." At this he threw up his hands and waved them in the air.

His squaw and his children, his father and his brothers, Canonicus our sachem, all who dared to stand before him and to speak in his direction told him he was dead. And so he was dead.

But he was not dead!

Must the people be right in this word? Or was this one more thing which we took upon the word of the fathers of our fathers, as Chepassôtam had said? And did they know the whole truth? Could Williams tell us more? Could his god-book tell us more? But Williams was gone. Would he ever be back?

"You are not dead," I declared to the Assoko-man, "for I would not speak to a dead man!"

"Kat?" he said.

I said within myself that this was my Fool. Though all the people think him dead, yet I would look upon him as my Fool. I would hear him as my Fool. I would speak to him as my Fool. I would talk of him as my Fool. I would feel his breath in my face. I would know his heartbeat once more. I would hear him laugh! I longed to hear him laugh.

"Assoko," I said, and his eyes grew wide, for none had spoken his name since his soul had flown. He swallowed, and I saw his tears gather like warriors at the hilltop.

"Assoko!" I declared, and he burst forth with waters that fell on my soul like the cool rain of summer upon the dry fields. I was washed in the flood, like no bath I had taken for moons upon moons. And I found myself weeping, no shame in my heart and no fear for the eyes of our brothers upon us. He lives!

And then came the silence. Pregnant with laughter. The sound that I longed for! The laughter I lived for! The laughter of men who have nothing to dream of but long days before them of victory and slaughter, of gaming and feasting, of warm fires and women, of sons and of daughters who rise up and bless them.

We laughed like laughter was our breath, the ground beneath our feet, the skies above our heards, our very hearts and souls. Could laughter call the soul back home again?

And then we were clean. Or surely the Fool was! And I was awake.

But he left. For though he lived, still his soul had flown. Laughter could not bring it back. And though I warned him not to seek Sowaniu, still his heart had told him he must seek a new soul of the gods. Thus he walked north—and I walked with him—to Providence, where the wife of Roger Williams took him in. Williams would return, she said, and speak then of new souls to Assoko.

I did not want to leave him there, but that was his desire. And I was not his master.

The days were lonely without the Fool, but the fire of the vigil of my vengeance kept me warm.

PART THREE

I Am the Stone

"My heart is all one stone."

—Wequash

CHAPTER FIFTEEN

Stone

Wawequa. The brother of Uncas. His arm it was which brought the tomahawk down upon the head of our prince. The tale was loosed in the forest—like the fires that burn the brush of summer—by the tongues of the men of the Mohegan.

Wawequa. Another name to hate.

Uncas laid his knife to the shoulder of our murdered sachem—said all tellers of the tale—and cut himself a portion. "It is the sweetest meat I ever ate," cried the mad dog. "It makes my heart strong!"

Uncas. His name was like the hard blow to the stomach when you least expect it. It made me sick. And all sickness cries for the cure. I knew the cure my heart sang for. I had rehearsed it within me day and night for most of the summers of my life. My knife was sharp and ready. My tomahawk was hungry.

"The wampum that we sent for the ransom of our sachem," said Kattenanit, "did it mean nothing to the Mohegan?"

"Uncas filled his own baskets," I replied, "and claimed it as payment for the courteous lodging of our prince."

"And the English," asked my son, "did they not know that Uncas held him?"

"They knew," I said, "for Uncas brought him before them. Even gave him up to them."

"Why did they not release him to us?"

"They held him under the pledge that he was yet the prisoner of the Mohegan."

"Then they honored Uncas over our sachem!"

"As they must, for it was Uncas who captured him. But their hearts were black. For it was they who decided our prince must die."

"The English?"

"The English."

"Why, father?" cried Kattenanit my son. "Why did they do this?"

"They said their god had told them so."

"What?" cried my son. "The god of Williams?"

"I do not know," I said. "I do not know. For this is by the tongue of a Pequot who was among them. Perhaps his tongue is also the tongue of Uncas, and thus we cannot trust it. I do not know."

"But the English ..."

"Not all the English did this," I said. "Yet many of the leaders from among their many towns were in the council. And a handful of their preachers."

"But he walked in peace with the English!"

"They said that he was haughty. That he conspired to unite all Indians against them. That it was not safe to let him go free. And so ..."

"Our prince said he loved them!" cried Kattenanit. "And that his feet had not moved from them!"

"He spoke his heart," I replied.

"I would speak my own heart!" declared my son. "And I would know theirs. For this is a wound. And the fever will find it!"

"We have no tongue we can trust," I said.

"Roger Williams will come back," said Kattenanit. "And I shall speak to the English through him."

"Speak then, and give them your heart," I said. Yet my own heart was hard and I did not much care if the fever found the wound.

"I am too old to walk with the warriors," said Canonicus our king. "And the sons of Chepassôtam our beloved are too young to walk in the moccasins of their father. Yotaash his brother lies under the earth, dead in the wars, and his soul has flown. And so Pessacus the youngest must stand now as the father of our people." Our aged sachem looked upon the solemn council that sat about the tired fires of his warm wigwam. "If you will have him, I will sit with Pessacus in council and kingship. And the Narragansett will once more have two to lead them."

Pessacus was but twenty summers. Yet his brother my prince had been younger still when he first wore the mantle of the sachem. We would follow Pessacus the brother of Chepassôtam. Whom else did we have in whose veins ran the blood of our kings?

A new powwow was among us, from the town of an under-sachem of the Narragansett. His name was Nickeétem, which means "I am well," for many were healed by his strong medicine. Our city was glad when his wigwam was raised in our midst.

"Do you know I am the grandson of our powwow who is gone?" I asked him when first we met.

"You are Katanaquat," he said to me, looking upon me with eyes that were deep like the sea. I saw at once dark shadows that I knew. I felt the faint, cold touch of a familiar wind. And I wondered, *Has the old Snake shed his skin and come back to us in the shape of Nickeétem?* "And you," he continued, "would now be a powwow, if the word of your grandfather were straight and strong."

"This word was an arrow," I said to the medicine man, "that flew as straight as any shaft flies. But the strong wind can cause the straight shaft to fall to the side of the target."

"What is this wind?" he asked. And his fingers played with the bones about his neck. They were the bones of the hands of men.

"The wind that drives the Rain From God," I answered, and I laid my hand upon my heart. My wind. My wall.

"Nopatin your father?" he asked. "The East Wind?"

"No," I declared. "Though Nopatin my father would blow for me as I bid him, it is not his breath that moves the shaft of my grandfather. It is my own." And I stared into his shadows. Yes! I knew them well.

His brow was troubled, and proud anger rose within him. His own anger? Or that of the guardians and masters of his soul? *Another doll on strings!* I thought. *Another dog on a leash. Another man who has bowed so low that his back will not straighten unless some invisible rope pull him up. But a man nonetheless. And a liar no doubt.*

"Do you mock the gods?" he asked, his eyes tight lines of hard and sharp contention. And I felt he spoke in chorus with the shadows of his soul.

"Do they not mock us?" I asked. And I stood tall in the warfare that so few among us dared. No longer could I lean upon my right hand or my left to find my Fool, to touch my prince. So on my wall I stood—and shook my fists.

"It is not good what you say!" he warned.

"I am well," I replied, and I bent my head to honor him. This was our way. For he was now our powwow, and his word, his medicine would do us good. All for a price.

I left the tent. Katanaquat wore no leash, let the powwow know this now.

The English of Massachusetts sent two messengers to Canonicus. The old sachem made them stand long hours outside his door in the driving rain before he called them in.

"Have you been weeping?" he asked them. "Or do the gods urinate upon you as you have done upon the Narragansett?" They did not know what to answer. Canonicus spoke few words to them, all with sand and flint. Then he sent them to Pessacus.

Our new king made them wait many hours more, then led them to a simple tent where they traded words into the middle of the night. The English would know our hearts toward themselves, toward the Mohegan, they said.

"Chepassôtam our beloved was your friend," said Pessacus our sachem. "And yet you gave him up to the hands of evil men. We do not understand your hearts. For never have we done you any wrong."

The English gave us answers, but their words were as fog through which we saw neither sun nor sky.

"As for Uncas," Pessacus declared, "the Narragansett will soon go to war against him. Not as Chepassôtam warred by a great army, but by small bands of beavers who will chew the poles from his wigwam one branch at a time until his tent collapses and he can stand no more!"

They were fishing when we fell upon them, seven braves and five squaws of the Mohegan. We killed all but one, and sent two hands and a foot to Pomham, our former under-sachem, in invitation to join us in the war. He would not receive the gifts, but sat down even closer to the Massachusetts English. They sent him soldiers and built him a fort. For he feared we would fall on him too.

The English called us to themselves, with Uncas and with our Niantics, to make a truce. We made one, which was to last until the next Moon Of The Planting. So we sharpened our arrows and hunted through the snows. But my soul kicked against the peace. My heart burned for the battle.

"It is time again to fight," I said to Kattenanit my son, in the Moon Of The Planting. But his thoughts were not of war. Though his hands were much skilled in the carving of the wood, there were more bowls in his baskets than war clubs.

"I have not the heart for the fight," he replied.

"You have not the heart for many things which make the man!" I said in anger. And I threw my soup into the fire. It hissed like the snake and spat brown smoke into the room.

"Katanaquat, my lord!" cried Ohowauke my second squaw. "The broth is rare! We have so little." She took the iron pot from the fire to save it from the fate of its little brother.

"Send Winaponk into the woods to slay the moose!" I growled. "And then we shall have meat in plenty until the beans sprout!"

"He is not old enough to hunt moose!" argued his mother. "He is only nine summers!"

And I rose to stand before my squaw.

"He is old enough to do whatever I ask of him," I said. And I turned to the boy. "Go!" I commanded. "Take your bow and your arrows and find us the moose. Or the bear. Or the pigeon. Or the hare. But do not come home until your shaft fells the bird or the beast!" He looked at me with wide and startled eyes.

I picked up his bow and flung it at him. His arms flew up to protect himself, and the small weapon bounced from his legs and rattled to the floor.

"And do not lose one arrow!" I shouted as I gathered a handful of the thin shafts of his own making and threw them at his feet. He moved to stand behind his mother.

"You are worse than the bear itself when it is wounded and backed in its lair!" cried Ohowauke.

"The bear can howl in its own lair as it pleases!" I said. "Now move away from the boy, squaw!"

"No," she said. And my heart spat fire.

I struck her in the face, and she fell with her heavy metal pot upon the floor. The boiling soup leapt upon her limbs, upon the boy, upon his face. And cries of pain and anguish rose that brought men running to my door. Squaws came in great number, entering the house to give their hands to the comfort and the care of the wounded woman and her wounded child. Silvermoon sang with Quanatik my daughter for healing and for strength. The burns were bad. The pain was much. Metauhock my girl-child sat with wide eyes in the shadows, her slender arms wrapped tight around the scraggled neck of old Cold Tongue.

I left the wigwam. Kattenanit followed.

"Father!" he cried with his hand upon my shoulder. I pulled it from me and turned to face him.

"Why do you not go wipe up the spilled soup?" I said to my son, my first-born, with the anger of scorn in my eyes.

"Why do you not go wipe it up yourself?" he cried. "For a man is not a man who slays the doe for protecting the fawn!"

I swung at him, and his hand took mine while it flew. He was strong. He was a man himself and not a child anymore. Twenty-two summers had raised him tall and dark and broad at the shoulders. The son of his father in all ways that eyes could see. But beneath the bark ran the sap of another tree.

"I am a warrior, Father," said my son. "Not a daughter!" He threw my hand to the side and stood back from me. I did not move toward him. "But the warrior does not have to love blood to be the man! It is enough to stand strong against the foe. It is enough to be the shield for the weak, for the old man, the child, and the squaw."

"And so you stand strong now for my squaw and her child! Against your father the foe!" I taunted. "Is that what the warrior does? Pushes the face of his father into the lap of the squaw?"

"You are wrong, Father," said Kattenanit my son. And I knew it was so. But the bear was wounded and against the wall. I raised my hand again. But he gave me his back and walked away.

"Do not mock me!" I cried.

He turned once more to face me. "It is not mockery to walk away from an angry man," he said. "It is wisdom."

*　　*　　*

"Where is the Fool?" I asked of Williams, who had come again among us at last. His sorrow for the death of our prince was deep, and it touched me even in my darkness.

"He is well," replied the preacher, "and has gone to live among his cousins on the island of Capawack, which the English call Martha's Vineyard."

"And they received him as one who yet lives?" I asked.

"As one who has been raised from the dead," said Williams. And I wondered at his words.

Kattenanit spent much time with Williams. The two spoke much of Chepassôtam, of the English, of the god-book, of Jesus Christ, and of peace. Canonicus too heard Williams gladly. Long nights and loud laughter warmed the wigwam of our ancient king. He loved this English man, as Chepassôtam had. As many of the Narragansett did. As I would if my wall had not grown heavy with the thick vines and the long thorns of my anger and my pride.

The wall was strong. The gods would not get in. And I could not get out.

Do not move, I said to myself. *Do not so much as breathe.*

We lay upon the wet ground beneath the tall grasses, still as logs. The winds walked through the marsh, bending the tops of the slender green shafts as they came. They did not walk alone. Fourteen warriors of the Mohegan crossed the wet fields with them.

Less than thirty paces from us now, they were not speaking, but I could hear the squeezing, squeaking sound of their moccasins against the rain-soaked earth.

Twenty paces.

Ten.

We rose, twelve warring men of the Narragansett, and loosed our bent bows upon the Mohegan. *"Jûhetteke!"* we cried in chorus. *"Fight!"*

But we had not caught them with their fingers in their belts. Several bows were quickly loosed in our direction, and men of both sides soon fell wounded. My eyes were hunting for one man alone.

"Uncas!" I cried, and I lunged toward him through the wet green. But my foot found a muddy hole, and I tumbled violently into the grass. A Mohegan was upon me, but it was not Uncas, and I felt his steel kiss my arm. A cold and wicked kiss, and one I must return! But could I rise? The warrior kicked my head. My face went down upon the slogged earth. Black water splashed my eyes, filled my gasping mouth. I tried to roll. My legs were wrapped in the sharp green ropes that rose on all sides. I tore myself free and flung myself back from the dark, painted form that reeled toward me. I was on my back in a pit of cold green, while the tomahawk of death fell upon me like the hawk from the blue sky. But it buried itself in the mud, and its wielder fell into the dark juices beside me like the stone that is thrown into the swamp. He was dead, struck from behind. A war club of the Narragansett found his head before his axe found mine. No time to give thanks. I must rise!

I leapt to my full height and swung my own club in an arc as a shield. None stood near me. The grasses were trampled in a circle of war, and the red blood of battle was splashed like bright roses upon the green carpet. The Mohegan were fleeing, Uncas with them. Four were dead. And two of their wounded were in our hands. Tantaquigeon! The brave who had first overtaken my prince as we ran from the battle of the Great Plain. His head was bloodied. His chest was torn. He stood before us with cold eyes and closed lips.

I walked to him swiftly, looked once into his soul, raised my club above my head, and laid him dead upon the ground.

"You are drunk on your hatred and your violence," Williams told me as we sat at his table in Providence. "If you continue to slake your thirst on the blood of the men of Uncas, you will wake one morning to find the soldiers of the English at your door."

"Why should they be the shield of the Mohegan dog?" I barked.

"Uncas has pledged himself their ally," said Williams. "And though I would rather run the gauntlet with one leg broken than trust the man, he has kept his pledge. And he comes when they call."

"The Mohegan dog!" I repeated, and I would have spat had I been in my own home.

The preacher sighed and sat back in his chair. The fire in the hearth climbed lazily up the stone chimney. Mary the wife of Williams laid meat before us on earthen plates, and drink in cold pewter. The house was filled with the pleasant smells of smoking ironwood, roast ham, and raisin pudding. Nopatin my father, with Kattenanit my son, sat also at the table. Outside, several warriors of the Narragansett lounged beneath the apple and the oak.

Williams spoke thanks to his god for the meal, and we ate.

"Vengeance belongs to God alone," said the preacher as he sawed his meat. "Those who walk in hate will not see God."

"I do not wish to see god," I said. "My eyes are tired of the shadows of the gods!" And I set my drink aside. It was beer. I asked instead for fresh waters from the cold river.

"Roger does not speak of the spirits, Father," said my son, "but of the One True God whom none may see unless they die."

"I do not wish to die," I said.

The wife of Williams gave me new drink, and I lowered my head to thank her. Her face and her form were yet fair, I thought, while the beauty of Silvermoon was worn out like the skins that cover the wigwam day and night for many seasons. What did it matter? There were other women among the tribes. More wives to be had, if I wished any.

"He speaks of heaven," said Kattenanit. "None go there but those who wish to see God. Those who turn from their evil deeds to follow Christ."

"Are you now a preacher?" I asked my son, putting down the drained cup and wiping my mouth with my arm. "Am I now a doer of evil deeds?" And I felt the anger rise within me. Must I sit and hear myself shamed? Must I bow my head to this talk of peace and friendship when my heart calls me to war? When blood cries for blood? Who are these men to throw water upon my fire? Are they not friends? Are they not family?

They are fools! All of them fools! Our prince is dead! Uncas is alive! Peace is for women who weave baskets in warm wigwams.

Vengeance belongs to God alone? No! "Vengeance is mine!" declares The Rain From God.

Kattenanit looked at me with strong eyes, but he did not speak.

"Let us council of beaver skins and wampum," said Nopatin my father. And so we did.

"She is gone, Katanaquat," said Silvermoon my wife, my first love, the echo of my ancient dreams, the distant chant of my hardened conscience.

"Did she take the boy?" I asked, staring into the vacant corner where her baskets had been. Where her rugs had lain. Where the small bow of Winaponk had leaned against the wall.

"With Quanatik," she added.

I heard a quiet sigh. Metauhock our girl-child, whose mother Teeshkatan had died in childbirth, turned in her sleep upon the bed. The sun slept also.

"The second squaw did not wish to speak with me of her leaving?" I said to the dark and empty absence of Ohowauke my wife. My once-wife. Of Winaponk my son. My second son. Of Quanatik my daughter. My first daughter. My shining-eyed daughter. Though she was the child of Ohowauke, her eyes were mirrors of the soft and silent light of Silvermoon.

"She spoke of this often," said my first squaw, "but you did not hear. For you were always shouting. Or worse.

"Even the dog, if too often whipped, will run away."

I looked at my wife, my first and now my only wife. My heart cried out against me. Against my anger. Against my pride. Against my meanness and my violence. Against the vengeance. Against the fire in my bones.

Then I crossed my wall and shouted back. I cursed my conscience. Cursed my heart. Cursed all songs of love and mercy. Cursed the younger days that rose within my memory to shine their warm light in my darkness.

Black clouds formed within my soul and crossed before my eyes. Hot tears swelled within the clouds. I fought them wildly with my will. And won.

"Come," I said to Silvermoon, a dull command, a dark and selfish word. I held out my hand to her.

She stayed her place, a hard and vacant stare upon her mask. Was I the stranger in this wigwam that she looked at me this way?

"Come," I said then to the shadows and the long unspoken words of love that hung like empty baskets from the grey poles on the wall. Nothing moved. And no one spoke.

I lay awake alone. Silvermoon slept sitting, her back against the tentside, her blankets wrapped around her to the neck.

He was an old man, our king. For more than eighty summers he had seen the sun come up each morning upon the lands of the Narragansett. Now those lands were fewer, and his days were fewer still. Yet he faced east. Soon his soul would fly beyond the sunset to Sowanniu.

He loved the English always, though they sometimes did him wrong. But he loved Roger Williams most of all. The sachem and the preacher were as father and son. Each gave much to the other. Each walked freely upon the lands of the other. And if these two had not loved as they did, the peace would not have lived so long.

Williams was in our country now, in his new trading house at the mouth of the Muscachuge. He did us much good from this house, and we traded with him often.

In the summer of my forty-sixth year, on a cool morning in the Moon Before Summer, Canonicus called his people to him.

"My eyes are heavy," said the old sachem, "and they will not open to another sunrise. Send at once for Roger Williams, for I wish to look upon his face before the night falls long and evermore."

Too late came the English preacher. With many tears he closed the empty eyes of the great king our father, the grand sachem of the mighty Narragansett, the strong heart and the wise tongue of the People Of The Little Bays And The Great Waters.

Our king was buried in new cloth given by Williams.

The Narragansett wailed and wept for many, many moons.

Mixanno, the eldest son of the dead king, became chief sachem with his cousin Pessacus.

I painted myself black, and sank into the shadows of my great, grey wall of stone.

When a man is cold, do you take his coat? When a man lies sweating with the fever, do you pay the powwow to let him lie alone? Do you pull the cup of water from his lips and hold it from him?

The god of the English. The god of Roger Williams. The god of Wequash. The god toward whom my prince once leaned. This god who is a father. This god of mercy. He reached into my heart—he cared nothing for my wall—he reached into my heart and poured cold water on the only fire of love that still burned bright enough to give light to my eyes.

Kattenanit, like the fish upon the hook, was drawn from my heart by this god. Drawn from my house and from my people. I could not save him. I did not know which way to aim my bow! For how can the shaft find the heart of the wind?

"Do you love cider so much that you leave your lands to beg for apples at the door of the Massachussetts English?" I said to my son, my first-born, my now-grown, the fruit of my loins, the apple of my eye. And my words were sour.

"I wish to learn more of the One Great God," he said simply.

"Cannot Williams fill your ears with news of his god?" I challenged. "If this god is in all places, then why must you leave the Narragansett to find him?"

"Williams has told me much," replied Kattenanit, "and I love him for his kindness and his open heart. But there are few among us who care for his God-talk. We like better his cloth, his tobacco, his beads. And Nickeétem opposes him. I feel the cloud of the powwow upon me in this place!"

We sat beneath Old Willow, our backs against the rock, our bared feet swimming in the shallows of Red Creek.

"His cloth is good," I said, "but his tobacco is better." I lit my pipe and drew from it noisily.

"In the village of the Nonantum of the Massachusetts, there is a sachem named Waban," said my son.

"More wind!" I coughed. For Waban meant wind in the tongue of the Wampanoag.

"Waban has opened his wigwam to the preaching of a man named John Eliot."

Another English god-preacher. Another English hand upon the shoulder of the Indian!

"He is a good man," declared my son. "Like Williams, he speaks true and walks without looking behind him. The men of Waban hear him gladly, and many now call upon the One True God."

Many old and addled men! Many silly women! Many small children!

"Many warriors. Many braves. Many strong and straight men," said my son. "Even Cutshamakin of the Massachusetts."

"When he wakes on the Sabbath with a toothache," I jeered, "then he calls on this god for a day or two!"

"Many warriors stand with God," declared my son.

"And you wish to stand with them and stare into the heavens!" I growled at the murmuring waters and the darting dragonfly. "Like the dog who joins his brothers in baying at the coon up the tree!"

"I wish to learn more of the One Great God," Kattenanit repeated.

"One Great God! Which one great god? There are more gods than there are fish in the great salt sea!" I cried. "Go down upon the sea in your canoe, and call for this One Great God. Soon it will rise from the deep spouting, and you will wish it had not!"

"I would bathe in its fountain!" declared my son.

"Go then!" I cried, stepping into the cold waters of Red Creek, swinging my arms about my head like the man who chases the hornet. "Go and whistle at this god who swims in the fog of the morning. If you see him, throw a net upon him and he is yours!

"Go then!" I commanded, gesturing northward as the wind blew. "Go and feed your prayers to this god who lets men nail him to the tree."

I climbed from the creek and swung my fist into the face of Old Willow. The bark tore my knuckles. I washed them with my tongue.

"Drink his blood and eat his flesh!" I mocked. "Then lay his bones beneath the earth and watch them get back up again! But when his ghost haunts your dreams, when his shadow clings to your legs and pulls you toward the deep swamp, do not cry for Katanaquat! For the ears of your father no longer hear the pleas of the weak. I will not throw you the vine to pull you out. If you are the man, then your own feet will find hard ground. And if you sink, you sink. I am not your keeper!

"Go!"

"You were among them!" I said to Nickeétem. "Among those who came to Teeshkatan my squaw when the papoose would not be born. When the boy-child would not come into the light."

"I was among them," said the slant-toothed powwow. I wondered that his words could ever be straight, for his mouth was full of crooked yellow spikes, like the palisade of some long-abandoned fortress. *Such teeth,* I thought, *are better fitted for the gape of the wolf.* "But our medicine was not good on that day," he said.

"And why was it not?" I asked. "And why could so many do so little? Does not the fire burn higher with many logs?"

"The tall flame makes much light," said the powwow, "but it can devour the meat before the man can eat it."

"Did you burn her with your much light?" I cried.

"I know well when to pull the log from the fire, and when to blow on the flame!" declared Nickeétem. "I did not burn her. Nor did the other medicine men. But none can know the mind of the spirits."

"Not even the powwow?" I asked. But I knew the answer, for who can fully know the mind of any other, unless he opens it? And who can peer into the heart of a god?

"The powwow knows what he is told, sees what he is shown. My guardians see much that my own eyes do not. But they do not tell me all," replied Nickeétem.

"Then you do not know why she died," I said.

The powwow looked at me with the dead eyes of my grandfather, and his voice became soft and low like the purring of the cat. "Perhaps," he said, "it is because The Rain From God swings his war club in the face of the spirits."

"I am a man!" I declared. "I stand where I stand."

"You stand on the rock in the midst of the swamp!"

"If the whole earth is a swamp, then I stand secure!"

"The whole earth is not a swamp!"

"I stand where I stand."

"Do you fear me?" he asked.

"I fear many things," I said. "Does not every man?"

"Do you fear me?" he asked again.

I looked long upon him. Did his guardians stare back at me? Did they tell him what they saw? Did it matter what they told him? I was a man! And the powwow was a man. I did not fear him.

"I stand where I stand," I said. "And I fear no man."

I entered the country of the Mohegan alone.

I knew the sun was now hidden behind the walls of the west, for the dusk was heavy. I could taste the dew in the air. Nanepaushat walked in his sleep above the trees, his eye cracked open to the earth. There was nothing in the new sounds of the night to cause alarm, and the peaceful shadows of the forest held their places as they should. But I sensed that I was not alone.

Obediently I sank back into the blackness of the laurels on the riverbank, sliding silently under the leafy blanket of the tangled thicket.

Two—no, three men—stepped suddenly into view only a whisper to my left. Uncas! And two warriors. One was Wawequa. The other was not known to me. There must be more. But soon the three melted into the dark woods, and none came behind them. If I was swift, if I was silent, I could overtake them!

I rose like smoke and blew upon the night wind toward my prey. If I were the smoke, I could enter their mouths, their ears, their eyes, their nostrils. I could cut off the breath of life from within. If I were the wind, I could jump upon their backs and push their faces to the earth, where the twisted root of the great oak moans for water in its thirst. Where the dark heart of the grey stone sings its cold, quiet song to the spider, to the salamander, to the tiny bones of the dead leaves of many autumns. My tomahawk cried to my heart as I ran. It pleaded. It begged. For blood.

Three shadows. Black against black. Just ahead of me.

Only two leaps.

Only a heartbeat.

Now!

I did not know who it was that went down beneath my blow. I did not stop to see. No matter! For no man stands again without his head. I swung at the second, and buried my axe in his flesh. His ribs held the iron, and would not let it loose. I pushed him from me with my foot, and drew my knife from my belt. My eyes were upon the third.

In a dream, in the land of day-is-done-but-not-yet-night, we danced the dance of death. The third man and I. Was it Uncas?

"I am Katanaquat!" I cried to the man-shadow.

"Ungh!" it coughed at the revelation, and I knew my man.

"Uncas, you dead dog!" I spat. "Your scalp will ride home with me tonight upon my belt! Your ghost will howl forever in the cold winters of the mountains of the north. Your soul will gasp for air beneath the dark waters of the great salt sea. You will never know warmth. And if you find your way, in the madness of your wandering, to the courts of Sowanniu, the great dog which guards the gate of Cautantowwit will tear you in pieces and feast upon your bones!"

He said nothing, and I lost his shadow for the moment in the thickening darkness. There he was again! A purple shade against the dim half-light of the squinted eye of the moon. I closed on him, but a sudden cold wind swept past my face. A spirit? No! The war club of the Mohegan! It had nearly kissed my skull.

Uncas came on, and we fell back from the eye of Nanepaushat into the cavernous forest. The ambush was done, the battle was pitched, and the advantage was no longer mine. My tomahawk was snared by the bones of a dead man, lying in the bushes drinking blood. I held a knife, my foe a club. A finger against a foot! Where was he?

I went down. The world was bright for one moment, like the splash of the lightning in the midst of the storm of night. Then it was full of the shadows of shadows. And pain. Heavy, black pain. My chest.

I was on my back upon the earth. I heard the breath of my foe above me. I saw, without seeing, his form. I bent my feet before my face. I pushed them with great force into the heavy air. My heels hit flesh. Uncas stumbled backward.

I rolled. I rose. I ran. Through the deep blues and the blurred blacks. Under the tall legs of the pine giants. Into the grey, splintered garden of the leaning birches. Touching my sweating hands to my sticky, wet chest. Listening for the sounds of pursuit. Hearing only the falling of my flying feet, the wheezing of my tortured breast. Wondering if my heart would burst beneath the frenzy of my flight.

Why had I come alone?

Why not? My heart had led me to the man! And it was one against three. The Rain From God had fallen on two. A mighty deed! Yet Uncas lived. Cursed be the spirits and the night! He lived! And while he lived, my soul could not sleep. Not for one eve. Not for one hour.

There was none to hold me in the city. None to whom I leaned.

My sachems were not the men that their fathers had been. They now paid tribute to the English, and fled from the sound of the horsemen of Plymouth. Pessacus had to beg permission to gather chestnut rinds on the island of Quinunicut, called Rhode Island by the English.

Our powwow struck his hands with the gods and filled his many baskets with the goods of our people. Though his medicine was weak in war, it was strong within the wigwams of the Narragansett. All was well for the medicine man.

The children of my grandfather, the dead powwow, with Mishtaqua their ancient mother, were gone among the Niantic. And thus I went also, Silvermoon and Metauhock coming with me. We raised our wigwam beside that of Nopatin my father. But Cold Tongue would not move from the city of Pessacus and Mixanno. Perhaps his soul was wedded to the soil on which he lay so many seasons. I bid him farewell, but he did not see or hear me go. The old dog was blind and deaf. He only barked while sleeping. In the long, cold winter that followed, he was added to the soup of a few meager meals.

Uncas mocked Mixanno, jeering his dead father, abusing the names of his ancestors. If the Mohegan were not silenced, surely he would call up the ghosts of the dead and the bloodlust of Chepi!

Did the Mohegan want a fight? We would fight him, Nopatin and I. But our chief sachems had first to beg the English for the right to redress the wrong! And the English said no, for they favored Uncas, who slept at their door.

We moved on Uncas anyway, an army of the Narragansett. But the English who lived within the country of the Mohegan ran from their houses to warn the sachem. Thus he was ready when we came upon his fort. Should we throw ourselves against the rocks? We went home.

Mixanno died, leaving Quaiapen his widow with two sons and a daughter. Cojonoquant, the cousin of the dead sachem, rose up to make himself chief. Yet he fell as much as he rose, for the man was always drunk with strong water. Scuttop and Wequachanuit, the sons of the dead sachem, also stood to claim the kingship. Even Quaiapen their mother gathered men about herself and raised a palisaded town which the English called Queen's Fort. She changed her name to Magnus. We called her the squaw sachem.

And so the tribes of the Narragansett became as the branches of the dead pine. The needles fall. The boughs are cut down. They are taken from the one trunk and cast upon the many fires. At last they are ashes good for nothing but for mourning or to be thrown upon the ice of winter and tread upon by the foot of man. Oh! for the days of my wise prince and his great uncle!

But we were not ashes yet, just scattered branches of the one great tree.

* * *

"I can no longer sleep within these wigwams," I said to Nopatin my father. "The knife of Uncas hides in every bush. The eyes of Uncas peer across the river into my dreams. Either I close his eyes forever or I must flee!"

"Flee?" said Nopatin my father with great amazement. "Is this my son who speaks? Does the rain halt in its falling and climb back to the clouds?"

"I do not climb back to the clouds," I replied. "But neither do I fall to the ground. I am like the cold fog of the morning that stands confused between the heavens and the earth."

My father was silent.

I picked up a rock and tossed it into the Pocatuck. "I am like the heavy stone that is cast into the stream," I said. "The waters flow above me to the sea, the fish swim all around me, but I do not move.

"The waters are my days and my nights. They pass me continually, carrying my dreams far beyond my eyes."

"The fish are the peoples of the earth, the tribes of the forests and the shores, and all the peoples from over the great salt sea. They come and they go and they come again.

"But I am the stone that does not move, and no fish stops to counsel at its feet. If I do not move soon, the mud of the river will cover me."

"And Uncas?" asked Nopatin.

"He is the man who crosses the river, who stands on the stone, who pushes it deeper beneath the black mud," I said. "Either I cause his foot to slip, or I must roll with the waters to the sea!"

"His foot must slip one day," said my father.

"I cannot lie beneath these trees waiting!" I cried. "Will you not arm yourself and call your warriors to follow us against the Mohegan?"

"Uncas cannot die," said Nopatin my father.

"All men die," I said. And I ran my palm across the scars upon my chest.

We sat upon the eastern bank of the Pocatuck, my father and I, and watched the blue-green waters slide on southward to the sea.

Chapter Sixteen

In the Pines

Silvermoon did not go with me. She asked, but I said no. For the dog who is dying wishes but to die alone, alone beside the quiet stream where he once drank upon the hunt. Alone beneath the tall pines where the hot sun does not touch the earth. Alone.

Though I had no dream of dying, still my heart was cold as death. It beat unto itself alone.

Tall pines are better than tall grasses for the wigwam of the lone warrior. Hidden from the eyes of Keesuckquand, sheltered from the storm, the floor of the pine wood is a home of its own. I made it mine, just north of the Great Swamp, between the Yawgod and the Shickasheen.

Within a natural circle of seven tall trees that stood upon a small rise like ancient giants in the midst of the dark forest, I raised my house upon twenty bent poles. I covered it with the bark of the birch. Mats I had in plenty from skins I hauled from the village of Nopatin and from pelts I bought from the men of the squaw sachem. Her fort, though half a morning north and east, was the closest of the great villages of the Narragansett.

My days were passed in hunting or fishing and gathering berries in season beside the Great Swamp. Though no corn would grow upon the shaded floor of the pine woods, I planted some seed by the banks of the Shickasheen. I planted beans and squash also. Only then did I wish my squaw was with me, for this was not work for the warrior. But I must live. Tobacco I raised at the edge of the wood.

I bought a canoe from the men of the Queen's Fort and brought it down the river to my gardens.

Around my wigwam I buried—from tree to tree of the seven— sharpened logs, each next to its neighbor, and each twice as high as a man when he stands. And thus a wooded wall was pitched, with a gate like the doors of the English, of plank, but on hinges of leather. I chiseled three small windows into my wall, about the size of two hands, at nearly once and half again the height of a man standing. I placed a stone beneath each of these holes on the inside of my fort, so that I could stand at them and look out. At three places also within the wall, I laid several logs upon their sides—and then upon each other—in the fashion of the steps of the English. When standing on these, I could see to both aim and loose my arrows into the forest beyond. On one of the pine giants whose branches climbed lower than the rest, I hung a strong vine. With the vine I could raise myself into the lowest branch. From there I could ascend into the heights, even cross to the boughs of other trees. I did not know if I might need their shelter from more than the rain and the snow.

I dug two pits for fire, one within my wigwam and one without, but still inside the wall.

And there within my house I laid my head each night when not abroad upon the hunt in the trade.

"Do you not wish to hear the voices of your people?" asked Nopatin my father as we sat about my fire in the Moon Of The First Frost. He came to my wigwam each time he walked beside the Shickasheen to the trading house of Williams. With him was Mattachuk my next younger brother, the son of Moapitug the second squaw of Nopatin. Thirty-four summers had passed since Mattachuk had been a papoose. He was now a warrior of the Narragansett with many children of his own. I wished for one moment to be in his moccasins, walking the sunlit paths with my father, talking of warm days behind and glad days ahead. But no such days lived in my heart, and I blew the thought into the fire.

"I hear your voice now," I replied, "and I am glad for your feet upon my floor. But it is enough that you come when you can."

He sighed, and his eyes walked my walls. The wigwam was covered inside with mats made by many hands. The hands of Silvermoon. Ohowauke. Quanatik. Teeshkatan. Taquattin. Mishtaqua. And Hassamet the mother of Assoko. "You lie here wrapped within the arms of many who have loved you," my father said, spreading his hands out to the colors on my walls. "Perhaps you hear their voices while you sleep."

"I hear the owl in the forest. The wind above the trees. The rain upon my roof," I said, "when it can find its way through the pine boughs!"

"Do the spirits visit you?" asked Nopatin the son of the dead powwow.

"I have my wall," I said. "But they come as they come to any man. The forest is full of them. I thank them for the harvest and the hunt."

"Kattenanit asks for you," he said. And my heart turned one eye toward the light. "His name is now Joshua, and he calls upon the great god of the English." My heart shut both eyes, closed both ears.

Joshua! What name is this? Not the name I know him by! Not the name of the Indian. When the man changes names, sometimes the man changes.

Joshua! It is the sound one makes when scoffing. When coughing. When hit unaware on the flat of the back! A mocking and a cry!

"He has taken a wife," my father continued, "and she is large with child. He wishes you to come to him when the papoose comes into the world." Nopatin looked upon me. I could feel his steady gaze, though my own eyes wandered in the dark world where men muttered what none could hear or understand. "I am going to him when the time comes," I heard someone say with the voice of Nopatin. "I will come to you then. We can walk the path together."

"Do not come," I said to the muttering men and the shadows in the darkness. "Kattenanit my son is dead. Why should I go to look upon his bones?"

We slept, and our breath was white upon the cold air. I rose three times within the night to put more wood upon the fire. Once, my father sat up as I lay the log into the low flame. "Silvermoon sings for you," he said quietly. He covered himself and went back to sleep.

In the morning my father walked north with my brother. The day promised snow.

Was this a game of the gods? Or did Weetucks sit with his brothers on the shore, smoking and blowing, while a great fire rose upon the sands?

The winds blew warm in the midst of the Moons Of The Snow. The fog rose thick along the rivers and the bays. The snows turned to water and lay in cold puddles upon the hard earth. The icy brooks bent and cracked and opened up their mouths toward the heavens. The hunter shed his coat as if it were summer. The black bear came forth from his lair to blink and to wonder and then go back to bed.

For days the fog was so heavy in my woods that I could not see my wall from my wigwam. It was one thing to live with this fog in my soul. That was my choice. That was my war. It was another to wake with it soaking my blankets. I would find a hill where my eyes could see the sky!

I painted my face for the journey, and filled my back bag with meal to last a week. I took my bow, my arrows, my knife and my tomahawk, my skin for water, my pipe, and my tobacco. I put small fire into a large shell lined with clay and filled with the rotted powder of the yellow birch. This I bagged and hung at my belt. For who could make new fire in this dripping mist?

I tied my gate shut on the inside, pulled myself into the pine, and dropped into the low grey cloud outside my fortress. My feet found the path that walked north, and I followed it blind to the edge of the forest. There the Yawgod flowed with ice, and there the light broke dimly through the steam of the melting snow. Everywhere, the world lay wrapped in a warm, misted cloak of silver and white. Never had a winter awakened like this in the midst of its long night!

Beyond the village of the squaw sachem I wandered, and the winds blew warm upon my shrouded path. I crossed the frosty Wanasquatucket upon the bridge of the fallen spruce, into the lands of Roger Williams. Providence was not far, but who could tell if he walked the right path in this strange and smoky dream?

Sometimes I saw deer moving like herds of ghosts among the bush and briars.

Sometimes the fog flew from me and the clouded skies called out my name. *Katanaquat! The Rain From God! Do you like the weather?*

Katanaquat! called Kaukant the crow. And the birds of winter twittered like bats within the mysterious mist.

Katanaquat! shouted the cracking ice of the melting rivers. And I dared not get too close to the slippery waters.

Katanaquat! spat the breaking branches as they fell beneath the heavy, wet snow that crowned their weeping heads.

"Katanaquat!" said the preacher, as I stood at the door of Roger Williams.

"Your son asks for you," said Williams, as we sat at his fire after meat. "And Assoko calls you in his prayers."

"Voices from beneath the earth," I said. "My ears have long been closed to the spirits."

"Why do you run from God?" asked the preacher, and he leaned toward me as the father leans toward the child who has sand in his eyes. To gently wash the face. To help the child to see. To send him on his way again to laugh and play.

"I do not run from God!" I declared. "He has not called me. And I stand where I stand."

"And where do you stand, my friend?" asked Williams.

"I stand in the forest, my eyes to the east," I said, staring into the fire. "I am Narragansett. I am the son of the East Wind. I am the Rain From God. I am a warrior of my people. A hunter and a man of medicine. The father of many children and the husband of ..." My words caught me waking. The words of another man. The words of a once-man. The words of a no-man. The words of a stone.

I was stone. Cold stone. And a stone stands where it stands.

Unless someone rocks it from its table.

"You stand where all men stand," said Williams. "Beneath the wrath of a holy and offended God."

"What have I done to offend this God?" I asked, my eyes hot with the flames of the dancing fire.

"You were born an offender, as all men are!" he answered. "Like the snake that is hatched with fangs readied to strike at the hand that would lift it."

"And so God sent his Son to take the serpent in his hands?" I said. "To let it bite him till he died? I do not understand this God. This Son who dies."

Williams stood and paced before the fire, a sermon simmering in his pot. I had eaten his soup before. I could eat it again.

"He did not simply die beneath the bite," said Williams, "and let the serpent crawl away. He took the serpent's poison too. And now no man need fall beneath the fangs of sin!

"God so loved the world that he gave his only begotten Son, that whosoever believeth in him should not perish, but have everlasting life!

"Though the world stands guilty and will one day be burned, God sent not his Son into the world to take vengeance upon it. No! God sent his Son into the world to save it, to rescue it! To ransom each man with the wampum of his Son's own blood.

"Jesus ran the gauntlet for your life and mine, Katanaquat, not for his own. He died at the stake in my place and yours, not because he was guilty. And not because he was weak. But so that we might live!"

The shutters were opened at the windows, for the night was warm. Williams pointed out at the faded blue snows of the evening, as the fog lifted ever so little to let the dim light of the cloud-covered moon kiss the earth.

"Though your sins be as scarlet," said the preacher, "they shall be white as snow. Though your crimes be as blood, they shall be white as the linen on Mary's table!

"If you are willing to come to him, if you are obedient to his Word and his law, you will eat the good of the land."

I sat on my wall within, my feet to the outside. A dangerous stance.

I saw something shining far off in the fog. Was it the sun upon the sea? Was it Sowanniu? Was it the light of the house of a friend? Why did I see it at all, where never it shone before?

Or was it light after all? Was it not the form of a man? Was it a ghost? A ghost walking? A ghost singing?

A song. I heard a song. Not the same song that the wind drove through my heart so long ago. But one like it. One that came from the same tongue. One that called with a clean voice through the crowded trees.

"He that would come to God," said the voice of the preacher in the fog beneath the trees, "must believe that God is. And that he rewards those who diligently seek him."

I shook my head, and I saw again the darkening snows outside the window of the good man of Providence. But something else was out there now. Something old and angry. Staring from the shadows like the wolf into the house. Into my eyes. Into my soul.

I pulled my knees up to my chin and slid from off my wall into the darkness on the safe side.

I crossed the Pawtucket, now called the Blackstone by the English, into the country of the Wampanoag. Though the fog was heavy still, it pushed its way south before the strong breath of new winds from the north. The mists began to sink, and the cool winds blew, until the air was once more clean around me. As the winter awoke from its dream of the summer, I found my senses sharpening, my feet moving more surely on the path that led to … where? Where was I going?

Though the colors of the melting winter returned to the earth around me, they were in shadow still. For the sky was darkening with the clouds of a ripening storm. Did the cold winds bring snow? I had no coat!

Dark light fell from the gathering clouds to paint the hills and trees—hills and trees that I had once walked with my prince. Hills that led to English Medfield, Dedham, Mistick, Concord, Woburn. Trees that stood above the Wampanoag, the Massachusetts, the Penacook, the wigwams of John Sagamore, of Chickataubet, of Cutshamakin, of Waban.

Waban! And my son! No longer did they live beneath the trees, my father said. But in a town of their own. Natick. A town filled with Indians who prayed to the One God.

Natick on the Charles. On both sides of the Charles, with a bridge between the sides. A bridge of wood and stone. Built by their own hands— Indian hands. And better than any English bridge anywhere else upon the river! Why had no tribe ever done such a thing before?

I would see this great bridge. This town of praying Indians. The houses they built and the wigwams they raised. The longhouse of worship within which they sang. Where Eliot preached. Where no spirit came but the one Holy Spirit. Where Joshua Kattenanit sat with his God-book and called on the One Great God.

Tomorrow was their Sabbath, Williams said. I would cross their bridge tomorrow, stand upon their streets tomorrow, see what men had wrought beneath the hand of this almighty God.

Tonight I would sleep beneath the shelter of a rocky crag. And cold the night would be.

The new day dawned in darkness, a boiling darkness in which the warm winds fell back from the hard steady blows of the gales of the north. The skies were in turmoil. The clouds marched like armies. The drums rolled above them. The lightning fell swiftly, like arrows on fire. But still the rain waited, though loud was the war cry.

I passed through the trees where the wigwams sat scattered, through small Indian towns and snow-covered cornfields. Past fences and cow sheds and dams on the creeks, where the waters spread backward to fill up the low spots.

I traveled a path that was widened by horses, by wagons and cattle, by many men walking. I passed by the houses of English all dressed for the Sabbath day meeting. They traveled together on lands that had once been the lands of the red man.

At last I crested the great hill of Moodnock, and there, spread before me like pictures sewn on skins, were orchards and wigwams, houses and fences, streets and gardens—with one great longhouse standing in the center of the town. And a river, the Charles, flowed through the midst of it all.

Natick, the Place of the Hills.

The dam broke above me, high in the heavens. The waters of winter fell hard on the white earth. And I walked the wet, widened road that led down to the gates of the town where the Indians prayed.

The cold rains fell. But I did not feel them. They pelted the puddled earth and the bark-covered wigwams. They rattled the wooden shakes upon the empty homes and the crowded longhouse. They roared in my ears. But I did not hear them.

Before me stood a house of plank and beam—a house filled with braves singing praises to the One God. Braves who had buried their hatchets and scalp knives. Braves who no longer bowed down to the pow-wow. Braves who did not fear the gods or their medicine. Braves who no longer danced long at the fire, or howled to the spirits. Or hid from the shadows.

They had what I fought for. But they had it by bowing. They had it by crawling as dogs to the door of the One God. By weeping and beating their chests in their misery, praying to Jesus to take all their sins from them. Making him lord, and then they were his servants!

My once-son was in there. The son of my once-love. The son of my once-life. The son of my once-dreams. The son of my blood and the son of my pride. He was not Kattenanit! Now he was Joshua!

What did he look like with hair cut short like the English? With shirt and shoes and pants and hat? Would I know him? Had he too died and been raised from the dead? Why did he call me to come and be with him, his father who scorned him, and coughed at his Great God?

Who was this God that he caused men to praise him? To change names and families? Spit at the spirits? Rise up in the morning and build a great city with stone and with wood and with bridges that Weetucks could walk on?

My wall. Was it strong as the wall of this Natick?

The rain, it was falling from God. It was washing the sins of the Indians of Natick. Whiter than snow. Whiter than the linen on the table of Williams. The rain. It was falling from God.

But my son, he was stolen. My prince, he was dead. My Fool, he was gone from me. Uncas still lived. And the fire of my pride and my hatred and vengeance yet burned like the coal in the palm of the powwow.

I would not bow down to this god in the heavens! His rain would not cover the fire of my own heart. For I had rain too, and it fell where I bid it. Who was this God that he thought himself greater?

"Katanaquat!" I shouted to the Father and the Son and the Spirit who heard the praises of the Indians of Natick.

"Katanaquat!" I cried to the wet missiles that fell from the embattled heavens.

"Katanaquat!" I wailed to the spirits and the shadows and the powwows and the preachers and the white snow and the linen and my once-son and his Waban and the bridge of stone and timber and the rolling Charles River that ran down to English Boston by the Bay of Massachusetts on the salt sea shores where once ran Wampanoag and Patuxet in the merry games of harvest.

"Katanaquat!" I howled to the thunder as the lightning lit the dark day with its fire, and the cold rain sang its war song in the valley of the Charles.

"Katanaquat!" I chanted to my heart, but no strength filled it. Only darkness as the rain fell in the puddles at my ankles.

The door of the longhouse swung open, and I saw the wondering faces and the forms of the praying men of Natick. Men like me, after all. Not spirits of men—but men in the flesh. They came forth into the pouring rain, into the rain from God, searching the street for the crier in the storm. One man saw me first.

"Father!" cried the voice of my once-son. And he came to me running.

"I have no vine to throw you!" I cried, and I fled in great fear of the shadows of memory. Fled like the coward who runs from the cold wind. Flew through the streets past the fences of Natick. Back down the wide roads that led to the rivers that led to the forest that led to the trails that led to the dreams that I dreamed in my darkness within the birch wigwam within the high walls that I built in the pine woods. Alone.

I stood at no door on my long journey home. I ate at the table of the wilderness. My suppers were sour. My nights were as my days, and my days were as my nights. I took the loneliest paths. I cut new trails over hills that were empty of men. I came at last to the door of my pine woods, and entered the quiet beneath the tall trees. This was home now. Nevermore would I walk abroad in the midst of dreams.

It was not good for the man to live alone, Roger Williams once told me. For God had made the man first, and found him to be lacking. So He put him to sleep and took from him a rib—like the powwow pulls the sickness from the man who suffers—without a wound, without cutting the flesh. From this rib God made the woman. And when the man awoke and saw his squaw, he cried, "This is now bone of my bone and flesh of my flesh!" And the two were one together. And it was good.

I woke from a dream of Silvermoon, a dream that had visited me now most every night for many moons.

In the dream I saw her standing in a mighty fire, crying to me, pleading for me to pull her from the flames. But I could not, for I was sleeping. In my dream I was sleeping. And when I woke within my dream, I would see the fire but Silvermoon was gone. Had she lived? Had she died? Had she been here at all? And then I would lie down to sleep again, within my dream to sleep again, and the fire would rise once more with my once-love within it.

Then I would wake. Really wake. And my own fire would be burning low within my wigwam, and I would not know if I slept or if I was awake. I would rise to put my hands above the flames. And if they bit me, I knew that I was not dreaming. And then I would go outside and shake my head. Too many nights of such dreaming! Too many hands in the fire!

Nopatin my father came to me. The child of my once-son was waiting to be born. Would I go?

I would not, for one trip to Natick had been more than enough.

He had heard of my going, for my once-son had told him. But why had I fled?

Ask the wind.

Would I not walk awhile with him?

No, for my legs were lame.

So are your excuses! argued Nopatin my father.

Was Silvermoon well?

Why did I ask?

A dream. Do not worry. She comes to no harm. Just a dream, and I wake, and I wonder.

She is well.

I am glad.

The winter was hard. My meals were sparse. The spirits crept under the tall trees and whispered outside of the walls of my wigwam. And sometimes they came in the door and stood laughing. *The man! He is so strong! He stands where he stands! What a warrior! To hide in the pines like a squirrel in his tree!*

And I cursed them for their cursing me.

Uncas found me. In my fog, beneath the tall trees. In the summer, in the morning. When I rose, he fell upon my fortress shrieking. Well I knew the voice that cried the loudest!

Arrows pierced my tent and blankets. Stones fell on my roof. Yet the foe had neither breached my gate nor scaled my palisade. So I had hope.

My fortress sat high, and none could look into it but from the trees. Yet I could look down on the ground that surrounded it. Was I encircled? No, for the shafts that impaled my wigwam were all from the east. Did Keesuckquand fight with them?

I ran from the tent to the eastern wall, an arrow taut upon my bow-string. There upon the stone of one window, I rose to my height and peered out. Just a moment was all that I needed. I saw many warriors. Fifteen or twenty, some in the open and some behind shelter. The shelter was sparse for no brush grew about me. Just trees, but a tree is the best shield I knew from the sharp bite of flint.

Did they see me? I did not know. But I would not stand in one place. No warrior stands in one place.

I leapt to the steps of the logs nearest to me and rose above the wall to aim at the man whom I knew to stand closest. He danced with his arms wide, his arrow in flight, and I shot at his chest as the Fool shoots. Or as he once shot. The shaft flew swift and true, and laid the dancer upon the needled carpet. Soon all the rabbits had fled to the trees. And I was now lord of the hill.

"Come and wake me from my sleep again, my friends!" I taunted, from my little window on the east. "Just give me a moment to get back into my bed!" And I watched as a few men ran southward from shield to tall shield.

"Come and join me on my island!" I shouted and I ran to my south window to follow the rabbits. "I have strong water and women. Come and join me!" And I climbed again to rise above the wall to hit the hare as he runs. Another went down, my shaft through his leg.

I ran back to the east window, and saw that Uncas was calling to his men to circle the fortress. I would follow the litter! Two more fell as they left one tree for the cover of the next—one I killed, the other tumbled down the hill, an arrow in his side. They could not keep this up for long. They would not wish to. Not for Uncas. Not even for the scalp of Katanaquat. Not with their own blood adorning the pine wood.

More arrows came over my wall. But they fell behind me in the dirt and on my wigwam. Yet they came from the south now as well as the east. And soon they might fall as the rain from the four winds. But I had a secret.

I ran to my tent and threw open a small wooden box. Inside was a pistol of the Dutch, a gift from my father. He said I might need it, alone in the pines. I had fired it twice just to hear its sharp thunder and see it spit fire. The balls had flown somewhere. I did not know where.

How to load it? I had practiced in my mind many times. The powder. The shot. The rod. The flint. I ran to the wall once more.

The rain of carved death had ceased, for the foe did not know where I was within my walls. I rose again upon my east logs, long enough to let myself be seen, and then raced in a circle from window to window to see where the rabbits had run. They had fully surrounded my lair.

"Send more rain, little storm clouds of the Mohegan!" I shouted. "For I am thirsty and dry." The arrows began to fall again within my palisade, and this time from many directions. As I peered briefly out of my southern window I spied Uncas my target. A shaft fell from the north within an arm of me.

"Thank you for the arrows, my friends!" I cried. "I was running low! I have sent my own shafts out on the hunt, and they have not come home yet!" My words called forth a new shower, and I watched carefully as the shafts descended. Then I was silent. For long moments I was silent. The vast wood was silent too. But with one eye I watched as the hated sachem stepped quietly to the side of his shield of pine.

"Uncas!" I cried. And he did not move. "Do you not know that it is foolish to stand by the tree in the storm?" Still he did not move, but his dark eyes found my window. Found my one eye. He pulled back his bow and stood, waiting. Waiting for me to rise. I aimed my pistol at his painted chest, but did not raise it to my window yet.

"What if the lightning should fall with the Rain From God?" I cried, hoping to pull Uncas closer by my taunts. But he stood like the pine, straight and unmoving, his shaft pulled tight to his ear. Waiting. Waiting for me to rise. But only my hand rose, and only enough to let my pistol wink its eye at the forest beyond.

I pulled the trigger and the gun belched loudly beneath the still pines. Fire leapt from my window, with the black smoke of vengeance, and I heard the alarmed cries of the warriors who surrounded me. The ball flew, but my eyes could not follow it. I heard the smack of shot against wood, as pine bark splintered on the tree next to Uncas. With an angry bellow, he leapt behind the towering shield.

The rabbits scampered away from my fortress, circling to the east, where they gathered together beyond the bow shot of my arrows, beyond the reach of my lightning. I saw arms flying and I heard tongues rattling in hot argument. I heard the voice of Uncas above the rest. But none came any nearer to me.

Then I remembered my tree. My rope. My tower. What if I climbed into the skies to send rain down upon the heads of the Mohegan? Yes! Let the Rain From God fall!

I pulled myself into the laddered branches of the pine, and hurriedly climbed the boughed steps into the prickly heights. Like the squirrel who runs from tree to tree across the forest ceiling, like the hunter who leaps from rock to rock across the creek, I made my way from one pine tower to the next until I was only four trunks from the quarreling foe. I was so high that I could hardly see them through the thick green, but that was good with me, for here no shaft could reach me from their bows. Yet my own fire—the lightning and the hail of my little gun—could fall like the talons of the eagle upon their heads. I loaded the pistol once more.

"Katanaquat!" I shouted to the wondering pines and the Mohegan hare. And I threw my lightning down upon the foe.

One man fell with my hail buried in his shoulder. He rose again for one moment, staggered toward the nearest tree, and sank to the earth dead. Uncas looked about with wild amazement on his face, and I laughed aloud.

"Katanaquat!" I cried from my safe perch in the pine, and I shook the branches violently. With great shrieks and wild gestures, the Mohegan warriors and their sachem ran as one man to the west.

I had won.

But they will return, I said to myself as I crawled more cautiously across the sagging beams of the ceiling of the great forest. They would come for their dead, of course, and I would surrender up the bodies. But might they not also come with many more warriors? Or with fire upon their arrows? Or with guns of their own? Or while I was sleeping? And so I had not won! For I must flee. Uncas would not let me lie in peace upon my bed.

The thought of running was bitter to my soul, but what could I do? I was now within the pine tower that led down into my fortress. But my heart was hot within me and my eyes were dark—for Uncas still lived! And I did not watch so closely where I placed my groping feet.

My moccasin slipped from one branch, and the force of it pulled my foot from another. One hand held firmly to a bough above my head, but the other merely clawed at the bark before my face. *Hold tight!* I said to myself, even as my feet floundered in open air. My free hand found a branch, but it bent beneath my weight, and I sank for one moment while my legs searched desperately for wood that was good to stand upon. They found some, but I was no longer upright! My body swung sideways and backward beneath the bending boughs, wrenching my first hand loose from the strong branch above me. For a heartbeat I lay in the high branches upon my back, rocking gently upon the needled, outstretched arms, like the papoose of the English in its cradle. I stretched my own arms out to steady me, like the man who lies upon the cracking ice. For what if the ice breaks and sinks beneath the cold waters?

It sank, and I fell, a hopeless plummet through the scraping, stabbing gauntlet. Then all was black.

How long I lay upon the needled carpet I do not know. But at last I pulled myself to my wigwam, for I had fallen within my walls. I rolled myself upon my bed. One leg was broken—below my knee and above it, I was sure—for the bones cried terribly in their anguish. So too did the ribs which had suffered beneath the Talking Rock so many long seasons ago. My eyes swam like frightened fish within the puddle, and they would not be still. My head shouted louder than the cries of many warriors, and it hurt worse than the toothache. My flesh was torn in many places, and it ached to be whole.

I slept. Perhaps a day I slept. And when the light returned to my eyes, I thought for one moment that my fall had been a dream. But with the turning of my head came the thunder of the drums and the storm within my ears. Though my eyes no longer swam, still a mist hung before them. It was not the mist of the morning. A fever burned within me, and I knew that I must find the powwow. Either that or die upon my bed beneath the pines.

I tried to rise, but the spears of my own bones forced me painfully upon my mat once more. Yet I must move! And so I cursed the spears and forced myself upon the floor to face the earth. I would crawl like the snake, if I must, from my wigwam to the Shickasheen. There my boat could carry me over the shallow rapids to the waters of the Pasquiset, and further to the villages of the East Niantic. There I could lie in the wigwam of the pow-wow. There the medicine man could call upon the spirits to heal me.

My parched lips called for water, but the water bag hung higher than my rebel limbs dared reach. It was not far to the Shickasheen, but I had never walked it on my belly.

As I dragged my broken body across the forest floor, my bones cried out in protest, and the thinly scabbed wounds of my fall opened their mouths anew to chew upon the sap-sweet, needled earth. I did not go far before my flesh decried my will and lay at last unmoving. But for the rising and falling of my wearied lungs, I was stone. I slept again.

When I awoke the darkness met me. And the air was heavy with the sickening stench of dead flesh. To my right, only a short crawl away, was the black form of the Mohegan who had fallen to my hailstone from the trees. The beasts of the wood by night, thanking the spirits for their meal, were even now upon him. I could hear the tearing of flesh, the sound of sharp teeth upon bone. Would I be next? Did they not see me? Could they not smell my blood? Sense my presence?

Where was my knife? My bow? My arrows? I had none of these things! For the gods had sucked out my reason while I lay upon my fever bed. I had crawled like the dumb slug which slides upon the rock in the night only to die there in the hot light of the morning. Did I dare to move? Did I dare to rise up as a man and frighten the beasts away? Could I rise?

I must.

With one great pained and clouded effort, I pushed myself from the ground to stand upon my good leg at the foot of the dark, sticky pine. Low growlings rose from the dinner table of the dead Mohegan. Whether they were lynx or lion, I do not know, for the dark threatenings that rumbled in their throats reached my pounding ears in confusion. They might have been man-eating Mohawk for all I could tell! Black spirits—like bats—flitted about my head. *Be gone from me, cursed things! Unless you come to ransom and to rescue me, be gone!*

I could not walk, for my broken leg was a swollen, useless thing. I wished to cut it from me and throw it to the beasts! I sank upon my good knee and slowly moved myself sideways beneath the trees, away from the shadows and the sounds of the gruesome feast. None pursued me. The further I traveled, the lighter the dawning sky became, until at last I heard the sound and saw the sparkling waters of the singing Shickasheen. With the red glow of morning peeking through the pine and the sycamore, I fell in exhaustion beside the river and slept.

When I awoke again, the sun was high above the trees. Though I was out of the thickest pine, my canoe was not in sight, and my fever held me to the earth like the strong bonds that hold the captive to the pole of his torture and his death. My limbs were swollen. My wounds were hot. My back was cold upon the earth. I could not move. I wondered for a moment, *Am I living? Am I dead?*

My eyes were opened to the treetops and the great, bright, hard, unblinking stare of Keesuckquand.

"Here I lie," I said to the sun god, "the slug upon the rock." And my words echoed within my cracked head, like the shouts of the man within the great cavern. The stones fell from the cavern walls and rattled at my feet.

"Here I die," I said to the cool earth around me, "like the branch that is cut from the tree. Here I have fallen, and here I shall rot."

The Shickasheen sang its dancing, mocking song of life as my heart sank like the stone sinks beneath the mud. The warm, blurred colors of autumn crawled like snakes before my eyes. The dreams of the night were mixed with the dreams of the day, and voices rose within me.

"All men are fallen," I heard myself say in the words of Roger Williams. "All men are so fallen under the wounds of their own sins that they cannot rise to God's heaven."

"Who then will lift us from the bloodied earth?" I heard myself ask in the words of Kattenanit my once-son.

Jesus will lift all who would ask him, who know that their own arms are helpless, their own legs useless, their own strength weakness, said the words of Williams. *All who call upon the name of the Lord will be saved.*

Unto thee will I cry, O Lord, my rock. Be not silent to me, for if you are silent, I become like those who go down into the pit, shouted the words of the god-book of Williams.

I am poured out like water, and all my bones are out of joint, whispered the god-book to my fevered soul as Keesuckquand stared down upon my mangled form.

My heart is like the wax of the candle, and it is melted within me.

My strength is dried up like the slug upon the rock, and my tongue cleaves to my jaws. You have brought me to the dust of death.

I closed my eyes.

For dogs have surrounded me, the assembly of the wicked have besieged me, said the god-book to the dried slug.

"Save me from the mouth of the lion," I heard the god-book say through my own cracked, shivering lips.

I slept. I woke.

And though my pain was constant and the fever yet raged, strength was in me to move once more. Did the spirits pity me and breathe upon me in my sleep? Did the god of Williams come to save me from the mouth of the lion? Or did my own medicine return in small measure to put hope into my heart?

I forced myself to the waters to slake my thirst, then returned again to the shadowed shelter of the pines, for I found it impossible to crawl among the rocks and branches along the Shickasheen. Once back upon the needled carpet, I followed the sound of the flowing water southward toward my canoe. The sun was not yet fallen beneath the trees, and if I could but climb into my boat, I might live.

The trees thinned as I neared the clearing where my tobacco grew. Within a small grove of water willow my canoe was tethered. Though my pain roared within me and without, I rejoiced to see the bright green blanket of the open field. I rose triumphantly upon my one leg to stand upon the ground of my deliverance.

Then I saw that my field was spoiled. My tobacco was cut. Great stones from the Shickasheen were scattered upon the soil. Ivy from the sycamore was strewn among the rocks. Worse yet, and the death of me for sure, was the sight of my staved canoe, broken and splintered. The wings of my safety and my healing were clipped. I was fallen again, never to rise.

I sank in sudden and utter despair upon the ruined field, my bones collapsing within me like the bundle of dried sticks that is cast upon the fire.

The fear of death was upon me. And none could help me but the spirits. Yet it was they who plotted my demise!

Let them come then! Let them all come! If they wanted me so badly, let them come as an army and take me! Let them finish their work! I would die as a man!

My heart cried out to the trees and the skies. To the beasts and the birds. To the spirits and the shadows and the ghosts and the gods.

Come then! Come and take me! All or any of you! Come!

If you want this worm, then pull it from the earth! Impale it upon your hooks and cast it in your sea.

Come then! Come and slay me! Sink your knives into my heart. Tear my flesh and gorge yourselves. Take my scalp and hold it high.

If you want this dog, then come and put your ropes about its neck. Drag it home and tie it at your door. But do not make it run this wicked gauntlet any more!

For one setting of the sun, one rising and one setting more I lay, with my face in the damp soil beneath the wet ferns beside my field. I did not rise to eat the berries that grew within my reach, or to pull myself to the stream to drink.

I lay in front of my wall—the wall within my crushed and battered soul. I lay there naked with no weapon by my hand. I waited for the gods to come.

The beast trod around me. The bird settled by me. The serpent slid over me. The spider and the many-legged insect walked my flesh like the hunter walks the forest. The wind passed above me, softly and surely, through the tall trees. But none took my challenge. No spirit fell upon me in the night. No vulture fell upon me in the day. No serpent vision. No demon visitation.

Had they not heard? Had they not seen?

They heard, whispered the wind with the tongue of eternity.

They saw, said the moon with the voice of the Holy Spirit.

I also hear, said the singer of the Song On The Wind.

I also see, said the echo of the light beyond the stars.

And the God Above All laid his shield of mercy upon me.

For a heartbeat, two heartbeats, an infinity within three heartbeats, the eyes of my darkened heart opened.

Who is the fool? I am the fool. For I bow my heart before the beasts of the earth. Before the spirits that crawl by night and the gods that fly by day. Before the memory of my ancestors! Before the souls of my enemies.

Who is the fool? I am the fool. For I crawl like the snake beneath the rotted pine. I hide like the toad beneath the shadowed rock. I slink like the fox into the darkened den.

But I am a man! And a man is something more.

Where is my wall? Where is my medicine? Where is the shield of my soul and the strength of my heart? Like the frightened, wounded warrior before the axe of the enemy, I am fallen to my knees. I beg for life or for death. For mercy or for one last stroke against my shivered, bloodied body. And I ask it of the sun! Of the shadows! Of the darkened souls of the dead!

Where is Katanaquat? Where is the strong one? Where has he flown? I see his hand on the end of his arm, I know its scars. I see his foot at the end of his leg, I know its form. I feel his heart beating in his chest, but it is not his heart! For it beats like the broken drum. It rattles like the broken pot. Broken at the feet of whom?

The One Great God. The God who is Only.

He lives. My soul tells me that he lives.

For though I know the spirits—know them as I know the faces of the leaves of every tree—still they are not him. Though I have seen Chepi in the black heart of the dark swamp—seen him in the eyes of Uncas, in the madness of my dreams, in the storm that howls unending—still that devil is not him.

The One Great God.

He lives. My opened eyes do not lie to my broken heart! They see of a sudden what has always been. That all that lives about me—on the earth and in the sea, in the heavens high above me—sings the same song, walks the same path, breathes the same breath. It fits. And Someone, Something, made it so!

Sowanniu? The Southwest? The great god Cautantowwit? He did not make all this. Only a piece of it. Maybe none. For I do not see his mark upon these trees. I do not see his hand upon these stones.

What am I, that I breathe against the gods? A man! And what is a man but something more than beast and bird? Than sea and all that dwells therein.

Man is lord. Lord of what? Lord of all his hand may touch. And what of all it cannot reach?

The skies. The gods.

And who is lord of them? The great god of Sowanniu? He sits alone in palaces of wood and skin. Stands upon his mountain. Looks afar to watch the children of his making.

But who made him who watches? Who demands the sacrifices and the smoke of Cautantowwit?

And why do the feet of the god of Sowanniu touch the earth and not the floor of heaven? Why does he not fly like Keesuckquand across the blue sky?

And why does Keesuckquand not walk the new path when his eyes awaken? Is he held within the cage? Does he pace within the prison? Is the leash about his neck? Is he not free?

Then who is lord above the sun? Above the stars?

And who is the fool? I am the fool. For I bow to the prisoners of the earth and sky! And though I watch my wall against them, still they strike all flesh beside me. Still they shake me from the tall tree. Who can stop them? Is there one who can stay their hand?

The One Great God. The God who is Only. The God who is Ever. The God who is All Places. The God who made all that my eyes can see. All that my heart can sense. All that lies beyond the door of death.

For what are the spirits to him? Dried leaves and ashes. He coughs and they scatter. He laughs and they fall.

And what is my wall against him? A weak and tiny thing. Sticks and grass. One breath and he fells it. One step and he climbs it.

Yet he does not raise his foot.

He calls. He whispers. He knows my path.

And who is the fool? I am the fool.

Yet I am Katanaquat, and I will not be the fool.

I shall lift my eyes from the dust. I shall wash my face in the river. I shall sharpen my arrows anew. I shall spit in the face of the spirits.

I shall walk my own path.

And if the Great God wants me, let him say so to my teeth. Let him chase me through the wood and put his hand upon my shoulder. I will turn then. I will face him. I will hear his words. Would not any man?

* * *

I opened my eyes to the darkness of the midnight hour. My heart was beating strong within me. My eyes were clear. I shivered beneath the clean sweat that covered me like a blanket of dew. My fever had fled.

I crawled to the singing Shickasheen and laid myself in. With no canoe to carry me, I was my only boat, my pained and tortured limbs my only oars.

The waters moved me slowly through the lands of the Narragansett and into the country of the Niantic. In the village of the sachem Manomik, an ancient powwow set my broken bones and tended to my wounds. I rested there until my strength returned, until my legs could stand and walk, until my arm could once more swing the tomahawk and bend the bow.

I walked with a limp, and stumbled if I all of a sudden turned. I hobbled like the skunk walks, but still I forced my legs to run. For the hunter must chase down the deer. The warrior must be swift upon the path.

But I cursed my leg, for it would not be straight!

Manomik, when he heard me mock my bones, rebuked me. He said that no stone which has rolled for fifty-two summers should moan if one side is now flat.

I ate much good soup of salmon and trout, and I liked it well, but I longed for the clam and the oyster. Yet I did not return just then to the shores of the Great Bay—or to the salt-sands of the Niantic and Nopatin my father—for my heart would not let me. My pride would not release me.

CHAPTER SEVENTEEN

Short Walk through Long Winter

The many seasons of my life thereafter—until the war of Metacomet and the English—were like one long and dreary winter. There was little color to speak of, and little warmth but for the heat of the battle and the hunt. For as the snow covers the earth with one great, cold, white blanket, making all things look alike, so did my cold heart cover and color the days of those long years.

I went north among the Shawomet and the Nipmuc and east among the Wampanoag. But the trees were thinner to the east. The paths were wider with the horses and the wagons of the English. Many English towns had grown up beneath the green. Many ancient wooded giants fell beside the towns.

I did not live alone, for I had learned the folly of the lone wolf. But neither did I stay long with any one people. A summer here. A winter there. My hand to help gather the harvest. My club to help threaten the foe. My bow to help bring down the deer. My chant in the chorus of voices around the fire.

The spirits troubled me some—as they trouble all men—but I spurned them and mocked them openly now, for I walked the path believing at last that the One Great God was god above all. Many thought this strange, but I did not spit at them, for each warrior must carve his own club for the battle. Each man must climb his own hill to see the rising sun.

But the One Great God did not own me. I was my own man still. And I did not go north among the Indians who prayed. For if the One God wanted me, he saw my path. He knew where I slept.

* * *

Nopatin my father was ill unto death, but I did not know, for none could find me. Kattenanit my once-son was with him at his dying and helped to place him in the grave. But I arrived at last too late for these things, and both my father and my once-son were gone—my father to the judgment of his soul, and Kattenanit my once-son to his home and family at Natick.

Silvermoon came to me beside the grave of Nopatin, and wept with me. But I did not speak to her, for how does the man speak to the memory of his once-love when the moon shines through her eyes to lay its cold light upon his conscience and his pride?

Metauhock my girl-child—no longer a girl-child—stood straight like the tall pine beside my once-love, and hummed quietly, mournfully. Our hearts were like two trees, a wide muddy river between us.

Ohowauke my second squaw was gone. Gone to the Mohegan, with Winaponk my son and Quanatik my daughter. This was much smoke in my eyes, and it darkened my days.

Mattachuk my next younger brother begged me to raise my wigwam beside his, but I would not. The rain cannot stay long in one place, but moves with the clouds upon the wind.

Would I run with him against Uncas to avenge some late, foul deeds of the crooked Mohegan?

Again, I would not. For I had no heart to bend the bow against my own son Winaponk who now walked armed beside the warriors of Uncas.

Would I fall upon Uncas if the chance arose to find him alone and without Winaponk?

I would fall as the stones fall upon the bear beneath the deadfall! cried the tongue of my vengeance.

And so I was convinced to stay long enough to attempt once more the life of the hated sachem.

We soon moved into the country of the Mohegan, several war parties of the Narragansett, but things did not go well. For we fought like women throwing stones, and I never once saw Uncas.

Some of our warriors, armed with guns, fired balls into an English house. Others much frightened an English woman by killing a Mohegan who stood at her side. Though no English were hurt, the United Colonies—the English of Connecticut, Massachusetts, and Plymouth—demanded that we pay a fine of many hundreds of thousands of white wampum beads. This was more than the shells upon the beaches of the Long Island! Unable to gather such treasure, and unable to stand in war against the English, the sachems of the Narragansett and the Niantic offered our lands as a pledge for the debt.

But a second King Charles arose in England across the salt sea, and he was not pleased with this deed of the United Colonies. Since the Narragansett—under Pessacus and Mixanno—had once declared themselves the subjects of the English king, the second Charles claimed our lands as his own and put them under the protection of the people of Rhode Island. These were the people of Roger Williams, of Providence and the many towns that stood near and upon the once-lands of the Narragansett. These were our friends.

Yet it was a dark and threatening thing—like the not yet fallen thunderstorm that hangs above the trees—to have our lands so tossed about like the sticks thrown by the gambler in the games.

And our own kings and princes! They were like the waves of the sea, tossed one way and then another by every wind of each new season.

Wequachanuit the son of Mixanno changed his name to Moosup, for he hoped for more medicine from the spirits. Then he changed it again to Canonicus, after our late grand sachem and great king of many seasons past. For the grass had grown long upon the grave, and the name could be used once more. But the name did not change the man, and the Narragansett were no better off.

Scuttop the second son of Mixanno, with Quinimiquet his sister, submitted to the rule of the United Colonies, and then the Narragansett knew not where to bow!

Cojonoquant the drunken one sold much of our lands for strong water. He signed trees away like the brave who surrenders his goods in the dance. But when the tree is fallen, who can stand it up again? Many old and trodden paths now ended at the fences, fields, and farms of the English.

Pessacus, with the squaw sachem and Ninigret of the Niantic, was called often to Boston to explain what they had sold and what they had not, to whom they had sold it and for how much. Soon the English would wish to know which bushes we most often stood behind to relieve ourselves!

Across the Great Bay, in the country of the Wampanoag, our old foe Massasoit was many years departed. Metacomet his son—called King Phillip by the English—was now chief sachem, and rumor was alive in the forest that he was plotting a war of all Indians against the English. Because of this word, which was not yet true, even our friends of the colony of the Rhode Island were suspicious of us. And they wished us to give up our arms.

Can the hunter give up his bow? Can the warrior bury his tomahawk and his knife? Will the brave surrender the gun for which he has trapped many cold waters and traded many skins? Foolish men of the Rhode Island! Does the sailor go to sea without his ship?

Not only were the tallest trees fallen along the shores of the great salt sea, not only were the wisest men gone from among the tribes of the eastern wood, but also many of the best of the first English had now gone to their graves. Winslow. Bradford. Winthrop. Their souls were flown.

And though the blood of the fathers lived on in the flesh of the sons, the hearts of the sons did not beat as the hearts of the fathers. The love that now walked the paths between the towns of the English and the cities of the Indian was not as the first love. Many wounds lay open and unhealed. Many covenants were broken. Many insults were long endured. And many eyes grew dark and narrow within both the wigwam and the stone-chimneyed house.

CHAPTER EIGHTEEN

In the Fire

D oes the rain grow old? Does it not fall in its youth upon the earth to dance and to sleep and then hide in pools and puddles, sinking last of all beneath the dark, warm soil to rest forever in its dreams?

I was an old man now, with seventy-four summers passed since my father lifted his first papoose to the crying skies of the thirsty spring. Among those with summers as many as mine was one old preacher of the English, one who yet walked in love with the Narragansett.

"Katanaquat, do you not wish to see the children of your children as they grow to be strong and good within the villages of the Praying Indians?" asked Roger Williams, as we sat together upon the slatted bench outside his house in Providence. His thick, wavy hair was as white as his sins were washed clean. My own, like my heart, was yet dark as the night.

"I wish to see them grow strong and good within the villages of the Narragansett," I replied. "But it is enough to know that they grow strong and good."

"I wish they could grow strong and good within your villages too," said the preacher. And I was surprised to hear him say it. "For it is not the cut of the hair, or the clothes, or the christenings which make the Christian," he continued. "It is the heart. And the heart can grow strong and good no matter where it walks, so long as God lives in it."

Can the One Great God live in a heart? He who made all things? He who stands upon the stars?

"Job asks for you often," said Williams, for the name of my once-son had changed once more.

A great tragedy had come upon him. His home had burned, and in its flames he lost his first wife and their three children. A terrible thing to fall upon a man! And though I had not known them while they lived, still I felt the heavy ache of loss. The children were of my blood, and the wife was bound by love to the heart of my once-son.

Williams told me of a tale within the pages of the Bible—as the Christians called the god-book—of a great sagamore named Job. The One Great God allowed much suffering to come upon this Job, and the great evil spirit Satan came against him so that his children were slain, his beasts and his fields destroyed, and his wigwams fallen. A great sickness was then sent against his flesh so that he broke out in sores from his head to his toes. He tore his garments and lay upon the ashes of his mourning, but still he did not curse the One Great God. False friends came to Job to counsel him about his wickedness, yet there was no wickedness in the man. Then God himself came to speak with this Job, and he told him of many great things done by his own hand that were greater than all the works of all men. When the Great God saw at last that Job was bowed fully before him, he restored to him his health and his lands and his medicine. And many more children were born to him, so that his last days were greater than this first.

My once-son was now Job, but his sufferings were not done. He married again, and three more children were born to him. But after the birth of the third, his new love took ill. It was not long before he buried her beneath the soil of the Place of the Hills.

Were his latter days greater than his first? Was this not instead the piling of sorrow upon sorrow? For now he was the father without the squaw, and who would look after his house and his children?

"Why does this Great God, whom you call the god of love and mercy, bring such miseries upon the children of men?" I asked.

"Should we not better ask, 'Why does this great God, who is holy and just, not slay us all for our great wickedness?'" answered the preacher. "Should we not better ask, 'Why does this great God, who alone is good and righteous, bother to shower his mercy upon us at all?'"

I thought of Uncas who yet prospered though his heart was the foul swamp of wickedness. And I wondered where justice lived.

"If I were the Great God," I said with eyes squinted to the blue skies, "I would slay the murderer and the thief and let the good man live in peace!"

"If a man so much as holds hatred in his heart, Katanaquat," said

Williams, his old and hardened hand upon my scarred and painted arm, "then he is a murderer. If he so much as covets the possessions of his neighbor, then he is a thief."

I looked at the preacher with wonder in my eyes.

"Then I have murdered men most every day of my long life!" I exclaimed. "And there are none upon the earth who are not murderers and thieves!"

"None," agreed Williams. "And so the question remains, 'Why does the Great God not slay us all?'"

"Do you know?" I asked.

Williams took his hand from my arm and folded his own arms one over the other, like the elder who sits in counsel around the fire. He sank a bit upon the bench and sighed deeply. His eyes closed for a moment, and a strange, contented smile grew upon his face.

"I do not know," he admitted at last, "for God has not told us the reasons why he does all the things that he does." Then the good man sat up straight and leaned toward me, a warm strength within his clean eyes. "But we do know that God mixes everything, both the good and the evil, in a stew of his own will and his own making. And all who love him may eat of his stew with the full assurance of its great and final goodness for their lives and for their souls. Indeed, all who love him desire this stew, whether it be bitter or whether it be sweet."

"And those who love him not?" I asked.

"They eat. Perhaps they enjoy the meal," said the preacher, "but in the end they die. And without hope."

"We all eat the same stew?" I asked.

"We are all in the same stew," he answered.

"And he flavors it with the tears of men!" I grunted.

"He makes his own tears, and the blood of his Son, to fall upon the fields of both the good man and the bad man," Williams replied.

"Rain from God," I said with a grim smile.

"Let his merciful rain wash your soul, my Rain From God," said Williams firmly. "Repent of your ways! Call on him while you may, and he will show you his love in abundance."

"He has my once-son in his hands. Assoko too. Is that not enough?" I said. "And are they bait for my own heart? I will not bite!"

"They would willingly be bait, Katanaquat!" said the preacher. "For though God called them, they walked to him upon their own feet. They answered him with their own tongues."

"Then I will wait for him to call me too!" I said.

"Are you deaf?" replied the preacher.

In many places that I walked, men told me that Assoko searched for me. And that sometimes my once-son was with him in the hunt. But always I was elsewhere. Like the hummingbird, I would stand still only long enough to suck the juice of the flower, and then I would be gone.

Why did I not go to them? Can the brave walk upon the clouds of the heavens? I do not know. But the longer I denied myself their company, the harder it was even to face north.

Fear? I must now say it was so. Fear of bowing. To anyone or anything.

Pride? It is poison. Let no man say that it is medicine and strength!

Metacomet.

The hot and hungry coal lay smoldering upon the warpath beneath the dew-damped leaves. Hard, dry winds blew long and cold above its hidden head. The time was soon for it to rise and break its fast, but not yet.

There were others among the old English who walked in love with the Indians beneath the tall trees.

One was John Eliot, of whom my once-son told me many seasons past. He preached like Williams preached. Only more so, and with great effect among the tribes of the Massachusetts. An English man named Daniel Gookin also walked with Eliot to do good to the Indians. And upon the isle of Capawack—called Martha's Vineyard by the English—lived an English governor named Mayhew. He also loved the Indians. And they so loved him in return that they even called him Father!

I wondered at these things. I knew the love of Williams to be true, but could the hearts of these men be as true? As clean? As straight?

The Indians who prayed now numbered in the thousands. Who could have dreamed it? Conquered not by bow or sword, but by the Great Invisible! My once-son was among the conquered, also was my Fool. My heart fought with me often as I thought of them. Yet though I heard them call to me, I shook their pleadings from my ears like water.

I am Narragansett.

My hair falls long as the hair of men should fall, like the wind-blown boughs of the weeping willow.

My flesh is dark and painted with the colors of the earth, like the many leaves of the warm autumn.

My clothing is little and free about my loins, for Pussough the wildcat cannot run with trousers on his legs!

My moccasins are made of the skin of Noonatch, and they know their way home through the woods.

My wigwam is beneath the tall trees.

My blood flows with the rivers to the bays.

My eyes look east, where Keesuckquand rises each dawn to look upon the mountains and the marshes, the islands and the waters of the great salt sea.

I am Narragansett.

I stand where I stand.

But my heart, like my flesh, was not so firm as in the days of my youth. It ached with the scars of my wounds. It limped as I walked. It softened with the sagging of my muscles. And it staggered under the weight of Uncas my burden. Yet I shouldered my vengeance like the hunter who carries the meat of the dead bear. Though the meat now stank, I had no better food.

My wall was grown over with grasses and brush, and its logs were bent from leaning on them. Yet I manned it still, and kept a wary eye out for the shadows on the other side.

I dreamed of Silvermoon, and I often woke with weeping. Sometimes, too, the fire-dreams returned. While my once-love cried to me from within the awful flames, my heart would break with the emptiness and impotence of my ancient, sleeping arms. Nothing could ease the deep pain that arose within me in the black of the night.

Canonchet the son of Miantonomi my prince was now a sachem of our people, a very hopeful spark within the fires of the Narragansett. The wisdom of his father burned within his heart. The pride of his people was strong within his eyes. The strength of his years was ripe and full. Here at last was the true son of our late prince!

Tatuphosuit the son of Uncas our enemy was now a sachem of the Mohegan, a rotten apple from the tree of the proud Pequot. When he smiled, all men watched their backs. When he spoke, all men heard the smooth and crooked tongue of Uncas his father. When he lifted his war club, even the papoose covered his head. Here was the very reflection of the dark shadow of his father the king!

Tatuphosuit killed one of the lesser sachems of the Narragansett, a cousin of Canonchet, and Uncas tried to buy the life of the murderer. The English were concerned that war might break out. Williams came among us to know the truth.

"If Uncas can pay to have murder undone or have one of his men die in the place of Tatuphosuit," argued Canonchet, "then all our young sachems will be tempted to kill and murder! For then they need only dip into their wampum baskets to clean their own hands of the blood!"

"Your words are wise and true, Canonchet," said Williams, "and I will send them to the English."

We wished only to avenge the murder. This was our way. But the English would not let us. They feared something worse.

To our east, across the Great Bay in the country of the Wampanoag, the dormant fire of Metacomet arose from beneath the leaves and swept in sudden fury through the dry, sun-smitten forest.

A Praying Indian named Sassamon brought words to the governor at Plymouth that Metacomet was planning for war. Shortly thereafter this Sassamon was found dead under the ice of Assawomset Pond, killed by the men of Metacomet.

Three men of the Wampanoag were accused by another who had seen the murder. They were taken and tried in the English way. They were found guilty of the murder. They were hung. Metacomet was enraged, for this was the death of three for one, he said, and now blood must be shed for blood. The fire had been waiting for the tinder!

From Mount Hope, the last of the lands of the Wampanoag, the men of Metacomet fell upon their neighbors the English in the town of

Swansea. Nine English were dead before the French guns of the Wampanoag. And the fire spread.

The Podunk and some of the sachems of the Nipmuc joined King Phillip in his war against the English, and the English rose up from every town to fight back. Even did they come from New York and the Long Island, where many of them now lived, having taken the lands from the Dutch.

Others of the tribes of the Indians were neutral in the conflict. But who can sit still in the forest when the fire burns out of control?

And the Narragansett? We met with ambassadors from Boston, Roger Williams being the tongue for both sides, at the Great Pond between our chief city and the trading house of Smith. There we declared ourselves the friends of the English, having no alliance with the Wampanoag. And if any of the men of Metacomet should flee to us, we said, we would deliver them up to the English.

Yet the English did not trust us, for some of our Niantic rose up with Metacomet, and always the tongue of Uncas spoke against us. The men of the Mohegan sachem, with the Pequot who were among them, fought with the English, and the smoke of the fire rose to fill the trees.

"I would fight," I said to Canonchet the son of Miantonomi, "but these old legs will not run. And these old eyes would not know the foe from the friend!"

"It is a bad war," said the sachem of the Narragansett. "For all men now carry guns and spit fire. Women and children of both red man and white man are dying. None can walk the woods in peace, or sit by the river to fish. Nor can we gather the harvest but with weapons in our hands."

"Our young men are itching for the battle," I said, "and I wish that I were young again."

"You have scratched the warpost long enough, great Katanaquat," said my sachem. "You should be glad to sit and eat soup in the wigwams of your children!"

"Salmon soup is very good!" I said. "But I am glad to eat it alone. And I would rather run with the warriors."

"You would draw us into the fire," said Canonchet, "and I am afraid that our young men will do just that! I have warned the English who are on our lands to fortify their houses or else leave them. For the days are hot and the grasses are dry."

Where does Noonatch run when his whole world is in flames?

The Wampanoag came to us with their women, their children, their old men, and their wounded. Take these who cannot fight, they begged, and protect them as your own. Canonchet received the refugees. For this was our way, though we had promised otherwise to the English. There were relatives and friends among these poor and frightened souls, and who would send the naked out into the storm?

Canonchet was called to Boston. Williams went with him. Though he came home with a coat trimmed with silver, our sachem was angry for the treatment he received.

"The English will think us their enemies if we do not give up our refugees to them," he said. "Yet I say to them now, No! Not a Wampanoag, nor the paring of the nail of a Wampanoag!"

I liked this talk well.

One thousand of the English came against us, with one hundred and fifty Mohegan under Oweneco, the eldest son of Uncas. The mad dog himself, like the Rain From God, was too old to fight, but his children swung the war club for him.

And where was my once-son to lead the Narragansett on my behalf? Praying to the One Great God in a town of wood and stone! Yet even the Indians who prayed were not trusted by the English, and many were taken from their towns and sent to Deer Island in the Bay of the Massachusetts. Was my once-son among them? The Great God knew. I did not.

Like the whirlwind on the water, the English blew through the woods. They attacked the village of the Narragansett squaw sachem Matantuck, burning more than one hundred wigwams, killing seven of our people, and taking nine captives. At least the prisoners of the English would not be tortured at the pole!

Our warriors at last took to the woods against the English and followed them always as the hunter dogs the deer.

* * *

Canonchet moved us onto an island within the Great Swamp, and many of our sachems brought their people to us there. We raised a fort and planted our wigwams within. The fort was surrounded by a palisade like the one I had built within my pines, yet of larger trees, sunken all around into a thick hedge. Two separately fallen cedars created the only bridges by which a man could cross over the mire to the island. Near the largest of these trunks we built a block house to protect the gate. Daily more Indians came among us, until there were many thousands within our walls. Only Ninigret did not come, for he sat upon his lands with some of his people and declared himself the friend of the English and the enemy of none.

The weather was extremely cold, and the cracks in my old bones ached. The ice and the snow were in most places two feet—and in many places three feet—deep. Though the fire of my wigwam was warm, my flesh was not. As each day passed, my strength was less, like the waters that seep from the pouch that is not sealed. Outside my tent there was much activity, and the hope of our people was high. We were many in a strong place, and the powwows and the elders were certain that none could come against us. But I had nothing to say in all this, for I was like the old stump that sits in the marsh while the birds and the bees and the beasts rise up around it in the dance.

Silvermoon came to me. As I sat on my mats like the rotting stump, she came to me.

She fed me soup, and it warmed me as nothing had for many moons. For many seasons of many moons. Still I did not speak.

She sang me songs, and it took all the strength that an old warrior can muster just to hold the tears behind my eyes. I felt I was dreaming, but I knew I was not.

Only my nights were now lonely, and I spent them in wonder. For how could my once-love still care for me? I who had left her so very long ago? Her presence was a gift, while also a torture. For I did not have words, and I feared that my tongue would trip up my feet. Then who would lift me up when I lay naked in my shame upon the cold floor? But I had to speak at last.

The fire burned high, and the pot boiled quickly. As my once-love filled my bowl, I looked long upon her. The years had not been kind to her, but no more brutal than to many an old squaw. Her hair was long as it ever had been, but greyed and brittle like dried and dirty straw. Her form was bent. Her legs were bowed. Her breasts were emptied bags. Her hands, like mine, were crooked things, but strong and filled with purpose as they went about their work. Her face was sagged and wrinkled. But her eyes! Her eyes were filled with the light of the long and lonely night, deep and forever, dark and clean. Something within her was very young still. Or older than both of us. The soul of the woman was stronger than the flesh. And the flesh of the woman was stronger than my own. But it did not matter that my once-squaw was stronger than her once-warrior. For I needed her.

"You are like the mountains and the heavens," I said aloud to the soul of my once-mate. And she turned her eyes upon mine. As if my words were like the air which we breathe each moment without thought, she looked upon me. As if I were Katanaquat the never-left, she looked upon me. As if I had been at her side always and had never ceased to whisper in her ear, she looked upon me. And how could this be?

"Like the spirits themselves," I continued, "you are always here." And I knew then that though I had left her, she had never left me.

"I am an old woman fussing over an old dog!" she said. "That is all."

"Have you forgiven me?" I heard my tongue say. And I lifted my head above my wall.

"Forgiven you?" she answered, like one who does not understand.

"For leaving," I said, and I stood up behind my wall.

"The leaving!" she said, and her eyes flashed. I sat down again behind my wall and turned my eyes into the shadows.

"Those waters long have passed into the sea," she said. "Each day brings new waters down the hillside." And I turned my head slowly toward the light.

God's favor is new each morning, Williams once said.

And is it like this? Like the undeserved and unexpected gift?

"But have you forgiven me?" my tongue said once more, and I stood again at my wall and looked with dim hope beyond the crumbled stones.

"You are an old dog!" said my once-love with a cough and a lonesome smile. "It was a young man who left me!"

"I am the young man still," I cried, "though dressed in the ragged skins of the old dog!"

"Are you?" she laughed.

"Have you forgiven me?" begged the old dog who lied about being the young man.

Silvermoon blew my question out of her cheeks and drew up a stool beside me. With some effort she sat, then looked again into my eyes.

"When you left, I forgave you," she said. "But when you did not come back, I grew angry in my heart.

"I chewed on the meat of my anger for many seasons until only the bones remained. Then I sucked on the bones until even the taste of the meat was gone. Then I carried the bones about in a bag which rattled your name whenever I walked. Then I lay them near my bed and saw them only when I slept or when I woke.

"Then I arose one morning and looked upon the sad, dry bones, and I wondered at my foolishness.

"'These are the bones of a dead man!' I said, and I threw them in the fire."

I sighed sharply. "Then you have forgiven me!" I said.

"I am an old squaw, and I have no teeth with which to chew!" she declared. "You are an old dog! Drink your soup."

She stayed with me that night and all nights thereafter, and I was warm.

The cold settled around us like the wolves that surround the wounded deer, and the waters turned to ice about our island. Should an enemy come upon us now, he would need no logs to cross the mire, for the frost was as hard as the rocks of the earth.

I slept with Silvermoon upon my bed, and dreamed.

The fire-dream! But this time I was in the fire too, crying out for someone to deliver me—deliver us—before the flames consumed us in their fury. I could feel their sharp tongues as they licked my flesh with their molten blades. They roared like the bloodthirsty warrior. They danced like the bloodthirsty brave. And then I heard the distant thunder.

I awoke in a chilled sweat, and saw that my once-love—my once-more-love—was well and slumbering still. My own fire flickered low at our feet. The thunder still echoed in my pounding ears. My heart prayed.

Gunfire.

A few distant shouts in the frosted air beyond our walls.

Cries within our fort. More shots without, but closer now.

The war cry. The warning. The loud and confused waking of four thousand sleeping souls of the Narragansett.

Thunder from our walls and from our block house. Frenzied cries within our wigwams and our streets. The screams of women. The wailing of frightened children. The sound of running, crunching feet upon the frozen ground.

I tried to rise, but my head was heavy and my legs did not wish to support such a weight. I made them obey, and I pulled my cloak about me as I hobbled to my door. I pushed open the mats that separated my sleeping world from the world where men howled. And I saw that the battle was brought to our island in full.

Upon the palisade, many warriors fired their guns and their arrows into the swamp beyond. At the main gate, open but for the brush that was strewn before it, we were gathered in force. I called to a brave who was running to join them.

"What comes?" I cried.

"The English!" he shouted. "With the Mohegan! They are upon the log, beneath and around it! We must drive them back!" And he raced to the front to add his fire to the defense.

"God!" I cried aloud. "Do you see?" And I stumbled back into the tent in numbed astonishment.

Silvermoon was awake and clothed, her eyes filled with the darkness of dread and doom.

"We are many," I said to her absently, and my hands found my bow. I fastened my quiver at my side and selected a shaft. I went to the door once more, and stepped out into the brutal winter air. "Stand here!" I commanded my squaw, pointing to the doorway. "I will return," I said as I started toward the main body of the defenders. "But if I do not," I shouted back to her as I stood in the wild and crowded street, "take my pistol from its box. It is loaded. I have shown you how to ready and to fire it. My knives are also there." I stumbled on, then turned back once more to shout, "But you are a woman, and perhaps no harm shall come to you."

What difference did her gender make within the hot moment of this cold nightmare? Did not the hailstorm descend upon each one alike?

Many of our men were fallen. Others were dragging the dead to one corner of the wall and throwing them like clamshells in a heap. I tried to push my way to the front, but could not for the frantic movement of the many warriors. Some were filling the positions of the fallen at the wall, but many were shrinking back in the fear of death. Guns! Though they made much noise and did much damage, never had the Indian learned to shoot them like the English. Never did we aim them so straight as the shaft upon the bow. Some of our boys had never held one in their hands. I hugged my bow as if it were my life itself.

Suddenly, like the beaver dam before the waters of the strong flood, the wall of warriors at the gate collapsed, and the English entered with their muskets flashing and their long knives waving. We showered them with shot and shaft, but still they came on steadily. And then we fled.

Like the hare before the pack of dogs, the Narragansett raced to and fro in the streets. Many ran into their wigwams to defend their homes and families. Many more passed out the back gate or scaled the palisade and fled into the swamp. Where had I seen this before? Upon the hill at Mystic, when the Pequot died beneath the covers of their beds! I hurried back to Silvermoon as fast as crooked legs could carry me.

"We are undone," I said as I entered the wigwam. "Come and sit at my back upon the bed!" Silvermoon moved behind me, the pistol in her hand. "It will spit only once," I said of the gun, "but men die if it spits true. Hold it out before you like the finger that points. When it points at the foe—and not before!—pull the trigger." I readied my bow.

Silvermoon began to chant, a plea to the spirits. A strong cry for help and deliverance. But it rang in my head like the death rattle in the hands of the powwow, and I asked that the song should cease.

"The spirits love blood," I said. "And my own blood would please them well! We will not beg for their mercy. The night cannot be as the day!"

"Who will deliver us?" asked my love, and I saw that she stood in the fire of her fear.

"The Great God sees," I said. "But if we die, we die." I turned to her fully. "I am with you," I said, choking on the dust of the seasons of my long unfaithfulness. "And you are with me. I would die no other way."

The gunfire had lessened, but the howling of our women and our children was increased. On all sides I heard the shouting of men and the crashing feet of running warriors. A new sound now reached my ears, and the chill of recognition climbed my spine into my head. Fire! The village was on fire. Like the death-blaze of the Pequot on the hill so long ago. On that past day, it was the Narragansett who watched as the Pequot died. Now it was the Pequot and the Mohegan who watched as the fortress of the Narragansett became the pyre of the funeral of a nation.

"Shall we run?" I asked to the fear in the eyes of my love.

"To where?" she coughed as the smoke from without filled the wigwam within.

I bowed my head into my cloak and closed my eyes, for the sting of the vapors was too much and the stench too strong.

We are a dead people, I said within myself. *We can no more escape this fiery fate than the turtle can outrun the dog. Great God who sits upon the stars and captures the hearts of men, even you can but watch as we melt in the midst of this boiling pot! And even if you were to put your foot upon the fire, still we would be crushed beneath your moccasin. We are a dead people. I am a dead man.*

Shouts. Shrieks. Shots.

And laughter.

Who could laugh in the midst of such carnage and confusion!

The door flew open, and I did not even raise my bow. I saw the pistol come up from behind me, but my hand moved to push it down again. We were dead already. Why send more souls to the winds?

Laughter.

I raised my eyes to the black clouds and the dark forms at my door.

Laughter!

"Kat?" said the cracked and aged tongue of the phantom of my Fool.

"Manitoo!" I cried, "It is a god!" And I fell upon the floor at its feet.

The old ghost helped me stand. And three young phantoms under the command of the old ghost without a soul, guided us, carried us— Silvermoon and me—through the red and choking corridors, past the hot and charring palisade, out into the cold and smoking swamp. Hurriedly we struggled through the snow-laden ice and brush that covered the cracked and crusted floor of the Great Swamp. Behind us, lighting our way through the shadows of the dark cedars, was the massive torch of one thousand flaming wigwams of the mighty Narragansett.

PART FOUR

God Is an Ocean

"The most holy God be pleased to make us willing now to bear the tossings, dangers and calamities of this sea."

—Roger Williams

CHAPTER NINETEEN

The Song of Jacob

Was this another world? Had we crossed the Great Salt Sea? Had we passed into the realm of the spirits themselves? Was this Sowanniu? Heaven? A dream?

Men walked as friends, both red man and white. And though the war was on their tongues and raging in the lands beyond the waters of their northern bays, the fear was not within their hearts.

Their streets, their paths, their open fields were free of death and battle. Their homes were filled with prayer and plenty.

This was Capawack. The Vineyard of Martha. The isle of Father Mayhew and his beloved children. Where praying Indians lived in praying towns overseen by praying magistrates and praying sachems. Where non-praying Indians lived in peace with both praying Indians and the English of the island. Where a band of Christian red men, armed with powder and ball and commanded by Christian Indian officers, arrested all agents of Metacomet who set foot upon their shores.

Another world. A dream.

In this world of peace and dreams, beside the warm fire within the wigwam of the Indian preacher Hiacoomes, I sat with the ancient phantom of my Fool. And I found him not the phantom after all.

Assoko was old now, as ancient as I was. But still the waters flowed strong and clean within him. Sitting before him, I felt the strength of younger, warmer days move through his eyes into my tired and tortured soul.

His hair was yet black as mine was—for the head of the Indian does not fade to white with age as the head of the English—and his long locks lay across the rough and wrinkled field of his ancient wound. Had the soul returned? Had the Great God given a new one?

His face had fewer wrinkles than my own, but they were straight and deep, like painted stripes that will not wash away.

His dark eyes were clear like the waters within him. And though I glimpsed islands of sorrow, the stream itself bubbled forth from some secret spring of joy. And this I seldom saw within the eyes of men.

He rocked slowly in his chair, a heavy smile upon his silent, furrowed face. His chair rocked with him, for it sat upon curved slats that let it move like the cradle of the English papoose. I wished to ride in it myself, but I did not beg the privilege.

"Where is my son?" I begged instead of my Fool, for I knew that the two, though separated often by the sea, held hands across the waters.

Assoko widened his bright eyes, bent his brow curiously toward his thick nose, and held his lips tight in the same strange smile. He looked both troubled and amused, and I waited to hear which it was. If either.

"Job is ..." the Fool hesitated, and his rocking stopped while his tongue searched the inside of his mouth, pushing first one cheek and then the other. "Job is not himself," he said at last. "He pretends to be someone else just now. But God is with him." And he smiled, showing large teeth that were broken like the stones of an embattled wall, yellowed like the leaf of the willow at autumn.

Not himself? What kind of riddle was this?

Hiacoomes added his words to those of the Fool, and I was much glad for it, though the understanding troubled my heart.

"Job is spying for the English," said Hiacoomes, "at the fires of the Nipmuc. We are praying for him, for if he is discovered, it will surely mean his life."

"Why does he do this?" I asked. For who would risk his life in such a way? And to what end?

"Many of his people have been hurt in this great war, and he plays the spy for their good, as well as for the English," said the Indian preacher.

"For the English!" I coughed.

"The English are our brothers," said Hiacoomes, "for they pray to God as we do. Jesus makes us one."

"The English have not treated the Praying Indians of Eliot as brothers!" I declared. "For they fence them like their cattle and ship them to cold islands! And if one of these Indians so much as prays for Metacomet in his sleep, they hang the poor dog on a pole!"

"Much wrong has been done by all," nodded Hiacoomes. "God brings this war upon us all for our many sins. When the scales are balanced by the blood of the children of men, the war will cease."

This Hiacoomes. I had heard of him. For he was the first among the dark men of Capawack to pray to the One Great God. Thirty summers and more had passed since he chased the spirits from his door. Now he was the preacher to his people on this island, and an elder much respected among the tribes upon our greater shore. The powwows could not kill him with their medicine. And many of the medicine men forsook the gods and began to pray to God themselves! Hiacoomes was not like Squanto who played his own game. Not like Wequash who ran to the oak along the Pocatuck, but strong with the strength of God upon his head and within his soul. And this I had not seen within the eyes of my own kind. Though I knew that Hiacoomes was only one of many of the Indians who prayed, I had not walked north to look into their souls. And when they walked south, I looked another way. I took another path. I coughed while they spoke. I stood where I stood.

But here I was.

Another world. A dream.

And my once-son was elsewhere again, beside the fires of his enemies. Listening. Watching. Waiting for news that would help win a war for the English. Against the Wampanoag. Against Metacomet the son of Massasoit. Had I not also fought the father of this son? Were not the Wampanoag my enemies as well? Should I not find pride in the courage of my once-son? Should I not pray for him as well?

For what if he were caught in his game? I did not wish to dwell on such things! The pain of my fear was too great. And I found myself wishing that I could walk backward through the seasons to the memory of the quiet green forest with Kattenanit my young son at my side. To play again the father and never to leave.

* * *

"Once more our prince is dead!" I cried to my Fool, though he was no longer my Fool alone, but the Fool of others. The Fool of God. "Words have come over the salt waters, and once more our prince is dead!"

Captured by the English. Shot by the Pequot. Beheaded and quartered by the Mohegan of Oweneco. Burned in the fire by all. His head sent as a trophy to the magistrates of English Connecticut.

But before he died, Canonchet the son of Miantonomi, great prince and sachem of the Narragansett, told his captors that it was good that he should perish at their hands.

"It is well," said our prince. "I shall die before my heart is soft, before I have said anything that is unworthy of Canonchet to say."

Killed but unconquered.

A prince to the end.

My soul wailed unceasing.

The great canoe of Metacomet, filled with the wardreams of many tribes, went slowly down before the guns and arrows of its foes. Many braves died in the cold waters, while the oars of King Phillip drifted to the sea upon the current. Few now paddled with Phillip, but still the sachem fought against the flow. It was sink or swim! For nothing else was open to him now. There was no shore to heave to, no home to run to where he might lick his wounds and fight another day. He must battle on until the night fell long at last upon his sad and wearied soul.

The warriors of the Narragansett kicked their sunken feet as well, hard against the flood. But when the waves fell over them, they did not rise again.

Was I mad? Was my heart bewitched? Were my senses deadened as I walked in this dream? Did some spirit stick a sword into my soul, that it bled upon the floor? Was I too old, and my medicine so weak, that I spilled out like the waters from the cracked and broken cup? I did not know, but I woke often weeping, and only the song of Silvermoon could dry my aching eyes.

*   *   *

"Father?" said the impossible echo of the never-be that haunted my days and confounded my nights in this other world. This dream.

I turned from the table where I sat with Assoko, and my eyes fell upon a man. His face was the face of my once-son, and I hardly knew my own heart for the joy that erupted from within.

I staggered from my seat, like the old dog that rises when his master calls, and fell into the arms of the form of my once-son, my here-son, my never-be.

And I wept like the babe who cannot be consoled though it wakes from its nightmare within its own bed at the breast of its mother, to the song of its father with sunlight to chase every dark fear away.

And my wall fell in pieces beneath the deep waters of wells I had filled with the sands of my sins that now burst forth with new life, like strong water breaks through the skins with the strength of its own desperate arms.

And I knelt on the floor, sobbing long in my anguish. But none tried to lift me. They knew that my sorrow was washing my soul, like the Fool as a child when he wept in my wigwam.

I muddied the floor with the tears of my penance. And nothing could still the hard rain as it fell.

Like the ancient warrior who dreams that he wakes to the morning of his youth, I woke at last upon this isle of dreams.

The Great God called, and I turned to face him. But not as the warrior who faces his foe. For when he called, I turned and saw Assoko of the new soul. And Kattenanit my son, who was now Job of the new name and the new heart, with the children of his loins playing games upon my bed. The bed where I woke to the gift of my once-again lying at my side in the still of the red dawn rising, the memory of the silver moon reflected upon her sleeping face.

I turned and saw Indians praying. Preachers preaching. Strong warriors lifting their eyes to the skies with great songs of rejoicing and tears of repentance.

I turned and saw English men feasting with sachems and laughing with braves as they toiled in the fields.

While the Moon Of The New Green rose out of the Salt Sea, I heard the voice call me, the voice of this Great God. But though his voice called me, I saw not his face and I knew not his form. For my heart did not know how to answer his call. I turned and I looked for him time and again. What more could I do?

"Like Wequash, I am a dead man walking if I find not God," I said to the men who had risen from the grave, as Job and I walked with the Fool upon the shore. "Though I am awake to his call, I still sleep in my soul, and my heart cries to stand from its bed and rejoice with the warriors who sing to the skies."

"It is Jesus for whom your heart cries," said Job, and we stood to look out upon the wide waters that reached to the shores of the smoking lands of the Wampanoag and the Narragansett. "For none other can open your eyes to the Father."

"The Father!" I cried. "And the Son! And the Spirit of Holiness! Three Gods but One God! I cannot conceive of it."

The wind tossed my hair like the waves of the harbor, and the sea called out my name.

"God is an ocean," said Assoko. "Cast yourself in."

I laughed at his words, and reached with sore effort to pick a few small stones from the shore at my feet. I cast them in instead.

We walked slowly on, and I moaned all the more of my prison, my plight, and the darkness of my night.

"God is an ocean," said Assoko once more. "Cast yourself in."

"And if I die?" I asked my Fool, to test his wits. To wrestle with his words.

"It matters not," he said, more quickly than I thought my Fool could answer. And I rose to the challenge, and wrestled with him more.

"It matters not if I live or die?" I questioned, for I knew the Fool loved me, and I longed to hear him say so. My heart begged for his tears to fall for me, his laughter to rise for me, that I might stand from my grave and join him in the strong, mad, joyous chorus of our youth. But I could not tap his sorrow to touch his joy, for his tears sprung now from deeper places. His tongue drew waters from a different well.

"It matters not," he said to my amazement. "For you will be in God."

"Which God?" I cried to Assoko of the new soul. To the winds that blew forever. To the sun that gazed upon us. "The Father? The Son? The Holy Ghost? Which God?"

"All are God," said Job. And it was the voice of every preacher I had ever heard. All of them sitting upon my old wall. All of them speaking as one to my soul. All of them smiling and pointing toward Something that sang like the Song On The Wind to my heart. "And God is all three," said the voices. "But they are one God only."

"One God," I said, trying very hard to hear the Song and understand the words.

"One God," echoed the Fool. And I looked upon him with new eyes. For he was not the fool, but I.

"The Father is a spirit," I said aloud, rehearsing the words that I had heard many times from many lips through many seasons of many years, "like all gods are spirits. Like the false gods are spirits. Like the demons and the angels who fell. Yet he is a great Spirit and the Only True God!" I said. "Is this not so?"

And the voices said that this was so.

"But what of the Son?" I said anew. "How can he be God who walks as a man?"

We stopped again in our crooked march across the salted stones of the shores of Capawack. Behind us lay a wall of tall trees. Beside us, tied to large poles that were buried in the sand, lay several canoes. Before us lay the salt sea.

"Tell me!" I cried to these men who prayed freely and surely to the One who stood outside my reach. "How can this Jesus be God? For he walks as a man!" I looked upon my own wrinkled flesh. "A man, it is said! Flesh, bones, and blood! Blood that he sheds upon the earth! How can he be God? And how can it be he that my heart seeks?"

"God is an ocean," said Assoko. And he reached to pick up a large conch that lay unbroken among the rocks. "God is an ocean!" he said again, more loudly and excitedly. "God is an ocean!" he proclaimed to the gliding gulls and the rolling blue waters. And he began to dance. Upon the sea-washed stones and the salted sand he danced. Not the dance of his youth—though I doubted not it still was in him—but the twisted, near-falling leaps of the old man with fire upon his pant legs. And he laughed.

That wonderful laughter that—even in the smallest dose—strengthens the heart. Then he spun toward me and cried, "Listen!" And he held out the conch to my faltering hands.

I put the great shell to my ear, and I heard the faint roar of the ocean as it spilled into my soul. As I had heard it many times before, this echoed call of the great salt sea. And I thought it to be the souls of dead men who had drowned, souls now imprisoned who cried out to all who would listen to their mournful tales of storms and death and the darkness beneath the great waters. "God is an ocean!" declared Assoko.

"Yes!" cried Job, and I passed him the conch, for his eyes asked as much. He raised it to his ear and listened. "Yes!" he cried aloud once more. "God is an ocean!"

"And who is the fool?" I asked, for this game had me puzzled, and bothered besides.

"What do I hold?" asked my son to his father, lifting up the great shell.

"It is a conch, my son," I said, "though you seem to think it something more!"

"And Jesus is a man, Father!" he replied, "Though you seem to think him something less."

"Yet he is something much more. He is God. Flesh filled with God!"

He lifted the shell to my eyes once again. "What did you hear within?" he asked.

"The sea," I said to my soul and to my wondering heart.

Within the shell, the sea.

A mere shell, but filled with the roaring of the vast ocean. Though my eye could not see it, the ocean was there. This was more than a mere shell upon the wet shore.

And Jesus. He was more than a mere shell upon the wet shore. He was filled with God. And God filled all things! So this Jesus was more than— much more than—a man.

My eyes opened within and my heart rose up to cry, *Manitoo!* But my lips were silent, for the heaviness of understanding was upon my soul. And fear came upon me so that suddenly I shook as though the spring winds had shifted and cold, icy breezes had come to the island to wrap us in winter anew.

And who was the fool? I was the fool!

More than a man, this Jesus! Who could face him? Who could turn and truly face him? For he stood as a man and lived as a man and died as a man. But he was God!

Cloaked as a man, the Great One had walked in the midst of his people. Yet they knew him not! He slept in their wigwams. He gave them his words. He sat at their shores with them. Fished from their boats with them. Yet they knew him not!

And then he let them take him and beat him and lead him to the poles of his torture and his death. A twisted ransom for all their dark deeds.

And for mine.

But then! To the terror and amazement of all men, he rose from his grave. And who can now hide from the wrath of the Tortured One? Did it not fall even now upon Metacomet? Upon the brave men of the great Narragansett? Upon the pale English as they slept in their houses beneath the tall trees of the Massachusetts hills?

Did not God come at last in his wrath to destroy us?

The Son came not into the world to judge it—for judgment is already upon us—but to save it, I heard the voice of Williams say within my heart.

God so loved the world that he gave his only begotten Son, that whosoever believeth in him should not perish. But have everlasting life!

Though the world stands guilty and will one day be burned, God sent not his Son into the world to take vengeance upon it. No! God sent his Son into the world to save it! To rescue it! To ransom each man with the wampum of his Son's own blood.

His love and his mercy are given to lead us to repentance.

Let his merciful rain call you to repentance, my Rain From God. Call on him while you may, and he will show you his mercy in abundance.

I dropped the conch upon the stones, and it broke into a hundred small and scattered pieces, like Jesus was broken, his blood spattered abroad over nations and tribes, over all tongues and peoples. But who can know that he has done this so long ago, unless the news comes forth to him with words that he can understand?

Words of the blood of the God-man. I had heard these words so many times, but seldom with my heart. For they fell on my ears like the seed of the corn that falls upon the trodden path beneath the high wall. And Kaukant came—for the Watcher let him come. And he crossed my wall.

And he ate up the seed before it could find any turned soil within which to root itself.

But my soil was now turned. My wall was now fallen. By the hard hoes and the painful blows of many sad seasons. By the strong hand of the One Great God. And now the words were true words, for they broke through to my heart and slew me where I stood.

I was conquered.

"I see now," I said aloud to the preachers, both English and Indian, who spoke to my heart through the wall that was fallen. "I see now that God can live in a man, and that One Man can be God." I raised my eyes to the men who walked with me upon the salt shores.

"But I must think on these things alone," I said to my son and my old friend the Fool. "Go home, and I will come to you later, for I would sit and watch the sun go down beneath the sea."

I climbed upon a large rock, and sat staring out upon the dark blue waters. "Go home," I said again. "I will come to you later."

The night came upon me, cool and full of strength. The tides rowed in upon the shore and pushed their boats close to my rock. Their hands reached out to pull the sands into the sea, and I watched them gather carefully the many pieces of the broken conch. One by one they took them and they hid them in their bosom, until the shattered shell was fully gone back to its home beneath the deep—like Jesus once more risen to the skies, through the clouds, beyond the sun, above the stars, to heaven, his only true home.

"God," I said to the deep sea and to the heaven high above it, "I come to you."

I untethered a canoe from one of the great poles, and pushed it out into the grasping surf. I threw my best leg in before me, and pulled my twisted bones behind it. A paddle lay on the floor of the canoe. I took it in arm, and with it I shoveled the sea.

Soon I came to the white, rolling breakers. Though they did not rise so high, still they stood as a wall between me and the One Great God. As the dark sea fell upon the face of my boat, I lent all the strength of my arms to the plow.

Forward. Into the surf we plunged, my boat and I, and under the beating we rose to do battle. The wall must be taken, the palisade breached, before the spoils of war could be won.

Then suddenly, darkness came out of the night. Not the darkness when Keesuckquand sleeps and the moon hides—for great Nanepaushat rose full in the black sky—but darkness invisible, cold and contemptible. Serpents on wings and great whales that grin terribly. Chepi and all of his foul and cruel followers!

Why now did the gods come? What was their great contention? Why did the spirits care that one old warrior rowed out into the deep to meet God upon his ocean?

Though the surf coughed in my face and wrapped its cold arms around me, the spirits shouted in my ears so loudly that I could not hear the ocean in its great and constant pounding. My heart filled up with fear, as the waters filled my tumbling, tossing canoe. And the hungry beasts of the swamp of Chepi swarmed over my wall in its crumbled ruins. To slay me? No! To turn me back!

Why? To save me from the monsters of the deep? No! Because they were afraid! The spirits were afraid!

And full of hatred. Full of envy. Full of anger. Full of curses and great omens. Against the One Great God!

From my side of my wall, they cried against the One Great God! And I knew then that my side had always been their side.

My wall was a mockery! Bonds and a prison of my own making. It shut nothing out but the love that warms winter, the grace that delivers.

And the warfare I waged was a sham and a laughing thing. Yet it was true that the spirits would slay men. Slay them with dreams of vain gods and great omens. Set them to warring against their fears and their families. Like the cat with its ball, the gods played with the soul!

My wall! It meant naught to them! They stood on the other side when it served their will. They crawled under when I did not look, and laughed in their loincloths. It is the Great God only whom they fear! I saw this now and heard it loud.

The stronger their warnings, the greater their curses, the harder I rowed through the pale, pressing surf.

"God!" I cried to the rolling black pastures beyond the bright breakers, "I come to you!" And I broke through the surf, and I forced my old arms to drive my boat onward. Out on the ocean where God waited for me.

God is an ocean, said my heart. *Cast yourself in.*

God is a demon! shrieked the spirits who had dogged me all my days. *You will perish forever!* they cried.

"God is an ocean," I said to the shadows. "His Son is a Savior. He walks as a man. Does not hide in the shadows. His blood is my portion. My only strong medicine. God is an ocean. I cast myself in."

And I stood for a moment in my rocking vessel, and I heard the screaming of the lying spirits, and I looked upon the rolling waters, and I saw the fish leap with the moon upon their backs, and I fell into the deep with a great cry of joy.

Perhaps I was the fool for my plunge. But none can tell me so to make me yet believe it. It was what I had to do. I would not ask the same of any other man. It was where I had to stand alone. I know this to be true. He knows it also who pulled me to shore—who lifted my legs and pointed me home.

"I am in God," I said to the wide, astonished eyes of my Fool and his preacher. To Silvermoon and Job my son. To my grandchildren and the praying warriors of the God of the deep sea and the distant stars. And I threw my weary, sea-soaked flesh upon my bed.

"You could have perished!" they said when I told them of the battle. Of the victory.

"If I live, if I die, it matters not," I said. "I am in God."

Assoko laughed. Long and hard like the strong wind blows. I laughed with him, and it made me more weary still. But there is a strength of soul that no weariness of body can defeat. And there is a weariness of soul that no strength of body can sustain. My soul was alive with a life that it had never dreamed of though it had fought for freedom from the moment I was born!

"I am in God!" I declared, and I knew not how it could be so but that the Son of God had covered me at last beneath his bloody cloak. And buried me beneath the waters of the deep, dark sea. And raised me up again a new man though an old man. What a great and awful mystery! It filled me through and through.

"God is not found within the waves of the Great Salt Sea!" they cried.

"No, but he dwells there as elsewhere," I said.

"He is found in Christ Jesus alone," they cried.

"Yes, I believe this and nothing else," I said, "but Christ met me where the fish fly and the porpoise roll."

"It is his blood that cleanses, not the waters of the ocean!" they argued. "The seas will one day boil when the earth burns, but his blood is sprinkled in the heavens!"

"My heart knows your words are true," I said. "But God called me under, and would you not have me to do as he bade me?"

"Once there was a man named Peter," my son told me at last, "whom Jesus called to step forth from his boat upon the sea."

"What did Peter do?" I asked.

"He obeyed," said my son.

Conquered. But whole.

Katanaquat is dead. But he somehow lives anew.

Who is this new man? This man who now lives in the shell of the old man? Who knows all the ways that the old man had known? Who sees in his memory the paths that the old man had tread? Who feels still the pain and the call of the battle, yet who dreams like the child of the peace beyond knowing? Who walks in his stumbling like one who runs laughing? Who laughs in his new heart like one who lies weeping?

Katanaquat is dead. His ancient song falls like cold snow upon the harvest.

Who will sing the new song? The song of victory?

Jacob will sing it. For Jacob means "one who replaces another by force."

My name is now Jacob.

CHAPTER TWENTY

Is This Katanaquat?

The war was not over. Neither the battle on the main shores nor the war within my soul. Perhaps we fight until we die. I think it so. But let all men be sure that one will fight upon their right hand if they bend their knee to follow him. None can sit like Ninigret and say, "I have no foe."

The Moons Before The Harvest brought much sun and no rain, for the Great God held the waters of his mercies in the heavens until the fire of his wrath had cleansed the earth.

On the isle of Capawack, the seas brought some relief on all sides, and we suffered less than those who wandered and feared and fought upon the shores of my once-home. But my heart also thirsted, for the favor of God had been stopped to a trickle by dark thoughts that rose up to trouble me constantly.

Uncas! He lived, and I wanted to slay him. For nothing had driven me longer or stronger. And nothing but vengeance could wash white the black, aching seasons in which I was bound to his shadow. My wounds, in their ancient tongue, cried for the blood of the wicked Mohegan.

Our Father, who dwells in heaven, holy is your name. Your kingdom come, your will be done, on earth as it is in heaven. Give us this day our daily bread, and forgive us our sins as we forgive those who have sinned against us ...

You have heard that it has been said, "You shall love your neighbor and hate your enemy."

But I say unto you, "Love your enemies. Bless them that curse you. Do good to them that hate you. And pray for them who despitefully use you and persecute you."

Then you shall be the sons of your Father who is in heaven. For he makes his sun to rise on the evil and on the good, and sends rain on the just and on the unjust.

But Uncas!

"Vengeance is mine," says the Lord.

Who among men would deny me my vengeance? Who among men could declare Uncas innocent? Who among men would condemn me if I laid his foul, crooked form on the earth amidst his own fetid blood? Few among men! But I strove not with men. I wrestled with God.

My name is now Jacob. And vengeance is not mine to own. For if I take it up in my hands, then it owns me. And no man can serve two masters. For either he will hate one and love the other, or he will hold to one and despise the other. I cannot serve both God and vengeance.

I walked alone to the windy point of Wawitug on the isle of my waking. I took no meal, only water—though Silvermoon begged me to carry some corncake—for I fasted in order to clean out my soul before God.

The cragged stones off the shoreline stood like great, still gulls within the lapping waters, and I sat upon the hillside that fell sharply to the sea.

My vengeance. My anger. My hatred. My warfare. To put it all under the blood of the Son. How could this great deed be done? My soul was weary from the war, and all great deeds seemed higher than the old man could climb.

Come unto me, all you who labor under a heavy load, said Jesus my master, *and I will give you rest.*

With my tomahawk I felled some small trees and stripped them of their branches. Then I sat a bit to let my strength come back to me. With the longest and the thinnest of the branches, I bound the trunks together side by side. This would be my raft. And I dragged it to the rocky beach, and lay upon it for a while.

I slept, then woke to drink some water and to pray.

I limped among the rocks upon the broken shore, lifting one and then another to carry each and set it by my raft. At last I had a pile of stone that satisfied my wants.

I unbound a rope from about my waist and fastened one end to the flat boat. The middle of the rope I set beneath a heavy stone. Then I pushed the small raft out into the waters. It ran to its limit, where, held by its leash, it floated a few feet beyond the grey shoreline.

I lifted one stone from my pile, and stumbled with it in my arms out into the cold, sliding surf. I placed it upon my raft, and went back for another. In this way, I moved the pile from the shore to my boat. And then I sat upon the shore to find my breath and to let my bones sigh for a bit in the warm, smiling sun.

At last I gave the raft more leash, and with a long trunk that I had set to one side, I forced it out further into the sea. I wedged one end of my pole beneath the branches that bound my raft together, and I placed the other end beneath another large stone. Thus my raft was held fast in its place upon the waters. But I knew that the restless sea would not let it sit still for long, so I scrambled in haste—if haste you can call it—to the top of the hill that looked down on my boat and its cargo.

Its cargo! My enemies. Stones of my vengeance. All that cried, *Blood for the blood of my brothers!* Uncas. Wawequa. Tantaquigeon. Oweneco. Corbitant. The tongue of Tisquantum. The Nipmuc. The Pequot. The hated Mohegan.

The blood for the blood of my brothers? None else than the blood of my Savior. Of Jesus. None other.

I stood for a moment staring down at the stones as the small raft bobbed gently beneath its great labor. Then I squatted to embrace a large rock at my feet, and I struggled to raise up its roots from the soil. My bones shouted angrily, *What is this foolishness?*

Silence! I told them and lifted the boulder. I held it up for only a breath, for my arms could not keep it, then I thrust it out from me.

For one blurred moment, the great stone seemed to hang in the air, like the dragonfly as it ponders its next path. Then it fell.

"Who is a God like unto you?" my voice chanted to the heavens and to the Great One who sat above the heavens. "Who pardons iniquity? Who walks on the path past the sins of his people? Who does not hold to his anger forever but loves mercy greatly?

"He will turn again to look with favor upon us. He will have compassion on us. He will conquer our wickedness and cast all our sins into the depths of the sea. ..."

The great stone collided with the raft and its crew, smashing its bonds and plunging its face beneath the blue waters. The logs split apart and fled each from the other. The rocks rolled as one to the floor of the ocean, the depths of the sea.

My burden was covered. My soul was at rest.

Now it only remained to bless those who cursed me. And that would mean walking old paths one more time.

"You wish to return to the shores of the Pocatuck?" asked Job my son, and he shook his furrowed face in sad disquiet.

"Will you go with me?" I asked.

"I will go with you," he said. "And before you," he added. "For I will not let you walk first into the lair of the wildcat!"

"Behind you!" said the voice of my Fool from my back, and my heart was glad. For two may walk safer than one, but who can break the threefold cord?

The sun was a heavy club upon our backs as we sailed the still waters from the Vineyard to the shores of the Niantic of Ninigret. We saw from our boat that the leaves of the trees fell like dried leaves of autumn, though it was yet summer. The Weekapaug ran low, like the creek that is dammed near its source by the beaver. But her waters were not in the hills where the man could break their prison and let them flow free. They were held in the heavens, unwilling to fall.

At Nianticut on the Weekapaug, Ninigret entertained us well and gave us much news of the war. Though the tents of Ninigret were left unmolested, the country to the north and east was much in flames. Many wigwams, many fields, many forts, and many houses were destroyed. Much blood was upon the earth, and still men fought.

Phillip was loose in the woods, but his lands were in the hands of the English.

Natick was no more, and its great meetinghouse lay as ashes that blew with the dry wind to the sad Charles.

Providence too was burned. And I would sit nevermore at the old table of the gentle preacher Williams. Though his love for the red man had saved his own scalp from the knife, his labors were gone with the smoke of the fires that devoured the town on the lands he was given from the hand of our grand and gone sachem Canonicus.

Many of the Narragansett were fled to Ninigret, who took them in and gave them refuge from the fire.

Fire upon the earth. Fire in the heavens. All men thirsted for the waters of peace. But the blood was not done, for the sins were not paid for. Jesus the Savior is also the Warrior whose sword has two edges. Sodom once burned, with Gomorrah its sister. This is the judgment of God, I am told.

In the land of the Mohegan, Uncas sat upon his rich mats. There he drank strong water and cracked fleas with his rotting teeth. To his north upon his west, near the English town of Norwich on the Quinnibaug, a small band of praying Mohegans lived upon lands given them by James Fitch, a preacher of the One God. It was to the praying Mohegan that we traveled with several of the men of Ninigret. And it was there that we met Fitch, for he came among them often.

"This is Katanaquat?" asked the preacher, looking upon the old man who hobbled in my moccasins.

"He is now Jacob," said one among the Mohegan who prayed. "For he is now our brother in the One God."

The preacher spoke to me in the tongue of the Indian, and my heart heard his words with much gladness.

"Jacob you are?" he asked.

"Jacob I am," I said. "Though I was The Rain From God, now I am dried up by God in the heat of the fire of my trials. Now I am new like the silver that English men burn from the black stone. Yes, Jacob I am."

"Then Jacob you shall be, though many will think you are sprung from the earth! For they will not believe that you were Katanaquat," said Fitch. "Uncas must know this!"

"For this I have come," I replied.

"You must not go to him," said Job my son. "But call him instead to ourselves in this place. For though Fitch believes that Uncas will marvel that you are alive and a Christian, I fear that the sachem will marvel but a moment and then set his dogs upon you!"

"If I live, if I die, it matters not," I said. "I am in God."

Assoko rocked gently upon the yellowed grasses beneath the dried and cracked shelter of the shedding chestnut. His face was empty of thought, but that was no clue to his heart, for even the face of the waters of the teeming sea may sometimes lie like one who sleeps. But under the skin there is much that moves waking.

"Kat?" said Assoko at last, his eyes still dim with the hot, lazy shadows of late noon. He looked to me, and puckered his thick lips while flaring his nostrils. "It is not good to test God," he said.

Uncas did come to us, not for the rumor that Katanaquat was here—for he thought it a ruse—but because of the drought.

The streams were but damp mud in some places in the country of the Mohegan. Crops spoiled in the fields. Apples fell withered and hard from the trees like the leaves that fell early and dry. And men did not hunt who were fighting at war.

The powwows danced themselves to sickness, their own waters foaming from their demon-driven limbs. But no rain fell.

So Uncas walked north with a pack of his people to ask the God-preacher to call on the God of the English.

I saw the mad dog coming as I sat beneath the chestnut with my Fool. I groaned within, for his sight was not a good one to my soul. Assoko sat motionless, as though he were dreaming, but his eyes fell like shafts upon the old sachem.

I rose, for I would not sit—not in this moment—as the hated-forgiven Mohegan walked near to our tall tree. His eyes were like watchmen—the eyes of the serpent—that darted about while his head was held upward. His chin pointed out like the gun when it thunders. His hair was cut back from the sides of his head and gathered in one long, black tail behind him. Two strings of red wampum encircled his neck and fell down to his black, painted belly. A thin knife at his back was his only weapon. His arms were still strong, though his legs were bent sideways.

He walked as he always had, no man before him, a curious swagger, though slowed by his seasons. And spread out behind him, in numbers of fifty or more, were the women and warriors who came with him now on his humbling mission.

He saw me, but his eyes were not quite as keen for his long years. Thus he did not know that an old enemy stood in the shade of the chestnut. I was readied to cast the name of Uncas before the procession, when Assoko suddenly threw back his head and wailed.

"Weak woman!" cried the heart of the young warrior within the frame of the old Fool. "God!" cried the heart of the old Fool within the soul of the young warrior. And Uncas stopped dead in his tracks.

The old sachem swung his head toward us like the hunter turns his bow upon the prey. His dark eyes opened like the frog upon the swamp flower, and his mouth fell like the deadfall. He stood like stone and studied us both in his trance.

Arrogance burned hot upon his cold visage, but the fire was slowly tempered as the lines of fear rose white within the wrinkles of his ugly face.

"Warriors of the Narragansett!" bellowed the frozen cavern beneath the sharp nose of the stunned sachem. And the guards of the Mohegan pushed swiftly forward through their ranks to stand before their king. The startled braves searched the land in vain for the warriors of the Narragansett. Their gaze beheld only two old and crooked hunters who looked on them with tired eyes. Assoko rolled his head from side to side, moaning and praying. I stood with my arms crossed, my back leaning slightly against the tall chestnut.

"Uncas of the Mohegan," I said quietly. "You yet live."

"I do," coughed the mad dog in his wonder. "And is this Katanaquat?"

The Fool threw back his head and laughed, and the guard of the sachem drew back with mutterings. "This is the Fool!" cried some old men among them. "A ghost!" screamed the women. "A god!" wailed the warriors.

But Uncas sighed deeply and sank his old roots into the dry path.

Some of the Mohegan who prayed came forth from their wigwams and lowered their eyes at the sight of the sachem.

"Is he God?" I shouted to the praying Mohegan, "that you bow to the shadow of the old man?" And I shook my head.

Uncas snorted. But I held up my palms.

"This is not Katanaquat," I said to the eyes of my ancient foe. "And it will not bite." I bowed my head too, but only to wipe clean the tears of my victory. Hatred was gone, and I could not believe it!

"You mock me," said Uncas.

"I do not," I spoke cleanly. "Your own deeds do mock you before the eyes of all who have watched you in all the long seasons that God has had mercy upon your black soul." And I closed my eyes for a heartbeat. "As my own deeds did mock me as well," I added.

The men of the Mohegan stood as still trees and waited for words from their sachem the mad dog. But he did not bark.

"I go to Norwich," said Uncas calmly, though beneath his calm the storms of shame blew strong, "to ask Fitch to call on this God who has watched me! This God has a good ear and hears when sir Fitch sings his Song."

"He hears all who sing his Song," I replied.

"And now you sing it too?" asked Uncas.

"Do you not remember the Song On The Wind?" I asked.

"I remember the dirge in the storm," he answered, "that sank into my spirit like the poison arrow!"

"Your heart was poisoned already," I said, "for the arrow was clean when it flew."

"I sing my own song," he replied.

"As I do," I said. "But now it is a new Song, and the melody can make the foulest clean."

"You chant and crawl in fear to the God of the white man!" Uncas spat.

"I sing and stand in gratitude to the God over all men," I countered.

Uncas moved toward me slowly, his old fists white and clenched and shaking, his purple lips moving without words. He stopped within a pace of me and whispered to my face, "I should have killed you in the summers when our bows were green and our moccasins were small."

"And I should have killed you a thousand times for the smell of your breath within the wigwams of the Narragansett," I replied, looking deep within his eyes. I saw no spirits. Just the carnage of the battle of the spirits. The ruins of another proud wall that thinks itself strong. The darkness of the heart that beats only for itself. "But," I said, "I can truly wish that we were brothers on the same soil. Friends and not foes." I swallowed heavily, for the words were strange waters on my tongue. Yet they were clean.

"You lie," said the black heart.

"All men are liars," I said to the carnage of the spirits. "But not all men lie."

He stared long upon me, then turned to the Fool. Assoko stared back, a stupid smile upon his sad face. I wondered what he saw. Then he stood—and Uncas stepped back, his eyes fastened to the scar on the head of Assoko.

"New soul!" shouted Assoko, pointing to his head and then his heart. "Old man!" he bellowed, striking his chest with his fist. And he burst once more into laughter.

Uncas pulled himself higher, his eyes wide with wonder. The Fool laughed the harder, and fell at last upon the ground in his private joy. There he rolled and shook and bellowed while the tears streamed from his eyes like waters over the falls.

I could not contain myself—for this was my Fool!—and I joined in his revel. I sat down beside him and laughed like the madman.

"Come!" cried the conquered sachem of the Mohegan, and he led his startled, staring people through the village of the Praying Indians and into the forest beyond.

"If God should send rain, will you not say it was your powwows?" probed the preacher of Norwich.

"No," replied Uncas. "We have done all that we can, and it is of no use."

"And if God should send rain," said Fitch, "will you tell all your people that this is the hand of the true God?"

"I will tell them so even now," said the sachem. And he made a great speech to the Mohegan who attended him. And he told them that if rain should fall that it was not the powwows who called it, but Fitch through his prayers to the God of the English. Yet this was not faith in the heart of the sachem, but wampum for rain. Would not all pay the same?

A fast was appointed in Norwich to entreat God for rain, and the praying Mohegan—Assoko and Job and myself among them—came to the town to join in the praying, for the drought had brought even more suffering among the English than among the Mohegan.

I searched for Uncas as the dawn of the fast began. I found him standing tall and silent beside the wide path as the penitent fasters walked past him to join in the prayers of the day at the meetinghouse.

"I pray now for rain for you, my sad and bloodied old foe," I said to the sachem. "For the Great God sends his good rain upon all."

He did not speak, but looked beyond me to the cloudless skies.

By midmorn the heavens were yet clear, and none could say that God had heard us.

At noon the skies were yet as dry as the dust upon the thirsty streets, and no omen testified anything otherwise.

By evening the bright face of Keesuckquand was yawning, but nowhere above us could even the smallest sign of rain be found.

When the sun at last was setting beneath the distant hills, and the day of prayer was ended with the songs of many singers, a wee handful of white and purple clouds rose silently above the red horizon. Yet no waters fell through the long, hot night.

The next day the sun hid above the thickening mat of gathering grey, and though the air was heavy with moisture, the heat lay upon us like the skin of the bear.

"The rains do not fall!" lamented Uncas as the dark day rolled over into the black night. "But if they do," he declared, "it will be for the prayers of the people of Fitch." And he hoped that his flattering words would yet win him one more bag of medicine. One more bottle of strong water.

On the third day, the skies opened up in their mercy, and the rain fell gently but strongly from dawn to dusk. The Quinnibaug rose more than two of the feet of the grown man.

I met him in the falling rain, my ancient foe of the black heart. The waters of the heavens flowed over his old, painted face, and I thought them to be the very tears of God. The wet dog had no words for me, and his eyes were empty.

"My name is now Jacob," I said to the ghost of the man I once hated. "And this," I raised my hands to the mercies that showered upon us from the bright grey skies, "this is *katanaquat*. This is the rain from God!"

Son of My Father

W hen the New Moon rises, it sheds no light, but hides in the palm of the great hand of God.

Metacomet is dead. The judgment is over. Sad feet kick cold ashes beneath the tall trees.

Ninigret smiles, for his people grow strong again, swelled in their numbers by the herds of the lonely Narragansett who wander from our ancient lands into the country of the Niantic sachem.

Uncas is gone but a summer ago. Gone to his just rewards. Gone from the earth. The air smells no sweeter.

Williams is gone but a summer ago. Gone to his just rewards. Gone from the earth. "Life is a brief minute," he once said. "Eternity follows." We will look for him on a longer, brighter day.

On the seventh of August, in the Year of Our Lord 1684, in the eighty-second summer of his long life, Jacob Katanaquat of the people of the Narragansett, son of Nopatin his father, died in great peace and in the grace of our Lord Jesus Christ in Christiantown of the Praying Indians of the isle of Martha's Vineyard.

At his deathbed were his ancient friend Assoko, his faithful wife Silvermoon, his eldest son Job Kattenanit with his wife Mary and their four children—John, Patience, Joy, and Jacob.

Also with him at his passing were the Reverend Mister John Eliot; the Major Daniel Gookin; the Reverend John Mayhew, the grandson of our beloved and lately departed Thomas Mayhew; and many of the Christian Indians of the island.

The words of the long path of Jacob Katanaquat, when written down here, make a book much too small to tell all things fully. But that they are true I declare by him who is true, for they stood before my eyes at certain times in former seasons, and they fell upon my ears in the last days of Jacob my father who told me all things.

I am Job Kattenanit, son of my father Jacob Katanaquat. This is my pen that has written his story. The words are my father's. The glory is God's.

One more tale waits for the telling, for my own path was walked over far different hills than the trail of my father. I will pen it for you, Lord willing, on some other day.

Though some of the Indian terms (and some of the archaic English terms) that are used in the story are easily understood in the context of the tale, several items may need some explanation. This short glossary will help you better enter the world of seventeenth-century New England. In a few cases, pronunciations are included for those words that are most apt to be mispronounced. All the Indian terms and names listed here are of the Algonquian languages of New England. Algonquian is not a tribe, but a linguistic classification of many tribes (including the Narragansett). Some of the following words are Narragansett; others originated in the varying tongues of neighboring Algonquian peoples.

assoko Literally "a fool" in Narragansett; one who is weakminded, retarded, or simple. As applied to this principal character in *The Rain From God,* there is no negative moral connotation attached to his name. The Indians, not understanding mental retardation or mental illness, had superstition concerning fools and thought them to be especially close with the spirits. Our Assoko is a unique fellow who, though retarded, is "no fool."

backbaskets Small reeded, leather, or wooden baskets, belted and worn on the back. For carrying food, pipe and tobacco, and other items.

beaming The second-to-last step in the week-long process of tanning an animal hide. After a fresh hide was scraped, washed, soaked in water, wrung, dehaired, and cured (in animal brains), it was then stretched upon a large frame of saplings and poles to prepare it for beaming. Indian women accomplished the hard work of beaming by forcibly rubbing the whole surface of the hide with a long-handled tool that had a working end of stone or horn set at a right angle. This both stretched and softened the hide. When beaming was done, the hide needed only smoking (over a smudge fire of green or rotten wood) to prepare it for its many, varied uses as clothing, wall coverings, weapons sheaths, etc.

Cautantowwit (caw-TAN-tow-it) The Narragansett creator-god who was believed to live in the Southwest and oversee the affairs of men and judge them at death.

Chepi (also *Hobomucko*) The devil of the Narragansett pantheon of gods. Not totally bad, Chepi nevertheless was associated with doom and gloom. He was also the patron spirit of the powwow, appearing in visions most often as a serpent (a very old trick!).

deadfall A common way of trapping animals in the seventeenth century. A heavy weight of logs or stone was propped above a trip log upon which meat or fish was attached. When an animal—usually a bear or a wildcat—attempted

to eat the bait, it would jar the trip log, and the logs or stone would fall
upon the animal, trapping and often killing it.

fire pot The fire pot was a way to carry smoldering fire in a world without
matches, flint, or steel. A pea-sized ember was laid in a clay-lined shell that
was filled with powdery rotten wood. The ember would start the "spunk"
smoldering, and the fire pot's airtight case kept it burning very slowly. The
shell was carried in a bag and would keep fire all day.

foot ball The author's invention, so named in our novel as a distillation of any
number of games the Indians played with balls of stone or wood—from a
form of kickball or soccer to lacrosse—upon the long shores of the sea.

harvest games (and Indian games in general) The Indians were very glad for any
leisure activities that pulled them away from the grueling daily work of sub-
sistence. But their games were not all idle fun. Among young boys especially,
many competitive games were played in preparation for manhood and war.
Running and wrestling, throwing sticks and rolling stones, outwitting your
opponent on the playfield—all helped develop the skills that a young boy
would one day need in the battle. But everyone enjoyed the games, and
much gambling accompanied them. There were special times of extended
games (such as at the harvest) in which everyone was involved in the
action—the men on the playing field, the women and the children in the
grandstands, and many others laying bets on the side.

Kaukant Literally "crow." In Narragansett mythology, the crow brought the
Indians their first corn seed from the gardens of Cautantowwit. In gratitude,
the Narragansett allowed the crow (but no other bird!) the freedom of the
fields. If only Kaukant could repay them for his centuries of mooching!

Keesuckquand Literally "the sun."

manitoo General term for a "god." Besides the specific gods for whom the
Indians had specific names, this term was often applied to any object, per-
son, or happening the Indians found extraordinary. The English and the
Dutch, when first encountered, were considered manitoos.

medicine (of Latin and Middle English derivation) The supernatural powers and
protection given to the Indians by the spirits.

Miantonomi (Mee-AN-ton-oh-mee) Historically, this great sachem of the
Narragansett is among the most famous of the New England Indians. Still
quoted today, his words and recorded actions show us an intelligent man
who did his very best to walk in peace with the English while leading his
people in their ancient ways. He seems to have considered the truth of
Christianity and was a close and personal friend of Roger Williams. His murder at the height of his political power—at the hands of Uncas' Mohegan
Indians and by the order of a few misguided English at Boston—is a black
moment in the history of mid-seventeenth-century New England.

moccasin game The most common sit-down game among the woodland
Indians, it was played by two teams of three men, usually with a large audi-
ence. A game could last for days or until one team lost everything but their

breechcloths. It was played with four moccasins and four small objects that were identical except that one was inconspicuously marked (the objects might be pebbles, foot bones or fruit pits—and in later days, lead bullets). Teams took turns guessing under which moccasin the opposing team had placed the marked piece. Score was kept with wooden tallies.

Nanepaushat Literally "the moon."

Narragansett "People of the little points and bays" or "at the small narrow point of land." Inhabiting lands which encompass most of present-day Rhode Island, the Narragansett were the principal power among the New England Indians after the Great Dying—a plague which decimated the coastal tribes of New England a few years prior to the coming of the Pilgrims in 1620. Untouched by the sickness, the Narragansett were able to subject many previously independent tribes—including the Wampanoag, whose chief sachem, Massasoit, celebrated the famous first Thanksgiving with the colonists of Plymouth.

nokehick (or no-cake) Pounded, parched Indian corn. This simple food was the traveling sustenance of the hunter and the warrior. It was mixed with a little water, hot or cold, and made a tasty and fully adequate meal on the trail. Every brave carried a small basket of nokehick at his back or in a hollow leather belt about his waist—usually enough for three or four days. But forty days' provision could be carried by any warrior with little inconvenience.

papoose Literally "a child."

powwow The medicine man or shaman. The term has since come to mean any great tribal or intertribal gathering. In *The Rain From God,* "powwow" is used only to refer to the medicine man.

sachem (SAY-chem) Chief, king, or prince; the head of a tribe or village. There were traditionally two main sachems among the Narragansett, one older and one younger. This co-rulership was unique among the New England tribes, but every tribe had at least one chief sachem, and all large tribes had many undersachems who ruled smaller groups of Indians.

sagamore Probably another name for sachem, but used sometimes in the same context as an undersachem or a lesser tribal leader (which is the context in which it is found in the novel).

snowsnake A winter game played with a long stick of maple that was very smooth and tapered near its "tail." The head of the stick was carved into some semblance of a snake. The game's object was to slide the snowsnake down a long, level track of packed snow. Men took turns flinging their snowsnakes and the distances were marked. Whoever slid his snake the farthest won all the snakes. There were also many side bets.

Sowanniu (so WAN you) Literally "the Southwest." Traditional dwelling of the great creator-god Cautantowwit. The New England Indian believed that his soul would fly to the Southwest upon death and there be judged by Cautantowwit. A great dog guarded the gates of the courts of Cautantowwit, and only those souls who had lived righteously were allowed to enter those gates. In *The Rain From God,* the word has been capitalized (Sowanniu) and used in a way to communicate the stronger sense of place and permanence (like heaven or paradise) that the Indian attached to it.

wampum (from the Algonquian *wompompeague*) Small beads made from the shells of clam and whelk. The beads were white and—more rarely—purple ("black"). They were woven into belts or strung on leather thongs. *Wompompeague* literally means "white strings." Wampum was the major trade currency of the New England Indians, both among themselves and with the Europeans. It was also an integral part of all treaties, ransoms, and various ceremonies. Wampum used in this way had "meaning" spoken into it, and people recalled the events by "reading" the wampum. The Narragansett and the Indians of Long Island were the principal producers of wampum.

Weetucks (more often called *Maushop* by the New England tribes) The human-like giant of Algonquian tradition. He was believed to be responsible for the creation of Nantucket Island (he dumped the ashes of his great pipe into the sea, and Nantucket was the result). He was a good creature and had been a great help to the Indians, chasing whales ashore for them to slay and eat. He lived on Martha's Vineyard at one time, and cooked whales whole over the smoking volcano that once stood on the isle. When too many Indians began to populate his lands, he packed up his backbasket and headed into the land of legend—never to be seen again.

wigwam The principal home structure of the New England Indian. It was built in two main forms: the domed wigwam (which was the most common) and the conical wigwam (which is more like the teepee of the western Indians). Constructed of poles and covered most often with bark of trees and mats of cattail rushes, wigwams could be moved from one location to another. Tribes and families moved several times yearly according to the seasons and the need to be near the harvest, the hunt, the fishing grounds, or the shelter of a wooded valley in winter. Sometimes wigwams were moved simply because they became infested with vermin and needed to be set up anew on cleaner ground.

The Muddy River and How I Swam It

For the average reader of modern historical fiction, the river of objective history runs wide and muddy, often clouded by the opinions and imaginations of the author of the work. Sorting truth from tales is not an easy matter, even for the historian who blows the dust from ancient tomes to get the news and views of history's original correspondents. Nothing short of the Bible is inerrant recollection of days past. All history walks with feet of clay. We know in part and see in part.

Yet the story of Katanaquat, though fictional, is based upon history as best I have seen it through the dark glass.

Characters

Some of the people you meet in these pages are real people whose stories were first told in the journals, diaries, pamphlets, books, and town records of the seventeenth-century New England colonists. You will recognize a few of their names. Hopefully you will know them better when our tale is fully told.

Among those of our principal characters who truly lived and walked the wild woods are: Canonicus, Mascus, Massasoit, Miantonomi, Tisquantum (Squanto), Sassacus, Uncas, Wequash, Kattenanit, Thomas Dermer, Roger Williams, Edward Winslow, and William Bradford.

Many other players are also resurrected from the dusty tombs of history, including most of the Indian sachems and all of our named English cast.

In all cases—though I have invented eyes and noses and lips and mannerisms and figures of speech—I have attempted to portray the character of these folks as the record best reveals it. The brave Miantonomi was assuredly a good and intelligent fellow. The cunning Uncas was undeniably a wicked and perverse man. The outspoken Roger Williams was fully a compassionate and courageous Christian.

In many cases, the narrative is woven through with the recorded words, thoughts, and sentiments of the historical characters themselves.

In some cases, the portraits differ greatly from the popular notions that many entertain today. My options were open. The waters were muddy. I picked my shoreline. I swam.

Many of the people in our tale—like Katanaquat himself—are the product of the author's historically informed imagination: Assoko (the Fool), Askug, Mishtaqua, Nopatin, Taquattin, and others. Yet I have made every effort to be historically and culturally accurate in the depiction of all tribes and peoples. Having done so, the picture that has emerged is one that doesn't quite fit the frames of either the politically correct or the traditional views of Native America and the earliest periods of English colonization.

Language

Since our narrator is a Narragansett, I have sprinkled a good deal of the Narragansett language (with many other Algonquian words) throughout the text. Most of the places mentioned by name—the bays, rivers, towns, and villages—are real, and I have used Indian place-names (in a spelling of my own choosing—because spellings differ widely in original sources) wherever I could identify them. The Indian names for many animals, as well as objects in nature, also appear throughout the book. In many cases, the names appear with an initial capital letter (Kaukant the crow; Keesuckquand the sun; Pussough the wildcat; Noonatch the deer) in order to personify these things in the way the Indian often did. My intention is realism and a strong sense of the Indian culture. My hope is that the meanings of the words and phrases will be quickly understood in the context and normal flow of the story.

And because pronunciation may be a harder hill to climb than the definition of the words themselves, I have chosen spellings that should make things as easy as possible for the modern reader.

Remarkably, many of the native phrases that have found their way into the popular Indian vocabulary of the twentieth century—and which many of us associate more with the Indians of America's west—are Narragansett (and generally Algonquian) in origin: i.e., *papoose, wigwam, moccasin, wampum, powwow, manitoo.*

Some other terms—like *sachem* (an Indian chief)—though in common use in New England literature during the seventeenth and eighteenth centuries, have fallen out of use. Even some of the meanings of the more familiar terms have changed through the years. The Narragansett language itself died before the middle of the last century.

For the names of my fictional Indians—with one major exception—I dipped again into the ancient well of the Narragansett tongue, utilizing Roger Williams' marvelous conversational dictionary and Native American "tour guide," *A Key into the Language of America.* In that volume, published in London in 1643, Williams chronicled the culture and language of the Narragansett Indians whom he loved and among whom he lived.

The major exception is the Indian character Silvermoon, whose Anglicized name is borrowed from a young Narragansett woman living in Rhode Island today. The teenaged daughter of Roland and Starr Mars, Silvermoon Mars is the same age as my oldest daughter, Jandy. Her name seemed a natural for the story.

Katanaquat, our narrator and main player, has a name that combines the phonetic beginnings of *Cautan*-towwit (the Narragansett creator-god) and *ánaquat* (rain), creating the fictional appellation *The Rain From God.* Apart from Katanaquat (and Kattenanit—the son of Katanaquat—an historical character whose name I do not know the meaning of and therefore invented a meaning), whenever an Indian name or word is followed in the text by an explanatory English word or by a phrase such as "which means ..." you can trust the word and its definition to be linguistically accurate.

Culture

The culture of the New England Indian is widely documented in seventeenth-century sources. I have tried very hard to walk in Katanaquat's moccasins, thinking his thoughts and speaking his heart. I have tried very hard to reconstruct his physical and spiritual worlds, his tribal life and family relationships, from the details that are chronicled in the volumes of history. As many of us know, the politically correct views of the late twentieth century do more to revise and reinterpret history than they do to accurately depict the "way it was." Folks in days past simply did not think like we do today. Should that be such a surprise?

The New England Indians did not worship one Great Spirit as is often conceived. They had a virtual pantheon of gods, called *manitoos.* They had gods for men, women, children, animals, sun, moon, fire, water, rain, snow, directions, seasons, winds, houses, crops, and even colors. Yet, remarkably, there is a distant memory of the One Great God in their mythology: a Creator and Provider who made man and woman; a garden; a fall of sorts; a flood. The shadow of the truth often lies long upon the land even after the sun has fallen below the hills of time.

Of the spirits and the gods, the Narragansett had three who reared their heads highest:

1. *Cautantowwit* was the distant and unseen creator whose great gardens and green courts lay to the Southwest. He was mostly benevolent, yet often sent misfortune when angry with his human subjects, and was the final judge of each man. At death, the soul (if not hindered by the direct efforts of the spirits or of living men) flew to the Southwest. If it had been good during life, it would be allowed entrance into the courts of Cautantowwit. But the wicked soul was turned away and forced to wander in eternal restlessness. The Narragansett communicated with Cautantowwit through sacrifice, prayers, praise, and dance. Yet none knew him, and his face was a mystery.

2. *Weetucks* (or Maushop) was a benevolent, human-like giant responsible for the creation of various landmarks—islands in particular. He could walk on water and catch whales singlehanded. The smoke of his great pipe gave rise to the early morning fogs that hung upon the shoreline of the bays and rivers. Weetucks was the subject of many tales and legends around the fires of the Narragansett.

3. *Chepi* (or Hobomucko) was the devil of the Narragansett. His name was associated with death, the deceased, and the cold northeast wind. He inhabited the black shadows of the forested swamps. He brought calamity and illness. He appeared to men in visions as a man, an animal, an inanimate object, or a mythical creature. Most often he appeared as serpent. And this was the sign of the powwow (medicine man). Though most were terrified by these manifestations, many desired such visions, for Chepi did not appear to everyone, but to those who were called to leadership, great wisdom, and spiritual power ("medicine").

Because the natives of northeastern America lived under the constant dark shadow of the spiritual world, the role of the powwow (which means "a wise speaker") was a critical one in the daily existence of the Indian. The powwow was an essential link to the unseen realities that played with each man's fate.

By virtue of his intimacy with the spirits, the powwow advised his sachems on all matters of life. By the aid of the gods—some of which were familiar spirits which lodged within the powwow himself—he read the times and the seasons and the causes and the outcomes of events in the past, present, and future. He identified thieves and murderers. He danced and prayed for rain and harvest and hunt. He bewitched his enemies and the political rivals of his tribe, causing sickness and death by sorcery. He conjured sickness out of suffering friends and tribesmen.

He practiced scientific medicine as well, setting bones, dressing wounds, massaging, and prescribing certain natural cures through his knowledge of roots and herbs.

Sometimes he accomplished superhuman feats, causing rocks to move, water to burn, trees to dance, and the dried skins of dead snakes to come alive. Few could match or withstand his amazing powers—until the coming of the white man's God.

Events

The many events in *The Rain From God,* both the fictional and the historical, follow an historically accurate chronology. I have not applied dates to anything, however, because the European calendar was—for our narrator—a meaningless and unknown thing.

There is nothing in the fictional that could not have happened, and there is remarkably much that seems fictional that truly did happen:

I have stood on the stone table of the "talking rock." Several such "drum rocks" are scattered across the miles in Rhode Island, and archaeologists conjecture their purpose to be the same as you'll discover in the story.

The comet that preceded the Great Dying is a matter of record. The Indians spoke of it to the Europeans who arrived after the plague.

The Song On The Wind—and the subsequent experience of hearing it again as a hymn sung in the Plymouth meeting house—is a legitimate tradition among many of the New England tribes.

The lives (excluding early childhood, which predates the Pilgrims and the Puritans) and deaths of our story's principal Indian sachems—Miantonomi and Uncas especially—are recorded history.

The Pequot War. The burning of the Pequot fort on Mystic Hill. Squanto's duplicity. Wequash's conversion. Roger Williams' relationship to the Narragansett. The way the Indians fought and believed. The way the

English fought and believed. The Praying Indians and their towns. King Phillip's War. The Great Swamp Fight. The miracle of Martha's Vineyard. The climactic rain from God. All this—and more—really happened. Folks who were there wrote it down. Through a dark glass we can see it still.

Throughout the narrative, Katanaquat keeps us up on the changing times. His bits of news, as they apply generally to happenings among the tribes and within the colonies, are garnered almost exclusively from the historical record.

BIBLIOGRAPHY

The resources utilized for the writing of *The Rain From God* are too many and too varied to list fully in a popular novel of this kind. Yet the subject matter is so historically critical to the understanding of America's early heritage of the Gospel, that I cannot let Katanaquat simply tell his story and then say goodnight. Therefore, I have chosen to print an edited list of works that I found essential and most helpful in swimming the muddy river of the past. Some of these books may still be in print, but most can only be found on the shelves of your local library or through interlibrary loan.

Boissevain, Ethel, *The Narragansett People* (Phoenix, Ariz.: Indian Tribal Series, 1975).

Bradford, William, *Of Plymouth Plantation* (New York: Knopf, 1952). Originally published in the 1600s.

Chapin, Howard M., *Sachems of the Narragansett* (Providence, R.I.: Rhode Island Historical Society, 1931).

DeForest, John W., *The History of the Indians of Connecticut from the Earliest Known Period to 1850* (Hartford, Conn., 1852).

Eliot, John, *The Day-breaking, if not the Sun-rising, of the Gospell with the Indians in New England*, 1649.

Gookin, Daniel, *Historical Collections of the Indians in New England. Of Their Several Nations, Numbers, Customs, Manners, Religion and Government, Before the English Planted There* (New York: Arno Press, reprint, 1972). Originally published in Boston in 1792.

Mason, John, *A Brief History of the Pequot War* (Ann Arbor, Mich.: University Microfilms, Inc., reprint, 1966). Originally published in Boston in 1736.

Mayhew, Experience, *Indian Converts* (London, 1727).

Rider, Sidney S., *The Lands of Rhode Island as They Were Known to Caunounicus and Miantunnomu When Roger Williams Came in 1636* (Providence, R.I., 1904).

Simmons, William S., *Cautantowwit's House: An Indian Burial Ground on the Island of Conanicut in Narragansett Bay* (Providence, R.I.: Brown University Press, 1970).

Ibid., *The Narragansett* (New York/Philadelphia: Chelsea House Publishers, 1989).

Ibid., *Spirit of the New England Tribes: Indian History and Folklore, 1620–1984* (Hanover, N.H.: University Press of New England, 1986).

Tunis, Edwin, *Indians* (New York: Thomas Y. Crowell, 1979).

Various Authors, *King Phillip's War Narratives,* a collection of five contemporary accounts of the war, first published separately between 1675 and 1677 in London (Ann Arbor, MI: University Microfilms, Inc., reprint, 1966).

Vaughan, Alden T., *New England Frontier,* Puritans and Indians 1620–1675 (Boston: Little, Brown and Company, 1965).

Wilbur, Keith, *New England Indians* (Chester, Conn.: Globe-Pequot Press, 1978).

Williams, Roger, *A Key into the Language of America; Christenings Make Not Christians; and The Letters of Roger Williams—all from The Complete Writings of Roger Williams,* 7 vols. (New York: Russell & Russell, reprint, 1963). Key was first published in London in 1643. There was yet no printing press on the continent of North America.

Willison, George F., *The Pilgrim Reader* (Garden City, N.Y.: Doubleday, 1953).

Readers' Guide

FOR PERSONAL REFLECTION
OR GROUP DISCUSSION

Preface: I'm Your Brother

1. When I traveled north to Rhode Island to walk the ancestral woods and begin my research for *The Rain From God,* I stayed for four days with Roland and Starr Mars, a gracious and hospitable Narragansett couple who showed me the town and made me feel right at home. On a rainy morning, Roland took me to a small Connecticut church where he was the featured preacher for "Native American Sunday." If there was any other Indian blood in that congregation, I couldn't see it! Roland's sermon, entitled "I'm your brother!" was a rousing message of Christian unity. Sadly, there was hardly an "amen" in the house that day. Though the pastor and a few of his people politely asked Roland a question or two during the "fellowship" time after the sermon, no one even greeted me as I wandered—seemingly invisible—in their midst. I finally opened up a conversation with a man who was more interested in the cheese and crackers than in the koinonia of the saints.

Jesus commanded us to love one another (John 15:12–14), and he fervently prayed that all his followers would "be one" as he and the Father are one (see John 17:20–23). He prayed this so that our joy would be full, so that his glory would be seen in us, and so that the "world would believe that the Father sent the Son." If our unity can actually open blind eyes to the gift of salvation, then our disunity and lack of Christian love must be a stumbling block to faith. Jesus bought our unity with his precious blood upon the cross of Calvary (Eph. 2:14–16), and we must pray with him, "Father, make us one!" We must find ways to declare to one another—with our mouths, with our lives, and for the world to see—"I'm your brother!"

Personal Ponderings:

a) Do I see myself as a "brother" or "sister" to other believers? Do I take that reality seriously enough to become a servant and friend to my church family and other Christians in my community?

b) Do I acknowledge Christians of other denominations and cultures as "co-heirs of the grace of life" (1 Peter 3:7–9), as fellow members of the family of God? Are they welcomed in my heart and home? Do they know it?

c) What does the Bible mean when it says that we are "members of each other" (Rom. 12:5)?

Chapter 2: My Friends

2. Assoko, the Fool, was born retarded (with something like Down Syndrome). Today, we would consider Assoko a special-needs child, and he would receive focused and compassionate attention throughout his life, his needs being met by a myriad of public and private social programs developed to help folks like him. But many would still label him a "weirdo," and by a large number of his peers he would be disrespected, disparaged, discouraged, disowned, and discarded. Some would never consider being his friend simply because of the mental and social disability with which he was born.

But God uses the foolish things of this world to confound the wise (1 Cor. 1:27). He calls the weak to serve him, the messed-up to glorify him, the outcast to invite others into the kingdom. And so we, as God's people, must have that same heart toward the "losers" of the world, for we are ALL losers apart from the saving grace of God (Rom. 3:23–24; John 15:4–8). We must befriend the "Fools" of the world, patiently walking them toward the wholeness that can only be found in Jesus Christ.

Personal Ponderings:

a) Do I know any Assokos? Do I see them as Katanaquat did—special human beings with gifts and strengths all their own?

b) What can I do to befriend someone with special needs? To enter their world and let them enter mine, so that God can be glorified in our relationship and make himself known?

Chapter 5: The Song On The Wind

3. Katanaquat and his friends were in awe of the Dutch explorers with their armor, their muskets, their terrifying cannon, and their great sailing ships. The Indians thought the Dutch were gods!

Today, our society exalts men and women for their creative abilities, their physical appearance, their riches, fame, or position of power in our culture. Though it is a good thing to "give honor to whom honor is due" (Rom. 13:7), we must avoid getting so caught up in being culturally cool that we make idols of the gods and goddesses of our age. The character of an individual must always mean more to us than his charisma. Above all, Christians must "look to Jesus, the author and finisher of our faith"

(Heb. 12:2). We must be conformed to his image (Romans 8:29) and filled with his love. We must not let the world squeeze us into its mold, but instead let God renew our minds through a growing understanding of his good and perfect will as revealed in his Word, the Bible (Romans 12:1–2).

Personal Ponderings:

a) Is there a TV or movie personality, a popular music star, a sports figure, or even a Christian minister whom I admire highly? Do they exhibit Christ-like character? Why do I admire them?

b) Do I define myself by identifying with contemporary personalities and movements, or do I define myself through my relationship with God?

c) What means more to me (in terms of influencing my thinking and my behavior): the example and opinions of men and women in our culture or the life and teachings of Jesus Christ?

d) The Song On The Wind was a strange and apparently supernatural melody heard by many Native Americans in the New England woods prior to the coming of the English colonists (this is legitimate Indian tradition). In our story, Uncas hated the song; others were in awe. To Uncas, the song was a discordant wail and an unbearable shriek; to the others, it was an eternal summons, a deeply moving and transcendent call. Years later, Katanaquat heard the melody again as it was sung, with English words, in the Plymouth meeting house. It was a hymn of praise to the Trinity. The hearing of the Gospel is like the Song On The Wind. To some, it is foolishness, a stumbling block and a "rock of offense; to others it is the power of God for salvation" (1 Corinthians 1:17–19; Romans 1:16)! Some howl against the grace of God; others bow the knee in worship and repentance.

4. Jesus likened the sharing of the Gospel story to the sowing of seed (Matthew 13:3–9,18–23). Sometimes the seed falls on good soil, sometimes it doesn't. Sometimes it is received and sometimes it is rejected. How do I handle rejection of the Gospel by friends and family?

a) Do I get impatient, pushy, argumentative? Or do I turn the other cheek, go the second mile, let love speak where words have failed?

b) Do I take offense at rejection, "shake the dust off my feet" and avoid those who have rejected me? Or do I labor in prayer for the souls of those who don't want to hear, asking God to soften their hearts, commanding the Devil to take his fingers from their ears and his hands off their eyes? c) If I can overcome Satan through the blood of the Lamb and the word of my testimony (Rev. 12:10–11), then I need to talk about my Savior no matter what the response. Who do I know personally who has never heard the story of God's grace in my life?

Chapter 6: The Dying

5. The Great Dying was a terrible plague (it may have been smallpox) that swept the New England coastline prior to the coming of the Pilgrims. Some historians estimate that two thirds of the native population died. For those who survived, it was a time of deep mourning. One of the Pilgrim stories still found in most elementary school history books concerns Squanto, a Patuxet Indian whose tribe was entirely wiped out by the plague. It was on the fertile land of the extinguished Patuxet that the Pilgrims founded Plymouth. And it was Squanto (the "Lone Patuxet") who came to their rescue in their first harsh year in the wilderness of the New World.

Squanto was a "man without a country." Before the Pilgrims, he was taken in by the neighboring Wampanoag, who mourned with him in his deep loss but could not comfort him. It was not until the English arrived on his own home turf that he found new meaning in life through coming alongside the Pilgrims in their own need.

Personal Ponderings:

Jesus said, "Happy are those who mourn" (Matt. 5:4). That's a strange one!—but it comes with a promise: "… for they will be comforted." The Greek word translated "comforted" is a form of the word used to describe the "Comforter" or "Counselor" (the Holy Spirit) in John 14:15–17. This word also means "to come alongside." And the message Jesus is declaring here is that those who are willing to come alongside others in their sorrow will discover that God has come alongside them. When we wade into the woes of this world in order to bring hope and comfort to others, we find God right there with us—and we ourselves are comforted. "Weep with those who weep," brothers and sisters (Rom. 12:15–16); it's a "win, win" situation.

a) Who do I know in need of comfort? How can I sincerely mourn with them, coming alongside them in their sorrow and pain?

b) In prayer, I will commit to mourning for the sins and the sorrows of this fallen world I live in. And I will rejoice in the God who sent his Son to save us.

Chapter 8: Plymouth

6. Though Squanto was a "godsend" who taught the Pilgrims many things that helped them survive in a wild land where they were strangers, he was also a self-serving man who used his position among the English to win him favor and power among the neighboring Indian tribes. He was not always honest or fair in his dealings with other Indians, and although he lived among a strongly Christian people until his death, we don't know if he ever repented of his sin and surrendered himself to Jesus Christ.

Sometimes, in the church, we abide sin in our midst because people are "useful" to us or we are afraid to rock the boat. A wealthy but worldly congregant is a big giver, and we don't challenge him to holy living because he might be offended and take his money elsewhere. A hardworking but unmarried couple is serving faithfully in children's ministry, but we don't ask them to give up living together in fornication because we're afraid they will go to another church. The most talented worship leader in our congregation has a problem with anger and control, but we leave her alone because she deals very poorly with correction and we're afraid of the conflict. A young man is living an openly homosexual life, but we don't deal with his sin in a biblical manner because we're concerned about being labeled "homophobic" and "gay haters."

God is not happy with "sin in the camp" (Num. 21:4–9). "Christ Jesus came into the world to save sinners" (1 Tim. 1:15), and he submitted himself to a brutal and bloody death in order to win our salvation. When we let people live with their sins—out of convenience or fear—we may be helping them die in their sins! Our pews will be filled with compromise, and God isn't going to come to our church either!

Personal Ponderings

a) Do I hate sin? Do I love the sinner? Do I care about souls? Do I care about God's glory, God's reputation, God's presence in our midst?

b) Why do I let sin go unchallenged in a brother or sister's life? Is it because of unrepentant sin in my own life? Is it because I am afraid of conflict? Is it because I don't love them enough or care enough for God's name?

c) Am I my brother's keeper? Will I love him enough to personally confront him with his sin and walk him through to victory?

d) What sin in my own life holds back God's full blessing in my family, my church, my job, my ministry?

Chapter 14: Bitter Water

7. When a New England Indian lost his scalp, even if he lived, he was considered a "dead man," a man without a soul. He became an outcast from society, and had to fend for himself in all things. Nobody cared about him anymore.

In Jesus' day, it was those smitten with leprosy who were put away from the rest of the community and treated with fear and scorn. For the Jew, the tax-collector, the Samaritan, and the hated Roman were "lost souls."

But who are the lepers of today? Who are the "untouchables" of modern America? Will we dare to love as Jesus loved, going out of our way to minister to the Samaritan, heal the leper, and call the tax collector and the sinner to follow him? Do we dare to believe, as Katanaquat eventually believed of Assoko, that no matter what sin has done to a man, he is still a man?

Personal Ponderings:

a) Are there people in my life whom I treat as "lost souls"? Why?

b) Is anyone really lost to the grace of God (is there anyone who cannot be touched)?

c) Do I really see myself as lost without Jesus, a sinner with absolutely no hope of salvation apart from the grace of God through the cross of Christ? Do I know that my own righteousness is like dirty rags in the sight of God? That without the righteousness of Christ I am a traitor, a thief, a murderer, a pervert, a fornicator and a fool? And if I know this, then why am I afraid to touch the leper?

d) Do I know how much God loves me—really, really loves me—no matter what?

Chapter 16: In the Pines

8. Katanaquat hardened his heart and cut himself off from all the society he had ever known—from friends and foes alike. It wasn't that he wanted to be alone so much as he didn't know who he was anymore. He was a man seeking a reason to live—but his sin, his sorrow, and his pain pulled him from the relationships that could heal him and the responsibilities that could keep him whole. He hungered for relational reconciliation, but his unrepentant soul would not admit it. He yearned to know God, but not on God's terms. Estranged from family, unwilling to heed the counsel of those who loved him best, there came a day when his enemies found him alone beneath the pines. And this was a diversion he welcomed, for he was a warrior first of all.

But pride comes before a fall. And that fall was a sudden, violent one. Broken and dying, unable to command his own body or loose his soul from the prison he had built for it, he found himself alone with the Spirit of truth. He humbled himself and opened his heart to a startling conversation with the Almighty. And he heard from God.

God opposes the proud, but gives grace to the humble (James 4:6–10).

Personal Ponderings:

a) When did I last hear from God?

b) Does God have to knock me out to speak to me? Or do I "seek him early" in order to hear his voice and know his will?

c) What "walls" are in my life which keep me from surrendering fully to the work and will of the Holy Spirit? What hindrances hold me back? What sins so easily beset me, keeping me from running the race that is set before me (Heb. 12:1–13)?

d) The Bible says I need daily encouragement to keep my heart from being hardened by the deceitfulness of sin. In what ways do I cut myself off from the fellowship and encouragement of fellow believers?

e) Who do I know that needs a word of encouragement or a nudge to return to consistent fellowship?

Chapter 18: In the Fire

9. "When you left me, I forgave you," said Silvermoon to Katanaquat upon their reunion late in life. "But when you did not come back, I grew angry in my heart. I chewed on the meat of my anger for many seasons until only the bones remained. Then I sucked on the bones until even the taste of the meat was gone. Then I carried the bones about in a bag which rattled your name whenever I walked. Then I lay them near my bed and saw them only when I slept or when I woke. Then I arose one morning and looked upon the sad, dry bones, and I wondered at my foolishness. 'These are the bones of a dead man!' I said, and I threw them in the fire."

Think of the wasted years that Silvermoon "chewed on the bones" of her anger and her unforgiveness. Think of the freedom she gained when she "threw them in the fire." She was free to love again—to love even the one who had caused her so much pain.

Jesus said, "If you forgive men for their sins against you, your heavenly Father will forgive you too. But if you do not forgive men for their trespasses against you, then your Father will not forgive your sins" (Matt. 6:14–15).

If we want to be forgiven, we must forgive. If we want to be free, we must free others from the offenses that we hold against them. The Son will only set us free when we set others free. That's the way it works.

Personal Ponderings:

a) Am I a forgiving person? Do I forgive others as Christ has forgiven me (Eph. 4:30–32)?

b) Am I holding anyone hostage to unforgiveness? Who? How has this held me back in my walk with God?

c) Do I love my enemies? Am I free in my soul to bless them, to pray for them, to do good to them (Matt. 5:43–48)?

Chapter 19: The Song of Jacob

10. Jesus seldom healed, delivered, or ministered to someone in the same way twice. Isn't it strange that while trying to follow him we end up creating (and sticking to) formulas for doing things that he did in instant obedience to the Father's voice. Some of us lay hands on people for healing. Some of us anoint with oil. Some of us will only call the elders of the church to pray for us. Some of us go to mid-week healing services. Some of us wait for the popular healing evangelist to come to town. And almost all of us think that some of us are wrong in our approach to the matter. So it goes with many spiritual issues in the body of Christ. But what does God think of all this?

Katanaquat baptized himself. That's a bit unorthodox—but it was okay with God. Because God is not into "doing church" one way; he's into new wineskins for new wine (Luke 5:36–39). He's into changing hearts and transforming lives in every way imaginable. All he requires for us to come to him is that we "believe that he is, and that he is a rewarder of those who diligently seek him" (Heb. 11:6).

Personal Ponderings:

a) Have I been baptized since I believed? What does the Bible teach about baptism?

b) What "wineskins" in my life are getting old? What spiritual habits in my life (prayer, Bible reading, witnessing, worship, going to church) have become "formulas," lacking life? What can I do to breathe life into these areas?

c) In what area of my life is God challenging me to stand up in my boat and "cast myself in" in order to be changed by him? To go deeper in my relationship of worship and devotion to him? To more effectively minister to others?

Chapter 20: Is This Katanaquat?

11) The final victory of soul in Katanaquat's conversion was his meeting with his old enemy Uncas. Katanaquat traveled purposefully to the lands of Uncas in order to bless the one who had cursed him. And there, Katanaquat extended forgiveness to the man who had murdered his friends, betrayed his tribe, opposed him in war, wounded him in battle, and brought more misery into his life (and the lives of the Narragansett) than anyone else he had ever known. Though Uncas would not receive the grace offered, the offering was accepted by God.

Upon the cross of Calvary, Jesus hung between heaven and hell. The Son of God, the Son of Man, a spotless lamb, a bloody sacrifice, a sin offering like none ever before or ever again—once, for all—and yet millions would scoff at the death of the Holy One. But the sacrifice was not in vain.

"Father, forgive them …" Jesus gasped. And the Father forgave us. Though the nations rage against the Son, still the Father honors the sacrifice and stretches a merciful hand toward the rebel planet.

"It is finished!" Jesus said.

What am I going to do about it?

The Word at Work Around the World

A vital part of Cook Communications Ministries is our international outreach, Cook Communications Ministries International (CCMI). Your purchase of this book, and of other books and Christian-growth products from Cook, enables CCMI to provide Bibles and Christian literature to people in more than 150 languages in 65 countries.

Cook Communications Ministries is a not-for-profit, self-supporting organization. Revenues from sales of our books, Bible curricula, and other church and home products not only fund our U.S. ministry, but also fund our CCMI ministry around the world. One hundred percent of donations to CCMI go to our international literature programs.

CCMI reaches out internationally in three ways:

- Our premier International Christian Publishing Institute (ICPI) trains leaders from nationally led publishing houses around the world.

- We provide literature for pastors, evangelists, and Christian workers in their national language.

- We reach people at risk—refugees, AIDS victims, street children, and famine victims—with God's Word.

Word Power, God's Power

Faith Kidz, RiverOak, Honor, Life Journey, Victor, NexGen — every time you purchase a book produced by Cook Communications Ministries, you not only meet a vital personal need in your life or in the life of someone you love, but you're also a part of ministering to José in Colombia, Humberto in Chile, Gousa in India, or Lidiane in Brazil. You help make it possible for a pastor in China, a child in Peru, or a mother in West Africa to enjoy a life-changing book. And because you helped, children and adults around the world are learning God's Word and walking in his ways.

Thank you for your partnership in helping to disciple the world. May God bless you with the power of his Word in your life.

For more information about our
international ministries, visit www.ccmi.org.

Additional copies of THE RAIN FROM GOD
and other RiverOak titles are available
from your local bookseller.

If you have enjoyed this book,
or if it has had an impact on your life,
we would like to hear from you.

Please contact us at:

RIVEROAK BOOKS
Cook Communications Ministries, Dept. 201
4050 Lee Vance View
Colorado Springs, CO 80918
Or visit our Web site:
www.cookministries.com

RIVEROAK®
Good News in Fiction